"Now and again you must look in the Second most Obvious Place."

CJ West

A Demon Awaits

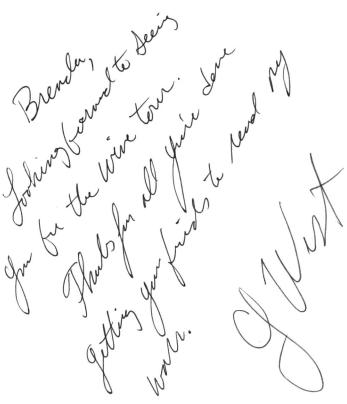

Brenda,
Looking forward to seeing you for the wine tour. Thanks for all you've done getting your friends to read my work.

J West

22 West Books, Sheldonville, MA
www.22wb.com

Cover design by Sarah M. Carroll
Author Photo by David Ciolfi
Cover Photo by Lyndsi West

ISBN 10: 0-9767788-2-3
ISBN 13: 978-0-9767788-2-0

Acknowledgements

Special thanks to Reverend Leo Christian for his help understanding the difficult path Oliver undertakes in this book trying to atone for his sins. Reverend Christian has a capacity for understanding and forgiveness that few can match. It was truly a pleasure getting to know him and seeing the world through his eyes. The parable *Two Boats and a Helicopter* is taken from a sermon I attended many years ago.

Thanks to Stephanie Blackburn M. Ed, L.M.H.C. for her vast supply of psychological and psychiatric materials and her help understanding Heather Lovely as a practitioner and the process of client evaluation and testing.

Thanks to Danielle Williamson from the Worcester Telegram & Gazette for her insights into the life of a newspaper reporter. Danielle helped me understand how a young woman in Cassie's situation is likely to view her work and her world. She surprised and delighted me. When I met with her I'd been developing Cassie for six months and I couldn't help feeling that Cassie Corcoran was sitting across from me.

Thanks to Jennifer Rowe, Assistant District Attorney in the Norfolk County District Attorney's Office. Jennifer has a gift for making complex questions about jurisdiction and trial procedure very clear. She helped me understand what I needed to know about the legal process with ease.

Thank you to my pre-release readers Paul Babin, Jady Bernier, Frank Cinnella, Sherry Davis, Pamela Goodliffe, DMD, Trish Moore, Kerilynn Newman and Jennifer Wolfe. And my utmost thanks to my wife Gloria who still gets excited about my work.

In loving memory of Doris West, hero, role model, fantastic Wiffle ball pitcher and much, much more to a great many children.

Then came Peter to him, and said, Lord, how oft shall my brother sin against me, and I forgive him? till seven times?
Jesus saith unto him, I say not unto thee, Until seven times: but, until seventy times seven.

Matthew 18:21-22

Prologue

In a moment, dear reader, you shall learn of my most perilous trial, the outcome of which cannot be known until death delivers me to the threshold of my ultimate fate. First, let me assure you that I wasn't always the creature you see before you, burdened by a multitude of sins. I was once an obedient and loving son. The journey from reverent child to wanted fugitive began with small deliberate steps. Headlights awakened me one night and I followed my instincts out onto the grounds of the winery where my family lived. I crept into the processing room and caught Charles Marston coating the downstream side of the disgorger filter. That discovery changed my life.

It was months before my father noticed the murky film the Saccharomyces bailii created on the surface of the sparkling wine. A week later they threw out every last bottle and I started hearing whispers about financial problems. It was still another month before my parents hurtled to their death in a car crash. They left me a bankrupt winery that I was forced to sell along with my childhood home. I was thirteen years old. I was alone. And I knew who was responsible.

Had I thought to bring a camera that fateful night, everything would have been different. They would have believed me: my parents, the police, the probate judge… I'd still own the winery today. I didn't have a camera then, but oh how I made up for my youthful lack of preparation.

Criminals are creatures of habit and Charles Marston turned out to be no different. The police were handicapped by laws, procedures and a presumption of innocence or at least an attempt to keep up the appearance. I had no such encumbrances in my pursuit. I eavesdropped and spied. By the time I was eighteen Charles had perfected his craft. He had bankrupted three more wineries and bought them for himself. I had learned a great deal as well. I invested in high-tech surveillance gear and spent my time reading news clippings and corporate filings. Charles' victims never came together to discuss their misfortune, but my research led me to them. Their anger was easy to tap into and soon I made allies eager to share what they knew of his scheme. I collected a series of similarly-contaminated bottles. Each had been pivotal in a Charles Marston takeover.

The night I watched Charlie Marston leave for college was the night I crossed the line from citizen enforcer to revenge-crazed psycho. I had planned to trap Charles Marston and his banking partner, Bill Caulfield, by using their greed against them. I was ready to bring them down, but when I saw young Charlie tearfully leaving *my* childhood home, bringing those two men to justice wasn't enough.

It took three years lurking around campus, but I discovered something that meant the world to Charlie. He had a deal in the works to play pro football. I paid an opposing player fifty thousand dollars to end that dream and later I blamed it on Charlie's father. I was becoming as ruthless as Charles and Bill, but I didn't care. The injury decimated the young superstar and he fell hard. When his girlfriend left and he turned to drinking I made him my playmate. I showed him things he never would have seen without me and in return, he let me walk right into the family and rip it apart from the inside.

I'll spare you the details, but know this: Charles and Bill deserved what they got and more. I hadn't bargained for the collateral damage and that's what's weighing down my soul now. I was too blind to think it through. I conned Sebastian into scaring away the winery employees. He was angry that his father was fired and he signed on to my plan eagerly. He kept a lid on things so I could trap the Marstons in their own house. Thanks to him I tortured the Marstons and Deirdre Deudon for two days without interruption. He got a suitcase full of cash, but that proved too much for his conscience. He foolishly brought it back and got busted.

I tricked a young husband and wife, Deirdre and Henri Deudon, into a violent confrontation that ended in her shame and his death. Deirdre would have committed adultery on her own, but I brought her husband to the scene in time to see her with me and Charlie. She hired TJ Lynch to kill me and I gave him what all hired killers deserve: a bullet in the forehead. Deirdre will chase me to the end of the earth now, desperately trying to finish TJ's work as a sign of loyalty to her dead husband.

I paid to have Henri's sister-in-law, Monique, killed just to confuse the gendarmes and get Charlie back to the United States. That was the lowest. I thought nothing of paying to have her shot. She left behind two kids and a husband that really loved her. If I'd been thinking, I would've walked away then, but I lusted for revenge. When I finally had Charles Marston pinned to the kitchen floor, I pummeled him unconscious before I realized what I was doing. It was over too fast. Charles is dead now. If I could bring him back to torture him again (longer this time) I would.

As for me, I wasn't supposed to live this long.

Charlie was supposed to kill me that night in the house. I had the perfect scenario planned. If he pulled the trigger, the police would find the evidence I left behind and arrest him for murder. There were enough pictures to link Charlie to everyone I killed and the houses we destroyed together. He should have been headed to jail, but instead of killing me, he tied me up and ran for the pictures. I'll never know how he figured it out and I'll never understand why he let me go. I wouldn't have done the same for him.

Even tonight when I broke into his house to grab the money I hid under his couch, Charlie kept his cool. He stood there with a shiny handgun glinting in the lamplight and hid the telephone behind his back to let the emergency dispatcher listen in. He could have killed me. No one would have blamed him. No one but Charlie would have called the cops. And no one could have predicted what the cops were about to do to me. Charlie is watching, but it's out of his hands.

Clean-shaven and neatly dressed, I look like a respectable college kid to a stranger, but the Westport cops will always see me as the lunatic with long hair and glasses that terrorized three families.

Chapter One

Surrounded on the dark grass and empty handed, Oliver Joyet couldn't fight off five cops armed with clubs and guns. Betrayed, outmaneuvered, he stood motionless as they approached. Officer Pinto led. His intense hatred vibrated through the night air. Even in the dim light from the porch, Oliver could see the bruise bubbling up beneath Pinto's collar. The other cops circled while Pinto moved in alone with his nightstick held high. These same officers had tormented Pinto at headquarters, humiliating him for his mistake, but now they sneered as Oliver's eyes begged for an opening large enough to bolt through. The Westport Police wouldn't allow another escape, not tonight. Tonight Pinto would collar a sadistic menace and the Westport Police would right their sagging reputation.

Pinto's angry eyes burned into Oliver as he closed in. This same all-consuming fury had possessed Oliver just weeks ago. Nothing could have stopped him from avenging his parents as nothing would stop Pinto now. Cunning and deceit were worthless here in the single-minded darkness. Only brute force mattered and Pinto's rage-charged muscles swelled with so much adrenalin he glowed of invincibility. Unconcerned with his own welfare, Pinto's only goal was to destroy the man who'd shamed him. A solitary comfort remained for Oliver: the police couldn't beat him to death. Oliver would suffer, but Pinto's comrades would keep him alive. He'd survive to be tried, convicted, and incarcerated for life.

Oliver knew the blow would come, but not where it would strike. Empty hands extended, fingers splayed, he showed his submission and yet readied himself to ward off the first swing, maybe even tackle Pinto and force another officer to cuff him before Pinto released his full fury.

Pinto's supple arm lashed down without warning. Flicked with precision, the nightstick struck Oliver's collarbone with a crack. His shoulder collapsed inward. The burning pain anchored Oliver to the lawn where his knees gave way, beyond the dim light from Charlie Marston's house. Ironic they caught him on this spot. The isolation of the winery allowed Oliver to blockade the Marston house and rain torment down on the family for two days. The same isolation freed Pinto to dole out his retribution at a leisurely pace and synchronize his story with his fellow officers after his lust was satisfied.

Emotion arced from Pinto's nightstick. His frustration slammed into Oliver. Embarrassment for losing his weapon spiked into Oliver's shin. Locker room jokes about catching Houdini propelled a blow to the back. Disappointment from Pinto's neighbors fueled a mighty blow to the ribs. Pinto showed no mercy for being left alive at the scene. He drove the club down even as Oliver huddled defensively on the ground. The club whirred and struck the back of Oliver's head with a thunk that reverberated throughout his skull, shaking his brain tissue like so much molded gelatin.

Charlie Marston watched the onslaught from the steps with the gun still in his hand. Intentionally crippled by Oliver, his father killed and the winery he stood to inherit burned to the ground, Charlie called for help rather than shoot Oliver dead. After being held prisoner in his own home, Charlie was branded a hero by the media for helping his mother and Deirdre escape. Charlie could have killed Oliver the moment he walked through the front door and the police would have ruled it self-defense. Legal worries weren't restraining Charlie. It was something inside that kept him from doing what so many others could not resist. Adherence to some moral code, Oliver supposed. For all his mercy, Charlie Marston didn't intervene even as the beating dragged on.

Oliver had cast his own moral teachings aside. Temptation to exact revenge dropped him to the ground at Pinto's feet. He'd more than fallen, he'd savored his quest to torture and kill Charlie's father. Charlie screwed it up by refusing to shoot. Death would have freed him from his hate and taken him away from Charlie Marston, the winery, and all the other reminders of what he'd lost. The anger was gone now, leaving him empty and cold, lying battered at Pinto's feet. His obsession with getting even dominated the first half of his life. It might take forever to repay the debt. There was no escape. Payment was due and Pinto was the first collection agent to come calling.

Pinto kicked him squarely in the back. His body jolted, but he felt only a vague ache in his spine. His vision was clouding, his fingers numb. He couldn't take much more.

He couldn't blame Pinto. Oliver knew rage like his. He was blinded by it as he pummeled Marston near to death. Now he'd caused the same rage to spring up within Pinto. Did he touch others this way? Did Monique or TJ have children who would grow bitter and angry as he did? Would Caulfield or even Deirdre seek some heinous form of vengeance? Oliver hadn't solved anything. He'd multiplied Charles Marston's transgressions a dozen times. He'd been taught better. Reverend White and Aunt Althea had taken pains to teach him love and compassion. Unfortunately, Charles Marston's tampering had thrown him completely off track.

Another kick. The abdomen this time. Pinto was inescapable. He and his comrades would punish Oliver without mercy on this night.

Oliver didn't feel the boot strike the back of his head.

His vision cleared. The cold and pain faded.

He stood tall, transported into a strange new environment, safe from Pinto and the others.

Alone.

He felt vigor he hadn't known in months, his senses keen, but hemmed in by a fog that rose up like a wall, enveloping him in a twenty-foot circle. There was no scent here. The space smelled neither natural nor institutional, a completely blank olfactory palette. The smooth solidity beneath him could only come from polished marble, but fog blanketed the floor up to his knees. He doubled over and tried to fan it away, but the thick fog stayed put. This new place felt immensely vast, offering unbounded vision to eyes trained to see here. Oliver could see nothing but fog. A wave of vertigo struck. He felt himself high atop a mountain peak where a misstep could send him careening downward. He straightened, keeping his feet anchored in place.

He felt the curve of his collarbone with his fingers, sturdy and strong under his shirt without sensitivity to the pressure he applied. He sensed no bounds but those within him. Light glowed from somewhere behind the fog. The air, if it was air, hung around him cleaner than that from any forest or seashore. Oliver tentatively slid his foot forward to explore. His shoe made no sound whatsoever. The ring of light around him suddenly grew wider as if someone or something was upset by his insolence. Oliver froze. At the center of the clearing, only ten feet away, two figures took shape. They simply appeared. They hadn't traveled through the fog, but materialized plainly within his circle of view without a hint of their origin.

Seated in ornate wooden chairs with red velvet seats, which themselves had just appeared, looking younger and stronger than he'd imagined them, were his parents. Two feet separated husband and wife and only ten feet separated Oliver from the parents he hadn't seen since he was thirteen years old. They showed no ill-effects of the car accident that ended their lives. They sat comfortably, facing their son with looks of deep sadness as if they'd been watching him since they departed Earth. They said nothing. Restricted by something unseen, they were allowed to look upon their son, but not speak to him. Strangely, Oliver couldn't speak either.

The circle expanded further. Light brightened. Fog receded. Oliver inched toward his parents in the increasing light, his feet now visible upon massive marble tiles. Two confident steps brought clarity to the faces he thought he'd never see again. Brows furrowed as he approached. He heeded their unspoken warning and stopped. The light beside his parents intensified. Without heat, it didn't burn his flesh, but glowed so intensely that the rays found his eyes through his forearm. His parents didn't react. He shied away, lowering himself to the floor.

Oliver's heart sank. Had Pinto killed him?

Was this his judgment day?

Oliver's belief was never in doubt, yet fear filled his heart. He accepted Jesus wholeheartedly, embraced Him and His teachings, but the Lord had undoubtedly seen what he'd done in the last year, what he'd prepared to do for the last ten. Oliver heard the first of God's commandments as if Reverend White was reading them with his fiery intonation. So many were his transgressions and so great was the hate that had filled his heart. There was only one outcome for him. His sins so far outweighed any meager good he'd done. Oliver would burn.

He'd turned away so completely. How had he not realized that this is where he'd end up? The lake of fire and the worm that never dies had been ingrained in him as a youngster. So real, and yet he'd walked directly toward the lake for ten years without hesitation.

If he was dead, the time for repentance had passed.

The light dimmed and Oliver was lifted to his feet.

A booming voice filled his head. "What have you done, Oliver?"

God needn't speak. Oliver heard the voice echo in his mind. More than a voice, he could feel His feelings of intense sadness and disappointment as clearly as his own. This voice had always been with him, guiding him from the fuzzy boundary of his consciousness. Without a whisper of distraction the voice was beautifully clear. He'd recognize it now wherever he went if only he could be given the chance. Oliver had stopped listening to this voice a long time ago. Whether God had stopped calling him, he couldn't be sure.

Oliver raised his head far enough to see sandaled feet below a white robe. Ornate tree-sized oaken beams supported the seat of His chair. Oliver couldn't raise his eyes further. The light dimmed, but Oliver's shame kept him focused on the marble tiles.

"Good people, Henri and Monique. Was your heart so consumed by hate you could not see? Can you not see within their hearts now?"

Oliver's head turned from the light and was lifted. There on either side of his parents stood Henri and Monique. They appeared silently and without warning as his parents had. Henri stood beside Oliver's father. There was no reason to fear Henri on this day, no sign of the rage that gripped him after seeing his wife naked with Oliver and Charlie. He wore a pristine robe and an understanding look for Oliver's predicament, maybe because hatred had overwhelmed him minutes before he died. His farmer's hands were now

5

clean. The bulging muscles underneath his robe were at ease. The aches of his life of toil had been soothed away. Calmer, taller, Henri was at peace.

Monique was stunning. She stood next to Oliver's mother with her eyes lowered toward the floor. She was distracted by something beneath the marble. There was a hint of grief in the way she looked downward, but no malice toward Oliver. It was as if boundless pleasures failed to ease her worry for the man she loved and the two sons she'd left behind. Her husband would remarry young. If he arrived here with another wife, the reunion might be trying for Monique. She seemed full of yearning to help her sons grow. Oliver had taken them away from her and yet his presence seemed inconsequential. She met his eyes briefly without a hint of anger.

Henri and Monique exuded purity. Oliver hadn't answered God's question and couldn't imagine finding the courage to do so. He averted his eyes, ashamed, as the thought occurred to him.

Just then, the floor became transparent. The marble turned to clear crystal. The view dropped to Earth and the fiery depths beyond. Overcome by a feeling of plummeting downward, Oliver dropped to his knees and scampered back. He braced himself for the wind and the fall that never came. The view settled far below Earth's surface on a subterranean world filled with haze and gloom as chokingly thick as the room he stood in was airy and light. TJ Lynch lay across a narrow trickle of molten rock, hands shackled down on one side, feet on the other. His weary back bridged the space. If he rested, even momentarily, his body would be plunged into the molten rock, his flesh and bone scorched away with the flow.

A scaly demon with a bony head that matched TJ's and scales blackened from tail to snout by the acrid smoke, stood guard at TJ's feet. It systematically whipped metallic tendrils into his flesh. The lashes ripped TJ's skin open in perfect parallel strokes that nearly touched. The underlying flesh regenerated itself, leaving wavy scars that reddened and healed while Oliver watched in horror. Recovery pained TJ as much as the wounds themselves. His entire body was covered with fine lines, quickly healing scars that recorded the last few hours of his never-ending punishment. The lines began to fade as the demon rested, gorging himself on the flesh of TJ's thigh. No blood spilled. The flesh re-grew, quickly filling the empty space as the demon licked its hideously long incisors. TJ howled, his hoarse voice rising above the moans of the damned that filled the cavern. His torment supplied purpose and sustenance to the demon chosen to punish him for eternity. The monster coyly looked skyward. It knew it was being watched, yet made no effort to restrain its unholy glee for its work.

Somewhere Charles Marston was suffering a similar punishment. Even without seeing him, Oliver knew he was being offered a choice. He closed his eyes and when he opened them again the floor was solid. He clasped his hands and lowered himself, hands on the marble, head resting on his hands, eyes closed.

"Tell me what I must do, Lord. Show me the way to atone," he begged without looking up.

"You alone must find the way, Oliver. I gave you loving parents and when I took them from you, I showed you the way to me. You had wealth and love. You needed nothing, but hunger for revenge twisted your soul. You must learn forgiveness and repentance. I created Oliver Joyet and you corrupted him into the creature you named Randy Black. You scorned me. You mocked me. Now you must replenish what you have taken away. Until then I will call you by the name you have chosen. Until then the place you have earned will be one of everlasting damnation."

The room began to dim.

"How, Lord? Please. Show me how."

"You have many tools, Randy. The way will become clear."

The room faded into terrifying darkness. He needed to take drastic action to save his soul; drastic action that didn't risk his life. Dying now meant condemnation, an eternity shackled within earshot of TJ's agonizing moans. Whether he suffered at the hands of a scaly black demon or donned the white robe of everlasting bliss hinged on his adherence to this single command. He was strong, intelligent and able. He struggled to wake himself and rise to the task God assigned.

Chapter Two

Stepping over the gas cans that blocked the steps was one of the biggest mistakes Jo Caulfield ever made. Her husband swore he'd never seen them even though he'd walked through that same door just minutes before she saw them. If she'd stomped back in and confronted him, the whole mess might have ended right then. That's if Bill was to be believed. It was too late now. Their lives were ripped so far apart there was no putting them back together. No sense trying.

But could the cans have appeared while they argued inside?

Bill couldn't have missed them. The line of bright red cans was unmistakable. Either someone had been hiding in the garage or Bill lied. They both knew someone had been sneaking inside their house for weeks. The nasty tricks drove them crazy. The intruder who controlled the heat and the doorbell could easily put six gas cans in the garage. The pranks turned the solemn banker into a furious, raving savage. His anger was so intense, his loss of control so complete, it couldn't have been faked. Bill didn't sabotage his own house, but was he desperate enough to burn it down?

She knew it was Randy sneaking into the house though she wouldn't admit it. She wondered how many times he'd been inside and whether he was infatuated with her or if it was her husband Randy was targeting. She remembered talking to Randy at parties. She'd never told anyone about her arrangement with Bill, but Randy knew everything down to the clause requiring her to sleep at home twenty-five nights per month. Looking back, she wondered if he was that smart or if her marriage could only be explained by something so ludicrous. She'd underestimated him. He dressed and acted like an overgrown teenager and she treated him as such.

Bill said the whole thing was payback for a shady business deal. It was all over the papers when his partner, Charles Marston, was killed. Bill tried to convince the insurance company, but he could only tell them so much. Without evidence, he had to finance reconstruction of the house himself. At least the prosecutor dropped the arson charge.

Bill confessed to Jo days after she left. Cheating the Joyets out of their winery was Charles' idea. Somehow young Joyet discovered that Bill arranged the financing. For years Bill's career at the bank soared with the Marston fortune. Referrals streamed in from Charles. Everything was great until Randy Black moved in across the street. Then everything fell apart.

Bill loved her. He begged her to come back, but Bill forgot this marriage was a business deal. She never loved him. She liked him well enough and they made good roommates, but the dream life was over. Bill's reputation was ruined. He'd been forced to retire from the bank so there was no reason to continue the charade. The house would take a year to rebuild. If she had to wait that long, she'd take her share and build a life of her own.

The contract wasn't over, but it was time to move on. No one blamed her, least of all the courts. "Force majeure," her lawyer said and the quick divorce was just as profitable as staying married another four years.

When she walked into the I.C.U. as Randy's girlfriend, the nurses didn't argue. The policeman outside had no idea who she was, but she didn't look dangerous, not in a physically threatening way. She signed her maiden name, the only name on the visitor log for Randy Black. She entered the room alone and walked around the bed, away from his left arm suspended horizontally at the bedside, so she could sit closer to him. Half his body was encased in plaster. His head was wrapped in white bandages and his good hand was cuffed to the bedrail at the wrist. She put her hand in his and listened to the machine breathe for him.

She'd never met anyone like Randy.

She'd read the stories in the papers and though she didn't want to believe them, she knew Randy hated her husband. It had always been bubbling under the surface. Maybe he showed her that side of himself because he wanted her to know. He worked hard to make it end well for her and it had.

Looking at him now, he was a completely different man from the one who lived across the street. Clean-shaven, handsome. How many times had he asked her to leave the old duffer and move in with him? That would have shaken up the neighborhood. He wasn't the first neighbor infatuated with her, but she felt maybe he wanted something more than the others. She wished she could ask him what he wanted now.

Bill had married her to make men like Randy jealous. When she walked into a room, men snapped to attention. Bill was no different, mesmerized from the first look. She still didn't understand why she went to dinner with him or why she considered his unconventional proposal. In the end money won out. How much different would it have been if Randy had met her first?

Would she have avoided the disaster with Bill?

A simple life together might have saved them both.

She lingered at the bedside wondering why she'd done it. Why she'd made a mockery of marriage for three million dollars. What price would she pay later? The arrangement was over, but she'd never get the time back. She'd devoted herself to a dried up old man. Even though they'd never been intimate, she could never have another first wedding.

The man in the bed before her was witty and incredibly charming even covered with stubble and black leather. She imagined what their life together might have been had they met on different terms. It was over for Randy now. When he recovered he'd spend twenty years in prison. She wouldn't wait. She couldn't. Her life was just beginning again.

He never reacted to the caress of her fingers. She left him there in the dark with the machine breathing for him and went out to find her new place in the world.

Chapter Three

In Randy's next breath lucidity and vigor were replaced by a painful haze. Confined, cold and dark; this was not Hell. Hell was furiously hot and it echoed with sorrowful cries. The silent space around him hid behind a blurry blankness. Drugs. Had to be drugs. He shifted dozily and found his torso too heavy to budge. A fabric and plaster cocoon weighed him down on the bed. The exertion produced imperceptible movement but ignited blinding pain in his collarbone. Cracked ribs screamed in protest. His lower legs howled and the dull throbbing in his head intensified, competing for attention over the other injuries Pinto inflicted. Excellent work for one man with a nightstick. Randy's treachery had truly inspired him.

Pain sliced through the fog separating Randy from the world.

Garbled voices spoke nearby, but Randy couldn't make out the words. He heard footsteps pass on a tiled floor, but couldn't identify their source.

Fuzzy lights appeared, dim at first, but bright enough to distinguish shadowy shapes. The ventilator sighed its mechanical sigh and forced a puff of air into his lungs. The mouthful of plastic tubing felt like a Frisbee jammed down his throat. He gasped for another breath, his lungs empty. Nothing flowed through the tube. The horrid machine refused to give him air. A high-pitched alarm squealed beside his bed. The tube had to go. His left arm was encased in plaster and fastened to his side. It wouldn't move for weeks. Jerking his good arm upward proved futile as well. A handcuff bit into his wrist and stopped it inches from the bedside. The chain snapped taught then clinked against the bedrail. His good hand useless, he thrashed wildly for breath inside his plaster prison. His eyes were open but blinded by a combination of fright and narcotic haze. His efforts sent shockwaves through his battered body that would ripple through nerve endings for hours.

Her soft hand took firm hold of his jaw and yet he didn't see her until the tape was stripped away and the tube expertly withdrawn. Cool sterile air filled his lungs. Industrial-strength disinfectant told him he was in a hospital, most likely St. Luke's. Panic subsided with a second unassisted breath. She switched the machine off and it stopped complaining.

"Welcome back to the land of the living," she said, not knowing how prophetic her statement was.

No longer spurred by impending suffocation, breathing through cracked ribs proved excruciating. He tried to say, "Thank you," but all that escaped was a pathetic croaking sound.

She smiled, understanding. She looked at him familiarly as if she'd hovered over him before, reading his eyes for signs of recognition while he slept. How long had he been here? How much of his story did she know? The handcuffs were enough to make most people wary, but she had an inviting look in her eyes. Deirdre had a similar look the night they met in that hick bar. She knew he could give her the rush she wanted. The glasses and scruff had been replaced by handcuffs. They were a clear sign that he was trouble, but they didn't deter the woman at his bedside.

She beamed, her light blonde hair pulled back, her eyes surveying his.

The room behind her came into focus in patches. Windowless, dim, crammed with equipment and an intravenous hanging at his side. Probably I.C.U. That's why she responded to the alarm so quickly. No sign whether it was day or night. They wouldn't have kept him here long. He'd been here hours, maybe a day, but not much longer.

The playfully sensuous eyes looked down at him as she checked the dressing on his head. Smooth hands, twenties, definitely in her twenties. She read the monitors studiously then carefully withdrew his medication from a small metal bottle and injected it skillfully into his I.V., but there was nothing clinical in the way she caressed his forearm. She caught him admiring the snug fit of her scrubs and smiled an invitation he was in no shape to accept, nor would he be for weeks.

Randy recalled his vision like a hard slap to the face. The nurse was a distraction he couldn't afford. Women like her were in his past. It was time to make good on his transgressions and that would take a Herculean effort. Lying there in the bed he had no idea what God expected. Doing anything in his condition would be a miracle. When he healed, he'd be facing the consequences of his vendetta against the Caulfields and the Marstons. Salvation was a dim hope, but no trial in this world compared to feeling a demon gnawing into your flesh day after day. Randy would never forget the hideous incisors tearing into TJ's thigh. He'd do anything to avoid that.

The nurse jotted a few notes on his chart and exited with a flap of the curtain and a sly look back. A blue-uniformed shoulder appeared in the doorway behind her and disappeared as the curtain snapped closed. The Westport police weren't taking any chances. The officer in the doorway wasn't going to let him get close enough for a chop to the windpipe. He'd heard that story, not that it mattered. Randy could barely move.

For the next thirty minutes, Randy listened to the voices passing outside and wondered about his quest. He'd delivered justice to Caulfield and Marston, but his methods had gotten him here, battered, with his soul destined for Hell if he didn't make amends. Randy's tactics needed to change. He needed to follow His law and yet he sensed it was his ability to drive and fight and shoot that would redeem him. The idea defied logic, but he couldn't shake it away. He wondered if he was expected to follow his earthly punishment to prison; if it was there he'd find souls in need of saving. He doubted it was true as the curtain pulled open again. Worthy people would be found in thousands of homes around the city.

A short, stocky man in a dark suit pushed through the curtain and pulled it closed. Serious eyes surveyed Randy. He'd only been conscious thirty minutes and already the police were there to beat a confession out of him. The man hung back, eyeing the casts, the monitors and the I.V. as if he were concerned about Randy's condition. He stepped up to the bedside and lifted the handcuff chain with a smirk.

"You must be a very dangerous man."

Randy wasn't ready for this conversation. He didn't know a good lawyer and he wasn't even sure he *should* defend himself. Taking his punishment might be the right first step. He doubted he could repair the damage he'd done from within prison walls, but taking his punishment felt right.

When Randy didn't answer, Detective Al Ruiz introduced himself as the sole internal affairs officer from Westport. "I wanted to see for myself," he said, "what kind of man takes five officers to subdue and sustains such serious injuries without leaving a mark on even one of the arresting officers. Very kind of you, I'd say."

"Worried I'll sue?" Randy croaked.

"I'm not a selectman. It's not my money. I'm here to see why five good men risked their careers by putting you in this bed."

A few words would sink Pinto. Randy pissed him off. Maybe he deserved a good whack with the nightstick, but not this. Still, he said nothing to Ruiz. Maybe it wasn't time. Maybe he'd tell the story later. Or maybe turning the other cheek was his first step back. Randy watched Ruiz unlock the cuff that held his wrist.

Rubbing his face, he felt several days of stubble and immediately wanted to shave. The stubble felt unclean, a reminder of Randy Black and all that he'd done.

Ruiz cautioned Randy that once convicted, his story would carry less weight. The time to come out against the offending officers was now, while a jury could see the damage for themselves, before arraignment, before trial, before he went to prison. Ruiz had no doubt where Randy was headed. He didn't condemn his brother officers for what they'd done, but he stood ready to punish them.

Would speaking out bolster his defense? A jury might think so.

Randy had thought the whole mess backward and forward while hiding out with the blonde and he'd come up with a believable story. If Charlie believed his father had crippled him, it seemed natural that he'd want revenge. Of course he'd need to cover it up and that explained Randy's involvement with the family. Saving the bottles had been a great idea. Such an uncommon bacteria showing up in so many different places proved Charles tampered with the wine. The cops helped the case by putting Randy in the hospital. Putting Pinto and the others on trial might be enough to manufacture reasonable doubt. The jury didn't have to believe Randy was innocent. They just needed to be unsure. With so many competing motives, a skilled lawyer might muddy the water enough to get Randy acquitted.

Thou shalt not bear false witness.

The words boomed in Randy's head. A familiar voice, not his Aunt's. A Bible school teacher's or Reverend White's, perhaps. Incriminating Charlie to save himself was out of bounds. Randy couldn't do it.

Ruiz implored him to tell the truth about what happened.

Randy trembled and Ruiz realized he wasn't listening.

Punishing Pinto accomplished nothing. Another distraction Randy couldn't afford. What happened that night at the winery was obvious, but Ruiz was helpless without Randy's cooperation. His anger was building. Abiding this injustice wouldn't be easy for Ruiz. He glared, trying to understand what held Randy back. He'd never know.

The curtain swooped open and the nurse swept in, surprised to find Ruiz at Randy's bedside. Measuring the two men, she sensed Randy's unease and suggested the detective come back when Randy was feeling stronger.

Ruiz pleaded his case one last time, left a white business card on the table and headed out to complete a doomed investigation.

Randy wondered if he'd just taken his first step. He'd trained himself to drive and stalk and shoot with devastating results. His talents were suited to a war of men, not a war of faith. After what he'd seen, his psyche was in no condition to wage a spiritual war. His ravaged body could do little even if he escaped the bed. He knew then what he needed. He asked his nurse, Rita, for some paper and penned a message in a dozen shakily-formed words.

Surprise registered on Rita's face when she read them.

She hesitated a long moment then left to fulfill his request.

Chapter Four

The glint off the sharpened machete flashed so brilliantly it stabbed Randy's optic nerve. His thoughts screamed run, but he was surrounded by nothingness. His fingers clung to a rough-sawn beam and his body dangled down toward oblivion. The demon atop the beam stalked closer and Randy swayed hand over hand beneath, desperately trying to get away. The beam dead-ended in the darkness. Where Randy had hoped to find a cable or a pole supporting the beam's weight, he found nothing to aid his escape. Randy hung there, cornered. The demon closed in, waving the impossibly sharp machete. The scaly beast licked the scent of Randy's terror from its lips. Talons stretched down. A honed claw carved a perfect, bloody circle into Randy's forehead as he hung helpless.

The demon lapped blood from its claw with its long, forked tongue. Horror stole Randy's screams. The beast lashed down and buried the machete an inch deep into the beam. Vibrations numbed Randy's arm. Severed fingers spilled off the beam and disappeared into the darkness, dropping but never making landfall. Blood flowed from useless knuckles up and over the blunt edge of the blade. The demon screeched with glee as it freed the blade, eager for another bloody treat.

Randy climbed atop the beam and faced the demon one-handed. The creature attacked, leaping high, the machete poised to strike. Randy's heart drummed. As the creature reached the apex of its leap, Randy saw that the beam beneath his feet was a weathered cross.

The blade sliced down.

Randy gasped. He woke to disinfectant and fluorescent lights.

Another dream.

In the twenty-four hours he'd been conscious, he was either in a woozy, drug-induced haze or suffering a pounding headache. When he dozed, the dreams reminded him of what he'd done and shook him to his core. The circle on his forehead matched TJ's bullet wound precisely. The fingers reminded him of his most horrible deed. TJ had been dead an hour before Randy chopped off his fingers and left them for Deirdre and Charlie to find. The demon took no such pity. It reveled in its work while Randy was still alive, just as he punished TJ's conscious soul into eternity.

They were weaning him off the drugs. His head felt clearer, but he also felt the throbbing in his temples. His eyelids ached and he let them drift closed. When he did, he saw Charles Marston's battered face, then Henri's slumped body. His eyes blinked open again. Eternal punishment felt absolutely certain. Lying in bed wracked in pain was merely a prelude. When he reached Hell the pain would flare and fade over and over, an endless repetition that would dull all sensation until heinous torture numbed to monotony. He wished they'd give him something strong enough to make him sleep—strong enough to make him forget.

He grabbed a handful of his own hair. He was damned forever, without doubt, without hope. Idiot! He'd traded a few hours of fury for an eternity of suffering.

His chest seized. The infinite expanse of galaxies stretched out in his mind. Too large to comprehend. Too large to contain. What could create something so immense that man couldn't travel to its edge? Boundless. Indestructible. The universe must be reality. The *only* reality. What happened in this life was everything. The end. He'd live out his life in prison and then darkness. Nothingness. No trace of him would remain. His consciousness extinguished for all time. The finality made his pain here in the bed and what was to come pointless. He'd meet his end caged in jail, surrounded by cretins lusting for violence and sodomy. The only existence that remained for him, horrifying as it was, must be lived. The thought of his spirit doused forever sent painful spasms through his chest. There in the bed, the idea was inescapable. If anyone could hear him, he'd have begged for company. He'd talk about anything to push away the feeling of his soul being stamped out for all eternity.

But God did exist. He'd spoken to Randy and shown him the changes in Henri and the others. It wasn't a dream.

Randy trembled. He imagined a universe small enough to sit on God's desk. All powerful, He could create an individual reality to test each of us, so much simpler than the hectic chaos of six billion souls determining their own destiny. But what contained His world? Randy's thoughts circled from godless to God-centered. His view of Heaven and Hell was beyond what the drugs or his imagination could create. His vision was a divine gift. The dreams might be his subconscious prodding him forward, but they could also be a message from above.

Randy prayed for strength and the savvy to recognize the path.

One tortured hour later, Reverend Simmons of the First Congregational Church in Westport walked in with Rita's note pressed to a black, hardbound Bible. Randy hadn't been to the church in Westport since his parents' funeral fifteen years earlier. He hadn't attended service since leaving the Midwest. The separation helped explain his current crisis.

The reverend stepped through the privacy curtain as if taking the stage. Young, polished, tan, he looked more like Mel Gibson than a man of God.

Reverend Simmons browsed the monitors then the bandages, assessing Randy's condition without comment. Every clergyman heard deathbed confessions. The nurses had surely told him about Randy's treatment. He'd know about the injuries, the drugs, even how long he'd been unconscious. He'd know why Randy was here, too. Whatever Randy told him, his credibility would be thin. At least the handcuffs were gone.

Listening to Randy describe what he'd seen, any sane person would attribute the vision to the drugs, the injuries, or even stress. Randy had much to fear in this world and even more in the next. The reverend was an ally he couldn't do without, so he wouldn't risk scaring him off. He'd earn the reverend's confidence before mentioning his audience with God.

The reverend introduced himself with a firm handshake, retrieved a chair and parked himself by the bedside. His eyes skimmed the plaster casts and followed them directly up into Randy's.

He waved the note and tamed his booming voice to a sturdy whisper. "You sounded eager to see me." As the whisper faded, he glanced from the casts over to the devices behind the bed.

If the reverend knew why he'd been asked to come he might have been jealous. He saw a sinner beaten near to death, a soul in desperate need of salvation. Would he believe God had spoken to such a lowly man?

Randy waited a moment and asked, "Is it ever too late to be forgiven?"

"In the eyes of man, definitely. But only God knows His plan for you."

"If you've gone too far, how do you know you've redeemed yourself?"

"That's the problem with life after death, isn't it? You never know where you stand until it's too late. When you're kneeling before God to be judged, there's no going back to make amends."

"Guess that's what packs 'em in on Sundays."

The reverend's eyes widened with surprise.

Randy couldn't believe his blunder. No matter how scared he was, he couldn't stop the old Randy from creeping through. Fortunately, the reverend saw his embarrassment and took no offense.

"Imagine how good business would be if everyone knew Heaven existed, like they believe in this hospital or that machine over there."

Like me, Randy thought.

"You're going to walk out of here soon and I expect you'll live a long life. Your relationship with God has time to blossom. Don't try to repair it in hours or days. There's no magic bullet. Use this experience as incentive to make some changes. Start your journey."

"I have." Randy couldn't explain his urgency, but he couldn't deny it either. "I've done some awful things, Reverend. I need to turn my life around and I'm scared it's too late."

The reverend's eyes flicked toward the nurses' station. They'd told him Randy would recover. Randy couldn't tell him how he knew his time was short, but he was glad the reverend didn't argue the point.

19

"Are you familiar with King David?"

Randy nodded.

"King David was said to be one of God's favorites in Heaven, but did you know he wasn't always virtuous?"

Randy didn't.

"King David surrounded himself with protectors known as the Mighty Men." The reverend spoke with a voiceover man's melodic tones. "These men were fiercely loyal and supported the king to the death. One night while the Mighty Men were out fighting, King David spied a beautiful woman in an adjacent home, the wife of one of his most loyal soldiers. She eventually shared his bed and became pregnant."

So far, this was nothing compared to what Randy had done.

"King David took confidence in one of his most loyal Mighty Men. He instructed the troops to engage in battle and then retreat, leaving the husband of the king's pregnant mistress surrounded by the enemy. The husband was killed and King David eventually married the widow."

Here was a famous biblical persona mired in the same issues Randy got himself tangled up in. They had different reasons, but it seemed the nature of sin hadn't changed all that much in two thousand years. Sex, wealth and murder had a way of knotting themselves together. Randy felt somewhat justified. He hadn't initiated his troubles as King David had.

"And God forgave him?" Randy asked.

"Revelations tells us that he did. The key is true repentance."

Randy nodded slowly and waited for an explanation.

"True repentance means being genuinely sorry for what you've done. Understanding that you've sinned, asking for forgiveness and truly changing. Changing so completely that you know what you did was wrong and you couldn't imagine yourself doing it again."

Randy felt this way now.

"Could there be something more? Something I need to do?"

"Like going to jail?"

That wasn't his first thought. "I can't honestly defend myself."

"Don't give up. You're young. You have much to do in this world."

What could he do behind bars? Who could he help there?

"Let me tell you a story," Reverend Simmons began. "I was preaching in Alabama and there was a terrible flood. Everyone was told to evacuate, but one of my deacons stayed rooted on his porch and prayed all night. When the water reached his porch a boat came. 'The Lord will take care of me,' he said and sent the boat away. That night, the water crested above his gutters and he retreated to the roof. Another boat came and he sent that one away with the same faith that God would save him. At dawn he was standing on his chimney in water up to his neck. A helicopter hovered above him. Still, he refused to grab the life preserver and haul himself up. Five minutes after the helicopter left, he stumbled and drowned. When he met God he asked why he'd been forsaken.

"God said, 'I sent two boats and a helicopter.'"

Chuckling pained Randy's ribs, but his spirit appreciated the lift.

"God expects us to take care of ourselves?" Randy asked.

"Exactly. He doesn't wave a magic wand and make things better when we need help, but He may offer us an opportunity to grab hold of."

God wanted more from Randy. There was something he needed to do, someone he needed to help, or something he needed to change. Whatever it was he couldn't add new sins to the ledger before he accomplished God's work. He couldn't incriminate Charlie to save himself and he couldn't imagine earning his freedom otherwise.

The reverend seemed able to read his mind.

"I've ministered to many people, Randy, few so urgently as you. You're not dying, son. You'll be fine. Don't despair."

The reverend could see the words provided no comfort.

"What's frightened you so?"

"Hell." Randy trembled with the admission.

"Good work by my brethren, I guess. Scared you straight?"

Randy shook his head solemnly, deliberately.

The reverend straightened. His hesitation showed grave doubts he wouldn't admit aloud. He believed in God. God was the center of his life's work, but how could he believe God would speak to someone like Randy?

He'd sinned grievously. The drugs, the head trauma, the unconsciousness, they were all easy explanations for anything Randy thought he'd seen.

Randy needed no explanation. What he saw was real.

"You do believe in Hell?" Randy asked.

"Of course," Simmons said, "one cannot believe in Heaven without also believing in Hell."

"And you'd do anything to avoid it?"

"Anything?" the reverend squeaked. "I've spent the last ten years reaching for Heaven's rewards." The reverend grimaced, the lines in his face rippled outward.

He looked forty-five. Randy wondered what he had done for the first thirty-five years.

"If you knew you were headed for Hell, what would you do?"

"You can't know…"

Rita slipped through the curtain with a single step. She'd been listening nearby and curiosity finally brought her inside under the guise of checking the equipment.

The reverend hesitated, looking at Rita in her scrubs and waiting for a dismissal from Randy, but he was shocked at what he heard next.

"Let's say I know," Randy began strongly. "Let's say there's a limit to God's willingness to forgive us and I know I'm over the line. I need to get back across and sooner is better."

Rita fled as if Satan himself had spoken.

"Impossible. No one knows God's will," the reverend said.

"Not impossible. You believe He exists. You believe He has power over everything living and dead. What do I do if He said I'm over the line?"

Reverend Simmons held Randy's gaze, a dozen explanations swirling in his mind. He gave no indication what he thought. Instead he asked why Randy thought he'd crossed the line of God's tolerance. He might have been jealous. He might have thought Randy insane, but at least he was diplomatic.

Instead of describing his vision, Randy told the story of his parents' death in a car wreck when he was thirteen. He had followed the path to the

Narrow Gate until that day, but knowing who was responsible for their deaths proved too much to live with. Something changed within him then and though his aunt ministered to him through the next six years, he planned in agonizing detail to avenge his parents. The plot took nearly ten years to develop and it cost him much of the money his parents left. When it was all over, he'd committed adultery in horrific fashion and tempted a decent young man to do the same. He'd killed three people and bought the death of another. He'd destroyed a man's life and marriage. He'd never expected to see this day and now that his revenge had been taken and his heart had cooled, he knew how wrong he'd been. But was it too late to repent?

"Repentance is an absolute change—heart and mind. Start there," the reverend said.

God said the way would be clear. Randy needed to heed the signs, but it wasn't that simple. The reverend believed wholeheartedly in forgiveness, but he didn't understand that the task ahead of Randy would be monumental. Randy prodded, but the pastor offered nothing concrete.

"Nothing's a coincidence," the pastor said. "It's all in His grand plan."

Randy believed that more than ever. If he was meant to save people in prison, then prison is where he'd end up. If not, he'd be set free. He wouldn't break his way out and he wouldn't perjure his way out. If God wanted him free, Pinto's mistake with the club would get him released. If not that, some other opportunity would be revealed in time.

Randy would wait and watch for a sign, look for someone who needed help and pray for the vision to see his task clearly.

Seeing his parents, Henri and Monique was a great gift. The change in Henri was tremendous. The man had a right to despise Randy and yet he stood without malice and watched as Randy was shown what he needed to see. This more than anything spoke of the wonders of Paradise. Earthly concerns paled when compared to the Everlasting and though Henri must have remembered what happened, his anger had been lifted. The joy of Paradise must be great indeed.

Randy felt the smooth cover of the Bible the reverend left.

He would find his way there somehow.

Chapter Five

Judge McKinnon surveyed the eighty spectators that packed his courtroom to hear the verdict read. The big woman in the front row wasn't glaring at him today. She focused on the jury foreman as he handed the verdict sheet to the bailiff. She knew what was written inside. She'd cornered McKinnon in the hall a day earlier and cursed his one-sidedness. She called him a racist for letting a white man off after he killed a black and she continued to spew threats until a court officer hauled her away. She'd been the accused in this courtroom half a dozen times. She'd never had such treatment and neither had her son.

Was it justice?

What had this grossly obese woman contributed to the world in her thirty plus years? She'd given birth to four kids she couldn't support or control. The oldest, a gang thug, was shot dead by the man at the defense table. Few in the courtroom disputed that, least of all McKinnon. He also wouldn't dispute that her other children were headed for similar fates. Unfair? Sure. Why hadn't anyone told her to get an education? Why hadn't anyone shown her the ambition to hold down a job? Why hadn't anyone stopped her from getting pregnant before she graduated high school? They'd stolen her dignity, these politicians obsessed with reversing Darwinism.

The neighborhood was better off without her gun-toting son. They had one less drug dealer corrupting kids and terrorizing law-abiding citizens. Still, McKinnon needed a drink to help him forget he was letting a killer go free to save his job and whatever dignity he had left.

The verdict arrived at the bench. McKinnon didn't need to read the words 'not guilty.' Not one juror looked at the prosecutor or the mother behind him. They didn't look at Tomlin either. They believed he was guilty and they wanted to convict him, but the evidence wasn't there. Tomlin stared straight back at McKinnon. He was no stranger to the law. He'd heard the testimony and he knew the slugs they recovered were useless without the murder weapon. He also knew he'd gotten more than his share of breaks.

Seated beside his client, defense attorney Tom Gold restrained his glee. He was given a sympathetic jury and deftly created reasonable doubt in their minds. In minutes he'd be on the courtroom steps playing to the cameras. His client was a victim of unfortunate timing. He'd been driving in the wrong part of town on the wrong morning. McKinnon hadn't tipped the scales enough for the media to notice. To a casual observer the proceedings were fair and orderly, but to a trained litigator, the tiny manipulations reeked of malfeasance. McKinnon wondered why the prosecutor hadn't objected more strenuously. He hadn't protested a key inadmissibility ruling at all. He argued credibly and built a logical case, but there wasn't a lot of fire behind his words. Maybe he felt the same way about dead drug dealers or maybe he was feeling the pressure, too. McKinnon would never know.

McKinnon handed the verdict sheet back and watched it read, watched the subdued celebration at the defense table, watched anger grip the powerless family. A son and a brother was gone. McKinnon's leftist peers wouldn't think so, but the city was better off. Justice failed the boy, but he reaped what he sowed. McKinnon couldn't bring him back, nor would he, given the chance. He didn't want to face the angry mother again and he rued the day he'd meet an angry father who could deliver on his threats.

McKinnon thanked the jurors, dismissed them and adjourned court for the day. He turned his back on the whole sordid nightmare and disappeared behind the bench. The hall to his chambers was empty. He banged the door closed, tossed his robe toward a guest chair and dug behind some files for a young single malt scotch. The first gulp of fire didn't ease his conscience.

Tomlin perplexed him. The scruffy hair and goatee gave him the look of a fun-loving kid. Nothing about him said cold-blooded killer. Weeks in the courtroom told McKinnon much about the men who faced justice there, but Tomlin might have fooled him if he hadn't known the truth.

The prosecutor never told the jury that Tomlin was a former cop, fired for taking a bribe. It was an unusual offense for a man so new to the force. He didn't have the criminal vibe. He was young, affable, but someone had gotten to him. He didn't seem the type to gun down young kids either, but this wasn't some random thing. The victim wasn't selected by chance.

Tom Gold barged in like an old college buddy. He'd been doing it so long he didn't look over his shoulder anymore. The other judges knew they were connected. If they attributed McKinnon's favoritism to their friendship, so be it. Gold looked more the privileged, trust fund kid than a career criminal and McKinnon hoped what he was doing looked like favors for wealthy friends. The truth was too scandalous to believe.

How Gold and Scott Tomlin, the scruffy kid defendant, got mixed up in this was beyond McKinnon. Gold never lost a case, but Tomlin had to do more than pay to become a client. When Tom Gold appeared in court, most of the heavy lifting had already happened behind the scenes. The shame of releasing guilty men never showed on Gold. At least Scott Tomlin had hung his head for the verdict.

Gold spun a guest chair and sat, propped his feet on the arm of another and gestured to a spare coffee mug. McKinnon poured and passed it over, nodding to the ceiling as he did. The gesture had no effect on Tom.

"Don't take it so hard," Tom said. "That punk made his living selling drugs to school kids. There's no telling how many lives he screwed up or how many lives we saved today. The city's better off without him. The world's better off without him."

"Tell that to his mother."

"Some princess. Fat, lazy, baby machine. She should be next."

Tom believed it. So much for the defense lawyer out to save the little man from oppression.

"It doesn't bother you at all?" the judge asked.

"Bother me? I won."

Chapter Six

Cassie Corcoran weaved through the looping I.C.U. corridor, avoiding a wheelchair and a cart filled with medical supplies. Busy nurses noted her passing without eye contact. She found Randy Black's room easily. A dozen feet from the nurses' station, one of Westport's finest leaned against the frame of an open door. It was strange to find a Westport cop guarding a prisoner in a New Bedford hospital, but the reasons were spelled out in pages of notes from her meetings with Charlie Marston and Jo Caulfield. This one man had rained terror down on three families, ripping them apart in a matter of weeks. Meeting him in person would hone Cassie's hallmark perspective.

The cop barely shifted his eyes from his newspaper when Cassie passed. She glanced to see if he was reading something of hers. He was opened to sports, a full page about the Red Sox. When she stepped inside she realized why he took the duty so lightly. His prisoner was half-covered in plaster, his left arm suspended by two twisted cables. The body in the bed didn't jive with the story she'd been fed by the Westport P.D. Officers Alvares, Bindas and McGee all backed Pinto. They said he resisted and they restrained him, but it was nothing serious. None of them had a mark on their faces or hands. No doubt Randy Black was dangerous, but she knew Pinto had an axe to grind over the escape. The whole department did and their story was beginning to smell. She polished her notebook with a fingertip as she stepped closer. A police brutality angle might give her piece some balance. If only she'd thought to bring a photographer.

A blonde nurse leaned over Randy's bedside intent on his every expression. Their slow movements mirrored each other from arm's length. When Randy turned away from the shamelessly flirtatious look in her eyes, the nurse wheeled around looking caught. When she realized it wasn't another staff member, her glare hardened, ready to defend her turf.

Venomous looks from other women were nothing new for Cassie. She did what she could to look studious. Her long, fine hair lay straight down below her shoulders and the dark-rimmed glasses broke up the elegant lines of her face. Cassie wouldn't compete for his attention. The nurse could have the bum. After her ex-boyfriend moved back to Texas, the last thing she needed was romance, especially with a hoodlum like Randy Black. She'd seen too many guys like him in Dorchester. All she wanted was an interview, a chance to put a face on the maniac and give her story legitimacy. With it she might have another Wally Ramos. Her profile of the gang leader won her this job on the crime beat. Her Randy Black series could push her past Walter Macedo and cement her lead in the newsroom. All she needed was a peek into Randy's psyche, but first, she needed to get rid of the nurse.

"Who are you?" the nurse asked, standing to face Cassie who didn't have a ready answer. "Only family in I.C.U."

Cassie waited half a second too long before answering.

"His girlfriend," she said unconvincingly. "Are you almost done?" She sneered a bit too late, feigning the jealousy of a woman who'd caught her boyfriend ogling another woman's cleavage. Deirdre Deudon said he charmed her clothes off before she knew it. He was making progress with Nurse Blondie. What he expected to do with her in his condition was another matter.

A strained moment passed between them.

Randy hadn't recognized her, but he refused to expose the lie.

The nurse stood her ground.

Cassie took off her glasses and smiled to show her perfect white teeth. She eased around to the opposite side of the bed. The reporter angle wasn't going to cut it with the nurse, but Randy didn't balk. She gave him a flirtatious smile and squeezed between the nurse and the bed. If he was willing to play along, so would she. She'd wonder later if the rouse was borne of a reporter's instinct for the best path to the story or a woman's curiosity about the devilish man Deirdre Deudon warned her about.

"I was so worried about you," Cassie said. "I came as soon as I could." She leaned down and kissed his cleanly-shaven cheek. Her buttons were securely fastened. He wouldn't be seeing her cleavage no matter how far she bent, but he didn't seem to mind. She withdrew and regarded him from several inches, blocking his view to the nurse behind her. His measured look stopped her there. This was no Wally Ramos. Wally had the unsettled eyes of a feral cat, flicking, constantly classifying predator and prey. Randy regarded her deeply with a parent's concern. He knew she was in a tough spot with the nurse and he helped without knowing who she was or why she was here.

They surveyed each other intently, wordlessly as the nurse backed away from the bed. She promised to check on him then pulled the curtain closed and disappeared. Cassie barely heard her leave.

"Thanks," she whispered.

Everything she'd been told screamed crazed, psychotic killer, but he'd just allowed Cassie to wrangle her way in and displace a nurse who was obviously flirting with him. He could have turned Cassie away with a few words. What wild-eyed crazy would do such a thing? Not for Cassie, dressed like a bookworm. Before she came, she'd resolved to keep her distance, not to let him know anything about her save her name and the story she was writing for *The Standard Times*, but she'd kissed him within a minute of walking in. Utterly convincing as the nice guy, he'd disarmed her in moments. She needed to be very careful with Randy Black. He was more dangerous than she'd imagined.

She formally introduced herself and described the story she was writing. He looked surprised. Hadn't anyone approached him? Wasn't he expecting the media to pounce? His picture had been on television for weeks. The Marstons' side of the story had been rehashed over and over by every newspaper and television station in New England. His story was debated on talk radio as a prime candidate to bring capital punishment back to Massachusetts. Cassie couldn't believe she was the first to discover he was conscious. Hadn't the Globe tracked him down? He could be feigning modesty, but his act was entirely believable.

"I've spoken to Charlie Marston and Jo Caulfield. I'd like to hear your side of the events."

"How is Jo?"

"Getting a divorce. Thanks to you, she says."

"She's better off without him. How much is she getting?"

"Is this how it's going to be?"

"Something wrong? I could call the nurse back in."

"Cute." He enjoyed having her at his mercy. He knew he'd lose control of his words once they were spoken. Was he worried about her twisting them? How could she convince him that she wanted to understand how his life had come to this? Her readers would be enthralled to read the inner thoughts of a madman fresh off a violent rampage. He faced serious charges and had his defense to worry about. Maybe he was worried about poisoning the jury pool. Maybe she'd have to wait until he was in prison to get honest answers. Or maybe he needed money for legal fees. *The Standard Times* didn't pay for information. If he was holding out for money, he'd be disappointed. She sighed knowing she couldn't pay for his story herself.

"You want to tell the world my story. Tell them you caught up to the evil Randy Black and made him talk. What do I get?"

"A forum to tell your side. To let the truth come out."

Something she said struck him silent. He gazed at her blankly.

"You must have an incredible story to tell," she prompted.

He attempted a smile, but it fell flat.

He was nothing like the man he was built up to be. It seemed getting caught drained the spark from the crazed madman.

She stepped back, slipped her digital camera from her purse and snapped a shot of the bandages, the wires and the machines behind. An exclusive. It'd never make page one, but she hoped Bart would run it.

"I could use a friend right now," he said.

The last thing she wanted from this interview was a relationship.

"And if you had a friend, you'd give her a good interview?"

"I'd give her plenty to dig into," he said hopefully.

Cassie was no prison girlfriend. He was a great looking guy. Smooth with the ladies according to Charlie. If he wasn't facing multiple murder charges, she might have considered fixing him up with a friend.

"What are you looking for? Someone to hear your confession?"

"I spoke to the reverend yesterday. I'm all set on confessions."

Another surprise. The visitor log would have the reverend's name.

"I could use some company. I don't get out much."

"Enjoy it now. You won't be getting out for a long time."

Randy laughed. "I like you," he said, "so let's start here: how did the Marstons get their hands on seven wineries?"

Cassie knew offhand from her discussions with Charlie. "Charles Senior rescued them from bankruptcy. He turned them around one at a time and made them profitable."

"EEENNNNTTT," he buzzed with the little strength he had. "You don't really believe that?" he mocked.

"Why not?"

"If you're going to write my story you need better research. Find out why those wineries had problems. When you can tell me, we'll talk."

"Can you tell me why you bought a house right across the street from the Caulfields? Jo says you were watching them. She says you broke into their house and tore it apart."

"Research first. Talk later. You have much to learn."

"One more question." Randy snickered, but she went ahead anyway. "Will you be pressing charges against Officer Pinto and the others?"

A no-brainer. At least she'd have something to write for Monday's paper. Cassie opened her notebook, ready for a quote.

Randy didn't give her one. He barely shook his head. If she hadn't been intent on his face she wouldn't have noticed.

"You can't be serious. Don't you want to see them punished?"

"That's not my decision."

"Of course it is. You can't let them get away with what they did to you."

"Who says they'll get away with anything?"

Cassie imagined Randy tracking the officers down and strangling them.

He sensed the plot developing in her head. "They'll be judged in time. It's not up to me—or you, Cassie."

"Don't you want the truth to come out?"

"The truth is a difficult master. We only pretend to know it. Take the Marstons for example. You stormed in here knowing Charles Marston was a successful and respected businessman and I was a thug. I bet if you do some research, you'll discover that you're quite mistaken."

His smile said the meeting was over.

Was she really going to start digging that far in the past? She had two more articles roughed out, but until now her coverage was the same as everyone else's. Charlie Marston wasn't shy about interviews. Neither were Bill and Jo Caulfield. If she gained Randy's trust, she might have the story the other reporters missed: another Wally Ramos. She shook his hand and headed for the archives.

Chapter Seven

Scott Tomlin ignored the rapid fire clicking as Whitey investigated alert after alert. Wakefield was pitching that night for the Sox. When his knuckleball was working he was beguiling, but having a guy on the mound who threw less than eighty miles per hour made Tomlin nervous. The Devil Rays' batting averages kept them in the cellar, but they surprised the Sox more often than they should.

"Tom Gold walking in." Whitey paused. "Elevator up. Four."

Scott closed his browser and swiveled around to watch Whitey work one of the thousands of cameras they monitored. From here they could freeze Tom between floors and keep him in the elevator as long as they wanted. Tom knew the emergency hatch was welded shut, but he winked at the camera anyway. He knew he wasn't in any danger.

"Keep an eye on the front. Let's make sure no one's behind him," Scott cautioned.

"You really don't like this guy do you?"

"He's too full of himself. Attracts too much attention."

"Saved your ass yesterday."

What did the kid know? At five four and one hundred forty pounds, Whitey was useless on the street. If he didn't spend so much time in a tanning booth, his orangey skin would glow like the whites of his eyes. He worked the cameras and he was great with the systems, but he couldn't do the real work of this firm. Someday they might bring him in, but for now he was safer wielding a keyboard.

Scott kept his evaluation to himself.

"Bring me next time you go out on a job. I'll keep you from getting locked up."

Bad luck had gotten Scott locked up. Some guy backed out of his driveway without looking at 4:00 A.M. The car appeared in Scott's path, two blocks from a scene littered with dead gang bangers. His Viper would have been through in a flash, but the communications van was too sluggish. He caught the guy's bumper and careened into two parked cars before he got control. The windshield held him in, but that didn't ease the headaches he suffered for the next week. The other guys got bounced around, but they hopped out the back and hoofed it. Scott was too dazed to get out and run.

He felt like running now. Tom only came in on payday or when he had a new operation to discuss. It wasn't payday. One day out of court and Tom already had a new op. Scott already knew his next job was going to bring plenty of heat. They should lay low for at least a month afterward, but there was no money in that.

Whitey switched to the hall camera.

Tom got off the elevator and walked to the control room door.

"Tomlin in there? I need a minute."

"Keep your eyes on the alarms. I'll be back."

Whitey clicked the door release with a smirk.

Scott shook Tom's hand and waited for the electronic deadbolts to engage. Tom was halfway to the conference room when he turned, so Scott hustled to catch up. Being alone in the halls was a very bad idea.

From the outside, the place looked decrepit, but the entire building had been gutted and rebuilt as a fortress from the inside out. Twenty feet inside the brick exterior, a new building was erected without fanfare or permits, the materials hauled in and out through the loading dock. The thick concrete walls and electronic locks seemed like paranoia at first, but the stockpile in the vault required protection. Access to the inner shell was tightly controlled. If anyone fought their way inside, they could be secured and wiped out from the control room. Nothing messy. No bullet holes, no blood, just dead bodies on the floor to be hauled away and dumped.

When Scott caught Tom outside the conference room the vulnerable feeling subsided. He felt foolish clinging to Tom for protection. He was in charge of the team, but they'd been butting heads too often lately. If he crossed the line he'd find himself trapped in a hall like this one, hearing the hiss of carbon monoxide. He'd watched the desperate clawing once himself. If the boss' loyalties frittered off, it could happen to him.

Tom pressed his thumb on the scanner and unlocked the glass doors. The long mahogany table rarely seated more than three, another sign of the overkill all around this building. Scott hid his disdain as he faced Tom with the table width between them.

Tom described this new operation as a slam dunk.

The target was a Latino male age twenty-four. Arrested sixteen times, mostly assault. One drug conviction. The latest arrest was a rape and murder. No DNA and no witnesses. The assault was brutal. The damage was evident even though the body was badly decomposed by the time a hiker stumbled over it. The DA was pushing the family to let him drop the case.

That's when the father found Tom.

"This is way outside our usual field," Scott said. Ethan would say this was the type of guy they should be killing on a regular basis. Khan would be all over this one. He'd do it for free if they let him.

"It's ten K. Twenty extra if the father pulls the trigger." Tom liked this idea. "An easy snatch and grab," he said.

Easy for him. He'd be in his office when the grab went down. Scott would be wearing a dark hood, shoving the kid into a van at gunpoint. If the rest of his gang saw the grab, the street would light up like Armageddon.

Tom pulled a photo from his briefcase and slid it across the table. He refused to let go when Scott's fingers reached it. Scott let go, gave the subservient nod Tom was looking for and then took the picture. It was a good close photo against a white wall, probably taken in the courthouse. Tom didn't do these things himself. He only knew people who did things like this, that and collect the money. Tom didn't allow links to anyone dirty to linger. He wanted the photo gone in an hour. How they made sure to get the right kid, that was Scott's problem.

Scott recognized the address in the white margin as rough territory.

"I'm working the DA to drop the case. Follow him and get ready for the snatch. We're going to take the extra twenty so be ready for that, too."

Scott half rose from his chair before Tom pulled out another photo. Two new projects one day out of court! All these bodies dropping at the same time were going to make big waves in the city.

Scott recognized the photo from television news bulletins. Anyone in Southeastern Massachusetts would. The address was printed neatly.

"Why are we getting involved with this guy? He's a lunatic."

The answer was immediate. "We've got a big job coming up. Ten times bigger than anything we've done. It's going to bring a lot of heat."

Scott was feeling plenty of heat already.

"Didn't he kill two people in front of the family?" Scott asked. "You don't really think he's going to get off?"

"It's not as simple as the press makes it out. One murder looked like a professional hit. Single bullet wound to the forehead, but then he chopped the guy's fingers off after he died. The father got it worse. His body was mutilated then hung in his own house. There was all kinds of evidence left behind. Professional surveillance gear was found at the scene along with the murder weapons, but the motives get murky. That's where this guy was brilliant. He twisted things around to point at the son."

"That Marston kid? C'mon. He's straight as they come."

"Black left him holding a recently fired murder weapon. The kid tested positive for powder residue."

Impressive, even better than some of Scott's work.

"The DA knows he did it. He has a legal box full of sworn testimony from the family. He terrorized them for months, but I'm telling you, he covered his ass. The DA's not banking on a conviction."

"The cops roughed him up good from what I heard."

"That's not helping the DA either. Five Westport cops beat the snot out of him. No weapons recovered."

"So what's the deal?"

"Wire him up good. I want to know everywhere he goes, everyone he talks to, the works."

"Not the hospital?"

"Forget the hospital. He won't be there long." Tom indicated the address on the photo. "Start with his house. He's got a Chevy van and a fancy Mercedes. Do them both. We'll start working him when he gets out."

"What's our angle?"

"He's going to do some work for us."

"Are you kidding?"

Tom stood up. "No worries. It's going to be cake."

Scott stared down at the long scraggly hair and reflective glasses in the photo. The door closed behind Tom and he was alone. Tripp was bad enough. This guy was even more of a psycho. Chopping fingers off. This guy got his jollies freaking people out. Scott couldn't maintain order with guys like this around. Tom's caseload was about to get much heavier.

For a second, the brick walls of the precinct flashed to mind.

He could never go back and he'd never want to. After three months here, he realized the force was a joke. Thirty percent of the trash he locked up got out and re-offended. Most of them didn't waste much time. The slammer taught them to be more careful, but trash was trash. In or out they didn't change. When this group decided someone was guilty, they were punished. Zero recidivism. No parole violations to worry about, no bail jumpers, no liberal judges to hear appeals. The only way Scott's clients got back on the street was reincarnation and he didn't believe that hokey crap. Scott and his men sent them on the express elevator to Hell.

He walked back to the control room and put Randy Black out of his head. He needed to focus on the kid. It was going to get messy with the father involved. The guy would be insane with rage. He'd want to torture the puke. Scott didn't blame him for that, but he'd have absolute control over the situation. No way was the father going to see Scott's face. If he broke down when the police questioned him, he was going down alone. Better yet, let him finger Tom Gold.

Chapter Eight

Sunday morning bustled inside the I.C.U. Working families and friends, separated from their sick loved ones all week long, came in careful-stepping packs of two and three. Not too many to overwhelm tired patients. Nieces, nephews and grandchildren clung to their peers, especially after being forced to drive an hour to see pale grandma lying desperately still. The tubes sticking out of bruised, paper-thin skin looked ghastly to a youngster.

Randy watched them creep past his door content they wouldn't be coming inside. After Cassie left Friday morning, the other reporters caught wind that he was conscious. They lied and swindled their way into his room by the dozen. Randy tired of their prying and enlisted Rita to draft a list of approved visitors. There would be no relatives, no girlfriend to Rita's delight, no friends at all. Just two names made the list: Cassie and Reverend Simmons. Sebastian could have been on the list, but he didn't make bail. If he came, he might be looking to get even for being led so far astray, but he wasn't the violent type. The police would come as they desired, but the press was barred from the room. There was no excuse for the nurses or the cop at the door not to remember two names. Their appearance couldn't have been more distinctive either: a stunning blonde blossoming underneath thick glasses and a movie-star man of God.

The preparations made it all the more surprising when the young man in the dark blue suit stepped in and angled to the bedside. A good looking guy. Too polished to be a cop. The officer at the door shouldn't have let him pass, but Randy would discover that this man was a whole new class of liar.

Tom Gold introduced himself as a defense attorney with a sterling record. If he was that good, Randy wondered why he'd gotten dressed up on a Sunday to get a sure loser of a case. He couldn't be very busy. Randy wondered about his fees and whether he really needed a lawyer at all.

Tom handed over a card and Randy flicked it toward the bedside table. It came up short and fluttered to the floor.

"I wouldn't be so dismissive if I were you. Arson, assault, extortion, multiple homicides, resisting arrest... Did I miss anything?"

Randy wasn't sure fighting the charges was the right thing to do. He wavered between pleading guilty and fighting it out honestly in case God wanted him outside the corrections system. Tom Gold could be the proverbial first boat or the serpent in disguise.

Randy said nothing. Tom waited patiently at the bedside.

Certainly his other clients didn't have such moral dilemmas holding them back. They wanted to save their skin. They'd only want to know whether Tom could get them acquitted or not.

"And you can beat all those charges?"

"I've got a great track record. No one wins every case of course, but you won't find an attorney with a better record than mine."

Randy almost choked on his cocky air. "My case is complicated."

"Look at you. We've got a case against the Town of Westport for sure. A few pictures and we've got the beginnings of a conspiracy."

"Is that why you're here? To take advantage of the casts and wires?"

This guy was here because he smelled a big contingency fee. The injuries were worth a few million whether Randy went to prison or not and a million dollar fee was worth dressing up on Sunday.

"I'm no ambulance chaser. I don't take habitual offenders and that limits my clientele. The judges know me. They know I don't front for scumbags. Believe me, that gets me more than my share of breaks. The down side is that most defendants cycle through the system over and over. Not many cases like yours come along."

"So you have to chase fresh meat."

"I want cases I can win."

"You think you can win my case? You don't know anything about it."

"I know the prosecutors are worried. That's a good start. I know that if the police listened to you when you were thirteen, none of this would have happened. I know that if Ron Morgan says what we tell him to, the prosecution's case falls all to Hell."

Randy's breath caught in his throat.

He knew about Ron Morgan.

Was he working for the DA?

Could he possibly know what Charles had done?

The bottles were locked in the safe. He couldn't know about them.

The newspaper articles were still online for anyone to see. Still, figuring out the Ron Morgan connection was good detective work. Charles Marston was guilty, but what about Charlie? Could he make Charlie look like the moneygrubbing son eager to bump off his father? If he did, would Randy get hit by the next bus and dragged straight to Hell?

Tom Gold backed off.

He'd made his impression.

If Randy hired a lawyer, Tom knew the job was his.

Thoughts of Ron Morgan hung over the bed. Ron could push this case hard one way or the other with a few well-chosen words. And he could be bought. Randy had done it once already, but he couldn't do it again, not now. Could he win this case without accusing Charlie Marston of something he didn't do? Probably not.

Randy watched Tom Gold disappear through the curtain.

Being Randy Black was much easier the first time around.

Chapter Nine

Scott crouched atop the van and adjusted his headset.

Another van was parked on the opposite side of the wooden-framed building. A group of men clad in black huddled around the corner from the front door, low and out of sight. There were others at the back, but Scott couldn't see them. It was his job to nail anyone breaking out front after the team went in.

A voice sputtered in his headset. "Cell jamming active." The voice paused several seconds. "Land lines down."

A steadier voice spoke. "Power going down."

The lights dimmed. They waited a beat, but no one inside the building reacted to the power outage. At 4:00 A.M. they'd all be asleep. Scott signaled with two fingers for the men along the wall to move in.

Four men stalked onto the porch.

Scott aimed at the windows over the porch roof. The easiest escape would be two steps on the roof and a ten foot jump to the concrete.

The men burst inside the door and spitting noises erupted immediately. The headset burst with a constant stream of chatter.

"Clear."

"Two down."

"Back door. Back door."

Scott heard sneakers on pavement. The shots were too muffled to hear, but Scott knew they were coming fast. He waited for the man to break toward the front. He didn't.

"He's down. Say again. He's down. Body on the sidewalk."

The rear door of the van burst open and a man sprinted around the back of the house. He'd have the body checked and dumped in the bushes, gone from view in seconds.

The voices became frantic.

"Shit!"

Loud shots rang out inside the building. Not good. The neighbors were close. The cell phones were jammed for four blocks and the land lines were down everywhere in the area, but the gunshots would carry. Even before sunrise, someone would get up and get to a working phone. Cops could be rolling. Worst case ETA six minutes.

"Got 'em. He's down."

"Not there. Not the freakin' closet. That's not right."

"Shit. I'm hit. I'm hit."

"Get down."

"Damn it. I'm hit." Another voice. Two men down.

"That's not right."

Scott jumped down off the van and signaled for the lights.

"That's enough. Hold your positions," he barked into the mic.

Inside the front door he found a man sprawled on the stairs and another in the doorway that led to the back of the house. Pink paint marked the center of their chests, three splatters each. The entry had gone well.

Ethan and Tripp stood in the kitchen. No surprise those two made it through. Nothing stuck to Ethan and Tripp loved combat. No one took the job more seriously than Tripp and no one was better in a firefight. He stood over a man in jeans as if to claim the kill.

Sid and Khan lay side by side in the hall, the only two clad in black forced to play dead. The man in jeans and a blue bandana grinned from the cellar doorway. He'd caught the two big guys leaving the kitchen for a bedroom. The shots would have been fatal and the noise would have awakened the whole block. Power lifting made Sid so tight he shot with his arms bent and lumbered from position to position. He was just too big for armed incursions, but when someone needed an attitude adjustment, Sid was indispensable. He'd chat with Sid later and have him bring up the rear slowly, making sure no one got behind him.

Khan was just big and bulky. He wasn't particularly strong or a good shot, but he was committed, a true believer if there was one among them. He worked alongside enough addicts and convicts to want to kill them all. He'd seen junkies who cleaned up in the winter just to get into the program house while it was cold or to get medical coverage. He'd seen crackhead prostitutes with HIV pick up eighteen year old kids. That's how he got here. He pulled one of those kids out of a car and got fired for disclosing confidential patient information. The whore was risking the kid's life to make twenty bucks. No one cared that Khan saved the kid. He lacked finesse, but made up for it with heart. Khan was saving even more kids now.

"What are you smiling about, Tripp?" Scott asked.

"Hey, I did my job," Tripp said, indicating the bodies on the floor.

"Yeah, and what about your buddies over here?"

"I can't kill 'em all, not unless you let me go in alone."

Tripp would enjoy that. He might get them all, too, but if he didn't they'd light up anyone who came in behind him. Sid and Khan weren't ready for that kind of firefight. They'd go in fast and heavy—together.

"Casualties are unacceptable," Scott barked. "We can't leave you behind and we can't risk driving your bloody carcass back here. Who the Hell can lift you, Sid, for God's sake. Can you try not getting shot?"

Only four could enter from the front. He couldn't send a group in the back because the two teams would be shooting toward each other. Even knowing the layout and having the headsets to communicate, they hadn't defeated the inside team cleanly in four tries. Ethan and Tripp were getting in safely. Sid and Khan just needed some help.

Scott took a deep breath. "What happened?"

The man in the doorway spoke up, proud to have caused so much trouble. "They make a lot of noise coming in. We've got four or five seconds from the first shot until they get back here. The place is small and the angles in the hall are tough. We know they're coming and we know what they're after."

That gave Scott an idea for the edge he needed. He gave the team the day off and walked back to see how his sniper at the back door fared.

Outside under the lights, the second sniper was perched atop a van at the far concrete wall. The house had been erected inside a cavernous space surrounded on all sides by reinforced concrete walls three floors high. The layout of the practice house was exactly like the house they'd be hitting, down to the narrow back porch and alleys on either side.

It had been no problem for the sniper. The escapee had to choose the street or one of the alleys. The sniper had a clean line of sight to the doorway, the street and the yard. The guy chose the nearest alley, but he was dead before he left the chalk outline of the grass. It would have been easier with a rifle than with the paintball guns they used for practice. The first shot had hit its mark. Four more followed just to make sure. The body lay curled up at the foot of the porch, still breathing of course, but trained well enough not to move.

The contractors he hired for these hits were so good he wished he could afford them full time. Sid and Khan weren't soldiers, but they followed orders. The contractors wouldn't tolerate sitting around for weeks at a time. No telling what kind of trouble they'd be into.

Back inside Scott analyzed the retreats they'd been using to beat his assault team. He'd need three cameras to cover the snaking hallway. He'd fish them in through the windows the next night. Once his team knew where everyone was, things would come off clean. One more practice run and they'd be ready.

Scott convinced himself it would work. The stand-ins were pros and they knew precisely when the hit was coming. The Cottage Street Killers would be sleepy, drugged-out losers in complete darkness. They had firepower, but just basic notions of how to use it. Scott's team knew close combat. He had a superior force and surprise, but only one chance. One casualty meant failure.

The cameras better be the trick.

Chapter Ten

Randy Black lay shackled within sight of the Earth's great lava spring. Narrow molten rivers fanned out in a thousand directions, glowing red on the cavern walls and spewing noxious haze into the thickened air. Arched over the river, his bare feet gripped one bank while his arms and shoulders supported him on the near side. Shards of craggy shale bit into his skin. Each time he shifted, sharp points snapped off and burrowed in, leaving a series of barbed stones embedded in his flesh, impossible for him to remove.

After being propped on his elbows for two days, he made his first escape attempt. When the demon turned away, he draped the chain down into the molten river expecting the iron to fatigue and melt away. It didn't. Heat radiated upward instead. The oversized manacles glowed red-hot. They sizzled deep into his forearms. The demon grinned as Randy screamed himself mute. His body racked convulsively as his flesh smoldered. The manacles grew hotter each day. Eventually the searing pain lost its power over him. The horrid stench of his own cooking flesh made him heave, but there was nothing in his stomach to vomit up, nor would there be again. Once confined here, there was no escape from an eternity of brutal torture, grotesquely horrifying, yet somehow fitting.

He groaned when the demon bore down on him, a whimper in the lofty chamber of noxious fumes and agonized howls. Being alone here for all eternity might have been preferable to the unending chorus of shrieks and moans. He knew his parents could see his anguish as they looked down from above. Their only son was a miserable failure.

He jerked with the whip's crack. Flesh flicked from his ribs.

His eyes flashed open and he started, but couldn't move.

Florescent lighting replaced the reddish glow.

He felt his chest for a wound that wasn't there.

Pain flared in his ribs. This pain was no dream. It needled him whenever he moved. It had dulled in the last few days and he hoped it would be gone altogether in another week. Right then, the soreness had him board-straight in his hospital bed wishing he could sleep for more than ten minutes at a stretch. His eyelids ached. His brittle eyeballs sent painful jabs deep into his skull. He couldn't shake the constant grogginess. He could fall asleep at will, but the visions flashed right back. Forced awake, he lay there confused, regretting what he'd done and doubting he could ever make amends. There was no escape. Asleep or awake his fear burned like a bright light. The molten river, the demon, eternal agony, they never left him.

The physical danger had passed for Randy, so he didn't warrant the constant attention of the I.C.U. In the morning he'd be moved to a regular room. The thing he wanted most was sunlight. Bright sunshine would help him stay awake through the day. The police had tried transferring him to the prison hospital, but Tom Gold fought that vehemently. So far his new lawyer was proving to be an excellent choice.

His free hand bristled over the whiskers on his jaw.

He needed another shave. Rita would be glad to oblige, caressing his head and winking the whole time, but he'd have to wait. The surrounding rooms issued nothing but the occasional snore. The nurses spirited about under dimmed lights. It was still the middle of the night, hours before Rita started her shift. As he rubbed the stubble, he remembered the first day he ate breakfast with the Marstons in Piolenc. The hair, the glasses, and the crazed ranting irritated Charles so much he didn't recognize the man underneath. Randy would never see stubble and sunglasses the same way again. He wished morning would hurry up and arrive so she could help him get clean.

He wondered if the dream was a warning or the start of his punishment. He'd been vigilant, watching everyone and everything that happened in the

I.C.U. He couldn't have failed already. He'd been careful since landing here, very careful, and he could barely move. The dream could have been sent, but he credited it to a nervous subconscious trying to spur him forward. His subconscious was right; it was time to take action.

Instinctively he reached for the leather-bound Bible the reverend left. The rulebook would determine what happened to his soul.

As he flipped it open he heard his own words mocking the Lord, *"Vengeance is mine..."* The words terrified Charlie, but remembering them terrified Randy even more. He wished he'd never said them, never done what he'd done, but that was past. It was time to follow God's rules and it had been so long he didn't remember the basics.

His fingers found Exodus 20 and he began reading.

At verse three he found the first commandment.

Thou shalt have no other gods before me. Check. No problem there.

Thou shalt not make unto thee any graven image. Check. Bowing down to an idol seemed ridiculous. He hadn't questioned the validity of his religious teachings since he was a boy.

One day when he was about ten, he'd asked his father how he knew God existed. Randy had been feeling full of himself and his father knew it. He asked Randy to take off his clothes and climb a telephone pole. When he could create a handful of sand and bring it down, they'd talk. Of course God was supplying the matter in the pole and the air around him, so creating the sand was simple compared to creating Heaven and Earth from nothing. There was plenty of hydrogen in the air, something supposed to be the root of all matter. Randy couldn't imagine how so much had been created from nothing. Faith came naturally since that day. Even so, sometimes he shuddered when he thought about the vastness of it all.

He hoped the commandments were in order of importance until he read the third.

Thou shalt not take the name of the Lord thy God in vain. How many hundreds of times had he done that? That one was disturbing. He'd learned this commandment long ago, been reminded not to take the Lord's name in vain and been scolded dozens of times by his parents. But who hadn't done that? He'd expected to be rocked by the big three, but this one came out of nowhere. Reading it he knew that God wouldn't take mocking lightly. He was a jealous God after all.

Randy moved on shakily.

Remember the Sabbath day. He hadn't gone to church in ten years. He couldn't remember the last time. He prayed, but when was the last time he attended a service? He'd thought nothing of working Sundays in his quest to repay the Marstons, if plotting revenge qualified as work. It definitely wasn't holy.

Honour thy mother and father. Check. He'd spent his entire life following this one. He'd overdone it if that was possible.

Thou shalt not kill.

Thou shalt not steal.

Thou shalt not commit adultery.

He'd violated these three all on the same day and encouraged Charlie Marston to do the same. Were these earthly transgressions less serious than the earlier commandments? Did the magnitude of his penance have to be that much bigger because he'd violated so many? He certainly couldn't risk breaking these again. Not ever. But how could he make amends for taking four lives and tearing apart so many others?

He closed the book and stared at the yellowing ceiling tiles.

What could he do to offset the damage?

He wasn't damned already. God hadn't sent him to be shackled. But what could possibly balance the ledger? He couldn't imagine what could undo the mayhem. He couldn't create life, couldn't replace Henri or Monique. He couldn't even create a handful of sand. God said the path would become clear. He hoped it would be so clear he couldn't miss it. He reopened the book and continued.

Thou shalt not bear false witness against thy neighbor.

This was the most disturbing of the nine so far. Not because it was so terribly serious. It was near the end of the list, but if he was to avoid prison, he'd need to manufacture reasonable doubt in the jury's mind. That meant convincing them Charlie Marston killed his father and TJ. It was the only plausible alternative for a jury. The only way to avoid jail. Twisting the facts meant violating one of God's commandments. It seemed minor compared to what he'd done, but he was out of second chances. He had to live clean. He couldn't lie and he couldn't pay Tom Gold to do it for him.

Prison or damnation? It should have been an easy choice.

Fighting the charges Tom's way was different than climbing into the reverend's helicopter. He needed to build his own boat and he couldn't imagine where to get his first plank.

Thou shalt not covet thy neighbor's house.

His neighbor had stolen his house. Right or wrong, Randy had coveted the Marston Empire from the day they took possession. He still wanted it back. He deserved it. Tom had some wild-eyed ideas about suing the Marstons, but they seemed frivolous at best.

Randy closed the Bible and rested his good hand on top. With his arm suspended, he couldn't even clasp his hands to pray.

Big changes and difficult choices lay ahead. He had so many questions. He wished the reverend were standing beside him now.

A nurse stepped inside the door and hesitated by the curtain.

She saw his hand over the Bible. His story was famous among the nurses. She'd be thinking he was scared of going to prison and she'd be partially right, though she'd never believe the truth. Few would believe he'd seen God.

This nurse didn't find him deserving. She flashed a scornful look then turned her back and took a reading from the equipment against the wall. Three stiff steps and she parted the curtain and disappeared. She didn't have a word of support to offer. If she could have snatched the Bible from him, she would have.

Chapter Eleven

The van stopped two blocks short of the house and a man clad in black with a trim headset and a silenced MP-5 slung over his back jumped out and scurried across the street and climbed the fire escape. The shot was longer than they'd practiced, but within range of the MP-5. Scott pulled the door closed behind him and they rolled on half a block past the target. Word came back that nothing was moving inside the house. They stopped in range of the wireless transmitters and the monitors blinked to life.

Sleeping men were concentrated at the back. Handguns lay in plain view on tables. Two rifles leaned into corners of the narrow hall. There was no cash in view, but they were here because the Cottage Street Killers were getting ready for a huge buy. The stash would be somewhere in the house and their leader wouldn't be far, not until the buy was made.

Scum like this was the reason Scott left the force. Gangs like the C.S.K. operated in plain view. They sold drugs to kids, killed anyone who interfered and terrorized residents for blocks around. Few had serious criminal records because residents were afraid to testify. When they did, liberal judges made sure the thugs didn't spend much time in prison. On this morning, retribution was finally knocking. Scott's team was about to deal them the ultimate punishment and rid the neighborhood of this menace.

One man slept on the stairs with an automatic on the tread beside him. He'd been assigned the front door, but at 3:58 A.M. he was out cold. If they came in quietly, he'd never wake up.

The second van pulled up on the next block.

Scott knew they'd be scampering in several directions at once.

The first call came in over the radio. "Strike team in position."

Scott flicked a switch and spoke into his mic. "Cell jamming on."

A few seconds passed while the men at the back of the house worked at a tangle of wires. "Land lines out."

Seconds later came the final call. "Power coming down."

The scenes on the monitors remained unchanged. The street lights cast a pale glow through the windows. The lights in the triple-decker were out and they'd stay out. The strike team would be peering through night vision scopes. The thugs inside would be fuzzy-eyed with sleep and nearly blind when the chaos erupted. If they saw anything at all, it'd be muzzle flashes.

Scott prepped his team. "Three men room one, two men room two. Armed guard on the stairs. Asleep. Say again. Everyone asleep. We go in quiet and slow."

"Roger that."

"Snipers ready?"

"Front door secure."

"Back door secure."

Scott gave the order to move in and waited for the shadowy figures to slip into view on the monitors. He counted the seconds as the men made their way up onto the front porch and worked the lock. There were no microphones in the house. The only sounds he would hear would be communications from the team or gunshots from the C.S.K. if they were lucky enough to get one off.

Tremors jolted the man on the stairs.

His body arched as bullets ripped through him and then he slumped.

The impact against the risers could have alerted the C.S.K. and sparked a firefight, but they didn't rouse. The four men in black blocked a camera's view as they moved down the hall. They separated to cover the two doorways the man had been guarding, their pace deliberate, standing tall, peering aggressively through their night vision scopes, ready to silence anyone who awoke. Sid's bulging form hung at the back.

A whisper sounded over the headset. Unintelligible to Scott, it was a synchronizing cue for the team. The muzzle flashes appeared in the monitors this time, the guns aimed almost directly at the cameras in the windows. Bodies jerked and jolted. None rose in time.

The shooting ended as abruptly as it began. Six dead, all quiet on the outside. The ambushes that had plagued the team in practice were forgotten. These weren't soldiers. They were opportunistic criminals. Too lazy to work for an honest living, they stooped to ruining lives for profit. That choice led to their downfall tonight and Scott was proud of what his team had done. Khan and Ethan celebrated inside. Taking these dirt bags off the street meant a safer place for kids to grow up. Tripp moved from corpse to corpse, checking pulses, inspecting entry wounds. It was sick how he reveled in the gore. Scott would never have hired him, but that was Tom's call. He didn't understand ops, he never would. Pretty Boy was in it for the cash and tonight he'd be taking down plenty.

"Let's get the lights on and locate the package," Scott ordered.

Two men took defensive positions at the entrances while the others waited for power to be restored.

Light brought gruesome reality to the scene. Blood pooled around the bodies on the beds and one that had fallen to the floor. The shabby rooms were littered with dirty clothes, fast food wrappers and crumpled beer cans. The occupants had lived like undisciplined teenagers. They were little more.

The men searched with gloved hands tearing through closets. They flipped the mattresses up against the walls and let the dead occupants roll to the floor and lodge against the baseboards. They sliced mattresses and emptied pillows. The men didn't find what they were looking for, but they didn't leave the bedrooms. The money would be close to the bodies.

Scott was about to suggest ripping up the floorboards when his headset came live. "We got it. Room one."

Two men gathered in front of a bureau just a foot from the camera. Nylon bags appeared and the men began stuffing stacks of bills into the bags. The two men from room two joined them and in minutes they whisked out the back door with four bags stuffed full of bills that had been stolen from parents, burgled from houses all around the city or purchased with young women's flesh.

"Strike team clear," the men called as they dashed to the waiting van.

Scott called in the snipers, left his MP-5 in the van, and trotted inside.

The weapons they used would make this look like a well-financed gang feud. The silent gunshots wouldn't help the cops. They'd never know for sure if the neighbors had heard the shots and kept quiet out of fear. The cameras were altogether different. They smacked of professionalism. They had to go. Through the front door, he had the hallway camera pocketed in seconds. It had taken an hour to insert them into the window casings from the outside. Yanking them out was a snap. The investigators wouldn't notice fresh gouges in this rat trap.

Scott pocketed the bedroom cameras and was back on the front porch in seconds. He killed the lights and left the six dead men lying in the dark.

The scene changed as he bounced down the stairs and onto the lawn.

Something scraped overhead.

Ethan sheltered at the back corner of the van, his gun trained on the lower windows.

Scott whirled around and saw him, falling from the porch roof. The kid had been hiding upstairs. His foot caught Scott's shoulder and slammed him to the grass. He was skinny and fast, on his feet before Scott could get a grip on his SIG.

Ethan didn't fire when the kid stood up. A good four feet separated Scott from the kid, but Ethan didn't take the shot. A burst from the MP-5 would have ripped him open and ended it.

The SIG cleared Scott's hip.

The kid was coming level. No time to get a shot off.

Scott rolled away.

The kid buried two shots into the grass where Scott had been.

Scott stopped, found the hammer with his thumb, cocked it and snapped off a shot. The kid couldn't believe he missed. He looked down expecting blood to start gurgling from Scott's chest and didn't have the presence of mind to fire again. The slug ripped into the kid's abdomen. The pain stopped him cold. He clutched himself, wavering there until Scott came level on his forehead and dropped him. A soldier wouldn't have stopped firing. He would have killed Scott there on the lawn. As it was, four shots roared through the neighborhood announcing the conflict. Heads would be down a minute, hiding under pillows that wouldn't stop a .22. When another shot didn't come, the faces would be up against the glass.

Scott didn't waste time checking the kid.

He stood for the van, the SIG by his side.

Ethan hadn't relaxed when the kid dropped.

He hadn't fired a single shot. He could have tagged the kid on the roof or down on the lawn. He'd been waiting for the kid to do his work, but the kid was too slow, too afraid. Now Ethan's MP-5 was trained on Scott's chest. In an instant Scott saw months of bickering with Tom flash by. This was Ethan's opportunity for advancement. Tom had put him up to it and assured him of the lead.

There was no time to raise the SIG.

If he dropped Ethan, the others would join in. He'd be on foot, running away from seven dead bodies in a shitty neighborhood at 4:06 A.M.

When Ethan hesitated, Scott jerked his arm upward.

Spitting noises erupted before he located the front sight.

Pain exploded in his chest and his vision went black.

The last thing he felt was hands rifling his pockets for the cameras.

The cops on scene would know his face.

Would they understand he left the force for this?

Some would. One of them might even be recruited to take his place.

Chapter Twelve

Cassie sat in the front row of the courtroom on the aisle to make an easy escape in case the proceedings dragged or an urgent story broke. She'd been waiting half an hour for Randy's bail hearing and still the case hadn't been called nor had he appeared. She tapped her notebook and wondered about the biggest case she'd reported for *The Standard Times*.

Last week, seven members of the Cottage Street Killers had been murdered in their sleep. Alerted by the scanner in her apartment, she beat Walter to the scene and grabbed the story for herself. Several witnesses were still outside after talking to police. Most agreed there had been three shots fired, a few heard only one, but one guy said he heard four. Even four shots didn't kill eight men. She dodged around behind the detectives before the police tape went up and caught a glimpse of two bodies on the lawn.

The nearest victim looked more like a spy than a gang member. He was older, thirty, maybe thirty-three, clean cut, without a single tattoo. His face was familiar, though she couldn't remember where she'd seen him. Dressed all in black with army style boots, he couldn't have clashed more with the kid in jeans eight sizes too big and ratty dreads that hadn't been washed in a month. The SIG Sauer on the grass sealed it. A P229 went for eight hundred bucks. Not a punk's gun. The spy had five bullet wounds clumped together in his chest. None of it fit the official explanation or the witness statements.

The lead detective briefed the press about an invasion and robbery meant to steal drugs and money. The likely culprit was a rival gang a few blocks away. Cassie had been working the neighborhood for months. Gang membership was down and conflicts between the gangs were rare. They were being squeezed more by the cops than each other. Why would one try to wipe another out? Why now? The detective told her off-the-record that the case wouldn't be solved. The neighbors didn't see anything. The guns were probably unregistered and traded away or dumped by now. He just didn't seem willing to put in the effort. Not for these young men, not after what they'd done.

She had reported what she'd learned on the Internet site by 2:00 P.M., but it didn't make print until the next morning. The captain's briefing that afternoon brought television crews swooping in to steal the spotlight. They accepted what he fed them and served it up to the world's dinner table as they watched between bites. The crews were gone as quickly as they appeared. They didn't have time for backstory. They had pictures. They regurgitated what the cops told them and they left. It was quick and it was done—another inner-city tragedy served to the masses. They moved on to find something else that would grab attention for another ninety seconds.

There was more to the story and Cassie was going to find it.

A small group burst through the outer doors and down the aisle.

Cassie didn't recognize the lawyer wheeling Randy into the courtroom, but she assumed he'd set him up to look pitiful in the chair. Both lower legs were in casts and his left arm was white from his wrist up and around his shoulder. If she hadn't seen him in the hospital, she'd think it was a show for sympathy.

The bailiff called Randy Black on cue as they entered. The lawyer wheeled him to a microphone up front and stood beside him. The next ten minutes illuminated the side of the story Randy wanted her to dig for. She knew the Marstons' story well, but she found the tale Tom Gold weaved for the judge surprisingly credible.

It was a grand conspiracy according to Gold. The father perpetrated a fraud, driving winery owners into bankruptcy so he could buy their assets on the cheap. Randy was investigating the fraud to bring a lawsuit when Charlie Marston discovered his research. Angry with his father and afraid to lose his inheritance, Charlie killed him and framed Randy Black.

Randy squirmed as his lawyer spoke, but didn't interrupt.

The police report Randy filed when he was thirteen years old was trotted out. It accused Marston of tampering with large batches of wine. Gold assured the judge he could prove the accusations even now. The 911 call transcript was delivered to the bench. Randy called the police when the Marston house was engulfed in flames. The prosecutor stipulated it was Randy's voice, but argued it was a hoax to throw them off track.

Gold said that Charlie Marston stabbed Randy, bound him up and fled. The prosecutor didn't object and this shocked Cassie. Gold itemized dozens of pieces of evidence stolen by Marston from the defendant's home after he ran from police. Three police officers found Marston in Randy's study holding a recently-fired handgun. Ballistics linked the gun to a dead man in Marston's own home. Powder residue proved Marston had fired the weapon. Still no charges were filed—an absolute travesty according to Tom Gold.

The spectators erupted and the judge banged his gavel to quiet them.

Gold announced they were suing the Town of Westport for ten million dollars for injuries sustained during the arrest. They were suing the Marston estate for the fifty million dollar fraud perpetrated by Charles Marston.

Judge McKinnon was troubled.

The prosecutor protested Gold's theatrics. Randy Black was a cold-blooded killer. Nothing would convince him otherwise. Cassie had been just as convinced minutes ago. She wasn't anymore. To let him walk was dangerous, but was it more dangerous than freeing Charlie Marston? Cassie feverishly scribbled notes for a story of privilege and political favors.

After some deliberation, Judge McKinnon set bail at seventy-five thousand dollars. The prosecutor objected to no avail.

Gold got up from the table and wheeled Randy out. Randy recognized Cassie and his eyes never left her until Tom pushed him through the doors. She'd found a shortcut to the truth about Charles Marston. Cassie followed them out of the courtroom wondering if she'd get her interview now.

Chapter Thirteen

Tom Gold proved his worth. He drove Randy straight from court to the hospital where the doctor removed the casts from his legs then signed his discharge. The original court date wasn't for a week, but when Randy refused to delay the removal procedure, Tom called in some favors and had the hearing moved up. The casts made a compelling statement to the court and Randy left the hospital with his freedom and a clear conscience—on that account at least. Tom's statements pushed further than Randy expected. The prosecutor was enraged, but Randy could see Cassie's eyes opening to new possibilities as he wheeled past.

Randy thought about Rita as they left the bank with a cashier's check. She dedicated herself to helping people and yet she was drawn by his dangerous aura. The other nurses treated him like a leper, but Rita spent her free moments at his bedside. With the first two casts off, she would have climbed in bed with him. Oddly, he was glad to be going home so he wouldn't have to decide whether to let her in or turn her away. What a wimp he was becoming.

Tom led him into the precinct and the desk sergeant accepted the seventy-five thousand dollars bail. Somehow Tom even finagled the McLaren out of the impound yard.

Randy and Tom parted ways. Tom went back to his office. Randy rested his plaster-covered left arm out the window and used the other to shift and steer. He launched the McLaren down the highway one-handed. The Ten

Commandments didn't mention doing one hundred in a sixty-five, but if he'd read Romans more carefully, he might have slowed down.

The McLaren stopped fifty feet short of the driveway. Randy got out and stood on the yellow line to survey the demolition of the Caulfield house. Workmen's cars lined the curb. An excavator crunched into blackened walls, chewing and reducing the debris and dumping it into a ten wheeler. The landscaping around the property had been trampled flat and the manicured lawn was awash in muddy ruts. Randy wondered who would pay for the reconstruction. There wasn't a realtor's sign out front. The insurance company couldn't have approved Caulfield's claim. If they believed the stingy little slime ball, Randy would be subrogation target number one. He flashed to the mailbox for a second, but decided that was a surprise better left for later. Caulfield deserved everything he'd gotten. Hopefully Jo took him for everything in the divorce.

Randy climbed back in and zipped around the black Corolla out front. Once he realized who owned it, he'd be looking for the tiny car everywhere.

He hadn't been inside his house in over a month. Others had. There was a search warrant on the island in the kitchen and the front door was still unlocked. The police had been through every square inch while he was hiding. Unfortunately, Charlie had beaten them here and taken years of research and chucked it in a dumpster. The truth lay buried in tons of garbage. He could reproduce the photos, but that would take time. The news clippings were scattered to the wind. He could gather them again if he wanted the world to understand Charles Marston's fraud, but he was dead. The story wasn't worth the effort anymore.

There wasn't a crumb of edible food in the kitchen. The fridge reeked of sour milk and green-tinged meat. He should've stopped for something. He dreaded lugging the heavy plaster cast out again. He pictured himself walking sideways down narrow grocery aisles, loading his cart one-handed and trying not to knock items off the shelves with his rigid arm that always seemed to be in the way. He decided to ignore his hunger and ambled upstairs. He flicked on his computer to check the security system, smiling at his cleverness while he waited for the system to boot. TJ had found the dummy downstairs. He stole the computer and thought it was safe to come and go as he pleased. He never realized that just because wires are coming out of the wall doesn't mean they're attached to something on the other end. Charlie Marston had fallen for the same ploy.

Randy's joy was short-lived. The wireless system didn't respond.

The bathroom mirror swung out over the double sinks to reveal a deep compartment with a computer mounted against the studs and a bundle of wires rising up from the floor below. This system received signals from the cameras and sensors around the house. All the indicator lights were dark. Resetting the power strip accomplished nothing. He leaned over the sink and stretched with his good arm to plug the hall lamp to the power strip inside the cavity. The lamp clacked on bright as ever. The power was on, but every piece of electronic gear hidden there was dead. It would take days to reconstruct. The problem was troubling, but not insurmountable. Security wasn't a pressing issue anymore.

With no way to tell who'd been in the house and no energy to repair his security system, Randy lowered himself downstairs to find a comfortable chair and watch the progress across the street. Halfway down, he saw a blonde head of hair waiting for him in the sidelight. Cassie Corcoran was following her story. She'd been in the courtroom that morning and she'd found her way here almost as soon as he did.

What kind of a slant was her story going to have?

At least she wanted to hear him out before writing it. She'd worked hard enough to deserve his time. He let her in, angled himself over to the couch and propped a few pillows under his cast.

"Looking much better I see," Cassie said with a nod to his legs. She'd seen him wheeled into the courtroom that morning, but she'd also seen him in the I.C.U. The last minute entrance in the wheelchair must have looked like courtroom theatrics. Nothing he could say would convince her it was just fortunate timing, so he didn't try. She sat with the same notebook on her lap, ready to document his account of the atrocities. Randy had other plans.

"Interesting story your lawyer told this morning."

"Saved you some research, did it?" Randy asked.

Apparently she'd forgotten their deal. If she researched Marston and his winery dealings, she'd get her story. As far as Randy was concerned, that was the story.

"Did you at least look up the complaint?"

She nodded. Her long blonde hair lay flat against her shoulders. The dark rimmed glasses hid the intensity of her eyes. Every morning before work, the librarian swallowed the diva. Did being taken seriously really matter that much? She'd be stunning in a little black dress.

What a difference from Rita. Cassie encountered men like Randy every day. What would have been a titillating experience for Rita dimmed to a gleam of perverse interest in Cassie's eyes. She wanted the details. She wanted to feel what it was like to be bad, but that was the end. She'd report on him like a lab rat. When she was done with her article, she was done with him. Randy savored the challenge. Changing her mind would be a step toward convincing himself and maybe the Almighty he was worth saving.

She admitted she hadn't found anything on Charles Marston except that he'd acquired six wineries before he died. She'd listened to Tom's story in court that morning and she was intrigued.

He couldn't take his eyes off the smooth skin of her face. Something about the way the light blonde hair fell against it felt wholesome to him. There was purity in her search for the truth. The professional distance Cassie shoved between them was irritating, but as much as Rita's desire for a fling with a bad boy was off-putting, Cassie's coolness drew him in. She was the kind of woman he should have been pursuing for years. Winning her over suddenly became more important than anything she could print about Charles Marston. The first step was spending some time together.

"Can we get some dinner while we talk?" he asked.

"You're in no condition to date."

"You're not afraid of a one-armed man?"

She was already in his house. Any restaurant would be safer. Soon he convinced her to drive which meant they'd share a ride back. He didn't hide his interest and she didn't object to socializing with an accused killer.

She chose White's of all places. He wondered if she was toying with him, but she suggested it so nonchalantly he assumed she couldn't know what this restaurant had meant to him and to Bill Caulfield. Bill was a regular here when he still worked at the bank. He was here entertaining clients the night his house burned down. Jo called him home in a panic after the roof started leaking. When the fire started and the White's matchbook was left behind, there was a lot of evidence pointing to Bill as the arsonist. The clients had heard his angry outburst. The phone records firmed up the time of Bill's rushed trip home. The explosion etched the time of the fire in the memories of Bill's neighbors. White's had served Randy well, not so for Bill Caulfield.

Tonight Randy would make another pleasant memory here. He ordered prime rib knowing he couldn't cut it himself. As Cassie's delicate fingers sliced the pink meat into square chunks, he described what he'd seen that night when he was thirteen years old. She was riveted. She'd heard about his statement in court and now he was sure she'd look it up for herself. She took a full page of notes and picked at her salad only while he stopped talking to chew. He described the contamination of the wines in several wineries and the bribery of the wine quality panel in Piolenc.

Cassie noted everything. The story had been reported in various local papers in bits and pieces, but no one had ever put it together because the wineries were spread so far apart. Cassie was the first reporter to hear the case Randy had assembled for the police a month earlier; the story Charlie stole from him. She listened intently for an hour without interrupting. Still, Randy could only hope the full breadth of Charles Marston's deception would make it into print.

When she dropped him off, she gave him a familiar smile and he didn't try for more. He hadn't denied the prosecutor's charges and they hadn't talked about the crimes he was accused of.

She waited for him to clumsily angle though the front door and then she drove off into the night. She might not believe he was innocent, but she understood more about the Marstons and the Joyets than anyone.

Chapter Fourteen

The call Cassie dreaded all weekend came Tuesday at 8:45 A.M. She'd been tapping her desk and rethinking her piece for twenty minutes when Bart's name glowed on the plastic display. He had approved the copy. It wouldn't have run otherwise, but it was counter to everything printed about the trouble at Marston Vineyards. Cassie's was the only article brazen enough to challenge the official version of events.

She knew when the phone buzzed that someone had read her story over the long weekend and wasn't happy. Her first, most desperate thought, was of the publisher. He didn't read the entire paper before it went out, not on the Friday before a long weekend. She imagined he'd gotten an angry call and was worried about a lawsuit. Anyone but him would be ok.

The Marstons would be outraged by the accusation against their deceased patriarch, but aside from the statement Randy made when he was thirteen, she hadn't pointed the finger at them too strongly. Randy had offered plenty more but without verification. When she corroborated the facts about the denied loan application and the other winery failures, the Marstons would have something to complain about and lawsuits of their own to defend.

The arresting officers surely hated the photos of Randy battered in his hospital bed. Maybe some of them were innocent, maybe they'd only watched, but there was no disputing what happened. She cataloged Randy's injuries and questioned Ruiz's decision not to prosecute. The officers' families would resent the implications of favoritism and abuse of power.

They'd say Cassie tarnished the reputations of these brave men with wild accusations that didn't belong in print. She wouldn't be welcome in the precinct the next time she had a story to cover there. The officers' children would get harassed on the playground. Cops and robbers would take on a new, violent twist at their school.

Cassie picked up the phone and Bart's soothing voice asked her to come to his office without a hint of the trouble she expected. She left her cubicle and followed the aisle to the solid wall at the end, gathering her thoughts as she went. She'd taken the photo in the hospital room herself. The witness statement bore the Town of Westport seal. Her evidence was incontrovertible, her assertions, not necessarily so.

She turned the corner and felt a shiver as she saw Bart's door.

Melanie gave a cautious smile from her cubicle.

Did she know? There was no time to wonder.

Cassie knocked and stepped one foot into Bart's office, straddling the threshold. She hadn't been this nervous coming to see him since her first interview. He'd quickly put her at ease that day. She hoped this meeting would end as amicably.

Bart sat stiffly behind the desk in his trademark starched white shirt. The cuffs, neatly rolled up two times each, gave him a look of industriousness from the moment he arrived at his desk. Cassie's jeans were slovenly in Bart's eyes, but he didn't glance at them today. He'd told her many times how proper clothes inspired a healthy respect for the people's trust. He wanted to leave this office to Cassie, to leave her with the stewardship of the news desk. Part of that was carrying forward the professional image he'd cultivated since 1964, but he had bigger concerns today.

She glanced at the plaques and awards mounted on the wall behind him, tributes to more than forty years dedicated to printing the news. Bart met her with sorrowful eyes, more worried than disappointed, troubled about the flak her article caused. Bart knew about her father's illiteracy and how amazed her family was that she could make her living with words. This job was a source of pride she couldn't let go. Bart didn't want to see her lose it either. He frowned as she met his eyes.

"Close it," he said, and waved her to a chair.

She pirouetted through the door and as she closed it, she saw Walter propped up against the bookshelf. She immediately understood what had happened. Walter had tried to make her his protégé when she first arrived. When Bart took on the role of mentor himself, Walter was infuriated. He resented Cassie from that day, begrudging her every good assignment and undermining her at every opportunity. Her stance on Randy and the Marstons handed him a chance to discredit her that he couldn't pass up.

She relaxed into a chair across from Bart and left Walter unacknowledged behind her. If Walter was the only one complaining about the article, she'd be delighted.

Walter's skinny fingers gripped the vacant guest chair beside her. He stood where Cassie couldn't see and began his attack. "Every other paper is railing that this guy is out on bail and we run a police brutality angle? I don't know what's happening here, but I don't want to be part of it."

"Perfect. It's not your story," she said.

"I care about this paper's reputation—unlike you. You take a lousy picture with your camera phone and decide to run it. What were you thinking?"

"That was my decision, Walter," Bart said. "We were the only media outlet with access to that hospital room, thanks to Cassie. I chose to run the picture and the story. You can't deny what those cops did to him. If ever there was a picture we needed to run, that was it."

Bart's frustration was obvious, but Walter wasn't giving up.

"So, what? Everyone else has it wrong?"

"You can't argue with that picture. I spoke with the doctors myself," Cassie said. The photo wasn't professional, but it wasn't bad either.

"That picture doesn't explain a dead man hanging in his own foyer."

Cassie turned from Bart to Walter "Listen, this didn't just hit the Marstons out of the blue. The other papers don't agree with me, but they're not talking to Randy Black. None of them are."

"I think you're doing more than talking." Walter snickered.

Bart stood up behind his desk. "That's enough."

"My research is going to show just what Charles Marston was doing before he died."

Walter fumed. "You're wasting your time. If you weren't so enthralled with this bad boy, you'd know that." He turned to Bart. "I want some time on this. I think we need some balance."

"If I want balance, I'll let you know."

Bart lashed a finger toward the door before Walter could argue further.

Walter stormed out, incensed that he wasn't getting a fair hearing, and slammed the door behind him.

Bart settled back in his chair and waited for the hall to quiet. He didn't let himself break into a smile, but Cassie sensed the worst was over. She steadied herself for other complaints about her piece, but she could tell from Bart's ease that there weren't any. Walter would be at his desk scheming a way to get the publisher's attention. He wouldn't be above calling in a complaint himself.

"The photo wasn't that bad," Bart said.

"Thanks." She smiled, relaxed now in her chair.

"He's not going to give up."

"I know. But I'm right about the story."

"The light's shining on you, Cassie. This guy's not talking to anyone else. No one's coming at this from your angle and I'm betting they all have a Walter Macedo guiding the ship. They won't change course, not now."

"I've got dozens of pieces here."

"This could be the one that puts you over the top. Just make sure you've got the goods. People don't want to believe that this hoodlum's innocent. They've made up their mind and they're ready to lynch him on the courthouse lawn."

"They all want me to be wrong. Especially Walter."

"Prove to them that you're not."

Chapter Fifteen

Randy arrived for his appointment unsure how Tom Gold suckered him into a psychological evaluation. Weeks earlier he'd have relished the opportunity to match wits with this woman, but today he worried he'd tell her what he'd done or worse, what he'd seen. If she was qualified at all, she'd deem him dangerous and unstable—six weeks ago he was. Today he'd limit himself to short, simple responses, not a word about what he'd seen after Pinto hit him. With luck she'd report on the new Randy Black not the old.

The parking space directly in front of the building was fortunate for a man with one good arm, the revolving doors, not so. Stiffly through, Randy met the expectant gaze of the security guard in the otherwise vacant lobby. The guard signed him in and dutifully led him to the elevator. Hospitality aside, the office building was like any other until he got off the elevator on the sixth floor. Everything in the wide hall was white: the plush carpeting with fresh vacuum tracks, the pristine walls, the ceiling tiles, even the lone door at the far end was painted white. It wasn't creamy off-white. It was brilliant-sunshine, wake-you-up-in-the-morning white.

He knocked and the white doorknob turned.

Inside was more of the same. A white marble-topped desk, white leather couch, floors, walls; everything was white. Heather Lovely stood to one side and ushered him in. The room felt more cozy than institutional, almost heavenly. Her deep crimson blouse and light blonde hair commanded his attention. If the monochrome décor was designed to thrust her center stage, it worked. Randy hadn't been to a psychologist in a long time, but this had to be weird even for a shrink.

He took his seat on the couch and she stalked silently around behind him in white leather pants and matching pumps. She smiled faintly at his robotic attempt to track her as she circled. When he recognized the sadistic twist in her lips, he lay back, propped his arm up with the single pillow and surveyed the white on white décor in front of him. Once she'd lost his interest, she settled directly behind the head of the couch where he couldn't see her. Straight from the shrink strategy handbook; she could read his body language, but he couldn't read hers. He feigned interest in her desk and the winter scenes hanging on the walls until she spoke.

"I'm surprised Tom Gold took your case. He's got a thing about defending the innocent. All the papers say you've been a very bad boy."

What a hostile opening. The shrinks he'd seen after his parents' accident pretended to be his friend at least until he got to know them. Was this a criminal thing? Was she trying to shove him off balance and get him to admit something? He kept his cool and vowed to stick to his plan to give simple responses and show no emotion "Is that how this works? Guilty until proven innocent?"

"This isn't a courtroom, Randy. We're just having a chat."

"A chat that'll be replayed for the judge and jury." He didn't see a tape recorder, but assumed it was hidden in the furniture.

"Not necessarily. Your lawyer requested this meeting. Only information helpful to your case will be presented to the court. That's the law."

"Unless I threaten to blow someone up..."

Heather laughed. "You're done blowing people up. Aren't you?"

"Never started."

She implored him to tell the truth, explaining that she couldn't help him otherwise. He was beyond her help but didn't say so. When she asked how many times he'd been arrested, he answered truthfully: five—mainly because she had access to his criminal record. She asked why he'd started the fight at the Sportsmen's Club. He told her the men thought he was cheating at cards. He could hear her pen rolling circles on the paper as she made a notation. He didn't admit cheating and didn't deny it. She asked how he felt about those men and if he'd ever go back. They were lousy poker players. Randy would be back when the cast came off. He flashed to the Roman soldiers gambling for Jesus' meager possessions and didn't say another word about gambling.

He wondered if she'd be perceptive enough to see the change in him.

"Let's go back to the night you were arrested in Westport. What started the altercation with the police?" she asked.

"One of the cops hit me with his nightstick."

"Unprovoked? He just marched up and hit you?"

"They surrounded me first."

Randy didn't explain how he'd escaped a week earlier. He assumed she'd read the newspaper coverage and he could tell she wasn't buying his portrayal of the innocent victim.

"Do they deserve to be punished?"

"That's not up to me."

She pushed him to describe a punishment fit for Officer Pinto. No matter how she asked, Randy refused. She suggested he play the role of judge, parent, and teacher in turn, all without success. "It's ok to want justice for what they did to you." She came around the couch and indicated his cast. "It's perfectly natural to be angry with someone who hurt you."

"Vengeance is mine saith the Lord." The words passed Randy's lips before he could stop them. He'd mocked Charlie Marston with these same words, but this time he meant them literally. Vengeance wasn't his province any longer.

Heather Lovely stood speechless. She looked down on him as if something in his expression could tell her whether or not he was a sociopath. She expected to see one today and quoting the Bible reinforced her belief. She pulled up a chair, pokerfaced, opened a folder and removed a series of cards. She explained she was going to administer a Thematic Apperception Test. She showed him blurry images and asked him to explain what he thought was happening in the scenes. Randy had seen the sad boy with the violin before and explained that he'd just performed badly. He was pouting and thinking about how he could do better next time.

She showed another card, a figure on a bare mattress.

He thought of Rita immediately, but explained it was a young woman home from work, sprawled on the bed to regain her energy before going out with her friends. Today the shrink would get nothing but happy thoughts and positive vibes from Randy.

When she got tired of his Candyland view of her pictures, she dragged over a small table and they moved on to the WAIS-R. He didn't hold back on the IQ test. Being smart didn't make him evil. He told her how far it was from New York to Paris, repeated sequences of random numbers back to her and impressed her with a digit span of twelve. She gave him puzzles to put together and he assembled simple houses, a human hand and a few animals as fast as he could with one good hand.

Finally she handed him a booklet with hundreds of true/false questions. She watched as he breezed through questions asked a dozen various ways.

"If you found money, would you keep it?"

"Do you think your mother is an attractive woman?"

"If you were at a party, would you rather drink wine than talk to someone boring?"

As he labored for over an hour answering the same questions rephrased and paraphrased, he considered his own question for this test: "If you were a duck caught in the rain, would you be afraid of lightning?"

He laughed as he worked. He wasn't nuts. He was angry for the last decade, but he had good reason. He talked to God often now, but lots of people did. Most people just didn't expect answers—certainly not an audience in Heaven. He shivered, his eyes hovering on the next question but not reading the words. If it had been the drugs, or the whack to the head that gave him the vision, Randy was banking the rest of his life on a hallucination.

But it was more than that.

Randy had seen the truth.

Chapter Sixteen

When Randy finally answered the last question in the test booklet, Heather Lovely took it from him and tossed it on her chair. After two hours in her office he'd finished her battery of tests, but she wasn't ready to let him go. She turned quickly back to the couch and stopped directly in front of him, so he couldn't stand without knocking her over. She squeezed his knees between hers and leaned over him, resting her right arm over his cast and pinning him there gently, but forcefully enough so he couldn't move. She reveled in his vulnerability, meeting his eyes, looking him over then running her fingers from his knee, up the inside of his thigh all the way to his pectorals. She leaned closer still and held his gaze with a naughty, power-drunk smile.

This close she reminded him of a younger, devilish Elizabeth Marston. Now that the testing was over, the refined psychologist gave way to the aggressive harlot. Gold had said her opinions were well-respected in area courts. Her testimony could sway the jury. She knew what that meant to Randy and she was ready to take advantage. They both knew no one would believe the defendant was sexually harassed by the doctor. Randy had near zero credibility. Just being alone in the room with her was a risk. A few words from her could label him a sexual predator. Was that her game? Sex for favorable testimony? Was she testing again? Prompting for an angry response?

He reminded himself the session was being recorded, the equipment hidden nearby. She could edit out her inflammatory comments and include whatever she wanted the court to hear. Randy chose his words carefully.

"Shouldn't you be sitting in your own chair, Ms. Lovely?"

She grinned. Saying nothing she splayed her fingers and clamped down on his ribs. She was familiar with his injuries, but not his progress. A few days ago the pain would have been excruciating. On this day it was a mild annoyance. When he didn't flinch, she dug in with her long fingernails threatening to scratch him open through his shirt. She eased the pressure unexpectedly, even as he was bracing himself to be scraped open.

"Are you coming on to me, Ms. Lovely? Because I don't find violence to be a turn on."

The detachment in his voice derailed her.

She eyed him up and down one more time and retreated from the couch to her post behind him. Sitting up, he could see her, but he couldn't tell if she was hiding her anger or just trying a different tack. Surely the décor was all wrong for this woman. The room befitted an angel, but the psychologist was acting like a crazy slut.

"Did Charles Marston Senior deserve what happened to him?"

The old Randy would have screamed 'yes.' Nothing could have stopped him from doing what he did. The correct answer was 'no' of course. He couldn't admit what he'd done, not to her, not ever. He told her that Mr. Marston had broken the law and that he should have been punished by the courts. He didn't mention that the police ignored his pleas to do just that.

She ignored his monotone textbook response.

"How do you think we should punish criminals?"

"Isn't that why I'm here? The system sucks them in and spits 'em out."

"No better than before," she snickered. "Do you know how many convicts end up back in prison after they're released?"

Randy didn't bite.

"Over thirty percent." She was angry now, goading him to join her. "Surely you could do better than those candy-asses in charge."

Randy refused her invitation to play dictator. "We've been refining the system for two hundred years. Not just anyone could take over," he said.

"But you could. You're highly skilled. Isn't that right?"

"Doesn't everyone believe that? It'd be ok if *I* made the decision."

Her lips crinkled into a smile.

"What about Charlie Marston?"

Randy shrugged off the question.

"Does he deserve to go free? He killed his father didn't he?" She let the words hang in the air. "Does he deserve to inherit a fifty million dollar estate?" Heather Lovely knew exactly where it hurt. Tom prepped her well for this meeting, too well.

If Randy's parents survived, Charlie would never have lived in that house. She reappeared beside the couch while Randy was lost in the past. He tried to unclench his jaw and soften his eyes.

Then he saw the gun.

The stainless steel barrel aligned somewhere between the tips of her pointy shoes and his sneakers. She blocked the path to the door. He could barely move with his shoulder trussed up the way it was. Wrestling his way around her was out. Ditto jumping out the window. He'd probably get hung up in the frame and leave himself dangling six stories up.

Death terrified him at that moment. Not that he had anything worth living for. He'd welcomed death weeks earlier, but dying meant eternal torment. God hadn't given up on him yet. He had more to do.

She waggled the gun at him.

"Is this what he needs? Should we stick it in his mouth and pull the trigger? Makes sense to me. Cut the red tape. Save the taxpayers a few bucks. Elizabeth can leave all that money to charity. Don't you think?"

She looked at him as if she could substitute Randy for Charlie. Stick the gun in his mouth and shoot him here in her office, spattering his blood all over the fluffy white carpet. He hadn't seen a soul in the building except the security guard downstairs. No one else knew he was there.

She waved the gun again.

Randy's feet gripped the floor.

They should have exchanged places then, doctor and patient. The insane doctor tired of waiting for an answer. She turned and walked to her desk, slid the gun into the top drawer and locked it. She sat on the desktop twenty feet away and watched him curiously. She seemed pleased with his courage to hold fast. She certainly wasn't convinced of his sanity or his innocence. What she'd learned of his guilt she'd brought to this meeting. He wondered if her testimony had been paid for and this whole charade arranged merely to entertain the lunatic on top of the desk.

He didn't take the opening to rush out. He waited until she stepped over and held the door open for him.

She whispered in his ear as he passed, so close he could feel her warm breath, "Things are going to work out well for you Randy. Trust me."

He'd been in the room with this woman for three hours and he realized how little he understood about her. She was extremely volatile and she was going to testify with his life in the balance. Which woman would sit on the witness stand? The professional psychologist? The gun toting vigilante? The siren? The strange décor convinced him this was more than play acting. Heather Lovely needed the help she professed to give.

The elevator doors stood open, waiting for him as he made his way down the hall, but when he stepped in and pressed the button nothing happened. He waited with his eyes on the only door that led out of this hallway—back to Heather Lovely. A drawer rattled in her office.

After a dozen nervous beats, the shiny doors closed and the elevator descended. He crossed the street to the gray box van, preferring the comfortable automatic to the sports car until the cast came off. He was so glad to close himself in that he didn't notice the head of fine blonde hair watching from the Corolla across the street.

Chapter Seventeen

Cassie couldn't imagine what Randy was doing inside for three hours. He hadn't been anywhere except the grocery store in the week she'd been watching him and this was a strange place for his first outing. Where the building sat on the outskirts of downtown, close to the highway and too close to Acushnet Avenue she expected business to be slow, but in three hours no one came in or out. She watched the building for twenty minutes after Randy left and still saw no one. She wondered if he was making plans to continue his crime spree. She hoped he was looking for a job to get his life back together, but whatever he was doing Cassie couldn't afford to follow him much longer. She had to start filing stories again.

She strolled across the street and confidently into the lobby as if she were late for a meeting. The guard glared at her. She scanned the directory of tenants on the way to the elevator. Not recognizing a single company name, she decided to check out the fifth floor and maybe another on her way down. Before she pressed the call button, the guard barked at her to sign in and wait while he called ahead to confirm her appointment.

Randy's name wasn't on the clean visitor log.

"I'm meeting Bill..." she hesitated. "Walsh, I think it is. He's with TechNow Systems on five."

The guard grimaced immediately. He knew she was lying.

He called upstairs. When he couldn't confirm her appointment, he ushered her out the front door without giving her a chance to explain. They were very touchy about visitors at 125 Coggeshall.

Back in her car, she scanned the Internet for TechNow Systems. She found nothing, odd for a tech company. She searched for any company at that address and found information on two: Heather Lovely, a psychologist, and Omni-sense, a home security company. In an out of the way building like this, the other offices could be vacant. It made sense that there wasn't any foot traffic, but where were the 'for lease' signs? Someone had to be paying for all that office space. Surely one psychologist and a small-time security firm couldn't fill an entire six-story building. Randy could be housing his criminal venture inside. If he was, Walter would proclaim Cassie's mistake as loudly and publicly as he could.

Randy could have legitimate business with either firm. The Marstons told of a man who was totally unhinged and a master of all things surveillance. They thought him a ghost before they were finally able to catch him. Even then, it was him trapping the family and not the other way around. Security work might be his calling. Then again, the way the family described the dreadful things he'd done, a psychologist might be exactly what Randy Black needed.

Cassie was getting ready to head back to Randy's house when she saw a white Mercedes zip out from behind the building and race away. Cassie followed, doing her best to stay inconspicuous with her running lights shining from half a block behind. The Mercedes stopped at a florist. The woman who stepped out looked nervous as she rushed across the sidewalk. She didn't seem to notice the Corolla when she rushed out and sped off. Judging by the Mercedes and the white suit, Cassie guessed she'd found Heather Lovely. A senior member of the security firm would have known Cassie was behind her long before she turned into the cemetery.

Cassie parked outside the gates. She scooted under the stone archway and through a grouping of high monuments. The Mercedes peeked through the stones one hundred yards ahead.

Heather Lovely stepped out of the car in white from her shoes to a light jacket that was too much for the strong sun on this late spring day. She looked ghostly drifting through the cemetery. Closer to evening the effect would have been striking.

Cassie's black tank top was a magnet for the sun's rays. She slipped silently over the green grass, weaving among the headstones closer to where Heather stood. She ducked low and hid herself rather than pose as a mourner. From behind a large monument she saw Heather lay two full bunches of white flowers on a family plot. Heather kept her head bowed for several minutes, subtly bobbing with tears or words of remembrance. Then she stepped aside and paced back and forth. Her demeanor turned angry. Cassie moved closer for a better look, kneeling before a granite monument from 1993. Heather jabbed her heel into the grass, punctuating her assault with acidic curses. The bitter exchange ended abruptly and Heather turned for her car with measured strides.

After Heather drove away, Cassie stalked over to the two headstones with white bouquets. Harold and Annette Lovely lay side by side. They died the same day in 1982. Cassie didn't get a good look at Heather, but assumed she couldn't have been an adult back then. She was certain then that it was Heather Lovely she'd been following and here were her parents, taken from here while she was fairly young.

As she stood wondering about Heather Lovely's age, absently looking down at the grass, she noticed a single black rose on the next headstone. The name was Peter Lovely, born in 1964, died July 10th 1985. Looking back to the first headstone, Cassie was shocked to discover the parents had died on that same day three years earlier.

The date couldn't be a coincidence.

Could Heather have killed them all? What did Randy have to do with this? Maybe he helped her get rid of the brother back in 1985. No, Randy was only eight then, too young to know Heather, too young for his first murder.

Did she dress in white to match the flowers on her parents' grave?

The grass on the son's plot was torn up where Heather's heels dug in as if to stab him through the ground. Cassie carefully copied the names and dates and drove back to the paper to do some research on this very unfortunate family.

Nothing about the lives Randy Black touched made sense.

Chapter Eighteen

The laborer jumped away from the temporary fence post, waving his arms and screaming as the post pretzelled under the weight of the excavator's bucket. Ron "The Mower" Morgan jerked the lever and the boom swooped up.

Daydreaming again.

He hated digging foundations for his father, but he had to buck up. His degree in Business Management was a gift from the coaching staff and appreciative faculty. He'd never expected to work at anything except tackling running backs and sacking quarterbacks. Unfortunately, he wasn't strong enough to fight through a professional offensive lineman and he wasn't fast enough to play linebacker. A hard year on the Vikings' practice squad taught him that lesson in spades. It was a huge adjustment being relegated to the cab of the excavator all day, but he had two kids now and his father was tired of paying the tab. Digging holes was the best gig Ron could find with his qualifications.

He finished pushing in the fence posts, careful not to frighten off his new partner on the ground. The Latino guy had guts to stand under the bucket and hold those posts with Ron operating. He must have really needed the money. When the orange fence was strung around the open hole, Ron climbed down into his Escalade and headed home.

The first sign of trouble was in the driveway.

The long black sedan didn't fit with the pickups his friends drove. It could have been one of his teammates that made it to the show, but they hadn't been around in years. Ron parked beside the sedan, lumbered up the stairs and found the driver sitting at the kitchen table talking to his wife. It wasn't jealousy that quickened his pulse. The geeky-looking guy in a dark suit and glasses was no ladies man, but even if he was, he wouldn't be chasing a two hundred pound married woman with two young kids. The man in his kitchen wanted something. Ron drew a labored breath and stepped in. He had to handle this one. He couldn't go to his father again.

The man hopped up with an outstretched hand, sputtered his name so fast Ron couldn't catch it then asked if there was a place they could talk. Ron grabbed two Budweisers from the fridge and led the way to the back deck where he cracked his and took a long pull. The stranger set his full can on the rail and let his briefcase hang in front of his knees.

"What's this about?" Ron asked.

The man pulled a news clipping from his jacket and handed it over.

Ron didn't need to read it. He'd seen this article in his dreams.

"An old story," the man paused dramatically. "It's third down and a defensive lineman stunts right into the hole. He's unblocked with the running back in his sites, but inexplicably, he dives for the opposing tight end, crashes into his knee and cripples him. Funny no one picked up on it."

Ron's worst nightmare had finally found him.

Even with a full ride Ron needed money to live on campus. His schedule didn't allow time for a job. Fifty thousand sounded like a ton of money back then—even more now. He'd never met the guy who'd offered him the money and he'd never met the guy who he was supposed to take out. He took the deal, found his opportunity and slammed the guy. It had haunted him ever since. Now it was time to pay, but the cash was long gone. Ron didn't have much to give these days.

Ron outweighed the guy in front of him by a hundred pounds, but he was just a suit. If he pounded this guy another would come. He took another long pull and hoped the guy wasn't a cop or a lawyer for Charlie Marston.

"Today's your lucky day, Ron."

"How so?"

"Do as you're told and you'll never have to worry about this again."

79

"I'm not hurting anyone for you."

"I'm not asking you to. I'm here to give you some free legal advice."

"Sure you are."

"This can all go away easier than you think."

Ron wanted to know more, but it couldn't be easy. This man didn't come all the way upstate to solve his problems.

"There's going to be a trial in Massachusetts. You're going to be called to testify."

Ron gasped. He hadn't told a soul. This stranger knew exactly what happened and now it was going to come out in court. The guy who paid him must have confessed. Ron's wife was going to be shocked. His father was going to go ballistic. Ron needed to tell him before it went public, but he couldn't walk into the house and face him with this news.

"Charlie Marston has solid grounds to sue. That'd mean serious jail time and you'd probably lose your house, not to mention the damage to your reputation. You were something of a star at Michigan State, weren't you?"

Ron didn't care about his sack record being stripped. He couldn't feed his kids from prison. "What do you want?" he managed.

"Follow my advice. Say what I tell you to when you get on the stand."

"I can't talk about this in court!"

"You have no choice. But if you listen to me, I'll arrange immunity before you appear. It'll all be signed before you step on the witness stand. No one will know what you're going to say before you get there except me and you."

Immunity alone would have been enough. Having the load off his mind would have added years to his life. That was before he saw what was in the case. The bronze latches clicked open and he saw stacks of hundreds, double what he'd been paid the first time.

The stranger left Ron with the case, wondering where he could hide all that money in the tiny two bedroom house. He could never explain it to his wife if she ever found it.

Chapter Nineteen

Randy left the McLaren along the drive and hustled past a long line of cars. The bruises and fractures had finally healed and with the shoulder cast removed he looked as healthy as anyone. He'd abandoned the boots and leather for khakis, loafers and silk socks. The ensemble lent a civilized ease to his stride. He hurried when he noticed the parking area was quiet and the double doors at the back of the church were already closed.

Keeping the Sabbath holy seemed simple enough, but he'd gotten the time wrong. Everyone was already inside when the door creaked open. He felt like a politician strutting in late to make an appearance, but the last thing he wanted to do was call attention to himself. He hadn't been here in a very long time, but the people inside had seen his picture in the papers, on television and hanging in the post office. They knew what he'd done and he doubted they'd be ready to welcome him back if they recognized him. Strolling down the aisle during the sermon would cement those low opinions, but he couldn't wait for next Sunday, so he went in.

The church could have been a replica of the one his aunt brought him to all those years ago. The red velvet lined pews were about half-filled with wispy gray haired women. The choir sang "In the Garden" from the balcony behind him while the congregation sat facing Reverend Simmons.

The air inside was stifling, the congregation edgy. They sensed his approach over the sounds of the choir and stirred. A few heads turned, showed no sign of recognition and turned back, but one feeble woman in a lime green suit stared long at his features. She whispered to her neighbor and soon word spread through the pews like a brush fire.

The man alone in the very last pew had killed one of Westport's finest citizens. A dozen necks craned as the choir finished and the reverend took the lectern. Sweat beaded on Randy's forehead. He felt the eyes on him in the stifling air. A trickle traced the back of his neck, headed for his golf shirt. The reverend cleared his throat and delivered a sermon that sounded like it had been prepared for Randy's appearance.

"God sent his only Son to take away the sins of the world."

The baritone hung in the air.

"Did he mean only certain sins?

"Did he expect us to decide which sins to forgive?

"Did he mean for us to stone those who don't live up to our standards?

"Not Mary Magdalene!"

He paused to let the congregation consider their silent condemnations.

"Should we guard the church doors so the wrong sorts don't get in?

"No.

"Jesus said, let he among you who is without sin cast the first stone."

The reverend told them that the stones never flew and neither should they fly here in this church. He went on, finally extending a hand of welcome to Randy at the back of the church and encouraging the congregation to do the same.

Randy bowed as he was recognized and felt a breeze on his damp neck.

An awed stillness swept over the congregation. Slowly all eyes turned upward. The ceiling fan high above hadn't worked in four years. The congregation didn't have the budget to get it repaired, so they moved services two hours earlier during the summer months. Miraculously, the fan started working again on the hottest day of the summer, the first day Randy Black wandered into the church, precisely when he was welcomed by Reverend Simmons.

When the service was over, the reverend stood at the back of the church and invited everyone to the vestry next door for coffee and fellowship. Randy stayed seated in his pew and watched the congregants file out, shaking hands, hugging each other and chatting their way toward the exit. He heard the choir file down the back stairs. They unzipped their crimson robes and hung them up. Feet shuffled out.

Randy didn't have anything in common with the parishioners next door. They wouldn't be eager to get to know him over donuts, but Randy wouldn't skip out on the gathering. Today was an important day. The first day he felt well; the first day of his journey. The reverend would help him find his way. Failing that, he'd take all the encouragement he could get.

Randy sat in his pew several minutes admiring the altar and thinking about sacrifice and redemption. He turned for the back of the church and braced to meet the stoic faces next door. Two steps into the vestibule he heard a gasp. He rushed back among the pews expecting to find someone struggling against a heart attack. The organist stood above him in the balcony, clutching the rail, her eyes fixed on the high ceiling. The fan stopped when Randy walked out. When he returned, she looked back and forth from him to the fan expecting it to start again, but it didn't.

Randy raised his eyes toward Heaven, smiled at the woman and headed for the vestry. He'd already been convinced of God's power, but his heart felt impossibly light as he crossed the parking lot.

The white building with gray asphalt shingles reminded him of his parents dropping him off for Sunday school. He remembered the dividers they used to separate the second floor into rooms, the wooden benches that hurt after sitting fifteen minutes, and the ladies who tried to teach while struggling to maintain order.

Inside, the wooden floors were as worn as they had been fifteen years ago. The fifty-cup stainless coffee makers were the same. The Dunkin Donuts on the folding banquet table hadn't changed either. Randy had run circles through the legs in this crowd all those years ago, playing tag and getting scolded a dozen times an hour. Some of those people who scolded him might still be here. He scanned the older faces and found a few that seemed familiar, but even the older faces had changed. A few looked as if they recognized him, but he wasn't sure if they remembered him from his childhood or his wanted-poster photo.

He made conversation here and there. He met a retired carpenter, a plumber and an artist. Generations of families made Westport their home, defined by those that came before them and the way their work shaped the community. Randy would leave no such legacy. His education in winery operations had been cut short. He'd pursued another mission and completed it in spectacular fashion, but it wasn't what he wanted to be remembered for. No youngsters would follow. Randy was the end of the Joyets he knew.

He pondered this as he stood in a tight circle listening to old men chatter about trout and striped bass to come. The organist rushed in, buttonholed the reverend and talked excitedly about what she'd seen. Word rippled through the crowd. Astonishment lit up the faces the story reached. Eyes flashed in Randy's direction. Whispers were exchanged, but the idea was too scandalous to believe. No one dared approach Randy even after the coffee hour outlived its name. At seventy-five minutes, the crowd milled for the door. A few stragglers pinned the reverend for a question or a story, but no one asked Randy about the fan. Soon only a few volunteers cleaning the kitchen, the reverend, and Randy remained.

The reverend freshened his coffee and invited Randy to join him across a long wooden table. The reverend regarded him differently now, carefully, as if this were a special opportunity and he wanted to capture every instant.

"I didn't have anything to do with the fan."

"Nothing is a coincidence," Reverend Simmons said firmly.

His eyes didn't waver now. They admired Randy like a gift.

"Thanks for calming the natives. I thought they were going to drive me to the edge of town and start looking for rocks."

"God fearing people believe in the law. Always have. Sometimes they get a bit enthusiastic. But we all make mistakes and we all deserve forgiveness, most importantly, from ourselves."

Randy's head drooped. Mention of his mistakes weighted his heart with regret. He'd taken to revenge so wholeheartedly, he'd doomed himself. Looking back, it was foolish. Now, making amends was a lifetime's work.

"Don't look so glum." The reverend reached over and patted his arm. "Did I ever tell you what I did before I joined the seminary?"

He'd been a chemical engineer, a star that rose quickly to senior management in a Fortune 100 firm. He'd been a zealous leader, successful and ambitious. He pushed his team to the brink, expecting them to match his fanatic dedication. He took control of a foreign plant where costs were driving his bosses mad. He slashed budgets and expenses, keeping the pressure up until the plant turned a healthy profit. Months after his changes took effect the plant had a major accident. Hazardous gases drifted downwind and poisoned 1,500 people. They lay dead in homes, cars and businesses, on sidewalks, everywhere.

The morning after, he viewed the photographs and resigned.

It took the tragedy to teach him that profit shouldn't be our ultimate motivator. The reverend had killed 1,500 people. Indirectly, sure. He hadn't intended it. He hadn't even imagined such a serious leak was possible. But what did intentions matter? The reverend and Randy had similar burdens. Reverend Simmons had found hope. Maybe Randy could, too.

"I'm heading to court tomorrow morning," Randy said.

"And you're nervous?"

"Not exactly." Randy had resigned his fate to God's will. He was ready to sacrifice himself to further God's plan, but not knowing what that plan was, he didn't want to throw his life away in a meaningless gesture that left him powerless. "My lawyer and I can't agree how to proceed. There are extenuating circumstances. The jury might understand, but they might not. Explaining things means admitting I'm guilty."

"Sounds self-defeating."

"That's what my lawyer says. He wants me to lie in court."

"And you have a problem with that?"

"I do. Exodus 20:16."

"I see. So you've come to me looking for a boat?"

Randy laughed.

"Don't be swayed. Your heart will find its way to wherever God needs you." The reverend shot his eyes around the vestry. "I never imagined I'd trade a glass-walled New York City boardroom for a cramped office in a hundred year old building in Westport, Massachusetts, but here I am."

Chapter Twenty

Sebastian carefully dialed the numbers from the card and hunkered down against the partition as the phone rang. The man at the next phone had protected him through the last few days. He was here to listen and Sebastian would speak loudly enough so he heard every word.

When Randy approached him about getting even with Charles Marston, Sebastian never considered he'd end up here. Standing five-eight and weighing one hundred sixty made him vulnerably effeminate in this place. The other inmates spent their days working out and dreaming up ways to amuse themselves. Sebastian stood center stage in their plans from his first walk into the cellblock. Gallons of testosterone sloshed around looking for an outlet. Aggressive or otherwise, Sebastian didn't want to be the target.

He'd been offered a choice.

Protection came at a price, a price that meant more time—easier time.

The phone rang.

He wished he'd taken the money and kept running. He couldn't believe his father wouldn't take it after Charles Marston ruined his career. Sebastian risked everything to put things right and his father turned up his nose and told him to take the money back. His father wasn't angry anymore. He wouldn't lower himself to blackmail and he told Sebastian that it wasn't his fight and he shouldn't have gotten involved. Sebastian wished they'd had that conversation before Randy tempted him to get even with the Marstons. Sebastian's life changed once he lit that trickle of gasoline.

Three men knew Sebastian had ignited the fire that destroyed the Marston winery. Charles Marston died that night. The other two, Randy Black and Charlie Marston, were gearing up for a legal battle with Sebastian between them. The DA promised he'd only do twelve months, but after this call, he'd be pushing for more.

The line connected.

His attorney recognized his name, but had to find the file to recall the details of his case. Sebastian waited.

"I can't do it. I've got to tell the truth," Sebastian said.

"Can't do what?"

"I've got to turn down the deal. I can't let Charlie get away with it."

The line went silent.

The man at the next phone replaced the receiver, but didn't leave.

"This was a sweet deal. You're going to get two years minimum. It could get worse—much worse. You sure you know what you're doing?"

It couldn't get worse than what almost happened in the showers. If protection meant two years, fine. Charlie Marston would be pissed if Randy got off, but so what? Charles deserved what he got and Charlie was going to get more than his share. He'd own seven wineries and have more money than he could ever spend. Sebastian's father was the real victim. He was sweating it out in a third-rate vineyard in California while Charlie presided over the dynasty Sebastian's father helped create.

The lawyer protested again. He didn't want to try this case. Maybe they'd offer him a deal to plead guilty but not cooperate. Whatever it was, it'd be more than twelve months. Anything would be better than being someone's girlfriend.

He'd never be the same after that. Never.

"I can't lie under oath. I just can't do it."

The lawyer begged him to reconsider.

Sebastian suggested he work on another plea deal and hung up.

The man at the next phone fell into step as Sebastian headed for the heavy doors. He clapped him hard on the shoulder. "You did the right thing, man. Keep your head down and you're gonna be ok."

Chapter Twenty-one

Cassie pulled to a stop on Cottage Street and admired the blue and yellow house with scalloped trim. It would have been an ideal gingerbread design had it been painted brown. The chain-link-fenced lawn was quite welcoming compared to the towering tenements with porches that dumped out onto the sidewalk. To have the setback for a front lawn, this house had been standing here for a very long time. Cassie hoped Di Stowers was a longtime resident with an even longer memory. The neighbors around the former Lovely home hadn't been helpful at all. No one remembered the family that tragedy nearly erased twenty years earlier. This visit was Cassie's last hope to learn about Heather Lovely's childhood troubles.

Cassie checked her watch. She'd give Di Stowers thirty minutes. After that she'd declare Heather Lovely a dead end and get back to her beat.

Purple pansies lined the concrete walk from the gate all the way to the porch steps. A shriveled woman answered the door and led Cassie into a dark living room with short halting steps, her slippers brushing the linoleum. Cassie settled deep into a dilapidated couch that had little support left to give. The woman passed over a newer looking chair for another that Cassie assumed to be her regular seat. Beside the closer chair, a pipe lay canted on a small metal tray, a faded book of matches beside it.

"Your husband's?" Cassie asked.

The woman's eyes fell on the pipe. She gave a bittersweet smile. "Clinton's been gone a long time now. Just me here, alone, waiting to die."

The woman clutched a tissue from her sweater pocket and dabbed her eyes. Her emotions lay so close to the surface, just the mention of her husband brought her to tears. Cassie couldn't bear to watch. This poor old woman sat each day with only memories of her husband for company. Cassie wondered how long Mrs. Stowers could live here alone. Thinking about the gangs of hoods that roamed these streets made Cassie shiver.

Cassie's eyes fell on a corner table aligned directly in front of Mrs. Stowers' favorite chair. Pink and red Mother's Day cards covered every inch of the tabletop. Beyond the table, the doorway was also lined with cards taped to the trim, rising on each side and climbing across the top.

Cassie stepped over and browsed.

"I've never seen so many Mother's Day cards. Looks like you've been collecting them for years."

The woman sniffled then smiled through her tears. "Those are this year's, dear," she said as if receiving so many cards was completely natural.

No woman could have that many natural children, but looking closer, none of the cards had faded. The woman wasn't deluded. They *were* this year's cards. "Wow," is all Cassie could think to say.

"My babies," the woman said and indicated a stack of thick quilted books with a wavering finger. Each was stuffed wide with plastic pages.

Cassie brought the uppermost book and stood over the woman while she told of the fifty-two foster babies she'd cared for over the years. The home was modest and if the cards on the table were a sign, this woman had given her wards all she could. Cassie wondered how the missing husband had fit in. Was he a typical husband of his time, demanding as much as the children? If so, frail Di Stowers had been incredibly busy.

The book chronicled the lives of so many children Cassie couldn't understand how one person could love them all so much. They'd come to her desperately in need and she'd given what she could, then and later through life. The faces grew in each picture, a few pages reserved for each child. Di Stowers smiled as she encountered each one, remembering them as if they'd never left. The worn plastic sheets had kept them with her.

"Do you remember Heather Lovely?" Cassie asked.

"One of my older girls. Hard to reach then, you know." She frowned as if she'd failed Heather.

Cassie asked what she remembered of Heather and Mrs. Stowers indicated another book on the floor. Heather's page had only two pictures: a dour girl of sixteen wearing cut-offs on a hot summer day, and a graduation photo with Mrs. Stowers.

"Did she ever tell you what happened to her family?"

"Her parents were murdered. Stabbed, I think. Lucky she wasn't there. Her brother found them."

"And her brother died three years later to the day. Did she ever say anything about the coincidence?"

Mrs. Stowers held her breath, just momentarily, but long enough for Cassie to know she was suspicious of the coincidence, too. She wouldn't betray the child she'd worked so hard to protect and Cassie wouldn't ask her to. "Not really, no," Mrs. Stowers answered. "There was a fire. She lost everything including her brother. He was the last of her family. That's when she came to me."

"That must have been so hard for her."

"She didn't talk for months afterward. She was terribly skittish even when she moved out on her own. For years I worried that I found her too late," she murmured, "but things turned out all right, didn't they?"

Mrs. Stowers looked up at Cassie for forgiveness. How could this sweet woman who had done so much for so many strangers blame herself for Heather's trouble?

It seemed no one but Heather Lovely knew what happened to her brother in the fire. This had been Cassie's last hope of resurrecting the story and now it was time to let it go. Bart would support her, but she couldn't afford more time on this if she was going to keep Walter from stepping on the Marston story.

Cassie thanked Mrs. Stowers and headed for her car.

Sitting alone in the driver's seat, she wrote herself a reminder to mail the special greeting that meant more to Mrs. Stowers than any other. She'd send it the following May.

Chapter Twenty-two

Randy wasn't sure why he stood in the library window looking down over Pleasant Street. It could have been a fantasy about saving someone from the traffic below, not that he could get down there in time. More likely it was distrust for Tom Gold that had him spying on his arrival at the restaurant. Whatever it was, he felt a surge of strength watching the oblivious masses trudge by. He'd felt this way watching Charlie Marston from the fringes of the winery. Even after Charlie started looking over his shoulder, he had no idea how much Randy knew about him or why. The warm and powerful feeling of control was returning to Randy's chest.

When the fan in the church started spinning he knew he was on the right path. Witnessing this small miracle converted the reverend from skeptic to willing guide. Randy was given this chance because he *would* succeed.

His body was healed. What he needed was the confidence to take decisive action. The court visit would scare most men to death. Far more than prison, Randy hated the helpless feeling he'd woken up with that morning. A similar feeling plagued him from the moment he caught Marston tampering with the disgorger until the day he collected the first contaminated bottle—his first step to getting even with Charles Marston. Standing at the window, he could feel the helplessness ebb. The court battle would work itself out. He wasn't given this chance to rot in prison. He'd be in church again next week, but he'd also get back to the gym and downstairs on the shooting range. His time was coming. He could feel it and he'd be ready for the challenge to come whatever it might be.

Brimming with confidence, he watched Tom Gold's BMW turn off Williams Street and park directly in front of the restaurant. Tom hung up his phone as he got out of the car, glanced around the street and stopped for a moment focused on the statue of a whaling boat thirty feet below where Randy stood. Tom waited there as if he expected the figure in the boat to come to life and greet him. When it didn't, he turned and went inside.

Randy hustled down and entered the restaurant two minutes behind him.

The morning rush had receded to the office buildings along Pleasant and up and down Union. Tom waited in a back-corner booth where they could strategize about their court appearance without being overheard by the two older men reading newspapers at the counter. The men ignored each other and the television news murmuring from the set mounted in the corner. They wouldn't care what was said behind them. The waitress didn't seem interested either. She propped herself up on the counter by the grill and did her best to avoid eye contact with her four remaining customers.

Tom sounded his approval of the suit—Randy's only suit. Unlike Tom, Randy had never dressed for work. Actually he'd never been to work. If the judge froze his assets, he might have to join the working world. Strange Tom hadn't asked for a single dollar yet. They agreed on one forty an hour, but after a month, you'd think the guy would send a bill. Randy had no way of knowing how many hours he'd put in or how large the bill would grow before Tom sprang it.

Before Randy could question him about the bill, Tom launched into the lawyer pep talk, asked how he was doing, and started running through what he could expect to happen in the courtroom that day.

Not much happened in a pretrial hearing according to Tom.

"Have you thought any more about testifying?"

Randy cringed.

Thou shalt not bear false witness.

Tom kept guaranteeing he had things under control, but he pushed Randy to take the witness stand every time they met. Randy couldn't lie under oath, so he couldn't discuss his relationship with Charles Marston without sinking the case. Randy thought he'd already done his part. He produced proof that Charles had stolen six wineries. It was Tom's job to convince the jury to acquit. With the bottles, the stab wound and the 911 transcript, Tom had everything he needed to create reasonable doubt. Still he wasn't satisfied and that made Randy nervous.

The waitress interrupted them to pour coffee. Tom ordered a bagel and Randy ordered scrambled eggs and bacon. Randy watched the waitress wander back to the grill before questioning Tom. "Do you have it under control or not?"

"I do. But it'll look odd if you don't testify. Why wouldn't you if the Marstons did what you say they did?"

"You don't think the jury will buy it?"

"There's not going to be a jury."

"What?"

"I'm requesting a bench trial."

Randy was counting on tension and disagreement in the jury room. Twelve people could fail to reach a verdict, but a trial before a judge was completely different. He'd cut right through the extraneous crap Tom threw at him. He'd be connected to the cops who'd beaten Randy and hauled him off to jail. For an instant he imagined someone had gotten to Tom. The Marstons were influential people. Charlie could have paid him to throw the case. That might explain the delay in his bill, but would he risk disbarment for a bribe?

Randy shook himself. Prison was not his destiny.

"That makes no sense. The right jury would be more sympathetic than any judge."

"It's your best chance. The judge will be impartial and, believe me, after all the media coverage any juror will have a negative impression of you once he sees your face at the defense table."

The stalemate continued while they ate. They'd be in court in thirty minutes. Tom knew Randy wouldn't stand up and argue against his own lawyer, so he chose not to discuss the issue further. Randy was losing faith, but he wasn't sure if a bench trial helped him or not. They ate in silence and when the waitress brought the bill, Randy reached for his wallet to pay his share. Tom waved him off, paid and led the way outside.

The two men started across Pleasant Street to make the climb up to the courthouse. A black SUV and a silver sedan stopped, holding back both lanes of traffic as the men hurried across.

A sudden movement from the left caught Randy's eye. Thoughts of Tom Gold, the judge and the Marstons vanished as the black two door shot out from the parking garage and barreled toward him. The familiar head of dark hair behind the wheel reminded him of a night months ago. Deirdre accelerated, angling for Randy in the center of the crosswalk.

Randy shoved Tom back toward the restaurant and darted for the opposite curb. The car entered the crosswalk as Randy left his feet. He arched his back. His right hand found the trunk of a parked Malibu and he broke his fall, the force absorbed by his hand, his elbow and finally his shoulder as he rolled over the trunk of the Malibu. He found himself in mid-air for an instant then his shoes hit the sidewalk and he slid across and rammed into a concrete wall. Randy fell backward, disoriented by his flip and the sudden stop.

Deirdre's focus never faltered. She veered after him.

A plastic newspaper box shattered sending green shards and an explosion of fluttering real estate advertisements at Randy. The sheet metal box advertising *The Standard Times* held onto its treasure as it crumpled between the bumper and the telephone pole it was chained to. The black car spun, met the bumper of the Malibu and bucked to a halt five feet from where Randy lay on the sidewalk.

The airbag saved Deirdre's head from a nasty impact with the windshield and her chest from an up close meeting with the steering column.

Tom was on his cell phone on the opposite sidewalk, presumably calling an ambulance and someone to haul off the lunatic behind the wheel.

Randy came around, opened the door and faced her, wondering why she'd come back now. She must have heard the rumors about the beating and the problems in the commonwealth's case. She couldn't let him walk away, not after what he'd done to Henri.

Deirdre fought free of the airbag ready to spit venom. She eased somewhat when Randy extended a hand to help her out.

"It's ok," he said.

Her face paled, shocked by his tranquility. Her life would never be the same after what he'd done. She stood ten inches shorter and ninety pounds lighter, not a physical threat, but she could have concealed a gun or a knife.

She focused on his eyes.

Cars inched around them. Drivers gawked.

"I've seen him," Randy said.

Her face fell slack.

"He looks well. He's forgiven me."

She didn't scream. She didn't pound his chest.

Somehow she understood this wasn't the man from the farmhouse.

"I'm sure he's forgiven you, too."

Her eyes shifted upward involuntarily.

"He's worried about you."

Disbelief and anger colored her face. "You're insane."

"He's there… with my parents."

Deirdre turned away. He thought she was looking for a weapon, but she couldn't risk attacking again. Word was spreading along the crowded sidewalk that she was crazy or on drugs. No one dared approach. They were alone in the crowd until a cruiser arrived.

She turned to face him again and he offered his hand.

"You didn't?" she asked. "It's not possible."

Sirens raced down Williams Street.

'Why you,' was the question he expected. He deserved to be punished, but he'd been offered a second chance and nothing was going to stop him.

The first cruiser arrived and a young officer jumped out.

"What happened here?"

"I think her foot slipped off the brake and hit the gas," Randy offered.

"Are you ok, mam?" the officer asked.

Randy left them and started up the hill. Tom knew where the courthouse was. He'd catch up.

95

Chapter Twenty-three

The wiry black man thrust a plastic tray toward Randy. His blue uniform pants never left the swiveling chair beside the metal detector. A sign beside him prohibited cameras and handguns in the courthouse—not surprising. Randy emptied his change into the bin and stepped through the metal detector. The man handed his things back and motioned him forward.

Tom followed. As they walked the length of the hall, Randy was grateful to be entering through the front door rather than being escorted through the prisoner entrance in shackles. They passed a young woman calming a baby on a bench. Randy wondered if she was here to support a husband or brother or if she was on trial herself.

Tom led the way into the courtroom. Proceedings were in progress, but no one objected to their entrance while the lawyers spoke. Tom walked up front, beyond a railing that divided attorneys and court officials on the lower level from spectators and defendants free on their own recognizance above.

Randy's eyes flitted around the wide room.

The desks at front rose in tiers like an Aztec village. The judge occupied the uppermost tier at the center with clerks and others busy typing on keyboards and shuffling papers on three sides.

A single defendant stood shackled to a heavy rail. The judge and attorneys faced him, but his eyes were turned toward the audience. He flashed hand signals to someone in the crowd. Randy spotted her, an older woman, his mother. They weren't signing, but they understood each other from across the room. They'd been through the procedure enough times to develop a code of their own. How heartbreaking for a mother to communicate with her son this way.

The prisoner wasn't as old as Randy. He'd been arrested for selling drugs, bailed out and here he was arrested again before his first trial came up. This wasn't a brush with the law. This kid was a professional. No wonder Pinto had such contempt for criminals. The prisoner up front was a cancer to be removed from society. Stunned at how disgusted he felt and how much he wanted to see this man punished, Randy looked away.

There was no jury box. No guns on the white-shirted court officers stationed on the left and right of the lawyers. Oil portraits ringed the room. Retired judges, he presumed. The men and women at the tables up front wore fine suits and impeccably-groomed, short hair. These people were judged on a regular basis and they understood how critical their appearance was. The motley crowd on the rickety wooden benches varied from a few men like Randy, carefully dressed in suits and ties, to a frumpy fifty year old man in dirty, ripped jeans and a rumpled, plaid shirt.

"Randy Black," the bailiff called.

Randy hesitated. The name wasn't the one he expected, not here. He involuntarily flashed to the off-white plaster swirls and wondered whether it was an administrative mix-up or God following through on his promise. When he looked back down, Tom urged him to the front corner of the spectator area. Randy met him there and eyed the stack of papers he held.

The judge, the district attorney and Tom spoke without the tension Randy expected in such a proceeding. His life was at stake, yet this pretrial hearing seemed more like a Monday morning status meeting inside some huge conglomerate. Where was the grappling?

Judge McKinnon confirmed it would be a bench trial in his courtroom. The DA and Tom assented.

"No discovery problems?" Judge McKinnon asked.

The lawyers agreed there weren't. Randy disagreed silently. Tom hadn't shared any of the evidence against him. Standing there he realized he'd put his life in Tom's hands. It should have been obvious, but he felt dependent on Tom and the mercy of the court for the first time. He'd told Tom about the wine bottles, but hadn't handed them over for testing. His last thread of control provided little comfort.

Randy's eyes fell on the witness list.

Joshua Roundtree, Blake Wendell, Steven Bartlett... All the defrauded winery owners were listed, save his parents. Addresses and telephone numbers were aligned under each name. Lower on the list, Randy recognized the names of Officers Pinto and Frenet, and Detective Miller from news stories of his arrest. The final name, Ron Morgan, was a shock to see typed on the page, but his appearance was no surprise.

Randy listened to legal jargon about depositions and schedules. The trial date was set for September 19. He'd be free until then. Nearly three months! He'd expected a few weeks to prepare himself, but now he had time to rise to his calling. He hoped three months was enough.

The bailiff called another case as Tom led Randy out into the hall. Randy saw Cassie climbing down to follow them and he waited for her just outside the entrance.

Charlie Marston limped up and stopped nose to nose, his eyes angry.

"What'd you do to him? What could you possibly threaten him with?"

"What are you talking about?" Randy asked, puzzled.

"Don't play cute." Bitterness had seeped deep into Charlie Marston, a leftover from the days Randy spent tormenting him.

Randy raised his hands, showing them empty, though he didn't need to here in the courthouse. Charlie chose to ambush him in this hallway where Randy couldn't be armed. Deep down, Charlie was still afraid.

"Dude, I have no idea who or what you're talking about."

Tom pursed his lips and shook his head gravely. Randy was suddenly aware of the people all around, witnesses to everything said. The exchange could be a prosecution stunt to get the testimony they needed. The conflict he expected inside the courtroom had been moved to the hall.

"Really, I don't," Randy said.

"Why's he changing his story now?"

Charlie grabbed Randy's lapel in his left hand, his right clenched to strike. Randy couldn't understand Charlie's sudden anger.

"Who?" Randy asked, still confused.

"Sebastian Leonard. What did you threaten him with?"

Tom's eyes flashed.

Randy swallowed. He knew then that Tom was working harder behind the scenes than he'd approve. Sebastian was the weakness in their case. The prosecution must have offered him a deal to roll over. Apparently, Tom had outbid them. Randy stood dumbstruck, wondering how Tom had approached him in jail and what he'd offered Sebastian to make him change his story. Tom hadn't asked for hush money for Sebastian or Ron. Surely he wouldn't pay them off out of his own pocket.

Randy almost didn't see the fist hurtling toward his cheekbone.

Only the tug on his lapel alerted him in time.

He swatted Charlie's fist away with an open hand. He moved so fast Charlie couldn't change course. Randy twisted the fist over the arm gripping his lapel and pulled the hands tight. Charlie stood helpless, his arms tangled until he let go of the lapel and untwined them.

Before he could, Randy shifted his weight and landed a heel on top of Charlie's injured knee. He pressed the joint tight, not enough to collapse Charlie to the floor, but enough to let him know he hadn't forgotten Charlie's weakness.

"Don't make me hurt you, Charlie," Randy said.

A uniformed cop grabbed Charlie by the collar and pulled him back.

Convenient he'd waited for Randy to get the upper hand. The cop didn't ask if Randy wanted to press charges for assault. If roles were reversed, someone would have asked the question with a notepad in hand.

Cassie appeared from behind. "You ok?"

"I'm a big boy."

"You look good for a guy who's been in a murder trial, a fist fight and a car crash all before lunch. What do you have planned this afternoon?"

"I wasn't *in* the car."

"But you're a magnet for trouble."

"Maybe I should work with you. Think of the gas you'd save if you didn't have to follow me around."

Chapter Twenty-four

When the doors finally opened, Tom stepped out onto the Hallway to Heaven as he called the stark white corridor. He smiled naturally for the cameras, wondering what mood he'd find Heather in behind the white door. She'd be watching him now. She took perverse pleasure intruding into private moments as her patients rode the elevator and walked the hall alone. Watching him was no different. She rarely missed an opportunity to spy in spite of the conservative values she espoused. The illicit peeping was an aphrodisiac. Combined with a sense of absolute control over a powerful man she could be overwhelmed by lust.

She expertly read his emotions even after he learned to control his expressions for the cameras. Her training taught her to pick up subtle cues. She'd watched him for months before he learned her secret and those early views had given her a glance at his true feelings. Maybe that was what gave her such control over him. But Tom wasn't powerless. A snicker or smirk on the way in would set off a tirade that could last the entire visit. Mentioning her brother or her parents would spin her into a rage for days. Unfortunately, her happiness couldn't be manufactured. It depended on a delicate balance of brain chemicals that always seemed to be in short supply.

Years of exhaustive probing made his feelings transparent to her, but lately he'd been gaining ground. Once talked about in the open air, barriers dropped. She was the most forthright and aggressive woman he'd ever met.

He wondered if all shrinks acted this way when the meter was off.

And why wouldn't a group dedicated to finding and treating mental problems readily see them in their midst?

Were they all nuts or did she slip through?

Sane or not, she'd done more for his career than anyone. Her testimony and connections handed him more victories than he'd earned on his own. He didn't slow to knock. He walked in and found her where he knew she'd be: behind the desk watching him on the monitor. She was half out of her seat when the door opened.

She passed behind him as he crossed the room. Attractive as she was, she rarely stood still and allowed him a good look. She was always out of view behind him as if she were analyzing a patient rather than meeting a colleague. She took her chair as she usually did and waited for him to take his place on the couch. It was a power trip, but the firm leather was comfortable after a long day in court and upsetting her wasn't worth a better seat. He barely noticed the white on white décor anymore, but he did browse the fringes of her white sundress before he turned away to stretch out. He imagined the feel of her smooth white skin as he lay there. She rarely went outside, preferring the security of her office and the apartment through the door behind her desk.

"Judge McKinnon's going to hear the case," he said.

"Randy's not at all what I expected."

Tom waited almost a full minute for her to continue. It was a tactic she used with her patients. Most people couldn't stand the silence, so after a short pause, they rambled on. He knew injecting his ideas only encouraged her to avoid telling him anything and that his only power in this relationship was his patience.

"He's a smart guy. One thirty-five on the WAIS-R," she said.

She hesitated less this time. "I tried knocking him off balance when he came to see me, but he kept cool. I let him know I'd help him out for a roll on the couch and he turned me down flat. Can you believe that? He's nothing like his profile. It's almost like you sent me the wrong client."

She seemed disappointed. Randy's collarbone was still healing when he came to see her, but what twenty-eight year old guy would turn her down?

Women like Heather were in short supply and from the stories Tom heard, Randy was a dedicated womanizer. Nothing about Randy seemed to fit the stories. Why would a man who killed three people be so righteous about telling the truth on the stand? He was acting as if he were innocent. Tom defended plenty of creeps early in his career and they all tried to look innocent in court. Randy took it to the extreme. He was more believable than any of them. Tom knew better, but if the jury bought his act it would make defending him much easier.

Tom pictured Heather kneeling over Randy on the couch and shook the image away. "Are you ready to testify?" He hoped she wouldn't press for another consult and another opportunity to get Randy on the couch.

"Ready to testify?" She laughed out loud and Tom felt ridiculous. "It's not me you've got to worry about."

Tom had known this since his second meeting with Randy. The guy was facing life in prison and he wasn't going to play ball on the defense. That qualified him as insane more than anything in the file.

"I can frame him as an anti-social narcissist. He's bright. He's a cunning manipulator, but he comes across like a Boy Scout."

"And?"

"If you play him as a sociopath and he plays it straight for the judge, you're going to look like an ass. I wouldn't risk it. Not my license."

"What then? Did we do all those tests for nothing?"

"You've got the results. If he wants to play innocent, let him. I'll tell the judge how smart he is. You tell them how hard he worked to indict the father. It'll play," she said.

He felt her intense focus even with his back turned. They both knew the prosecutor wasn't a twit. He'd trot in the family, the winery employees, everyone connected to the siege in Westport. The commonwealth's case would look strong. The key was not giving them anything to appeal.

"What are you worried about?"

She hesitated, but not long enough for Tom to answer. "You think he'll go on a murderous rampage if he gets off?"

"I'll get him off," Tom said. "I know he's guilty, but sometimes, talking to him, I can't believe he'd hurt anyone. The prosecutor's having trouble believing the story himself. Think about it. He knew Marston stole the winery, knew it when he was thirteen, but then he spends ten years collecting evidence. Just when he can finally show the world the guy's a thief, he kills him. It doesn't make sense."

"Maybe it wasn't the world he wanted to convince."

Tom knew what happened. When Randy caught Marston tampering he turned sadistic. Killing Marston wasn't enough. He wanted to torture the whole family, but that didn't fit his client's personality at all.

"The DA was livid about the seventy-five K bail for two murders and multiple counts of arson. He couldn't believe it, but he wasn't angry at the judge. I think he's starting to see the holes in his case and he's thinking twice about the Marston kid."

"Not bad, Super Sleuth," she said.

"Black set it up. The cops found Marston holding the gun that killed that private detective—powder on his hands, no less. He admits stabbing Randy and fleeing the scene. Add in the bit about the broken knee that ended his football career and you've got motive to kill your own father. Forget about the inheritance."

Heather stood up somewhere behind him.

"Sounds like you're on your way to an acquittal," she said as she pulled up her dress and rested a bare knee on the couch beside him. She traced her bare shoulders with a finger and inched the straps down onto her toned arms.

"I like my chances," Tom said.

He kept his hands at his sides knowing patience would be rewarded. Her fingers found his knee and traced a wavy path slowly upward to his chest. He stiffened as her hand gripped the base of his short hair. She threw her other knee over and straddled him.

Randy had no idea what he'd missed.

Chapter Twenty-five

The BMW turned off the main road and passed between the police station and a cemetery, two places Randy wasn't in a rush to go. Tom badgered him for the tenth time to take the witness stand and point the finger at Charlie Marston. He couldn't understand Randy's hesitance to lie under oath. To him, perjury was preferable to prison. Randy ignored Tom's prompting as the car angled through a tight corner. He leaned in toward the curving cranberry dikes and watched the shoulder as the road leveled and entered a thick stand of pines. It became dustier and less populated with each mile they drove. Not the sort of place Tom and his fancy car would frequent, but he was dressed down in jeans and a polo shirt, casual for the fancy lawyer. There was even less goop in his hair today.

The road turned to dirt. Tom finally quieted, but he hadn't given up. Blaming Charlie would confuse the case enough to earn an acquittal. And earning an acquittal was Tom's only standard of conduct. When he realized Randy wasn't going to incriminate Charlie no matter what he threatened, he suggested Charles Marston could be tormenting Randy from the dead. The judge might be sympathetic to someone hearing voices. How ridiculous.

Randy shook his head. He knew where Charles Marston was and he was desperately trying to avoid joining him in the smoldering shadows. He wasn't going to lie under oath. Tom had already bent the truth too far for Randy. If they were going to win this case, it'd be through Tom's arguments and the evidence Randy supplied. Randy wouldn't sacrifice his soul to improve Tom's win/loss record.

The next mile was populated only by two shingled capes, spread so far apart the neighbors couldn't see each other. Tom parked by a weathered old building isolated at the end of the road. The 'rod & gun club' sign out front had an unpronounceable Native American name routed into the wood. As he opened his door, Randy wondered if Tom knew how much shooting he'd done. If not, he might earn back his legal fees with a wager.

Tom opened the trunk, handed Randy a few paper silhouettes and hoisted two large plastic cases. He unlocked the shack and led Randy inside for a brief restroom stop after the long drive. Out back, the land fell away. They crossed a deck that overlooked the expansive range, bordered on three sides by ten foot high berms covered in weeds and saplings. At the far left, a squat trap house sat surrounded by five concrete shooting stations and its own set of berms.

A steep set of stairs led to a row of benches nestled low at the base of the building, protected from the elements and any prying eyes that ventured this far out. They walked the distance of the range and mounted silhouettes on two wooden frames. Randy paced off one hundred yards from the targets back to the benches in the shadow of the weathered clubhouse.

Tom unlocked the first carrier and pulled back the cover. A lever-action Winchester model 94 lay in the case, looking good for a gun that was over twenty-four years old. The blued barrel had been cleaned and the action had been recently oiled. Tom opened the other case and let Randy remove an identical rifle. Each man loaded six .30-30 rounds into his rifle and they faced the targets over the bench.

"Let's see what you've got, Mr. Black."

Tom chambered a round, settled and fired, the report rattling through a nearby grove of pines.

The open sights were imprecise for Randy's taste. With the right bullet, Randy could hit a man with a handgun at this range. The rifle shot was little challenge, though he couldn't be sure how Tom had zeroed the gun. He'd have preferred to be more surgical with his shots, but without a scope or glasses to check his results, he simply ripped off a series of six shots, pausing briefly to work the lever and steady the sights on his target.

Tom took his time with his five remaining shots then set his rifle on the bench and started off across the range. Randy kept hold of the Winchester and pocketed a handful of cartridges before trotting to catch up. Tom didn't look back at the rifle he'd abandoned on the table behind them.

When they reached the targets, Tom proudly pointed out three heart shots and three headshots tightly grouped on his silhouette, but he shook his head in awe when he saw what Randy had done to his. He'd stitched a line of six evenly spaced shots almost perfectly flush across the head of his target, a perforation of sorts. Tom wouldn't make a bet now, but without a scope, Randy couldn't rise to his true potential. Playing it straight felt better.

As they turned back for another round, Tom asked where Randy learned to shoot, a question Randy ignored to focus on a figure now standing behind the bench. Tom walked calmly beside him in the middle of the green grass as if nothing were wrong. They were exposed, thirty yards from the berms that ran the length of the range. The man cloaked in shadow faced them over the bench within reach of the gun and ammunition Tom left unguarded. He could be anyone. There was no fence to keep non-members out. With cover behind the bench, he could drop Tom and Randy on the grass and take off. More shots at the club wouldn't put anyone on alert.

Randy casually shifted the rifle to his left hand, slipped three cartridges from his pocket and inserted them as he walked, careful not to look down or break stride. Tom was unfazed by the figure ahead. He didn't acknowledge the metal on metal of the bullets entering the magazine. If he recognized the man at the bench he could have offered Randy some comfort, but he didn't.

The figure lurking behind the Winchester grew clearer as they closed in. Randy didn't chamber the first round.

Thou shalt not kill.

Vulnerability ripened in his stomach. Killing this man, even in self-defense, might condemn him to Hell. He might earn divine protection if he chose not to shoot and died in the process, but he might not. Randy couldn't afford to take the chance. The gun in his hands was useless and he could think of no other escape.

Tom surged ahead. Randy followed nervously until the man emerged from the shadows and shook Tom's hand. Ethan introduced himself, but gave no clue how he was connected to Tom Gold. He eyed the way Randy carried his left shoulder and tested the strength of his grip when they shook. The blazer and thick-framed glasses dressed up the thug with sharp sideburns and nasty eyes. The knowing eyes would be equally at home beating a confession out of a witness or swindling a widow out of her nest egg. Whatever he was here for, Randy wanted no part of it.

Ethan and Tom moved familiarly as they packed Tom's rifle away. Randy packed its twin. He left the bullets in the magazine and sealed the case, keeping hold of it as they walked inside the clubhouse. Ethan's blazer flapped open when he held the door, showing a handgun on his right hip. No surprise. Tom Gold pushed for this case when no one else wanted it. He'd taken Randy to a shooting range deep into the woods because he expected something for his effort. Randy was about to find out what that was.

Ethan caught Randy measuring him and smiled.

"I've read about your work in the papers. Very creative."

Tom studied silently. Randy wondered if they were recording him.

"I think you've got me confused with someone else."

"Relax," Ethan said. "There are no secrets between us boys. I'm a fan. Too bad they couldn't print half of what you did. The pictures would have been something. Really, the fingers, sick! I hear that chick spent a month in the loony bin after you finished with her. And you were watching the whole time. Impressive." Ethan gave a thumbs-up.

Randy raised his hands.

"My client's shy talking about the past."

"Oh, but he shouldn't be. He's going away. Why not revel in his accomplishments?"

"My lawyer tells me I've got a solid defense."

Tom didn't flinch.

"That's what we're here to talk about," Ethan said.

Tom hadn't even hinted at this meeting during the ride. Ethan wasn't pushing Tom into this. They were working together. Randy imagined that whatever they wanted was something he couldn't do. If the shots with the Winchester had been a test, he didn't want any part of the assignment.

Randy leaned toward the cases down the table.

Tom motioned him to sit with a condescending smile. Neither man moved for a weapon. They weren't afraid of the loaded gun in the case. When Randy wouldn't sit, Ethan produced a briefcase from the floor and clicked it open. Randy backed away expecting a gun. What he saw was far worse.

The photo had been stolen and destroyed by Marston. The only digital image had been lost with the other files when his computer crashed. How did Ethan get the shot of Ron Morgan breaking Charlie's knee? Not damning evidence alone. The next picture was a candid shot of Ron with his wife and kids.

"He's agreed to testify for immunity. You know he can be bought and you know we can work the immunity deal. He'll say what I tell him to. That can be good for you or it can be very bad for you. It all depends on how well you behave for the next few days." Ethan was riveted to Randy's slack expression. This was the kind of pain Ethan reveled in. It left no sign of injury, but the terror of prison bars would torment Randy for days.

Randy sat down absently. Things were about to get much worse.

Ethan spread blueprints for a huge stone building topped with minarets. He'd seen it erected on the edge of the highway in one of the worst sections of the city. Now that he knew what it was, it made sense. The violence on Acushnet Avenue was nothing compared to what the imams saw in the Middle East. He imagined they planned to import some violence of their own. Whoever permitted this was turning Southeastern Massachusetts into a war zone. Randy was angry at the prospect, exactly the reaction Ethan had hoped for.

"Our mayor, in his infinite wisdom, has given this land to a Muslim group and allowed them to build a mosque in our city. Imagine the outrage if he'd given the land to the Catholic Church."

Strangely true. The Muslims thrived on chaos and savagery, yet it was politically incorrect to protest. They inflamed at every minor affront.

"We need to stop them from wreaking havoc on our city. No matter what our bleeding-heart mayor is thinking, we need to be prepared. When they start planning suicide bombings, we'll be there to stop them."

"Who put you in charge?" Randy asked.

Ethan ignored the question and indicated several points around the main chamber and two antechambers behind. "We need to hear everything said here, here, and here. We'll supply the electronics. All you need to do is get them inside before the official opening on Friday. No one should be there beforehand except construction personnel. The foreman is on board. We've made sure the occupancy permit will be stalled until you're done."

Ethan didn't wait for an answer. He rolled up the plans and put them back in his briefcase along with the photos.

"Get ready. We'll be in touch."

He turned and left without waiting for an answer.

Tom listened for the car to drive away. He didn't look at all embarrassed as he led the way to the car.

Randy watched the road on the drive back, his mind racing to make sense of what had transpired. Clearly Tom and Ethan were working together. If they controlled Ron Morgan, Randy had no chance of winning his case without them. He couldn't understand why Tom Gold would be involved in a plot against a mosque. Gold was a Jewish name. Was that why he had something against Muslims? Or was it money? He hadn't asked for a cent in legal fees. Not typical for a lawyer with a BMW and a mortgage.

An eerie feeling came over him as they drove.

Randy was the new Charlie Marston. Tom had slipped his way into Randy's life with charm and persistence just as Randy had slipped into Charlie's. Just like Charlie, Randy had no idea what it was that made Tom pursue him. And as long as Tom was in charge of his case, it would be impossible for Randy to break away from him.

Why would Tom target the mosque?

And why did he want Randy's help?

Chapter Twenty-six

Cars rushed down County Street one after another, a constant wash of noise. Voices carried up from the sidewalk. The speakers walking down the hill to work were obscured by the asphalt shingles beneath him. He lay prone on the roof with the rope coiled beside him. The brick chimney and the gabled dormer hid him from view.

His eyes stayed focused on the courthouse steps one hundred twenty yards away. Any further and he'd have trouble making the shot through open sights. Soon, a cruiser pulled up to the no parking zone reserved for prisoner loading and unloading. Two officers jumped from the car, one facing him, one with his back turned. A third officer escorted Sebastian from the back seat. A bulletproof vest covered his vitals.

The man on the rooftop waited, controlled his breathing and kept the front sight hovering on the center of the stairs. The Winchester made him feel like a cowboy on a rocky outcrop. The men paused on the steps ever so briefly. For a single moment the group parted, leaving Sebastian standing four feet from the nearest officer.

The gun jolted.

The report echoed over rows of rooftops.

The bullet struck Sebastian just forward and above the ear.

He dropped to the granite in a lifeless heap.

The nearest officer darted for shelter in the entryway. His partner vaulted the railing and dropped behind the heavy stone stairs. The third officer dove behind the rear end of the cruiser.

The shooter stood, lined up a sedan on County Street and fired through the hood. The car swerved with the impact and ground to a halt. Steam billowed from the front end. The shooter lined up and fired at three more cars, sending each skidding to a panicked stop. Traffic gridlocked. Cars backed up on County in both directions. Some unwise drivers stepped out of their cars, not having heard the shots from above.

The officers watched from their positions. The cruiser was useless with the traffic jam between it and the shooter and they weren't going to charge an elevated rifle on foot. He didn't waste his last bullet on them. He picked up five brass casings from the gutter, grabbed the rope and repelled to the parking lot below. He left the rope hanging from the tenement-turned-law-office and hustled to the gray box van. Not a great getaway vehicle, but the other choice was too conspicuous.

The van jerked out of the small lot and plummeted down Williams Street. The dead cars blocked traffic behind him, providing four blocks of open road down to Pleasant. Later he turned onto Route 18, then Interstate 195 and he was gone, sailing down a country road into Fairhaven before the police could even scramble themselves out onto the highway.

Sebastian had made three deals in the last few months.

The first gave him five hundred thousand dollars in cash and an opportunity to get back at Charles Marston. Guilt and bad luck had turned him around. He gave the money back and wound up in prison.

The DA offered him another deal. If he pled guilty, he'd do twelve months, but his cellmate changed his mind.

The final deal was the one they brought him here to discuss. The DA was outraged. Sebastian's defense attorney was befuddled. Now it was too late for Sebastian to explain any of his deals.

Chapter Twenty-seven

Randy tossed and turned, haunted by the sickening sensation of holding his own severed fingers. When he pushed that image away half-knowing it was his subconscious tormenting him for what he'd done, he saw himself shackled across the molten river with a demon at his feet. This sinister vision burned with a realism he'd seen and smelled. He struggled to keep his eyes closed, but no matter what pleasant memory he tried to conjure, he couldn't calm himself. His face burned with nervous energy and his heart drummed out a steady beat. Horrific, never-ending torture awaited him if he didn't redeem himself. The thought was inescapable while he lay alone in bed. He dozed several times only to be awakened by his own screams. When he fell asleep for the last time, he dreamed something new: a massive explosion, large stones flying, bearded men torn apart by flying debris.

Knowing the origin of the dreams didn't help.

After six fruitless hours in bed, the lightening sky forced him up. He felt his way into the bathroom, achy muscles pulling him along, sore eyes half-open as he warmed a facecloth and scratched away the stubble from his jaw line. Removing the nagging reminder of the old Randy Black soothed his nerves. He shaved so often now, he performed the routine automatically.

Downstairs he scrounged up a bagel and coffee. He had time to make bacon and eggs, just not the will. Occupying himself would have been preferable, but his mind was numb. He chewed half the bagel and found his way to the overstuffed chair facing the front yard and the construction across the street. He began his day mulling what he must do next, much as his night had begun. Little changed overnight except his position in the house. He hoped the workmen would arrive soon to provide a distraction.

His thoughts drifted to the encounter at the shooting range. He wondered how Ethan and Tom were connected and how Ethan could extort him to break into the mosque and still carry on like he was performing a public service. His save-the-world philosophy didn't fit the thug image. Thugs wanted an easy score, fast money, but Ethan rambled on about saving the city from extremists. He could be a disgruntled cop, soured after seeing so many criminals go free, but that didn't explain his interest in the mosque. A cop wouldn't risk his badge by approaching Randy for something like this. Ethan's vocabulary seemed a bit too refined for a cop. The glasses and awkward movements belonged to a guy who got bullied for years in school and who'd flunk the obstacle course at the police academy. Ill-suited as he was, Ethan overcame his deficiencies with fanaticism for his mission.

Tom didn't betray what he thought about the project, but he was ready to exploit Randy's vulnerability. Tom could hang a long prison term on him by throwing the trial. Their attorney-client relationship explained Tom's need to contact him day or night. No one would believe Tom was involved if the scheme was discovered. The blame would land squarely on Randy and Randy alone. He assumed the job was coming from Tom. Ethan was only doing the talking to keep Randy off balance.

But what did Tom care about the mosque? He was way too calm to be a fanatic. If a terrorist had bombed a relative, his emotions would have shown through. The spiel at the gun range was easy to buy into, but there was more here than patriotic duty and a healthy fear of terrorism.

There was a great divide between American and Muslim culture with both groups looking down on each other as animals. Randy remembered a morning disk jockey comparing an American prostitution scandal to one in a Muslim country. The American man loses his job, while the prostitute makes the front page of the paper. The results are much different in the Muslim theocracy. The Muslim man is whipped and the Muslim prostitute is stoned to death. To Randy it was a horrifying double standard, as horrible as another culture might see the celebrity status of the American prostitute.

Which of us was being brainwashed? Whole countries denied eye witness accounts and pictures of the Holocaust. How could millions of people stand together and denounce incontrovertible facts? How could they be willing to strap explosives to themselves and kill innocent women and children? The cowardly tactics incensed him. Savages seemed an apt description, but there was something more. They had a combination of fanatical commitment and desperation that Randy couldn't understand even faced with an eternity in Hell. Nothing could make him attack women and children. It was one of those things that was undeniably wrong. Then his breath caught in his throat as he remembered what he'd done to Monique Deudon.

Hate made men do horrible things. Not Randy. Not anymore. Everything he did from then on served a single purpose. He wondered if Ethan's assignment would move him closer to his goal or further away. He wondered how a Muslim leader could convince a man to sacrifice himself. How indeed could he convince his followers that horrendous atrocities served Allah?

Even as a Christian, he'd been taught that the Jews were God's chosen people. Many Muslims openly dedicated themselves to exterminating the Jews. Christians were a mere notch above. If the Jews ever perished the Christians would be next. Would God want Randy to intervene? Killing the leaders of the Mosque might save countless lives. Stopping them here would slow the influence of Islam, but this wasn't Satanism or some freakish murder cult. There were a billion people practicing a religion Randy knew little about. Could Islam really inspire suicide bombing? He hoped not.

He stared vacantly at the window knowing the path of least resistance wasn't the one he should travel. His path required more than blindly following Tom's orders. The reverend would have a reason to resist. He wouldn't condone hurting anyone regardless of their religion.

His eyes were drawn outside as the Corolla zipped into the driveway and squealed to a stop. The blonde head of hair bounced up to the door and a fist immediately began pounding. Randy dragged himself to the door and the second he opened it, Cassie pushed her way in and closed it behind her as if she were being chased.

"What the Hell did you do?" She panted, her face flushed from the rush up the drive. She grabbed a handful of his T-shirt, but stopped short of yelling again. She looked down, confused by his sweatpants and bare feet.

"Rough night. Couldn't sleep. You should've called. I would've showered."

"Funny. You take killing someone that lightly?" Her voice trailed off.

"What are you talking about?"

"Sebastian."

"Try again. Sebastian's in jail."

She glared at him in disbelief, losing a bit of fire, but still angry. Angry she'd trusted him. Angry she'd followed up on his leads. Angry she was beginning to believe. He half smiled realizing he'd been getting through.

"I've been here since last night." He held up his hands then gestured to his bare feet. "Go outside. Ask my neighbors." He paused a moment to let her take it in. "So what happened? Who *really* got shot?"

She hesitated, but she believed him. It took her a few seconds to see the truth in his eyes. She did, but just as she began to tell him about the gunman on the roof of the County Street building, tires squealed outside. Blue lights flashed in the early morning light. Three cruisers lined up along the edge of his lawn. One blocked the driveway.

Uniforms appeared in the sidelight behind Cassie.

Randy opened the door. "Can I help you gentlemen?"

The nearest officer, by far the youngest of the three, wore a Dartmouth Police Department patch on his shoulder. Randy recognized Detective Miller from the newspaper coverage. Miller was committed to putting Randy away, the man behind him a hundred times more so. Officer Pinto stood one step down from the landing. Randy met his eyes squarely and he scowled back without looking away. Pinto wasn't ashamed. He wasn't appreciative that Randy hadn't pressed charges. Pinto wasn't finished.

The Dartmouth officer stepped up to the threshold. "We're here to search the premises."

"Can I see your warrant?" The question was instinctive.

"Probable cause. No need," Miller said before the young officer could answer.

"Probable cause? Really? I'm relaxing in my living room and you guys come screeching recklessly up my street. That gives you cause to search my home? My lawyer's going to have fun with this one."

"Your van was spotted at a murder scene this morning," Miller said nudging himself between the younger man and the door.

"No, my van was in the garage this morning. Look for yourself."

Miller seized the invitation to push through the door and guide Pinto and the other officer into the foyer behind him. Pinto turned immediately for the kitchen and disappeared toward the garage as if he were familiar with the layout. The Dartmouth officer hesitated. Miller nodded and he rushed to catch Pinto. Randy hadn't intended to invite them in, but a search could only prove his innocence. He backed into the doorway to wait.

Miller followed and stood uncomfortably close, forcing Randy and Cassie deeper into the living room. Miller blocked the door with his hand resting on the 9mm in his holster. Cassie stood aside, her glances awkwardly shifting from Randy to Miller and back. She'd interviewed Miller and printed his picture half a dozen times for this case alone. They had an alliance to identify the bad guys and keep the public safe, but they seemed to be on opposite sides this time. Randy wondered if his friendship would make her job more difficult.

Pinto quickly returned from the garage, stood beside Miller and whispered a bit too loudly that the van's engine was cold. It hadn't been to New Bedford that morning, not in the killer's timeframe. Before Miller could decide what to do next, Pinto turned and climbed the stairs for the bedrooms. Another set of footsteps followed and then drawers and closet doors opened and closed upstairs. Stacks of clothes dropped to the carpet as they emptied every conceivable hiding place in Randy's bedroom.

There was only one gun upstairs, the .40 caliber SIG P229 Randy used in the basement for target practice. They'd never find it and even if they did, it wouldn't help them. Cassie hadn't said so, but it was a rifle shot that killed Sebastian. The only rifles Randy owned had been found at the winery

116

months ago. They were locked up safely in an evidence room somewhere. If they weren't, it wasn't Randy's problem.

Pinto hadn't smuggled a rifle in under his uniform. If he was above planting evidence, sooner or later he was going away empty handed. When he did Randy could continue his conversation with Cassie. Until then, he'd wait. He interlaced his fingers, rested his hands on his knee and closed his eyes. He wasn't going anywhere. He wasn't afraid of this search.

But the shooting was troublesome.

Sebastian was the government's star witness against Randy. His death helped no one else. No chance it was an old grudge that found him when he surfaced in jail. No chance. Someone was setting Randy up and they'd done a fine job.

A fleeting thought struck and Randy's eyes flashed open. If someone was setting him up, Pinto was doing Randy a favor by searching so zealously. Detective Miller and the two officers were unwittingly corroborating his alibi. They'd already proven that the van couldn't have been the getaway vehicle and when they failed to find the murder weapon, they'd vindicate him of the shooting. Randy suppressed a smile. Cleaning Pinto's mess was well worth the legal help he was providing.

Loud footsteps and curses sounded upstairs. They were beginning to understand that Randy had never really settled here. The house was a front for his dealings with Bill Caulfield across the street. The few neighbors who visited for a beer marveled at his cleanliness for a bachelor, but they didn't know Randy had little interest in anything here save the electronics upstairs and the gun range downstairs. His worldly possessions couldn't clutter a house one third this size.

Pinto raced around from room to room even after the younger officer had given up. When Pinto found the gun range, he left the younger officer to babysit and brought Miller down to see it. That wasn't what they'd come for and Miller had no interest in dealing with the paperwork given that their search was likely to be thrown out of court. They left thirty minutes after they arrived with Pinto begrudgingly leading the way. Randy could have taken his life at the Marston house or his job after the incident on Charlie's lawn. Pinto didn't care. Maybe he'd heard about the lawsuit. Maybe the heat came down on him anyway.

The door closed behind them and Randy invited Cassie to an early lunch. Before she could accept, the phone rang in the kitchen.

Tom Gold spoke into the phone the moment Randy had it to his ear, "You handled that well, Randy. If I didn't know better I'd think you didn't need my help."

He meant the cops. He knew, but they weren't even in their cars yet. Randy walked to the front window, checked for cars across the street and found nothing unusual.

"Oh, no. I'm better than that," Tom said.

Tom could see him now. Randy checked the caller-id—'unavailable.' He felt trapped, Goldfish-like, just as Charlie Marston must have, but Randy was smarter and tougher. He wouldn't be intimidated by his own red phone trick and he wouldn't be caged by a pretty boy like Tom Gold.

"What do you want?"

"You know what I want. Do your job and this one goes unsolved."

Tom hadn't killed Sebastian, not personally, but he'd ordered it. Randy should have been digging into his lawyer's background, but he'd been preoccupied. No longer. Tom Gold was priority one until he figured out what he was up to. Cassie stood in the doorframe and watched, no doubt wondering who was on the other end of the line. A minute ago, convincing her to trust him had been all important. Favorable coverage would have been nice, but it was mindshare he was after: hers. He needed her to believe, but as much as they both wanted to go, lunch had to wait.

"You'll never guess what gun killed Sebastian," Tom said.

The Winchester .30-30 Randy used at the gun club. He'd left prints all over the gun and the cartridges he'd loaded. If the shooter hadn't picked them up, Randy's prints would be on the casings lying at the murder scene.

Sebastian's murder was beginning to look strangely like Charles Marstons', but this time Randy was innocent.

Cassie looked at him sidelong as he grimaced at his own stupidity.

Prevailing in two murder trials back to back would take a miracle.

Chapter Twenty-eight

Cassie was suspicious when Randy retracted his lunch invitation. She knew he didn't have a job to go to and no errand could explain the tense phone call. When he wouldn't tell her who was on the phone, he saw the possibilities churning over in her mind. She'd stormed in to accuse him of murder forty minutes earlier, and done just that, but she quickly understood that something bigger was happening. Pinto's failed search proved Randy hadn't been at the courthouse that morning. She believed he was innocent of Sebastian's murder and now the reporter's mind was groping for a new suspect. She had learned about Charles Marston's dealings at dinner and she saw Charlie attack Randy in the courthouse. Conspiracies were blooming in her head. She stood in the living room matching players to motives and sorting the likely from the not-so-likely. Randy didn't offer to help.

Randy had the *who* sorted out. It was the *why* that troubled him.

He wondered what she'd write about Sebastian's murder even as he considered the best way to coax her out the door. She didn't have any reason to suspect Tom. That left Charlie Marston as her prime suspect. The rest of the local press raised Charlie up as a hero. In truth, he might have been. Randy couldn't warn her not to trash Charlie without the facts. Getting it so wrong could wreck her career. A story on Tom Gold, on the other hand, could win her wide acclaim and step Randy closer to freedom. No other media outlet would run that angle. Randy wished he could hand her the facts, but the story could earn her the fate that struck Sebastian that morning.

Randy needed to find out why Tom Gold had gone to such extremes to control him. Leading Randy's defense in the Marston trial gave Tom a distinct advantage in their dealings. Even so, he'd planned carefully and taken risks to multiply his power with the Winchester. The ballistics and fingerprints would render Randy defenseless in court. He desperately needed a counterweight for Tom's leverage, something to keep that Winchester hidden away. Standing there with Cassie, he struggled to recall something he might have done that could make Tom Gold bitter enough to plot against him so meticulously.

Randy stepped closer and admired Cassie's fine blonde hair and smooth features. She was so fair and yet followed such ugliness for a living. He could see that the killings and violence excited her. It didn't fit the librarian from Dorchester, but apparently she was tougher than he knew. He reached down and lightly rested a hand on hers. The touch broke her trance-like focus on the carpet. She met his eyes, warmer, calmer than before.

"It wasn't Marston?" she asked in a whisper.

"Not Marston."

"Who then?"

The truth could get her killed.

Randy led her toward the door without answering. The reporter had vanished when the police left. The woman remained, curious about the man a foot away. Randy hesitated to draw her close. Her investigation would keep her within reach. She'd probe his history and once she found the truth, it would push them apart forever. Any progress he made in the meantime would only be temporary.

He gripped the doorknob.

She caught his forearm. "Who?" she asked again.

"Someone who doesn't want me running free."

He pulled the door open.

"Why'd you go to visit Heather Lovely?"

"Are you following me?"

"Sometimes."

"That's a very bad idea. It won't end well."

"I have to follow my story."

Good, he wanted to say. He was glad she latched on to what he'd told her. He'd read his perspective of the Marstons in her last piece. If that kept up, Randy's neighbors might tone down their accusing glares.

"She's a shrink if you must know. My lawyer wants to prove to the judge that I'm not insane. Or maybe that I am." She accepted his answer, dismissing one theory to make room for others.

"Was Sebastian involved in drugs or anything like that?"

"No. He was angry and a bit too gullible."

Cassie's features scrunched together. "What are you talking about?"

"It's better you don't know. You wouldn't be safe otherwise."

Cassie descended the steps tentatively, still sorting the players out in her mind as she left. Randy had no idea what she'd print the next day.

At 1:30 P.M. Cassie heard voices arguing in Bart's office.

She stepped through the door and saw Walter slap his hand on two typewritten pages on Bart's pristine desk.

"Just the person I was looking for," Bart said when he noticed her in the doorway.

"What's going on?"

He was surprised not to see a story in her hands.

"Walter's done a story on the Sebastian Leonard murder this morning. We were just discussing the link to the Randy Black case."

Walter kept his hand rooted on his story and glared at Cassie, making a show of looking at her empty hands.

"Didn't want to incriminate your boyfriend?"

Cassie stepped up to the desk and read Walter's headline: *Murder Rampage Continues.*

"That'd be a good headline if it was true," Cassie warned.

Bart looked uneasy.

"Sure," Walter said, "a tall man fires a rifle from a building and drives away in a gray van identical to Randy Black's. The victim just happens to be the only person with intimate knowledge of the kidnapping and murder of Charles Marston. But it couldn't be your boyfriend." Walter snickered.

"I know how it looks…"

"Give it up. He killed Marston and he killed Leonard. Whatever's going on between you, it isn't worth your career."

Cassie flashed a look at Bart. He shrugged and pushed back from his desk. He was helpless without an alternative to print.

"I was there this morning, in his house. He didn't do it."

Walter raised his eyebrows. "Did you sleep over?"

"Screw you, Walter." Cassie turned to Bart. "Do I have to take this?"

Bart's eyes stabbed at Walter then drifted down to his article. It was the way every other paper would report the day's news. Deadline was coming and if Cassie didn't have a story, Bart would run with Walter's *Rampage*.

"Do you have another perspective to offer?"

She didn't have anything written, but she could offer the facts as she'd seen them, probably what she should have written in the first place. Unfortunately, she couldn't offer a conclusion. An open-ended piece wouldn't help Randy. Readers would assume Randy was involved whether he pulled the trigger or not.

"The police searched his house top to bottom right after the murder and they didn't find anything. The van's engine was cold and he looked like he'd just gotten out of bed. The cops went away empty handed. They started with the same assumption you did, Walter, but they figured it out. Randy Black couldn't have killed Sebastian Leonard."

"Our readers won't believe that." Walter waved his article in front of Bart. "If you want a non-fiction piece, here it is." He slapped the pages on the desk and stormed out.

"You aren't going to print that?" Cassie asked when he'd gone.

"You have something to offer?" Bart checked his watch. "You've got an hour and twenty minutes."

Cassie bolted for her desk.

Chapter Twenty-nine

Randy bounded up the stairs as soon as the Corolla drove off. He'd seen progress in her eyes that day. She'd heard the stories of his battle with the Marston family, but after seeing the change in him she wasn't sure what to believe. She couldn't know about his vision. Without knowing, she could only compare the actions of the old Randy against the new and know they were incompatible. He hoped she'd latch on to the new and forgive the old. Randy was still struggling with the metamorphosis himself. The tactics he learned fighting the Marstons would be valuable against Tom Gold, but his new spiritual boundaries rendered many of those tactics obsolete. He surged to the top of the stairs flush with adrenalin, but unsure how he might use it.

What little he had in the bedroom had been thoroughly rifled. Clothes hung out of drawers. Books, pencils and cables from the desk lay heaped in a cluster of junk. The large stained glass lamp on his bedside table had been moved a few inches, but they hadn't found the door formed by the cames. They'd been right to search around the bed. Randy needed a gun at hand when he was battling the Marstons and especially the private detective Deirdre had hired. Randy gently opened the door in the lamp and retrieved the P229 from the holster mounted inside.

He felt clever for the first time in a long while.

Randy halted outside the entrance to the bathroom, stopped by an eerie remembrance of what he'd done to Charles Marston's ammunition. The photo Ethan showed at the gun range only existed on Randy's security computer, a machine so well hidden no one had found it in three searches of his house. Ethan not only found the computer and downloaded the pictures, but disabled it to make sure he had the only copies. Tom and Ethan were way ahead of the cops. They were capable of anything.

Even though he could see the slug on the uppermost round, he detoured to his basement range, steadied himself and fired three times in rapid succession. Three hits in the ten ring. Satisfied, he returned to the bathroom and swung out the mirror. The two foot deep pocket had served him well. Disguised by a closet on the opposite side of the wall, the pocket kept his tools and security system concealed from prying eyes. The system had alerted him to TJ Lynch's final incursion and saved his life.

Tom Gold was a more formidable opponent than TJ or the Marstons. He knew Randy's entire history while Randy knew nothing beyond Tom's legal work and his hatred of those inside the mosque. Randy needed to know what was driving Tom if he wanted to bring his dealings to light and he had only two short days to learn what he needed to know.

Two black canvas pouches held his tools and a few odds and ends left over from the winery. He didn't have time to order cameras and another receiver. He groaned at the lifeless PC mounted in the wall and knew what he needed to do. He replaced the mirror and rushed downstairs with his tools. Gently, he pried the miniature cameras loose from the light fixture in the hall, the beam above the bulkhead entrance, the trim above the kitchen cabinets and two in the garage focused on the McLaren.

An hour later, he had a new laptop PC charging on the seat beside him as he cruised to a stop two blocks from Tom Gold's office on County Street. He pushed his way down a sidewalk clogged with pedestrians. At the intersection of Court Street, he saw the reason. Crime scene tape was strung around the prisoner entrance to the courthouse. A mob had gathered to gawk at two men poking around on the steps. The onlookers drawn by the blood where Sebastian fell wouldn't have guessed that the prime suspect in the shooting had just walked past.

Across County Street, a two story law office was similarly taped, but there was little to see. A rope hung down against the side of the building, but otherwise it looked normal. Randy wondered if they'd found the shell casings among the parked cars and whether fingerprints would survive the thirty foot drop.

Further down, the BMW was in Tom's reserved spot just off the street. Attaching the tracking device under the bumper took only seconds. Tom didn't appear in the windows nor did anyone pay attention to Randy as he exited the short driveway and hustled back to his car. He cruised down Williams to a small lot across from City Hall. Tom would pass close by and from here Randy could be on the highway fast enough to stay within range of the transmitter underneath the Beemer.

Randy installed an antenna on his new laptop and the software he needed to turn it into a monitor for the cameras and the homing transmitter. When he finished, he browsed Switchboard.com for Tom's home address, but they didn't have an address for Tom Gold or any of the unblocked numbers he'd called Randy from. One of the exchanges was in Marion. He thought about going out there and trying to work the address out of a field tech, but Verizon was tight with unlisted numbers. If he knew the street he might be able to get the number, but he decided to sit it out. The BMW would be headed home soon.

At 4:00 P.M. his patience was rewarded.

He followed the BMW onto Route 18 toward the highway, but surprisingly, Tom passed the onramp. He zipped around onto Coggeshall and parked in front of a six story building Randy recognized. The crazy psychologist's office was on the top floor. He wondered if they shared more than clients. Paying for favorable testimony was the easiest way to manufacture the kind of evidence Tom needed to win his cases. If that was true, Randy had wasted a lot of time taking those tests. If Heather Lovely was anything like Ron Morgan, he was in more trouble than he'd realized.

An hour later, the BMW headed east on Interstate 195.

Randy stayed well back, but within the one mile range of the transmitter. The BMW sped down the left lane of the highway and then squirted through traffic, across Route 6 and down a narrow road toward the ocean. Randy turned into a public landing and abandoned his car among the boaters. He followed on foot, hugging the shrubbery without hunching down and looking suspicious. Past a cluster of magnificent homes facing the water, Randy found the BMW parked in an otherwise empty garage. The rear of Tom's house followed the contour of the bay to maximize the views. There were no toys in the yard, little decoration on the outside of the house and no flowers anywhere. He had a seven thousand square foot house on the ocean all to himself. Lawyering was good to Tom Gold. The IRS would be interested in Tom's illicit income, but Tom's home wasn't so extravagant for a man in his position that they'd investigate without proof.

Randy wondered how he could get the proof he needed as he drove twenty minutes back to Tom's County Street office. He walked a few blocks to be sure he wasn't seen and slipped around back of the old shingled building. What had been the back door to an old tenement was now an emergency exit for Tom's staff. At 6:00 P.M. they'd all gone home. Randy picked the lock and walked in.

He mounted a single camera to watch Tom at his desk and climbed downstairs to add a simple listening device to Tom's phone line. Additional wiring had been added when the house was converted. Black unlabeled cables fanned out along the floor joists and made their way through tiny holes to the upper floors. Randy had to slip up and down the stairs twice to make sure he had the right wire, but then the work was simple. He tucked the tiny transmitter up against a joist where Tom would have to tramp around stacks of file boxes and look straight up at the ceiling to see it.

Randy flipped through a box full of paper files, but gave up after several minutes. The legal nonsense was impossible for Randy to decipher. If there was something hidden there, he'd never find it.

The next morning, Randy waited in his car in the Park-n-Ride in Mattapoisett, just off Interstate 195. Hidden by trees and the dozen or so cars left by other commuters, there was no way Tom could have seen him as he zipped by at 8:41A.M. The blip rushed across Randy's screen at seventy-eight miles per hour. Randy started the car and headed off to give Tom's house the same treatment he'd given his office the night before.

Chapter Thirty

Randy slipped in along the line of hemlock and blue spruce that separated Tom's yard from his neighbor's. Around back, the wide lawn opened to the bay, exposing him to anyone who floated by. The house stretched several times wider than the office and the clapboards gleamed with fresh paint. Unlike the office, the house was immaculate inside, a smudged window or a few carelessly dropped shavings would be noticed here. A sticker on the dining room window indicated an alarm system monitored by Omni-sense, a company Randy had never heard of. The windows and doors were alarmed and if he forced one open a cruiser we be there within twenty minutes. No dog reacted to his circling the house or his presence on the deck, but all the first floor windows were closed.

The five air conditioning towers hidden in the juniper were all idle. It was early, but the temperature was climbing steadily. The breeze off the bay would provide free cooling. If Randy lived here, he'd have his windows open to take advantage. He stepped back and circled the ocean side again, this time twenty yards from the house.

One of the windows over the deck was open. A small section of roof sloped gently down from the window and covered a slice of the deck. Randy could jump from the deck railing and pull himself up, but he feared tearing the gutter down. He searched under the deck and around the backyard until he found an old wooden ladder in the pool shed.

Up and through the window, he found that Tom's careful housekeeping extended upstairs. Nothing was out of place. He was always neatly dressed and even his car was neat, but Randy assumed Tom was playing the lawyer role. Being judged every day certainly made him careful about appearances. Here in his own home, Tom was just as careful.

The room Randy climbed into was at the head of the stairs, the only room with clothes in the drawers and closets: Tom's bedroom. The four cameras Randy had left weren't nearly enough for a house this large. He'd stick to the places Tom frequently used. The first camera fit snugly into the molding of the armoire that held a television and DVD player. Funny, he'd be looking right at the camera much of the time and wouldn't know it.

Downstairs, a second camera fit under the lip of the fourth tread. Focused on the front door and about half of the foyer, it was still low enough to go unnoticed. The next set nicely into a recess in the stone fireplace and then he added a final camera to cover the kitchen with the hall in the background. If he couldn't see into most of the rooms, at least the hallway view would let him know which part of the house Tom was in.

Finally, he trotted into the cellar and tapped the single incoming line. In another few minutes he inspected his work, made sure he hadn't displaced anything then climbed back upstairs and crawled out onto the roof.

Once the ladder was back in the pool shed, Randy trotted along the line of spruce trees, along the driveway and onto the narrow old road that led to the shore. He walked casually to the landing and slid into the McLaren. His car fit well in this neighborhood, although the only other vehicle here at the water's edge was a rusty old Ford pickup. Its owner was probably out digging clams. He might work in this neighborhood, but he definitely didn't live here.

Randy booted the laptop and tested the cameras, studying the views and labeling them so he could cut around the house quickly. The monitor had only been working two minutes when Tom walked into the kitchen and down the hall. Randy followed him up the stairs and into his bedroom where he changed his suit for a pair of jeans and a golf shirt. Lucky Randy left when he did. He wondered why Tom drove twenty minutes to the city just to turn around and come home. Nothing happened that quickly in court.

An uncomfortable feeling came over Randy as Tom reacted to the cell phone on the bed. He picked it up, answered, and immediately left the bedroom. Once out of view of the camera, Randy was blind. He split the views on the screen, putting a view of the stairway on one half and the bedroom on the other. Tom didn't appear for several minutes.

When Tom came back into the bedroom he went straight to the window, closed and locked it. He moved over to the armoire and stood a foot away. His shirt filled the picture and then slowly he worked his way down until his eyes and nose filled the monitor as if it were a dive mask. He knew. He knew exactly where Randy placed the camera. Tom tapped the lens once then picked up the phone from his bedside and dialed.

When the phone connected, he asked his secretary for his own voicemail. Tom's recorded voice played from the computer speaker "You've reached the law office of Tom Gold. I'm not here to take your call right now…"

Randy wondered why he'd be calling himself to leave a message.

When the recording finished, Tom turned directly toward the camera mounted on the armoire and spoke. "Randy, you should be hearing me from both ears if your transmitters are any good. Now stop wasting time. Following me isn't going to accomplish anything. There's a ceremony tomorrow at the mosque. Eleven o'clock. Be there."

Tom hung up the phone and walked directly to the camera and pried it out of the molding with a key. The image went black. The others followed soon after.

Randy wasn't used to being outmaneuvered.

Suddenly he didn't feel safe parked on the landing. He remembered Tom's three-inch group with the Winchester. He could have shot Sebastian himself. Randy couldn't investigate with Tom aware of his every move. He was running out of time. Not only was Tom going to get away with killing Sebastian, if he handed over the Winchester and those casings, he could send Randy to prison for life. Pretty soon his only choice would be to follow Tom's orders and bug the mosque.

Randy started the engine and headed home.

Chapter Thirty-one

Randy raced toward the opening ceremony twenty minutes early hoping to connect Tom Gold to the other players involved with the mosque job. The McLaren whipped by dozens of cars as Randy slowed to seventy, then fifty looking for an opening to pull off the exit. At forty the traffic beside him was stopped and the crash barrier was rushing toward him. Moving left and taking the next exit would have wasted several minutes he couldn't spare. He squeezed the McLaren over and angled to a stop where the ramp narrowed to a single lane. The driver in the silver Mercedes beside him waved a single-fingered greeting and angled left to block Randy from the exit. Instinct urged him to swerve in and capture the lane first, holding the McLaren an inch from the other Mercedes, but he relented, sat back and allowed the silver car to inch ahead.

The woman behind him earned a wave and a genuine smile for allowing him in. There he joined the intolerably slow line of cars crawling down onto Route 18. Underneath the heavy beams supporting Interstate 195 stood three men in black with compact automatic weapons. This was a mosque opening, not a presidential visit. The security seemed overkill, but, considering what he'd been asked to do, maybe not. In other countries Muslims had a tendency to blow each other up. Why not here? And didn't some Americans want a little payback for nine-eleven?

The men didn't search every car, but rather peered in, taking but a few moments to check front and back for obvious signs of trouble. The momentary delay for each vehicle had traffic backed up in every direction, a high price for such a feeble security effort. A determined bomber could pack his trunk with explosives and ram his way through the chain-link fence and into the audience where Randy would soon be seated. So much for security.

Beyond the checkpoint, traffic thinned and a thick wall of demonstrators appeared along the chain-link fence that lined mosque property. Red, white and blue signs and flags waved everywhere.

"Baby Bombers Go Home!"

"No Tax $ for Islam!"

"Cash for Christians!"

The most popular signs featured the mayor's name circled and crossed with a red diagonal line. By the number of signs, his land giveaway might have cost him reelection.

A policeman at the gate inspected the invitation Randy had found on his driver's seat that morning, a thick gold-lettered reminder that Tom and whoever worked for him could move in and out of the house without Randy knowing. The alarm system was useless without the computer and it was going to stay useless now that Tom had Randy's cameras. For now he'd sleep with his eyes open, which was actually preferable to the nightmares. He hadn't slept soundly since Pinto whacked him on the head.

The parking lot stood in the shadow of Interstate 195 high above. Now shielded from the traffic and demonstrators, Randy took his first unobstructed look at the new mosque. The shell of beige bricks stood tall and forbidding as any school or courthouse in the city. Few windows interrupted the brick façade as if the occupants took their invasion of America literally and designed the building to be easily defended. Randy imagined archers in the narrow windows that rose along the corners. The glass dome atop the structure was set far enough from the raised highway so that stone throwing would be futile. Someone would try from the ground, probably soon. Minarets topped with crescents flanked the dome. In this neighborhood they'd be useful watchtowers.

The crowd jeered Randy as he left the car and circled the building. On the backside, an emergency ladder fastened to the bricks led all the way to the roof. Three sets of doors, front, back and the side, governed access.

Surely they'd be alarmed, windows, too. Of the scores of chairs arranged before the building's raised front entrance, only a handful were filled. Technicians scurried about the microphones at the podium and the stacks of black speakers stage-side. A line of chairs waited for honored guests and behind them, a thick white ribbon waited to be ceremoniously cut by the mayor. Until then, the entrance to the building was sealed.

Randy turned away from the stage and circled back around to the highway side of the building. He crossed the grass to the chain-link fence just forty yards from the massive concrete supports. The grass and weeds had been trimmed short, whether to expose would-be snipers or just provide atmosphere at taxpayer expense, Randy wasn't certain. The mob of protesters ignored him here and with the chaos surrounding the entrance to the parking area, the other attendees ignored him, too.

Tom's BMW wheeled through security and parked in the middle of the lot. Another sedan parked next to it and a slight man in khakis and a blazer hopped out and exchanged a familiar glance with Tom.

The men walked twenty feet apart. Tom led and never looked back. Randy hustled across the lawn to catch up, losing them behind the building, but catching sight of them as Tom sat near the center of the audience. His friend positioned himself at the end of a row further back and began preparing a camera with a thick lens. Randy feigned interest in the protesters as he approached the photographer then casually slipped in two rows behind.

The man ahead looked like a junkyard dog dressed up in bows for a visit to the Westminster Kennel Club. His hair was cropped to a quarter inch, enough to show its color, but not enough to offer a grip to an opponent in a scuffle. A scaly dragon peeked over the collar of his blazer and as he worked the camera, tattooed letters appeared above each knuckle. His fingers moved too quickly for Randy to discern the words. Less imposing than Ethan, Randy assumed he'd been sent to catalog the faces they'd come up against later.

When the speakers were seated and the mayor was introduced, the photographer snapped pictures from one end of the stage to the other, recording the face of every honored guest.

A wide cross-section of the city filled the audience. Dozens of suits lined the front rows. Randy imagined these were a mix of cronies, contributors and contractors. Interspersed were three dozen dark-skinned, bearded men and a few women wearing headscarves Randy assumed to be Muslims. A few casually dressed observers didn't belong in either group. They'd be reporters or curious politicos able to score an invitation.

The speakers droned incessantly about culture and diversity. Randy lost himself wondering why Cassie wasn't in the crowd. This wasn't a crime scene, not yet. Someone from *The Standard Times* would be here photographing and interviewing politicians and demonstrators. A politically correct reporter would minimize the demonstrators and glorify the mayor's decision. Judging by the number of protesters, it would be a difficult piece for readers to stomach.

Tom took in the event as calmly as he would a court session. He never acknowledged Randy or the photographer seated in front of him.

Speeches rambled on about a great day for America. Over and over they said the mosque would bring diversity of thought and culture, enriching everyday life in the city. Randy wondered where exactly Muslims had assimilated into the culture. He never understood why liberals got so fired up about diversity anyway. Throwing different people together was the universal recipe for tension and conflict. Why import fifty religious zealots? This new group would incite trouble and then stump hard to quell any voice raised against them. As if on cue, the protests through the fence grew louder.

Four men on stage wore white turbans and one, wearing crimson, stood out from the others. He turned angrily toward the demonstrators, glaring at the people lining the fence as the mayor spoke. He cataloged the faces just as the photographer had captured his. When the man in crimson had his turn to speak and every politician had been thanked, the ribbon was finally cut. The photographer stood up and made his way for the sidewalk, abandoning his car in the lot. Randy followed.

Chapter Thirty-two

The audience filed forward to shake hands with the imams and tour the mosque. Little groups knotted in conversation at the front of the seating area, clogging the path to the steps. Randy had never been inside a mosque, but his curiosity would have to wait. If Tom Gold had his way Randy would be inside soon enough, but for now he needed to know more about the photographer striding toward the sidewalk.

Why had he left his car behind?

He strode across the forty yard opening between the gathering that faced the front steps and the security team holding back the crowds on the sidewalk. The intervening ground was empty, so following close meant being seen. Randy waited at the edge of the crowd and focused on the man's clothes: dark blue blazer, khaki pants, black sneakers.

When he passed the officers on the sidewalk and entered the crowd, Randy took up the chase. The man was engulfed by protesters at the corner. They circled him and shouted insults, momentarily refusing to let him pass. He was unfazed by the outcry. He had no connection to the mosque. If he hadn't been there to take pictures, he would have been among the most vocal in the crowd.

He removed the cover from his camera and snapped a few closeups of the most vehement in his path. The implied threat subdued a few of the more cerebral, but it took a uniformed officer to part the crowd and allow him to cross Coggeshall and start down Acushnet Avenue. The crowd was lighter there. Both men stuck out in their dress clothes, but the photographer focused singularly on the path ahead, striding two blocks before turning into a brick building and descending the stairs into a basement bar.

Two sides of the building were visible from the corner, but the alley at the back gave the photographer a chance to disappear over a cluster of lawns. If he knew Randy was following him, he might have chosen this bar to slip out the back door and lose him. Randy wished he'd taken the license plate or even the model of the car parked next to Tom's. Staking the car out and waiting may have been the best way to find him, but knowing the games Tom played, he might hustle back and find the car already gone.

Randy pushed through the door and descended the stairs casually, but once he stepped into the bar all eyes were on him save the dark haired man seated in a booth with his back to the door. The pale bartender looked like he never escaped this gloomy basement. His rolled-up sleeves revealed pale skin and a bony frame, kept unnaturally thin by whatever he took to keep himself awake overnight.

The photographer's blazer and camera hung alone on the pegs by the door. His military-green T-shirt revealed arms covered in green ink from his forearms to his wrists with dashes of red blood for color. They matched the T-shirt well enough to give a long sleeve effect. He stood at the corner of the pool table, waving the cue in Randy's direction.

Randy stepped past the hulking figure at the door.

The black muscle shirt stretched wide to display more pectorals than any decent woman would show. Muscles bulged in clumps up his arms, meeting at the base of his neck. His bald head looked like the uppermost in the set. Randy wondered if his dedication to power lifting left time to develop that muscle under his bald crown.

Closer still.

Demons took shape on the photographer's arms. Scaly limbs reached in unison, extending around the back of his hand. The claws faded at the first knuckle. The artist imagined the work of these hands was driven by the demons he created. Maybe he knew this man was possessed by a desire Randy hadn't seen.

Closer still, the photographer stood upright and waved his cue toward the man in the booth. Randy turned toward him.

"You mind?" Randy asked as he reached the vinyl bench.

"No, Randy, go ahead." Ethan smiled at Randy's astonishment. "You're grasping at straws, kid. I wanted to talk so I threw you some breadcrumbs. This isn't our first time doing this."

"Who are you?"

He ignored the question. "Tom thinks you're pretty smart, but I'm not so sure. Did you really think we didn't have pictures of these towel-headed cock suckers?"

Randy hadn't questioned the photographer's interest in the men assembled on the stage. He was used to playing hunter not hunted.

"You've got a golden opportunity here, kid. We're going to get you out of a lot of trouble and you're going to slide right into a great job."

They hadn't mentioned anything but the mosque. Was Tom running some sort of gang? If he was, why target the mosque? There wouldn't be anything worth stealing inside.

"He didn't tell you, eh?" Ethan sipped his beer. "It's a test. We need a new surveillance guy. Our last one got lead poisoning." He didn't try to hide his satisfaction with the joke.

"Why didn't he offer it to me straight up?"

"Not up to me, but it's a good gig. Best thing I've ever done. It pays well and you go home feeling good after a day's work. There's nothing like saving the world."

Randy snapped a look at the faces around the room. Is that what these guys thought they were doing? Were they police-force rejects turned vigilante? He hoped the government wasn't paying them on the sly.

"Listen, kid. I think you're going to make it. The job you did on Tom's house was good. We wouldn't have found the cameras if we hadn't been watching. Clunky old gear, but not bad. You'll find our stuff's much better. Do what you're told and everything will work out."

Ethan got up to leave.

When Randy stood, Ethan reached around and pressed his thumb into the clavicle that had been broken by Pinto's nightstick. He pushed hard enough to fold Randy's knees and put him back on the bench, but not hard enough to risk a fracture. "Just relax a few minutes. Have a beer. The boys'll let you know when it's time to go."

Ethan turned and climbed the stairs to the front door. When he cleared the doorway, the muscle head shifted over, his triceps reaching the door frame on both sides.

Following Ethan was the first step to understanding Tom's gang of vigilantes. Randy needed to know where he got the money to pay them and how they decided on their targets. Then he'd know how to shake himself loose. Randy stepped away from the booth toward the center of the room. The bartender took up a pool cue and blocked the way out back.

The photographer stepped closer and twirled his cue, the stick whistling as it cut the air. "You don't want to start this off badly. We're going to be buds." At close range the photographer's savage eyes lusted for a reason to attack. The demons on his arms wrestled for control of the cue. The guys in this bar weren't out to save anyone. They'd killed Sebastian. They'd have no mercy on the Muslims in the mosque. Tom's attack dogs had him surrounded and they were just begging for a reason to pounce.

Randy stepped into the center of the room.

The photographer spun the cue then raised the thick end high.

Randy approached calmly, "You don't want to do that."

"Ten minutes and you can go."

The photographer glanced at the men rooted at each door. Confident Randy had no escape regardless of the outcome between them, he stepped forward and swished the cue in a lazy V pattern, blocking any advance Randy might make as he looked for an opening.

Empty handed, Randy stood his ground, feinting from side to side.

The photographer saw an opening, grasped his cue and jabbed the blunt end at Randy's chest. Randy latched on and yanked, stealing his balance. Then he crashed his elbow into the cue between the photographer's hands and snapped it like a matchstick.

Randy snatched his end and came away with a club. The photographer was left with a flimsy stick. While he looked at his empty hand in surprise, Randy snapped down, cracking the cue into his shin. The photographer folded instinctively, clutching his leg as the cue snapped back up and connected squarely with his forehead, standing him straight up. Randy spun and kicked him in the sternum, plunging him backward onto the pool table.

The muscle-bound thug flinched as Randy headed for him, thumping the butt end of the cue against his palm like a club. Randy kept his eyes high. He'd fake a headshot to get him to cover up then go for a knee. All he wanted was to get past, not do any lasting damage.

Pool balls clinked behind him.

Randy turned.

A tattooed arm raised high and sliced through the air, the orange ball about to be released. Randy dropped to the tiles banging a knee hard as he flattened himself against the floor. The guard looked down at Randy. When he looked up again, it was too late to move. The 5-ball drove into his ribs and Randy heard a meaty cracking as it slammed home. He doubled over, low enough for Randy to reach up, jab the cue under his jawbone and topple him over into the nearest booth. The ball clacked on the floor as Randy jumped up. The door flung open and Randy bolted up the stairs, through the outer door and onto the street. The photographer would never catch him on one good leg.

One step on the sidewalk and everything went black.

Randy found himself on his back looking up at huge man, taller and wider than the power lifter, minus the bulging muscles. He had a strip of beard along his jaw that reached down and joined a goatee. He'd been hiding at the corner of the building, waiting for the door to swing open. Once again, Tom was two steps ahead.

Ethan was gone.

"Why didn't you just wait? Wouldn't that have been easier?"

Randy lay on the concrete until Tom's man offered him a hand up.

Chapter Thirty-three

The scant demonstrators that remained along the chain-link fence faced the empty rows of chairs and the pristine brick structure beyond with quiet contempt. The throngs that had packed the sidewalks were whittled down to the fanatical core. The media was gone. The remaining cops stood around and chatted by the gate, relaxed now that the power of the demonstrators had ebbed with their receding numbers. Randy's head throbbed. The egg forming above his temple was too tender to touch.

Rushing along the sidewalk, the parking area came into view behind the mosque. A dozen cars remained, but the photographer's wasn't among them. The guard stopped him at the entrance with an outstretched arm. Even though the protest had subsided, they weren't getting careless. The invitation wasn't in his pants or his breast pocket. Patting his jacket he remembered he'd left it on the seat of the McLaren.

The officer accepted his excuse and followed far enough into the lot for Randy to click the remote and unlock the car. When he saw the parking lights blink, the officer returned to his post and let Randy head inside for a quick tour. If he decided to follow Tom's orders, a look inside might make the difference between slipping in and out undetected and getting caught.

The first thing that struck him, after the newness of everything, was the complete lack of furniture. He stepped into a wide courtyard that took up nearly half the building. It seemed a waste of space, a tiny Muslim city inside the city. There was a group standing at the far end. A few wore long robes and turbans and Randy imagined this building was a little piece of the

Middle East, transplanted here in Massachusetts to give these men a place to mill about safely.

A bearded young man in white broke off from the group and offered Randy a tour. He explained in slightly accented English that the courtyard represented the courtyard of Muhammad's house, the first mosque. The tour guide looked on the walls in wonderment as if seeing them for the first time. His rapid-fire speech and enthusiastic gestures showed just how proud a day this was for everyone connected with the mosque. He was too young to be an imam, so Randy assumed he was an assistant of some sort.

The building was slightly askew on its lot to allow the main prayer hall to face Mecca. There were several rooms off the courtyard. Beside the main hall, a prayer niche also faced Mecca with a narrow pulpit erected against the courtyard wall. Worshipers would gather in the courtyard and hear sermons then go into the prayer hall for daily prayers.

Randy asked to climb the minaret and the young man obliged. The tower itself wasn't high, only fifteen feet above roof height, slightly lower than the glass dome over the prayer hall. The minaret was supposed to be used to call the faithful to prayer, but the sound of the highway above them would drown out calling voices. In the time of Muhammad, the faithful had been called to prayer from a rooftop. Randy had heard church bells in Westport every Sunday and wondered if the Muslims used something similarly loud to be heard above the city commotion. He didn't interrupt the history lesson to ask.

On the way back to the courtyard, Randy found a dozen twenty-two gauge wires poking out of a metal box mounted into the back wall. He didn't need to see the faceplate to know it was an alarm console waiting to be wired. The system still wasn't operational. If he came tonight, all he'd have to bypass was the mechanical lock on the back door. He hid his interest from his tour guide and followed him back through the courtyard to the front steps. The young man was proud to have so many visitors. He thanked Randy and quickly rejoined the large group outside the prayer hall.

The McLaren eased around the lot in a wide turn, slow enough for him to know that getting over the chain-link fence undetected would be the hardest part of the job. Twenty minutes later, sitting in his kitchen with a tall glass of water he considered calling Tom. He could do the job easily with the proper tools. It was wrong to help Tom's men attack the mosque, but if he was going to understand what Tom was doing and why, he'd have to get Tom's guys to stop leaning on him. Maybe if he did what they asked, he'd get some room to operate. He could deal with the consequences later.

The rattle of the garage door opener was a shock. The McLaren and the box van were both inside with the doors locked and there were no other remotes. The setbacks at the Marion house and the bar hadn't prepared Randy to see the BMW wheeling inside. He watched in awe as Tom parked in the empty bay as if it were his reserved space. The garage door rolled back down behind him. Tom reveled in Randy's surprise, hefting a metallic case around the front of the cars and over to the steps. He barely paused for Randy to get out of the way before walking in, thumping his case down on the kitchen island and taking a seat.

He must have programmed a remote for the garage when he and his pals broke in and fried the computer upstairs. Tom met Randy while he was confined to a hospital bed. He had plenty of time to go through Randy's house while he was recuperating. It would have been much easier than the work Randy had done to rig the Caulfields'. There was no risk of him getting up and coming home. No relatives to barge in. Tom and his men had weeks to comb through every square inch of the house.

Randy's stomach felt hollow, but there was relief in understanding what was happening to him. Tom's control wasn't permanent. Randy could sweep the house for bugs, change the locks and the frequencies for the door openers or he could simply stay somewhere else.

Tom had guts walking in here alone. He knew Randy was smart enough not to try anything, but it would have been safer to send one of his minions. He came personally to watch Randy struggle to control his anger. Tom's arrogance would be his downfall. The rifle and Ron Morgan's testimony hung over Randy's head. If Randy could find the rifle and make a deal with Ron, then Tom would be at his mercy.

Tom popped open the case and turned it with a flourish. The inside was padded with gray egg-crated foam. A single black device filled half the case. It flipped open to reveal a monitor and a few specialized keys. No wire, no tools, nothing else was inside the case but a small box.

"Go ahead, turn it on."

Randy clicked the power button and waited.

When the screen came to life, Tom pulled open the small box and removed what looked like a string with a knot in one end. He gave it a twist, clicked a button on the monitor and Randy's face appeared. Amazing.

The microphones were even smaller.

Randy turned and absently scanned his own walls. He'd known since Tom's telephone call that his house was bugged. He'd spent two hours trying to find the cameras and now he knew why Tom had tipped him off. The equipment was more impressive than anything Randy had ever seen. He must have had fun watching Randy search knowing the devices were impossible to find. Tom could leave the cameras behind when his work was done. No one would ever find them. No wonder Tom's men followed him so easily. Until now, they'd known everything he did or said inside this house.

"How many of these do you have planted in here?" Randy asked, indicating his house.

"Enough. Now, get yourself down there and get this done. That alarm system is going to be finished Monday."

Tom was holding it up. Whether it was through union labor or city permitting, Randy didn't know, but Tom had more reach than Randy imagined. Randy stared at him from three feet away wondering what twisted the wealthy lawyer into a vigilante kingpin. The imams hadn't been here long enough.

"You've got twenty-four hours," Tom said, then turned and left.

The garage door opened then closed behind the BMW, a reminder that Tom had unfettered access to every corner of Randy's life. That had to change. If there were cameras in his house, Tom was paying someone to sit and watch them. Finding Tom's camera operator was the first step out of this hole.

Chapter Thirty-four

Randy stood at the window fuming as he watched the BMW drive away. Tom had slithered in and taken hold of his life just as completely as Randy had taken over Charlie's. Tom saw everything he did and heard everything he said. He believed he controlled whether Randy would spend his next twenty years in jail or walking free, but unlike Charlie, who could never get his football career back, Randy's fate was yet to be determined. He felt a twinge of guilt for what he'd done to Charlie and his family, but pushed it aside to consider how to deal with Tom. Months ago, shooting him would have been the obvious solution. Not so now.

Going to the police was pointless. Tom would hand over the rifle and Randy would be doomed once they matched his prints and determined it was the gun that killed Sebastian Leonard.

The best course was to counterbalance Tom's leverage. For that, he needed to know how Tom profited by attacking the mosque. He wasn't fired up enough to start a holy war. It was about money with him. If Randy could expose the money trail, he could bargain for the rifle and his freedom. Tom was making sure Randy didn't have time to make that happen. The pressure would keep building until Randy wired the mosque. But why would Tom go through all this trouble? He found Ron and bribed him to testify. He had Sebastian killed and set Randy up to run into the men at the bar. Paying someone to plant the fancy cameras would have been far less trouble. Tom wanted something Randy wasn't seeing and it had nothing to do with the surveillance job Ethan mentioned.

Randy couldn't think clearly knowing he was being watched inside his own house. He took the case of miniature cameras to the McLaren and sped off, satisfied that he was alone while he drove. Cruising down County Street, he settled into a space across from Tom's office. When the laptop booted, he cycled through the cameras and tried the phone tap. He discovered that all his gear had been removed, just as he expected. They'd seen him place the cameras. The office was wired and monitored by someone who was paying attention. It wasn't some high school kid in a monitoring farm in India. These people didn't spend their time calming the nerves of suburban housewives. They were pros. They expected trouble and they were ready. Unfortunately, these were the same men watching Randy.

Inside the silver case, Tom's sophisticated monitor was slim but heavy. On his lap, it came to life quickly and showed two live feeds. The first was completely dark. Randy wondered if it was in a closet in Tom's office until he opened the case again and light appeared. It was the camera Tom had showed him how to activate. There was another feed working: Tom's reception area. The view was focused on the front door from somewhere on the stairs. No one moved, but Randy recognized the image.

The McLaren roared off to test Randy's hunch.

Back in his own garage, he opened the monitor again and let it scan for signals. Only the feed in the case came live this time. The cameras in his house didn't communicate with this monitor and the camera from Tom's reception area was out of range. He could test the range with the one in the case, but guessed it was less than a mile. So how were they watching his house? They weren't sitting in a van nearby, not in this neighborhood. They wouldn't rent a million dollar house. No, the signal had to be forwarded from somewhere nearby. Breaking into a neighbor's house to install the device would have been risky. More likely it was in Randy's own basement.

The electrical panel downstairs was neat. Beside it, separate telephone and cable wires terminated on a small piece of plywood mounted for the job. If not for his work at the Caulfields, he might not have noticed that an extra telephone circuit had been added. The connection snaked back behind the plywood and disappeared behind the fluffy pink insulation. It ended in a neat little black box. Only a few inches wide, it was tapped into the electric supply and had a thin antenna wire that stretched around the insulation and ran along the wall stud toward the first floor.

Ripping it out would blind them, but they'd know what happened and they'd just install another forwarder. He tried not to look agitated as he replaced the insulation. He opened the electrical panel and stared at the breakers as if he were confused, but he was really memorizing the numbers the Verizon technician had written on the little beige box. He did his best to look flustered as he returned upstairs.

He didn't write the number down until he was half a mile away in the McLaren. Ten minutes later he stopped in at a Wendy's restaurant and made two calls from his cell. An old friend gave him the number he needed for Verizon dispatch.

"I'd like to report a trouble," Randy said when the line connected. He read off the circuit number he'd written down.

The line went quiet as the operator opened a trouble ticket for the circuit. "Have you confirmed power on the remote end?"

"I just came from there. Everything's fine. I can see carrier. My equipment's got power. I'm thinking it's programming."

"Hang on." The guy resented the insinuation that one of his union buddies fiddled with the programming and screwed it up. It happened plenty often. "Looks fine. I can loop back the remote. Must be on the home end, but that's a T1. You want me to loop it?"

"No," Randy said emphatically as if he cared about uptime. "I just called there. Didn't get anyone. They must be on lunch."

The operator was unmoved.

"I guess I'm going to have to go there myself."

Still no reply from the operator.

"That's in the Coggeshall Street site, right?"

"No. That's your problem." The operator hesitated and gave him an address on Holly Street.

"Thanks. I'll call over there."

Randy hung up and sat wondering why the address sounded so familiar. When he saw the red star pop up on MapQuest he knew why.

Later that night, Randy sat behind the wheel of the McLaren parked on Sawyer, headed east. No matter what color the traffic lights were, he could swing onto Belleville Avenue, zip down Coggeshall Street and hit the I-195 onramp heading west in about thirty seconds. He sat only a few blocks from the mosque and if he'd been ambitious he could have wired the mosque and gotten back for the job he planned, but pleasing Tom Gold wasn't his priority. If he got lucky and found Tom's monitoring center in the basement of that bar, he might even find the .30-30. Then he could wipe it down and go to the cops. In a few short hours he could be free from Tom and ready to focus on a more important mission.

The photographer's jaunt into that basement made sense now. If Tom's team spent the day monitoring cameras there, then it would be easy to take a quick break and deal with Randy when he trailed the photographer inside.

He waited until 3:45 A.M. in the darkened car. Time enough for anyone who stumbled out at closing to find their way home or at least several blocks away. It was prime time for the nightshift in Tom's monitoring center to take a nap before the world awoke, but Randy knew they were too professional for that.

Alone on the sidewalk down Sawyer to the corner and up the Avenue, everything was quiet. A lone figure stepped out of the shadows as he approached. She wore black, bike shorts and a wide open tank top that made it clear why she was up this late. Her friends had all gotten their work for the night. As he got closer he could see aged red scrapes on her face. She looked cold in spite of the weather, begging with her eyes. He frowned, shook his head and stuck to the shadows against the buildings as he passed.

Two blocks ahead, the bar was dark as were the apartments upstairs.

He hesitated in a doorway across the street for a minute then made the corner onto Holly and around the back. He pressed his head against the vinyl siding, but heard nothing inside. No footsteps, no voices, but that didn't mean anything. If this was Tom's monitoring center, the crew inside would be quietly working computer monitors at this time of night.

The phone, cable and electric wires dropped from a pole to the back corner of the building. No way to tell what type of service came in from out here, but at the foot of the wall was a tiny window that shed some light into the basement. He guessed it was a storage room for the bar.

There was no speaker on the outside of the building to sound the alarm, but Randy readied himself to bolt as he worked the window latch with the back edge of his pocketknife. The latch slid aside and the window pushed open with a thump from the meaty part of his clenched fist.

The bar remained quiet. No one responded to the noise from inside.

Randy lifted the window aside and climbed in.

Cases of liquor lined the walls.

The flashlight was brighter than he'd hoped, but in the confines of the storeroom, it wouldn't alarm anyone unless they were standing outside the window Randy had just slithered through.

The beam found the telephone circuits directly below the wires on the outside of the building. What he saw next convinced him Tom Gold wasn't new to extortion. A stack of black boxes with flashing red and green lights was mounted on a shelf beside the electrical panel. A few circuits came in and one went back out. There was no monitoring station here. It was a relay. The building was being watched from the real monitoring station. Tom would soon know that Randy wasn't inside the mosque.

Randy tore a corner off a wine case. He didn't bother acting confused again. He copied the outbound circuit number as fast as he could, stuck the cardboard in next to his wallet and doused the light.

He hoped the operator hadn't seen him climb into the storeroom this late. Maybe he was sleeping, but Randy knew these guys didn't sleep on the job. This room was an early warning system. They'd get excited the moment he walked in and they'd be coming to find him.

Randy slithered out the narrow window and pulled it back into place.

One more phone call and Randy would know where to find them. First he had to get to the McLaren and get out of there.

Chapter Thirty-five

Randy peered up and down Holly Street looking for movement under the dim street lights. If anyone was responding to the alert at the bar, they hadn't made it there yet. The McLaren was just a block and a half away back on Sawyer, but after climbing inside the bar and finding the relay, he couldn't let Tom's men spot him on the deserted sidewalk. He headed off into the alley toward the backyards that faced the center of the block.

Over a low wall, he crossed a tiny enclosed lawn, hidden back here by the knot of houses that faced the streets in every direction. His knee nudged a metal barrel as he scooted around the base of a wooden porch in the dark. A yappy bark nagged from behind the door. Inside or out the little fuzz ball wouldn't have deterred him, but fortunately the dog was inside and the muffled barks wouldn't warn the neighbors of Randy's movements.

Across two more yards, Randy eased down a driveway in the middle of the block on North Front Street. The sidewalks were as quiet as Holly Street. Still, he cut directly across and followed a driveway around back into a tiny yard. He was close to his car now, though he couldn't tell which yard he was parked in front of. He found a short drive with a black Toyota taking up most of the space. Creeping around the Toyota, the McLaren came into view down the block. No one stirred along Sawyer. He stood in the shadows a moment and watched up and down. Apparently, Tom's men didn't work that quickly. He broke cover and hurried to the car.

It wasn't the engines he heard and not the brakes exactly. They didn't come screeching in. They'd been watching the car, waiting for him to appear. When he did, the large white vans rolled up and blocked him in on both sides. One pulled up North Front Street and stopped in the middle of Sawyer. The other came out of a side street Randy hadn't noticed and idled nose to tail with a parked white four door. The sidewalks weren't wide enough for the McLaren and there was no room to push in front or behind the vans.

Two men got out on the corner of North Front to his right. Another got out of the van further down Sawyer to his left. All three raced toward him.

Randy turned and ran back down the driveway, retracing his route over fences and through tiny green yards. He burst onto North Front at a dead run. The arm was little more than a blur in the dark. Well timed, the man had known exactly where to wait. He thrust his arm out to catch Randy under the chin and clothesline him to the ground.

Randy ducked, squatting, awkwardly running with his knees bent too far underneath him and his torso hunched forward, but somehow he kept his balance. The forearm skipped off the top of his head and Randy stumbled out into the street, straightened up and regained his stride. He raced through the opposite driveway and into the yard. Randy hesitated a second on the grass. The man behind him was the guy with the goatee. Apparently he had a thing for ambushes, but luckily he didn't connect this time.

To Randy's right was the little dog, a few more fenced yards and the bar beyond. More of Tom's men could be waiting there. He couldn't go back.

Goatee lost a lot of ground with his swing, but now he lumbered across the street and started down the driveway. He was too big to keep up with Randy through the tight little yards and over chain-link fences. Randy turned away from the bar, sprinted to the back corner of a yard, hopped up on a low wooden shed and vaulted a stockade fence into the dark. He landed in a pile of grass clippings that smelled like they'd been rotting for years. He reeked as he jogged off, shaking his foot as he neared the next fence. The big guy behind him struggled to get over the six foot wooden pickets.

Randy raced alone into the dark.

In the third yard, he found a toddler's play house with thick plastic walls and a bright blue roof. He squeezed himself inside and hunkered down to listen with his knees pressed to his chest. He took long slow breaths, silently filling and emptying his lungs.

He couldn't go back to the McLaren. They'd keep it blocked in until they caught him. An hour from now, they'd be forced to move along by people in the tenements going to work. If he could wait them out, he could hoof it up to the highway and catch a ride toward Dartmouth.

He hadn't seen any guns. They knew it wasn't some random guy breaking in. They wanted him alive to do the job in the mosque. They wouldn't really hurt him. Not yet. Could he just walk out and talk it over with Ethan? He considered it, but decided it was not a good idea.

The stench from his shoes made his eyes water.

The chain-link fence at the back of the yard rattled.

Jammed in as he was, he couldn't turn around to look through the finger holes in the bright red shutters. Light was coming in now. The sun was coming up and his hiding place would be impossible to miss with its white walls and bright blue roof. He hoped it seemed too obvious.

Garbage cans rattled in the yard next door, the opposite direction he expected a noise to come from.

The rattling stopped.

Footsteps on the grass would be impossible to hear.

The city was slowly coming to life. Soon the lights would be on. Someone in one of the houses around him would have their eyes out the window with their morning coffee. Someone would see the men in their backyard and chase them off.

The rattling started again, both sides at once this time. They knew they were close. They'd be searching this yard soon. The plastic house was impossible to miss.

A voice spoke, muffled by the plastic walls, then silence.

Glass shattered.

Noise on three sides was too much.

Randy burst out the tiny door head first, crawling, pulling at the grass to get his hips then legs through the toddler-sized opening. Lights flicked on in the house. They'd be rushing to the windows to see what happened. He didn't have to see the hole in the second floor window to know one of his pursuers had thrown a rock and scored a direct hit.

On his feet, he heard the splash of a steadying foot against chain-links. The heavy diamonds of steel rattled down several feet before the noise petered out. Randy darted for the driveway, his legs accelerating with every long stride to the street. He could see straight down Howard Street to the I-195 onramp beyond. That was his target now. Get to the highway and flag someone down.

Tall wooden pickets raced by on his right. Three small cars lined the narrow driveway leaving a few feet for Randy to race past. Just half a dozen feet from the sidewalk, he could see another block of row houses stretched out on the other side. Get past those and he'd be climbing the onramp.

He saw the heavy chrome grille first, a hungry square mouth closing fast as he ran full speed right for it. The van cut between the parked cars and capped the driveway, still rolling, trapping him between the bumper and the picket fence behind. His sneakers skidded to a stop on the concrete. He jumped back as the bumper splintered the corner fencepost.

The driver tried to crush him against the fence. Was the break-in that big of a deal? Were they running drugs or girls out of there? They were definitely tired of subtle cajoling.

The driver's door opened.

Randy turned for the sidewalk and a foot race to the McLaren. With the van moved, his car wasn't blocked in anymore. If he could get there first and get his car moving, he could outrun them to the highway and be gone.

He took only one step and a huge shoulder buried into his ribs, the arm wrapped around, but not quite closed as the man drove him into the van. The paneling gave in the center. Randy's head smacked something solid, a support maybe. He wobbled, got his right hand on the guy's throat then everything went dark. It was the biggest guy from the bar that hit him, the guy he'd jabbed with the pool cue. A black bag pulled tight over Randy's head.

Hot breath rode up over his cheeks.

A cord tightened around his neck.

Fighting to get loose brought a flurry of punches to his ribs, abdomen and solar plexus that dropped him to his knees. Footsteps rushed around him on the sidewalk. The hard plastic came next, digging into his wrists, binding them together with absolutely no slack. The door opened and they shoved him in face first. His knees rammed the threshold and he doubled over, his face on the dirty, rubberized floor. They dragged him the rest of the way in by his belt and let him writhe, curled up on the floor.

Voices panicked. The residents would be out soon, angry about the fence. The van sped away, made two rights and zipped straight ahead for half a mile. No stops. No turns. No sounds of anything but the men who kicked him when he rolled over and tried to get a look through the bag. Air was getting in. His face was hot, but he was getting used to the dark.

One of the men pulled his wallet and flipped it open. He didn't find what he was looking for because a few seconds later his fingers were back in the pocket. He lifted the chunk of cardboard Randy had written the circuit number on and stuffed the wallet back in.

Someone had been watching him on camera. They knew he was getting close. This was something bigger than the mosque. If they were dealing drugs or guns they'd kill him without a second thought. They were too organized, too businesslike. They were too big for Randy to handle alone.

The van bumped off the road, jarring everyone inside. With his hands behind his back, Randy's body floated with each bump, jarring and sliding around. After a dozen rough yards, the van bucked to a stop sending Randy sliding face first over the flooring until something metal smacked his head.

They wrestled him out. Dirt scraped beneath their feet as he tried to steady himself and match their strides. He stumbled down a steep bank and then his footsteps splashed. Knee deep in cold water with a man on each side, Randy was helpless. Blinded by the bag, he tried to keep track of the bank behind him. He could see only a faint glow that told him the sun was on its way up.

A palm slammed between Randy's shoulder blades and sent him lurching forward. He stepped fast, found his feet blocked by a leg in front of his ankles and he plunged down, gulping a lung full of hot air. He splashed face first, hands hard behind him. His head turned an instant before his nose buried into the sandy bottom.

A heavy boot stepped down on the base of his spine.

Jerking and twisting proved fruitless. The pressure held him there.

No amount of contortion could bring his head above water.

The men stood over him as his lungs began to burn.

There was no escape.

He hadn't saved himself.

If this was the end, he was surely bound for Hell.

He stopped struggling and played dead, hoping they'd pull him up.

His cheeks puffed full of air that his lungs rejected because it was poisoned by carbon dioxide. Pressure built. His body urged him to exhale. He lay still, trying to calm his heart and conserve oxygen in the cold water.

Only Tom's orders could save him.

They waited impossibly long then fished him out by the shirt collar and spun him around toward the shore. The exhaled air exploded from his mouth. Damp air rushed into his lungs. His heart raced to circulate the scarce oxygen. The black hood came off. Ethan and the huge guy from the bar faced him from high on the river bank. The guy with the tattoos had been holding him under. Goatee was on the other side of him in the water.

"Shit your pants boy?" Ethan asked.

The power lifter looked like he'd be happier back at the gym, but the other three were intent on every detail of his face, recording every nuance of his terror to recall later.

"Do your job tomorrow night, or we're not going to fish you out."

They left him there in the sand with his hands still bound. All four climbed into the van and sped off.

He needed to be more careful.

What if he'd drowned?

Chapter Thirty-six

The impressions notched into Randy's wrists by the Zip Ties had been erased by swelling flesh, but the red marks remained along with the terrifying feeling of being blinded and dunked under icy water. Violent images flickered to mind unbidden. Randy felt himself crash a wine bottle into the back of Ethan's head, snap a meat tenderizer down on his knuckles, ignite orangey-red flames that engulfed him. Each snippet brought an angry feeling of release, but no image could replace Ethan's sadistic grin from the riverbank. Hate bubbled high inside Randy's chest. He beat it back.

Love thy neighbor.

Turn the other cheek.

Thou shalt not kill.

Nothing that happened here could compare to the torture he would suffer if he failed. His earthly body would die from prolonged abuse, but in Hell the tissue would regenerate quickly and painfully, only to be ripped from his body again ten thousand times over. Jesus knew that life here didn't compare to the infinite. Placing too much significance on this life only led to trouble.

Justice is what Tom's men deserved. Iron bars tightly locked. Randy had taken his first step to sending them there, but he felt queasy about the risks as he peered into the darkness for anyone who might be watching.

He slipped away from the McLaren and carried the metallic case along the length of the loading dock. At 12:55 P.M. Coggeshall Street was deserted. Two blocks up, the mosque would be empty, but the surrounding slum would have its share of late night prowlers. The mosque leaders had been in slums before, but here the prostitutes stood out in the open. Some had gone electronic on Craigslist, but many were still out in the weather serving the computer illiterate and the electronically wary. Booze and drugs weren't far from most corners either. Would the imams chase them away? Would they improve the city for law abiding residents? Even Tom Gold, a defense lawyer, was tired of the system coddling criminals. Maybe a few severed wrists would help.

All was quiet and dark inside the chain-link. He felt a flash of shame paint his face red as he skirted inside the fence. If he'd been asked to go inside a church or a temple he wouldn't have, but something about the mosque was different. He associated Muslims with violence. They met opposition with horrific atrocities. They even fought each other with devastating results. Still, he assured himself he'd stop Tom and his men from harming them. He followed the drive across the empty parking area and around back. Alone there, he wondered if Tom was playing on his fear of the unfamiliar religion or reacting to his own. After tonight, the pressure would ease and he'd have a chance to figure that out. He kept his head down to avoid the cameras as he stalked along the brick wall.

The door near the minaret looked secure from the outside, but the lock was nothing special and he knew the alarm wires hung harmlessly from the panel inside. The dim security light betrayed his position by the door as he donned a black mask and scanned the weeds for the observer he knew would be watching. The watcher could have chosen a tenement or even a parked car. The massive concrete supports under I-195 would provide distance from traffic and the shadows would provide excellent cover. Not a single figure was recognizable in the gloom. Tom's man was watching. He'd know Randy was doing what he was told, but he wouldn't know this was the start of something bigger.

The door picked easily and Randy ducked inside and fingered the hanging wires with gloved fingertips. His footfalls echoed in the deserted canyon of tile and brick. The dim security lights added little to the moonlight shining through the dome, but after his tour days earlier and an afternoon studying his notes, he identified the camera locations easily. Ethan insisted he angle them to capture a wide view of the worshipers. He also wanted them placed high enough so a kid tracing the bricks couldn't stick his finger with a miniature antenna.

There was nothing inside the wide courtyard to boost himself up with. Not a chair in sight. He patrolled the corridors and offices carefully until he was confident that he was alone. Then he rushed around like a janitor with a job to do. Hearing his own hasty footsteps, he realized Tom could have the police waiting when he emerged, but he couldn't worry about that.

The narrow hall that paralleled the courtyard ended in a set of spiral stairs to the minaret tower. At the foot of the stairs, a closet filled with generically-labeled plastic jugs, rags and a dozen boxes of light bulbs housed the eight foot ladder Randy needed. He lugged it to the twelve highlighted locations on Ethan's map. One by one he puttied the cameras into place, thirteen feet high in the courtyard, the main prayer hall, and the kiblah. The clear adhesive and the beige cameras blended so well with the mortar he wouldn't be able to find them again himself, not without the monitor to guide his search.

Standing there near the kiblah, he gave himself some insurance. He attached the final camera but didn't activate it. If Tom and his men decided to remove the cameras to cover their tracks, they'd never find this one. These had to be expensive, probably highly guarded military technology. High-end equipment like this left a trail and Randy hoped he could connect the trail to Tom later.

The monitor picked up eleven camera feeds and sound from three microphones. Mission accomplished.

On the way back to the car, Randy wondered if they'd be monitoring these feeds from the bar. It was an ideal hideaway with no line of sight to the mosque. He'd given them everything they needed to eavesdrop without detection, but Randy felt more hope than guilt.

The McLaren lumbered away from the loading dock, jumped out onto Coggeshall and turned with its brake lights glowing. It swung west, accelerated all the way up the onramp and swerved out into the passing lane.

Chapter Thirty-seven

Sid followed the McLaren up the slope onto I-195, pushing the van to keep the streaking car in sight. The McLaren swerved around a group of cars going from the onramp to the left hand lane in one swoop, already moving faster than anything on the highway. Incredible how fast that winged car of his went from forty in the turn to ninety-five at the top of the steep ramp. The Chevy had balls, but that thing was sick. No way Sid could keep up.

Sid dialed his cell and waited. "He's done. We're on one ninety-five."

"Everything working?"

"Beauty. Watched him on the new cameras myself."

Ethan grunted on the other end.

"That car of his hauls ass. No way I can stay with him."

"Forget that. We know where he's going. Meet us at the airport."

Ethan didn't thank him for taking this job, but Sid knew he was glad. With all the gear they had on Randy, watching him wire the mosque was a snore. Sid's jaw still hurt from the pool cue, but he'd have plenty of chances to get even. He volunteered to babysit because Tripp would've been too distracted thinking about what he was missing at the airport. Sid didn't get off on hurting people, but Tripp was a virtuoso. He changed when he started cutting into someone. He focused every filament of his being on drawing out every last panicked breath. Most of the time, Tom ordered Sid to keep him from getting too creative. Without Sid watching, Tripp got lost in his work and sometimes he got sloppy. It was Tripp's show tonight. Torment is what they were getting paid for, the more gruesome the better.

The McLaren had long vanished from sight when Sid turned north onto Route 140 and hit the gas. Whitey would track him from here.

Khan called. They'd been seen grabbing the punk, but they got away clean. The kid was ready for action and the father was on his way. Khan urged Sid to get there before Tripp got anxious.

Sid didn't have anything against the ragheads. They could kneel down and worship Allah all they wanted. As long as they didn't bomb anyone, no problem. The kid they picked up tonight was pure evil. He dealt drugs and ruined the lives of little kids for money like the gangs they targeted, but he went far beyond the others. When his girlfriend dumped him, he raped and killed her then buried her in the Fairhaven woods. He covered his tracks well. The body wasn't found for months. Drug money bought him sharp lawyers and he beat the charges, but he didn't count on the father.

He thought he was invincible until Khan wrestled him into the van.

Sid followed the security fence along the outskirts of the airport. The landing lights were off and the road was dark. He parked beside the matching van and Tom's BMW. To a patrol officer this would look like a drug deal, but the cops knew to stay away until morning.

He stepped out of the van and heard the kid screaming threats and obscenities. Sid walked fifty feet from the vans to where the kid was bound. Even hooded with his hands Zip Tied and his legs encased deep in a stack of tires, he didn't get it. He still thought he was untouchable. He'd pissed off the wrong guy this time, a father with enough money and enough connections to buy him gift-wrapped and ready for roasting.

Tripp and Khan stood beside the tires. Tom and Ethan bracketed the father as he faced the kid. Sid had arrived just in time.

"Show your face asshole and you're dead."

Tripp obliged and the punk's expression flashed angry then pale. As soon as the hood came off, he recognized the man he'd seen at his girlfriend's door. He'd never expected to see him again, not vulnerable like this. He was king with half a dozen gang bangers around him, but he'd been plucked from his turf. The situation dawned and, for an instant, Sid saw the scared kid underneath. Sixteen visits to the precinct hadn't had the effect of this one moment. Consequences. Justice. Mortality. He wasn't afraid of what the cops might do, but tonight society was visiting payback on his ass.

The father stepped up and drilled him hard to the side of the head.

Tom screamed, "No! No! No!" He grabbed the father by his shirt and pulled him back. Tom inspected his soft knuckles, brushed them off and called Sid over to hold the light while he checked for blood.

Tom pressed his face directly in front the father blocking his view. "Listen," he said. "You can't afford to get stupid. You're suspect number one. No DNA gets near you. No damage to your hands. No injuries of any kind. Get it?"

All the rage the paper pusher could muster hadn't broken the skin on the kid's face or his knuckles, but he got the punk's attention. Tom signaled to the van. Ethan ran over and fetched an armload of dark clothes.

"Where?"

"Wal-Mart. Today. Cash. Different stores for the bat and clothes."

Tom nodded and helped the father into a navy blue rain suit. He balked at the face shield, but Tom didn't budge from his path until his face and hands were protected.

Ethan handed him an aluminum bat and all four men stepped clear.

The punk knew what was up. He deserved it, but he was stunned it could really happen. The middle-aged office jockey wailed away. On the street he'd be in fear of his life from this punk, but the old guy showed some guts once it became personal. He plunked down the cash and lied to his wife about where he'd be tonight. The cops would be at his door in the morning. They wouldn't push hard, but they'd make a show of it. Whoever was sent after the old guy had probably dragged the kid in at least once. The drug pusher deserved this. The city benefited from this. The cops would never say it themselves, but they knew. Everyone was better off with this kid in the ground.

The kid dodged as well as he could, but the tires kept him rooted in place. Even lurching left and right he could only protect his head. The old man missed once, but even the glancing blows made the kid howl in pain. He shattered both clavicles and then the kid hunched forward and slumped down inside the tires. The old man wailed him sixteen times before he tired and stood there panting.

Tom offered him a throwaway .38.

The father sneered not wanting to spare him any pain.

Tripp and Khan moved in with gloved hands.

They stripped the father with surgical precision from top to bottom, careful that the blood spatter on the face shield and the rain suit didn't touch his street clothes—or theirs. The father stepped out of the suit and inspected the damage until Tom pulled him away toward the cars.

Tripp stuffed the raincoat and pants down into the tires. The kid was bleeding all over now, swollen, not even mumbling any more. If he had any energy left to fight, here was his chance, but he just slumped as the items were packed down next to his legs.

The face shield and gloves went in next. Then the bat. Then the gas.

The father glared. Even knowing he was about to burn wasn't enough. Khan motioned Sid to get between them. The kid was covered in blood now. The father didn't make a break. It could have been Sid's muscles that kept him by Tom's side. More likely it was Tom's DNA lecture.

Sid wondered if this guy had more daughters at home.

It was at least fifty yards from the top of the hill to the group huddled around the kid. It had taken almost ten minutes to crawl through the long grass and up onto the weed-covered mound. Cassie had to be back in Dartmouth by now. The guys with Tom didn't seem alarmed, so she must have remembered to stay outside away from the cameras. He hoped she'd hold off long enough for him to figure out what Tom was up to out here.

The van that had been following Cassie led him straight here. Tom's BMW was parked alongside the other white van from the day before. They used flashlights and talked loudly. They weren't worried about company. But what were they doing off the end of the runway after midnight?

When he saw the kid in the tires, Randy started snapping pictures.

The digital didn't have much of a zoom so everything was grainy and far away. The only light came from the flashlights aimed in his direction. The camera captured them like enormous white orbs. Randy hoped he could enhance the shots later and get a face or two. He was probably wasting his time, but he didn't have a better idea so he kept snapping. The men were so focused on the kid and the guy whacking him that they barely glanced out into the dark.

The batter swung like he was fifty. Still, the kid was getting pummeled. Randy wanted to get up and rush them, but rushing six men from fifty yards away was suicide.

He snapped pictures until the clothes came off and the gasoline started splashing. The smell roused the kid, but he wasn't getting free on his own. The skinny guy emptied two cans, dousing the tires and the grass all around.

The vans rolled clear and waited for one guy left behind. He was fiddling with something in the dark about twenty feet from the tires. A lighter flared, showing close-cropped hair. The tattooed guy. Had to be.

Randy drew his SIG, but he couldn't shoot. He'd spent weeks lamenting what he'd done in Westport. Even if he was supposed to save the kid, he couldn't kill the photographer to do it. Randy braced his hand in the dirt.

A stick torched into flame. Tattoos hoisted it over his shoulder like a spear and jabbed it back and forth like a dart player preparing to throw. If the spear touched the gasoline, the tires would burst into flames. If gas had pooled in the sidewalls, the kid would be obliterated by the explosion.

Randy leveled on the stick fifty yards away—an impossible shot in the dark. He shifted for the wrist, but it was jabbing, getting ready to throw and it was nearly in line with the photographer's head. A bad miss could drop him where he stood. The arm pulled back and held steady.

Randy fired.

The report changed everything in an instant.

The kid snapped to life thinking he was being rescued.

Tatoos side-armed the stick in a pitifully low arc. It skidded into the grass, flared and dimmed. There was no gas to ignite where it landed six feet from the tires, but if it burned awhile, it might eventually reach the kid. No one wanted to take that chance.

A door hinge squeaked.

The spear bearer crouched low hunting for another stick.

A muzzle flashed from Randy's left.

No report, just a steady flash. The weeds around him kicked to life. Twenty maybe thirty shots buried into the hill. Randy rolled away downhill. When he popped his head up there were two of them at the vans. One bent over to reload. The other gun flashed when Randy's head appeared in the weeds. Randy rolled right, away from the shooters to get a look at the spear hurler. He had another stick alight, thicker and shorter. It burned bright as it turned end over end and bounced off the base of the tires.

Randy never fired another shot.

The fire engulfed the kid instantly. Amazing how violently gasoline shoots flames into the air. Explosive is the only way to describe it. Not as spectacular as Charlie Marston's sawdust, but just as deadly.

Tom and the old guy took off in the BMW immediately after the flames jumped to life around the kid.

The guys at the vans peppered the hill while their buddy ran to join them. He climbed in and they drove off. Their job was done. If they'd known it was Randy on the hill, they would have come at him hard.

Randy had missed his chance. Nothing could save the kid now.

His eyes followed the trail of fire and thick black smoke as it billowed up to pollute the heavens and blot out a wide swath of stars. Randy waited there on his knees halfway up the hill, watching for a sign. The remaining stars blinked at him. None recognized his effort. Nor did they admonish his failure.

He wondered if he'd gone insane. If the shrink caught him watching the stars, waiting for God to send him a message, she'd have locked him up. More and more it seemed his destiny. He hung his head and slumped back to Cassie's Corolla. Someone would see the fire. Someone would identify the body. The story would be in all the papers. Maybe then Randy would understand why it happened and why he couldn't save him.

Chapter Thirty-eight

Randy wheeled the Corolla down the empty street and around the cul-de-sac to check for anyone who might be watching his house. The McLaren waited a dozen feet back from the garage where Cassie had ended her wild drive. She'd convinced the big guy that Randy was behind the wheel and she'd kept off camera long enough for Randy to track him to the airport. It wasn't their base of operation as he'd hoped, but maybe what he'd seen was better. Cassie could identify the victim and explain why he'd been targeted. Maybe she'd even connect him to Sebastian and the mosque.

She'd do the research willingly in spite of the danger. She surrounded herself with petty criminals, gangs, and drug dealers. They were all violent, but she didn't know how vicious Tom and his thugs could be. He'd tell her they'd burned a man alive and that they'd killed Sebastian to keep Randy on leash. She'd try to be careful, but she was a reporter not a private investigator. She'd already put herself on the line by driving the car. She wanted the story, but it was wrong to ask her to risk her life.

He pulled even with the McLaren and saw her blonde hair spilled over the headrest. She'd come along to test his story about Tom Gold. She'd seen Randy go into the mosque and she'd seen the van follow her when she left. She'd want to know what he'd found. She deserved to know, but if she pushed too hard, she'd end up like Sebastian. He watched her sleep inside the car knowing he couldn't send her home alone. He wondered how he could make her stay and what Tom's men would do if they saw her come inside. They'd use her like they used Sebastian, but they'd keep her alive.

Randy slipped into the McLaren. She lay peaceful, oblivious to the danger trailing them. When his thumb stroked her forearm the third time her eyes popped open and flicked around the car with a start.

"Get some rest?"

She tossed her hair and pretended to be alert. "What'd you find?"

At 2:30 A.M. she should have been home safe, not dozing in his driveway. His mind raced to comprehend the events that brought them here so early. He'd wired the mosque for a brutal group of thugs and exposed her to them. He'd failed his first mission, watching helplessly as they burned a man alive. He still didn't know anything about the kid, Tom Gold, the mosque or even why they'd chosen to get him involved. Cassie was the only bright spot, but she'd only stay so long without answers.

"I can't get you into this. I'll give you the story when it's over. It's yours, exclusive, but it's too dangerous now. Way too dangerous."

"I didn't sit here until one A.M. to be brushed off."

"It's two-thirty. And you have no idea what you're getting into."

"Show me." The defiant glare was tougher than he'd expected.

Bringing her inside was a mistake. If Tom's men saw them together, they'd see Randy's attraction to her and they'd add her to their list of targets. They'd already found people hidden deep in his past. They'd find Cassie easily. Staying together was the only solution, but once he told her what he'd seen, there'd be no holding her back.

Randy led her to the front door, stripped off his jacket and draped it over her head. They scooted through the kitchen and down to the basement. He showed her the black box that forwarded the camera feeds then ripped the wires from the wall. Tom's men wouldn't rewire the router until morning. He still felt like he was being watched as he showed her Tom's sleek monitor. She didn't need to see the tiny cameras to know someone was stalking Randy. She wanted to know why as badly as he did.

Upstairs on the couch, she wouldn't stop pressing for answers. She opened her leather notebook and set it on the coffee table, ready to gather facts for a story she should be smart enough not to print—at least not under her own name.

"I'll make you a deal. Stay with me when you're not working, don't print any names, and I'll tell you what I know."

"I'm not a little girl. I don't need you looking out for me and I don't need you telling me what to print."

"I don't need to tell you anything."

Her face soured, but her curiosity wouldn't let her leave.

"Sebastian thought he was safe surrounded by cops until he got a bullet in the ear. The kid I saw tonight looked *real* tough until they lit him on fire."

Cassie straightened with excitement—not fear—in her eyes. Didn't she realize she was right in the middle of this?

"Where? Where's he now?" Wide awake, she was ready to get in her car and drive off to the scene. Anything for the story.

Randy clamped down on the pen in her hand. "No names and we stay together when you're not working." He locked on her eyes through the glasses. They shifted up and to the left, met his and danced away. She was searching for loopholes. "I'm not getting you killed," he said.

"Fine." She let go of the pen and folded her delicate fingers into his.

"They're tracking my cars. I'll need a ride now and then."

She agreed and Randy began pouring out his story. It was Tom Gold and his men out there. He wouldn't tell her where until the morning to keep her from rushing out into the night, but he described the BMW and the two vans. He described Tom's dark suit and the protective clothing on the guy with the bat. The tires. The gasoline. The silenced gunshots. The fire.

Randy slipped the digital camera from his pocket, but the lighting had been all wrong and the action was too far away. The best image he captured was an indistinguishable glow under the flashlights. No one would ever recognize the men in the pictures. Twenty minutes of questions and follow-up questions covered every aspect of what he'd seen, save the location of the body. She was eager to climb into her car and race to it, but he made sure all she could do was arrange her notes and wait for morning.

When they were done talking, he led her upstairs to the only bed in the house. She kicked off her shoes and folded herself beneath the comforter with her notebook on the night table ready for late-breaking ideas. Randy yearned to step close and kiss her. The desire held him there a few feet from the bed, but he didn't dare upset the balance between them. He felt her eyes follow him until he closed the door.

He chose a corner chair in the living room where he could watch the front door, the stairs and the hall leading through the kitchen to the garage. No one could get to Cassie unless they climbed in through an upstairs window. That wasn't likely. He tucked the SIG in beside the seat cushion where an accidental discharge would burrow harmlessly for the basement.

When he closed his eyes, he saw a determined Cassie struggling to break free from him to investigate her story. He saw a shadowy figure trailing her that he knew to be Tom Gold, even though he could only see a billowy outline. He saw the man in the tires surrounded by Tom's men and his eyes popped open. Sleep terrified him. He reclined and blended himself into the shadows. He held his eyelids apart until their weight overpowered his will.

Hours later Randy opened his aching eyes to bright sunshine. Days without meaningful sleep left him woozy, his muscles numb. Something had woken him. He suspected Tom's men were already inside fixing the wiring downstairs. He listened but heard nothing.

He eased upstairs, through the bedroom door and squeezed Cassie's shoulder ever so gently. She leaned toward him, not away. He squeezed again and released her, wondering if the events of last night had brought them past familiarity toward something more.

Waiting for her, he realized he hadn't had a single dream. He'd slept unmolested for the first time since his vision. Had he made the right decision at the airport? At least his subconscious thought so.

Cassie dressed, drove them to breakfast and let him buy without protest. Through the morning he regarded Cassie differently. She was braver than he thought, willing to chase her story in spite of the risks. She'd stay close to him, not for romance, but for the story. Maybe the time together would bring her around.

She gave him a long sideways look when he directed her down the pine-needle-covered logging road. Randy jumped out and guided Cassie as she reversed direction in a muddy clearing that had been used to load logs onto trucks. He watched the Corolla until it disappeared into the trees.

The hike through the woods to the church seemed like overkill, but he couldn't understand how they always knew where he was. The house was wired. The McLaren and the van had to be wired, too. Today it was just him out here on an old abandoned road. No one had followed Cassie's car. No way they'd find him out here. Fortunately, the road was dry and the only thing growing on it were scattered patches of five-inch white pine seedlings fighting for the scant sun. In five years, the road would be passable only on foot and only by swatting green branches aside with every step.

Reverend Simmons opened the vestry door and peered past Randy to the empty church parking lot, surprised not to find his car. If he'd known what Randy was facing, he'd have thanked him for the precaution. The inside of the building reminded Randy of his Aunt Althea. She'd taught Sunday school for decades. The narrow plank floors and the grooved paths from the door to the offices and kitchen hadn't changed a bit.

The reverend's office was cluttered with books. On the desk, a chart traced Earth's civilizations back to the Great Flood. Everyone on Earth descended from Noah and his three sons who survived on the Ark. Every detail of the reverend's reality was shaped by faith. The facts were all around his office. Reverend Simmons lived in anticipation of the infinite.

"Do you need anything?" the reverend asked.

He wished they could trade places. The reverend had made a mistake, but since then he'd dedicated himself to God's work. Randy had been so muddled by his own anger he'd completely lost his way. Here in the reverend's office, surrounded by reminders of his faith, Randy felt distinctly unworthy.

"Perspective, I guess."

The reverend listened as Randy described creeping up in the weeds to help the man trapped in the tires. The reverend squirmed as Randy described the man being beaten, how his desperate shot missed and how they burned him alive.

"You're worried you should have done more?"

167

Randy nodded.

The reverend considered his response then raised his arm and measured his wrist between his thumb and forefinger. "You shot for this from over a hundred feet away. I don't know much about guns, but it sounds like you were hoping for a miracle."

"In the daytime, I can hit a dime from fifty feet. An arm's plenty big."

"But it was dark. Are you sure you really wanted to hit him?"

He could have hit the thug center mass and traded one life for another. Trying for the perfect shot was a mistake. Randy's choice killed the kid, but who was he to decide who to save? If he'd had time to think about it he might not have fired at all.

"What do you know of these two men?" Reverend Simmons asked.

"The guy with the torch is a vicious thug. He burned a man alive."

"And what of the man who was burned?"

Randy knew nothing of him. He could have caused more mayhem in his short lifetime than all of Tom's thugs combined or he could have been worthy of sainthood. Randy had no way of knowing.

"Maybe it wasn't your choice that killed him. Maybe it was his time."

Randy looked down at his clasped hands and realized the reverend was right. It couldn't be Randy's obligation to choose who lived and who died.

"Maybe He has something bigger planned for you."

When Randy didn't respond he asked, "Are you ok?"

The reverend eyed his clasped hands, something he did unconsciously now. The bowed head made Randy look as if he'd lapsed into prayer in the middle of their conversation. He raised his eyes so the reverend would know he hadn't. "Do you believe me, Reverend?"

Simmons reached over and rested a hand on top of Randy's. "The Lord has put me here to help you. Only you know what you saw. Only you know what it means."

"Very diplomatic."

"I believe in *you*, Randy. Yours is a rare journey for someone so young. I want you to succeed and I want you to keep coming back to church." The reverend's voice brightened. "I've got a fan that only works when you're there."

Randy thanked him and wandered to the front of the vestry and sat in the window, recounting their conversation. He couldn't be asked to choose who lived. That was too much for any man. He tried to help. The reverend assured him that God saw his intentions clearly. What was in his heart counted more than any outcome.

He absently watched the street for Cassie even though she wasn't due for an hour. He was more consumed by thoughts of the man in the tires than watching the traffic, but he noticed a dark blue van as it cruised to a stop just off the church green. Twenty minutes passed then thirty. The driver never got out. Randy strained to read the lettering on the side, but it was too small to read from the vestry window. A feeling washed over him as he watched. This was one of the vans that chased him, one of the vans at the airport. Early that morning the van was white, but he was sure it was the same van. Painted. They'd painted it this morning. They knew he was inside and they were serious about following him. It wasn't paranoia. It was them.

How had they found him?

The car and van were both in the garage.

No one had followed Cassie's car this morning and she hadn't come back yet. She hadn't led them here. Still, they'd driven right up to the front of the church green and waited. They knew he was inside.

The waggle of the black sneaker grabbed him. He'd worn these same shoes almost every day for the last week. What else did he always have? His wallet, keys, watch and cell phone. Any of them or all of them could be bugged. He'd been unconscious for two days in the hospital, enough time for Tom and his men to plant cameras throughout the house. It wouldn't have taken long to plant a tracking device or two in his clothes.

They'd been following his every move. That's how they found him hiding in the backyard that morning. They hadn't seen him. They followed him to where he was hiding and flushed him out like an animal.

Randy rushed toward the back of the building to find the reverend.

Chapter Thirty-nine

They started arriving just after 2:00 P.M. in faux wood paneled sedans, Volvos with obscenely low mileage and other boxy relics only seen in rural parking lots and antique auto shows. Retired couples tottered out carrying large Tupperware containers, crock pots and platters covered in foil. They had already been to church that day, but they came back in twos, filling the parking lot and feebly marching inside the vestry. Cassie wasn't part of the procession that met Randy in the kitchen.

A new pair of tube socks appeared from a large plastic bowl, a pair of boots, in his size, from a cardboard box topped in foil. Jeans and a new plaid shirt completed the ensemble. Randy stripped off his clothes and stuffed everything he'd worn that day into a cardboard box. Before he dressed, the reverend checked his back for fresh scars. There were plenty of old scars, but no new ones had been added. The whole idea was a bit far fetched and Randy was embarrassed for bringing it up. The reverend held the box without judgment as Randy slipped the cash and his driver's license from his wallet and tossed it, his keys and his watch in with his clothes.

"You don't need those," the reverend said, motioning with the box for the SIG and its holster.

Just showing the SIG might save his life. Randy wasn't letting it go. He pulled on his new clothes and clipped the SIG inside his belt.

One of the younger men carried the box to an SUV parked at the back corner of the building. When the SUV left the parking lot and turned toward the highway, the van followed thirty seconds behind. If they stayed far enough back, they'd never see him deliver the box to Randy's back porch. They'd see him drive away and they'd know the tracking devices were at the house. Without the cameras to show them what was going on inside, it'd look like a drop off. They might not know he was gone for days.

Randy headed out back through the woods and found Cassie on the logging road already turned around. She laughed at the way the jeans ballooned out around his waist and the shirt buttons that threatened to pop if he moved too quickly. Not the impression he wanted to make on Cassie, but at least the goons were off them for now.

"Rummage sale today?"

"My clothes were bugged."

The Corolla slowed as she faced him with a confused grimace then turned back to the road. "Are all the secret agents wearing plaid?"

The time and money spent tracking him didn't make sense to Randy either. They'd plucked him out of jail and forced him to bug the mosque. Now that the job was done, Tom could send him to prison by surfacing the Winchester or just by bungling the Charles Marston murder case. So why were they still following him?

The Corolla headed east on I-195 toward Faunce Corner Road. They were following the path of the SUV and van, but without the tracking devices they were just another car in traffic. Still, Randy watched every van they passed for the thugs that had been chasing him.

Cassie turned into the mall and parked at the outer edge of the parking lot away from the stores and the congestion of cars and pedestrians. "Let's go sexy. Some black jeans and a few T-shirts and you'll be good as new."

"Good thing. I can't go home. I've got to convince some young hottie to take me in."

She'd already agreed to let him stay. She tugged her glasses as if they disqualified her and pretended not to notice the hint of romance in his voice. She was hiding behind her last veil of professionalism, showing him journalistic interest and nothing more. At least she'd come back. She could have taken the airport murder story and moved on.

She let him hold the door and they went inside.

"Learn anything about the victim?" Randy asked, catching up.

"They identified him around lunch. Just got off a rape and murder charge. Moved some drugs. He's a regular customer."

"How'd they ID him so fast? Wasn't he crispy?"

"Totally." She laughed. "He was grabbed off the street yesterday. Buddies called it in." She paused to angle Randy toward a storefront. "They said a large van pulled up to make a drug buy. Two guys jerked him inside and drove off."

How could their illegal business be common knowledge?

She asked his size and held up a pair of cargo pants with a thirty-two inch waist. She found a black T-shirt nearby and sent him off to change. The clothes fit much better and she admired her selections when he rejoined her.

"Why are these guys mixed up with a drug-dealing rapist? What's that got to do with me and the mosque?"

"I wish I knew. It would've livened up my story."

"You know you can't include me in this. You identify me or them and they'll be on you as soon as the paper hits the sidewalk."

She gave a condescending look. She thought the whole deal with the cars and cameras was overdone. She'd seen the charred remains, but she spent every day looking at victims. She was probably only letting him stay because she knew he had more to tell. She wasn't scared. Not yet.

"I kept my part of the deal," she said. "I described the vehicles and I helped the cops find the slugs in the dirt. They're all over me to know who you are. But you didn't see anyone clearly. Your camera certainly didn't."

"I'd know the big guy anywhere. Sucker covered me with a hood and held me underwater in the dark."

She put her hand on his arm, gently reassuring him. Their eyes met intensely. He could feel the pressure on his face again, the pain in his lungs. He stopped himself from reaching for her.

She heard horrible stories all the time. She craved real life drama. Still, she was softening. He could feel it as she led him off in search of a pair of sneakers.

Chapter Forty

Cassie carried two foil bowls off the elevator on the tenth floor and headed for her apartment. Randy followed down the carpeted hall, his arms straining to lug the week's wardrobe he'd purchased on their brief shopping spree. He said he was glad to be hidden away in her apartment, but she knew that was a cover. He wanted to stay close enough to protect her whether she wanted him to or not. He didn't explain, but something was happening to him. Leaving all of his possessions behind was extreme. The cameras alone hadn't driven him to this. If he really had tracking devices in his clothes, he was into something serious. Serious enough to change him from the wild man Charlie Marston described to the polite guy she met in the hospital. Whatever it was, it would make a delicious story eventually.

Randy set his bags down by the couch, quickly surmising the bounds of his space for the next few days. Ethics or not, he wasn't getting her into bed. Deirdre had warned her about being alone with him. She would have been shocked to learn that Cassie invited him to stay overnight and even more shocked at how gentlemanly he'd been acting. It wasn't lack of interest. Cassie saw the way he watched her and the way he shuddered just a little when their eyes met, but he hadn't made a single move. Surprising, disappointing even. Contacts might be in order.

Cassie set the table, poured two glasses of water and peeled back the cardboard lid on her dinner to reveal chicken kebabs, rice and salad neatly compartmentalized inside.

"Are you always this comfortable with an accused killer at your place?"

She still wasn't sure what separated him from the rabble she met around the courthouse and the precincts.

"No, you're special."

He chewed and considered another tack.

"Is your fearlessness what led you to reporting?"

Guilt more likely.

"Writers aren't exactly risk takers," she said. "We don't lock 'em up. We just compile their stories for the world to see. You'd be surprised how many of them want to be in the paper."

"Yeah, sure. They like what you write, *sometimes*. But what about when they don't? I'm sure there are days you'd rather do something else."

"It's important work. I'm helping people. Telling them things they need to know. Making the world safer, you know, truth, justice and all that."

Someone needed to point out the danger living all around us. Maybe he was trying to do the same thing, to drag Charles Marston into the light so he couldn't steal another winery. He asked again how she got started and he poked and prodded until he got to Wally Ramos. "So, what was so special about this guy? You changed your major from Business Management to Journalism. It had to be a big story."

"He killed a friend of mine." *And I could have stopped him,* she thought.

Randy squirmed in his seat. "How awful. I'm so sorry." He chewed a mouthful of rice and let the tension settle. "Did he confess?"

"Eventually. Turns out he stabbed another student years earlier. No one talked to the police and he got away with it. If someone had stepped up then, maybe Ariana would still be alive."

"Now you're that someone."

She wished she'd been braver then.

Cassie steadied herself with a long drink. She was in the classroom that day. She knew what Wally was capable of even then and she was afraid of him like everyone else. She saw him jab the knife in and run, but he saw her, too. All he had to do was point a finger as he ran out and she knew what would happen if she told. When she saw him again two years later, Wally was a hardened criminal. Getting away with the stabbing in school hadn't helped him. He stabbed a dozen more people and robbed a hundred at least by the time Ariana became his last victim. Cassie interviewed him after he'd gotten twenty-five to life. She told his story for her campus paper and landed her job at *The Standard Times* as a result.

Randy sensed how deeply the story affected her. Maybe he could feel her guilt across the table. He didn't ask another question about reporting.

After a few minutes Cassie had questions of her own.

"What happened to you?"

"To make me the derelict I am?"

"No." She couldn't help but smile at his humility. "Charlie, Deirdre, Jo, Elizabeth, they all describe you…"

"As a psycho," he finished.

Cassie didn't buy the conspiracy theory Tom Gold spun in court. When five people were genuinely terrified of one man, they had good reason. The stories meshed together too well to be fabricated. They depicted Randy Black as a raving lunatic capable of anything to further his twisted goals. But here he sat, calmly chewing his salad, no more a threat than one of the appliances on the counter. His story was similar to Wally's, but the two men couldn't have been more different.

"You believe all those stories?" he asked.

"Everything's a puzzle with you. Can't you just tell me what happened? They didn't make it up. They couldn't have."

Randy considered a long moment. He was choosing his words carefully, worried about damaging his case.

"Off-the-record," she offered.

If he wanted to keep his story private he shouldn't be here, but he was short on choices.

"I was angry."

Charles Marston had given him reason.

"What about now? You don't seem angry anymore."

"Things are different."

"Because Charles Marston's dead."

Randy shook his head.

175

"What then? Pinto and his buddies knock you straight?"

"That was a fair fight, huh?"

Cassie grabbed his wrist and stopped him from taking a bite of chicken. "What the Hell? What happened? People don't just change. Not like that."

Randy switched hands with his fork and chewed his chicken thoughtfully then said, "I was told I was over the line. I needed to straighten things out or there would be consequences. I'm trying to do that."

"Must have been some talk." She thought about who might have had such an impact. "The reverend?" she asked.

"Close." Randy shifted his eyes upward.

His meaning was unmistakable. Cassie pulled back slowly. Schizophrenics heard voices, but they were withdrawn and confused. Randy was neither. He was strong, sane and convinced God was talking to him. After the paranoia about the cameras and then the bugs in his clothes, talking to God should have closed the case on his sanity, but there was no doubting the effect it had on him. Cassie was suddenly unsure of her decision to let him stay in her apartment.

"I'm not nuts. Really."

God talked to Moses. He sent angels to Mary, Joseph and Lot. But would he come down to talk to a sociopathic killer like Randy Black?

Impossible.

But if she really believed he was a sociopath, she wouldn't have brought him to her apartment. Would she?

Chapter Forty-one

Randy woke in pitch dark to the musty smell of robes that needed laundering. A key scraped into the lock on the outer door. Cassie would still be asleep thinking he was on the couch. She'd taken the news well the night before. She'd gotten quiet, but she didn't look at him like a lunatic. She needed his protection whether she believed him or not and the arrangement allowed him to maneuver without Tom's guys following. Hopefully, he'd be back in the apartment before she realized he'd slipped out at 4:00 A.M.

The office lights flicked on outlining each panel of the closet door with a white glow. Randy pressed his eye to a crack between panels and watched Judge McKinnon shuffle in with a Dunkin Donuts coffee in one hand and a thickly stuffed briefcase in the other. Randy waited to hear his bulk settle into his chair then he made his appearance through the folding door, urging the judge to be calm with a raised hand.

"I needed to see you—without my lawyer."

"So you broke into my chambers?" The judge vibrated confidence even as he scanned Randy for weapons. He was used to being in control, composed even after a man stepped out of his closet at 6:30 A.M.

His hand disappeared nonchalantly below the desk for a buzzer to summon help or a handgun. Either would ruin the visit.

"Don't do that. I just want to talk. I need help."

The hand stopped, still out of sight, inches from its goal.

"I have a problem with my lawyer."

The judge was unmoved.

Glass crashed outside. Sheet metal warped and twisted under enormous weight. Randy showed his empty hands and walked past the judge to the window. Two black kids were jumping up and down on the hood of the judge's Lexus. They'd gotten over the ten foot fence topped with barbed wire and spray painted *die pig* on the car's roof.

The judge didn't call security. One phone call and the two would have been trapped behind the barbed wire with the vandalized car. Judge McKinnon wouldn't have heard the case, but the outcome couldn't have been more certain. McKinnon frowned through the window.

"Fans of yours?" Randy asked as the kids scaled the chain-link.

"Murder case," the judge mumbled. "A former cop shot their brother. I heard the trial. They found not guilty and the guy walked." The judge had more to say. Randy waited until the silence was awkward and the judge continued. "The kid was trouble, high up in his gang. I still can't figure out what an ex-cop was doing in the middle of a turf battle, if that's what it was. I don't know why, but I believe he shot the kid. I'm not sure what the jury believed. The kid dealt drugs, intimidated witnesses. He was a real prize. Sometimes that matters to the jury. Sometimes it matters a lot."

"So his buddies blame you?"

The judge shrugged as if it were a part of the job he took in stride.

"Don't you care about your car?"

"It's insured. The irony is that the shooter, the guy these kids are after, died outside a drug house a week after he was released. It hasn't made it to court yet. It was in the papers, but these kids don't follow the news. They are the news."

"Want me to go down and tell 'em? Might cut down your insurance paperwork."

The judge crossed his arms and sneered as if he'd been tricked into getting familiar. He walked back to his chair and thumped down. He was surprisingly calm, given that two hoods had trashed his car and he had an intruder in his office.

"My lawyer's got it in for me."

"What do you want, Mr. Black? Are you begging for a postponement?"

"I want you to tell me I'm not crazy. You know this guy. Don't you?"

"Mr. Gold's a regular in my courtroom. No one has ever accused him of impropriety."

"He's wired my house with cameras. He's got guys watching me everywhere I go."

"Are you feeling well, Mr. Black? Sleeping ok? Maybe you should see a doctor."

There was sympathy in the judge's eyes, but they leveled on Randy as if he were a threat to be neutralized. He had the opportunity to reach for the button, but he didn't. The court officers would be swift. They'd haul him away and that would really complicate matters for Randy. The judge wanted to help, but something prevented him from telling Randy what he needed to know.

Randy assured the judge he was fine. What he needed was to get away from Tom Gold, but Tom had fabricated incriminating evidence and he could put Randy away on a whim. He couldn't risk angering Tom and he couldn't go on doing his bidding.

"Mind your words, Mr. Black. I'm hearing your case and you must be careful not to prejudice my opinion. There are procedures..."

"You don't understand. Procedures aren't going to help me."

"What exactly do you want me to do?"

"Tell me he's dirty. Tell me what he's into."

The judge stared into Randy's eyes. He hesitated then looked up behind Randy again. He knew. The judge knew about Tom and still he offered nothing. "If you had evidence a crime was about to be committed, maybe I could help you. If you don't feel your attorney can adequately defend you, select a new one. I'll grant you the time you need to get another lawyer immersed in the complexities of your case. Otherwise we have nothing to talk about, Mr. Black."

Chapter Forty-two

Tom saw Gordon salivating before he made it halfway across the lobby. Tom set his briefcase on the counter, clicked open the locks and found the four envelopes with the names of the lobby guards printed inside the windows.

"Always good to see you, boss," Gordon said.

"Especially on payday."

Gordon stuck three envelopes in the small drawer under the counter and held his own. He'd tear it open as soon as Tom disappeared. Gordon did well for someone who saw as little foot traffic as he did, but if he knew about the other envelopes Tom was delivering, he'd want in.

Gordon called the elevator and Tom made his way to the fourth floor.

Debbie put her call on hold when the elevator opened. She collected her paycheck and waited for Tom to disappear toward the back offices before picking up. You'd think she'd realize a high-end security firm would know its receptionist was on the phone thirty hours per week. The conversations got so intimate that the guys clipped the hot bits and shared them. Tom wondered if she was waiting for the ax to fall. She didn't do very much, but she showed up on time every day and that was enough.

Rob Kramer wasn't happy heading sales and installation design. He and Debbie were the only two employees not allowed inside the two foot thick concrete wall that separated the office space from the secure area. Debbie didn't care, but it drove Rob crazy. He wanted control to set prices, define new service offerings and streamline the operations center. He sparked to attention when Tom turned the corner. He was out of his chair before Tom entered his office.

"Hey, Tom. What did you think about my proposal?"

"Our prices are fine, Rob."

"Don't you want to be more than a niche player? We could take this company big time."

Visibility was the last thing Tom wanted for this company.

"I like our client profile. Who needs mommies who can't remember the alarm code? We'd have to triple the staff. The guys don't want to deal with that crap."

"At these prices all we've got are judges, cops and attorneys."

"People who take security seriously. Just like us."

Rob slapped his paycheck on the desk.

"Is this about money?"

It wasn't. Rob wanted an empire, a horde of minions who followed him around. Having twenty people work for him was much more prestigious than dealing with the same few contractors for every new client installation. The empire wasn't going to sprout. Sooner or later Rob would figure that out and head for the door. Fortunately, Rob had never been inside the concrete wall. His successor would never get inside either.

Back at reception, Tom pressed his thumb to the scanner and the metal-plated door rolled aside to let him pass. It sealed securely behind him.

"Delivering joy all around the firm I see." The voice came from an overhead speaker.

The short hall had only one other door, an elevator. Whitey opened the elevator doors from the control room and Tom stepped in.

"All the way down," Tom ordered without reaching for a button.

The car hummed down then the doors opened to a cavernous space.

Rapid fire spitting sounded in front of him.

Paintballs slapped everywhere. Ethan and Khan were taking cover behind the vans. They had Tripp pinned behind a pile of lumber. Always the underdog. Tripp craved action. At least they were on the ground. Sometimes they climbed the steel beams or mounted the platforms twenty feet up. If they stayed on the ground, there'd be no broken ankles. As usual Sid passed on gunplay. He sat alone on the padded bench, curling more with his right arm than Tom could budge with both.

Tom whistled and the game ceased.

"Glad to see you guys keeping busy."

Tripp came out from behind the lumber. "Practice makes perfect."

The paintballers gathered around and Tom handed out the envelopes. There were no pre-printed checks in these. They were fat with old twenties. Keeping these guys on month after month was hairy, but it was the only way. They spent most of their time hanging around waiting, but they brought in the cash. They knew they were being watched everywhere they went and after what happened to Scott Tomlin they were smart enough to keep quiet. Tom gave Ethan a nod and they broke away from the men counting by the van.

Tom opened his briefcase and held out a page from *The Standard Times*. "Seen this?"

Ethan hadn't.

"Find her and have a talk. Find out who you were shooting at. And make sure we don't read anything more about white vans."

Ethan flashed a look at the blue vans parked behind him as Tripp and Khan caught up. Tom left the three of them huddled around the article. Sid was just leaving the bench when Tom stepped in the elevator.

Up on the fourth floor, Tom pressed his thumb to another scanner and faced the camera. A second later, a heavy door rolled into the reinforced wall. Inside, the control room was filled with the hum of tiny fans and the glow from a dozen monitors. Whitey watched three conversations at once, two in the mosque and one in a police precinct a dozen blocks away. The imams and a police captain spoke simultaneously over the speakers and somehow Whitey extracted the important bits. The action was recorded, but Whitey rarely had to go back in time to catch something he'd missed. Tom marveled that Whitey listened, acknowledged his entry into the control room and still managed the alerts from various motion detectors. When someone entered one of the monitored buildings, he identified them and decided whether to follow their movements or not. Judge McKinnon, the mosque and two police precincts were shown in red on the board, priority for the techs to monitor. They received thousands of alerts, but even with all that was going on, there were only three alerts Whitey hadn't acknowledged.

"Anything interesting?"

Whitey indicated a red-turbaned imam on the screen. "This guy should have stayed in the desert. He hates everything about America."

"Is he stirring up trouble?"

"Nothing concrete yet. He's working them. Brainwashing the poor bastards. I think a few are on their way."

"Already?"

"Give him six months and he'll have bombs strapped on their backs."

"Let's hope he doesn't last that long. Get me some good clips. We're going to put these bastards out of business."

"You got it, boss."

Tom handed over four envelopes for the control room staff. They all made the same on paper, about four times what they could make anywhere else, much of it in twenties. Even as skilled as they were, they couldn't afford to work for any other security firm. The pay cut would be a killer.

Tom moved toward the door, but Whitey stopped him and played a clip.

"Is that who I think it is?"

"Yup."

"How'd he get in the judge's closet?"

"Roof maybe?"

"Shit. And we didn't see this coming?"

"Nothing's moved. We show him at home."

"Damn it! He's found the fucking bugs!" Tom yelled.

He'd been in and out of the judge's office before the men could get over there and get eyes on him. Fortunately, Judge McKinnon behaved himself. He gave Randy the standard answers about changing his attorney that he'd give any defendant. Randy left disappointed but quiet.

"Where is he now?"

Whitey didn't know.

"What are they doing playing paintball?"

Whitey blushed. It wasn't his job to run things. Tomlin had always kept the guys in line. Wasn't Ethan smart enough to pick up the slack? To Whitey's credit, he caught Randy on tape. Another operator might have missed it.

"Get them into the vans."

"They've been all over downtown."

"I don't give a shit. Burn some gas for God's sake. They're not going to find him in the freaking loading dock."

Whitey made the call. He wasn't so bad, he just needed to adjust.

The guys wouldn't find Randy Black. They had a hard time keeping track of him when he had a tracking device sewn into his sneaker.

"Check every camera we've got aimed at that courthouse. Tell me what he's driving. How he got in. Anything that'll help."

Whitey had already checked all the cameras and come up empty.

Tom asked for a recording of the judge letting Randy go. Whitey had already burned the CD. Tom patted his shoulder, took the CD and left for the vault.

Only two handprints worked the vault door. Tom waited for the system to recognize his and retract the titanium bolts. Automatic lights illuminated an array of velvet-lined shelves filled with plastic trays. Tom moved down to Judge McKinnon's and set the clear plastic case in the very front. Dozens of CDs filled the tray, a few marked with red labels. Those Tom had watched several times. The judge had excellent taste in young women.

He stacked the remaining cash on the way out. Tomlin was right about whacking the kid. Any job under a hundred grand wasn't worth the hassle to organize. Only a fistful of hundreds remained after changing out the week's payroll. It was nothing like the bags of cash they took from the Cottage Street Killers. Nothing like what they'd get for hitting the mosque.

Chapter Forty-three

Businesses and middle-class residents had fled the area around the new mosque years ago fearing crime and violence. Who better to strap on explosives, march into a crowd, and detonate themselves into the afterlife than the very people who drove them away? Randy watched the disenchanted rabble flow across Coggeshall to the mosque. The people straggling across the street had no jobs to hold them back, nothing in this world they were particularly tied to. Inflaming the downtrodden would prove easy. Promises of rapture would go far with these intellectual and moral midgets. Randy felt guilty for his harsh judgment. At the same time he wondered if this was happening in other slums across America.

The stream of visitors flowed with frightful consistency for such a new enterprise. How many converts would they make? How many militants?

Randy flipped open the monitor and surfed from camera to camera until he settled on the man wearing a crimson turban preaching to a small crowd gathered in the courtyard. With a few taps on the monitor, he could hear the imam. The anger building inside was palpable.

Capitalistic greed oppressed these poor people. The rich forced these poor impoverished souls out of jobs and into rundown tenements. Children were thrust into schools crammed with violence and drugs while the wealthy, white children learned in mahogany-paneled rooms and prepared for the Ivy League. The white-collared thieves passed their wealth from generation to generation while their media bombarded the masses with half-naked gyrating whores. They fed the frenzied orgy of hormones and drugs to oppress those who didn't belong. Helpless victims filled the crowd. High school dropouts, drug users, prostitutes, all their problems were caused by oppressive capitalists. Western culture was to blame. Islam was the cure.

Did any of these people know income inequality was dramatically worse where this imam had come from? Did they take any responsibility for their own wrecked lives? Did they have any idea how much harder life would be in another country? Randy wanted to go inside and tell them to heal their own broken families. He doubted they'd listen.

When the speech ended, several men from the crowd filtered back through the courtyard. Soon three categories of visitors emerged. Some were curious about Islam, some brought true interest, while others came solely to agitate the clerics. One man asked tentatively about women and men being separated. He liked what he was hearing, but didn't want to sacrifice the company of attractive women for this new religion.

The cleric explained that men and women are innately attracted to each other. If left unsupervised together, they will have sex. He said this with the certainty of an animal breeder and warned that Zina will lead to dire consequences now and in the afterlife. He warned the man to protect his sexual organs from anyone except his spouse. The man seemed flustered and ready to walk back to his old life when the cleric offered some encouragement. There was a reward in Paradise for every time a man had sex with his lawful wife and he could have up to four.

It sounded like a cult indoctrination. Individual responsibility and free will never entered the discussion. Allah controlled all. People were savage puppets with unseemly desires that needed to be reigned in.

Randy switched views to a heated discussion. The crimson-turbaned man had retreated to a back room after his sermon. He angrily barked that the Holocaust was a ploy by the Jews to control Western banking and media. The two young black men had their backs to the camera.

"What about gays?" one of the men asked.

"We try to help them."

"Help them?"

"Homosexuality is wrong. Homosexuals are disturbed by something in their life and they need help." He said nothing of modern stonings.

The two men shared a look.

"If Islam is a religion of peace, why do you get so violent when someone says something bad about Muhammad or Muslims? Cartoons don't really hurt anyone, do they? What's the harm if someone draws Muhammad holding a bomb?"

The camera wasn't focused tight enough to see the imam's expression, but the two men got up and backed away toward the door. The imam swung his fist in the air. If he'd had a sword, he may have beheaded the two agitators there in his office. In America, he'd be prosecuted for murder. Maybe he knew this. Maybe he left such unpleasantness to non-clerics.

"Blaspheming Infidels must be punished," he shouted and described brutal dismembering and burning of their bodies in horrifying detail.

The two agitators backed out through the passageway and seconds later, they hurried across the parking lot. Two men raised in one of the roughest neighborhoods imaginable, ran in fear from a religious leader. Their friends would laugh, but their friends hadn't heard the gruesome depiction of entrails being pulled from their bodies while they were still alive. The imam had the will to commit heinous crimes. He was unlike any religious man Randy had ever seen. This was their leader.

Why did the mayor give land to such a dangerous lunatic? Tom and his men would see that exchange or one like it and they'd burn the imam like they burned the kid in the tires. Would the world be better off? Surely the crimson-turbaned imam was an exception.

Here was the difference between killing and murder. Killing the imam would save lives. Randy couldn't know who was in danger, but this man was bent on hurting anyone who deterred him. If Tom was only interested in him, staying out of the way might be best for everyone, but Randy was supposed to be saving people. Did that include dangerous fanatics? His face reddened as he watched the monitor. If he was asked to decide the crimson-turbaned man's fate, he would be frozen by indecision. Maybe his heart hadn't healed or maybe he recognized evil when he saw it.

Chapter Forty-four

Randy backed the blue Chevy pickup he'd just rented to the edge of the parking lot, angled to take off in either direction. He slipped in the back door of the vestry and found Reverend Simmons in his office.

"Sit down, you look stressed."

"Confused."

Randy sat and explained what he'd seen and heard. "How can someone claim to be religious and then encourage his followers to kill people? I want to understand. I really do, but, what kind of a religion is that? Are these people savages?"

"They're not savages, far from it. They're very pious. They take their religious life very seriously. I wish my congregation was committed enough to pray five times a day. The vitriol comes when their culture collides with another. Islam dominates so much of their life that they're willing to do extreme things in its name."

"Doesn't that make them dangerous? Like the Nazis and the Kamikazes? People have to think for themselves. We can't let them go around killing anyone who insults Allah."

The reverend didn't respond to the comparison. He said nothing about the nature of Islam, an interesting point given the Muslim tendency to denounce Jews and pronounce them unfit to inhabit this world.

"Why do you think they do these things?" the reverend asked.

"That's why I'm here. I don't understand how someone can strap a bomb to himself and walk into a crowd."

"Do you think they get these ideas by reading the Qur'an?"

Randy had held the Qur'an and read a few dozen verses, but understanding it was beyond him. He didn't answer.

"What if I told you to go and kill everyone in that mosque?"

Absurd. Randy would never do it.

"You wouldn't. But now imagine I'd been telling you to do this since you were five years old. Hard to imagine, but it's a different story, isn't it?"

Randy was stunned.

Earlier in the day, he researched suicide bombing on the Internet. He watched a Palestinian children's television show and was disgusted by what he saw. Assud the rabbit, a man dressed up like the Easter Bunny, talked about eating Jews. The twelve year old hostess implored the audience to take back control of a mosque in Jerusalem. She told the children that they weren't terrorists no matter what anyone said. What tragedy could prompt the producers to brainwash their audience? No loving parent could allow their child to watch, but a steady stream of young callers phoned in their support. The reverend knew that halfway around the world five year olds were being prepared for martyrdom. Why hadn't someone stopped this?

The reverend waited a long minute for Randy to reflect and then said, "These people don't want conflict any more than you or I. The average Muslim wants to raise his family in peace. But remember, they believe deeply. When their religious leaders order them to become a martyr, some of them step up to the plate.

"There's another thing you need to understand. Many of these people you're afraid of were raised in an environment of violence and desperation. Extreme poverty and minimal education breed hateful ideas. Once hate takes root, prejudice is taught to the next generation of children. From then on, peace is difficult to relearn."

Randy tried to imagine the reverend asking him to harm someone.

"What does the Bible say about killing?" the reverend asked.

"Thou shalt not…"

"Is that all? Should we tolerate evil in our midst?"

Randy wasn't sure.

"What was the first thing the imam complained about?"

"Homosexuals walking around everywhere."

"Not surprising. The Bible is abundantly clear on homosexuality. Leviticus 18:22 tells us homosexuality is an abomination. Leviticus 20:13 tells us to kill those who commit homosexual acts."

Randy just stared.

"Paul in Romans Chapter One tells us that a society of men that lust after each other will be thrown into chaos and suffer wickedness, envy, murder, deceit. He goes on for three verses describing the afflictions of a society that *condones* such acts. Imagine someone who follows God's law—strictly follows God's law—arriving here and witnessing a gay rights parade. Isn't that wickedness? How could they not see Provincetown and San Francisco as the new Sodom and Gomorrah?"

The reverend and the imam held surprisingly similar beliefs.

"Our culture must be a horrific shock. Imagine how our movies and music affect the people from his home country."

"You don't really believe our society is wicked?" Randy asked.

"Not entirely. But wickedness is prevalent. Morality and decency are slowly trampled by groups seeking more rights. Every year we take small steps toward deviance. What's next after homosexuality? Pedophilia? Bestiality? Fifty years from now will men be marching sheep and donkeys down the street and proclaiming their right to love them?"

Civilization wouldn't stop advancing, but that was the reverend's point. Without guidance, we were advancing toward immoral chaos.

"So what? Do we start cutting the heads off homosexuals?"

"You see my point. Faith doesn't come with easy answers. If you read the Bible—the book *you* base your faith on—the imam has a point. Religion isn't an a la carte menu. Some things are just wrong. No matter how many marches and protests, no matter how many judges stand up and say otherwise, those things are wrong."

"We're not going to start killing homosexuals?"

"Now you understand how the imam feels."

"He thinks we're vile." Randy was beginning to agree.

"Think about it for a minute. Being a good Christian in this country is difficult. Romans tells us to obey our country's laws. But our government here in Massachusetts has decided to let homosexuals marry."

"So, do we stone them or go to their wedding?" Randy asked.

"Jesus wouldn't want us to stone them. Would he? He'd counsel them. We know what they're doing is unnatural. They know it at some level, too. The physiology is all wrong. They're hurt and they need help."

The imam had said exactly the same thing. Randy didn't agree with his methods, but he and the reverend had much common ground. Suddenly, wiring the mosque didn't seem like such a good idea.

The reverend sensed his struggle. "Whatever brought you here is bigger than ideology. Isn't it?"

"The imam is being watched. When they hear what he's saying, they're going to kill him."

"And you're going to get involved? Like the young man in the tires?"

"I am involved. They're going to kill him if I don't stop it."

Reverend Simmons reached a hand across the desk and patted Randy's. "We're back to what we talked about before. No man should have to decide who lives and who dies. That's God's province. Let's call the authorities."

Randy didn't know what to believe. Part of him wanted to race to the mosque and warn the imam, but he was sure to stir up trouble. His sermon was filled with anti-American, anti-Christian rhetoric. Even through the camera, Randy had seen the hate in his eyes. He knew that hate would be contagious. Tom Gold was no better.

The reverend offered to call the authorities anonymously.

A good idea, but Randy couldn't take that risk yet.

Chapter Forty-five

Randy hunched behind the rhododendrons as the BMW downshifted and swung in with a whine. The driver's eyes caught the expanse of lawn and then a wall of leafy maple branches lying across the drive. The car stuttered to a stop, the ABS preventing a skid. Tom jumped out, cursing his misfortune just ten feet from Randy. He never heard the footsteps in the grass. He was still cursing when the fist drilled in toward his kidney.

Tom dropped to his knees and Randy fell on top of him with a forearm across the back of his neck, driving him facedown into the manicured grass. Spitting turf, Tom threatened to kill him, still not knowing it was Randy holding him down. With his wrist bent up behind his back there wasn't much danger of Tom hurting anyone. Of course, Randy had limitations, too. He couldn't steal the BMW and he couldn't kill Tom, but kidnapping didn't make the Big Guy's top ten. There were no cameras focused out here in the driveway, so Tom's buddies wouldn't know that Randy planned to spend some quality time with his lawyer to figure out what he was pulling.

The Zip Ties worked so well that Randy bought his own. Tom didn't appreciate the irony of his men teaching Randy such a useful trick. He lay facedown cursing and threatening until Randy taped over his mouth. He squirmed indignantly, screaming muffled curses into the tape until he saw Randy walk around the garage for the truck.

He could have stolen one easily, but that wasn't allowed. He went through the paperwork and rented a four wheel drive Chevy for three days.

The rope was already tied to a sturdy upper branch. A quick knot around the tow hitch and the Chevy dragged the big maple out onto the lawn. The BMW rolled over a few broken branches and into the garage. Randy's gloved hands left no prints. He kept his head down and rushed out so he couldn't be identified if there were cameras in Tom's garage.

The hopelessness of the situation hit Tom when Randy loaded him in the back of the cab and belted him down on the bench seat. If he'd known how completely he was about to vanish, he would have struggled harder. No one could see him lying flat. Even if his men were watching their equipment, it looked like Tom was at home, just somewhere off camera.

None of the cars they passed on I-195 could see up into the back of the truck. Tom struggled for a while, but his muffled cries drew no attention over the highway noise. He tried again on the off-ramp, but Randy turned up the radio, crossed over the highway and turned off behind a hardware store.

The logging road followed an abandoned railroad bed into one of the biggest pieces of woods in the area. Five miles long and two miles wide, the forest was frequented by hunters, primarily in deer season. There were no jogging trails, no hikers, just miles of swamp with a steady drone of highway traffic in the distance. Randy circled west and put a huge section of knee-deep swamp between Tom and the highway. If he ever got loose, he'd be wandering in head high brush for hours. He might be smart enough to walk in a straight line to get out, but Randy was betting the lawyer had never been this far from pavement in his life.

Randy blindfolded Tom and marched him two hundred yards into the swamp. Their legs tangled in waist high brush with every step. Tom stumbled over every hummock in their path. Green briars stabbed through their pants and sliced across their legs as they pulled taut, drawing streaked red lines across their legs. They circled and looped back on themselves until the hum of the highway was the only clue to their whereabouts.

Randy ripped the tape off Tom's mouth, but left the blindfold.

"Ready to cooperate or is this going to get rough?"

"You're screwed, Randy. I've got you—"

Knuckles met Tom's cheekbone, knocking him back into a toothy-trunked white pine. The next punch landed a few inches below his ribs. Nothing vital, not yet.

Tom collapsed against the bark for support.

Randy reminded him that he was miles from anyone who could help. Tom didn't care that Randy was the only way out. He wasn't afraid of being lost, not yet, but he tensed when tape stretched from the roll. It circled the tree and caught him under the chin. Randy made four tight loops that pulled Tom's neck back hard against the bark. When his feet were similarly wrapped and Tom was helpless, Randy snipped the Zip Tie and stretched his hands around the tree. Blindfolded and taped to the tree, Tom still fought to keep his hands free. Randy elbowed him in the ribs. He deflated and hung there by the tape while Randy stretched his arms back. The fingers didn't reach. Zip Ties were no good in a chain, so Randy went back to the truck for the rope he'd used to tow the tree. Cinched tight and wrapped over with tape, it would keep Tom there until Randy came back to get him.

Tom's life belonged to Randy, but he showed no fear. Randy wondered if he expected help to arrive or if he was protecting something so important it was worth his life. How far would he have to push to get answers?

Randy made one last trip to the truck then removed the blindfold. Tom was entranced as Randy twisted the wire around the chicken's foot and left it tethered to a sapling ten feet away. He let Tom wonder what the chicken was for, but it was obvious he didn't get it.

"It's going to get dark soon," Randy said as he cut away Tom's suit pant below the knee. "Know what that chicken's going to do when it gets dark?"

Tom had no idea, but sight of the knife made him nervous.

"Poor thing's going to be petrified. Dozens of coyotes out here all packed up. It gets dark, that hen's going to be calling up a storm, nervous as Hell. The only thing she's going to be calling, though, is coyotes."

Tom's color washed away.

"They're going to find you in the process." Randy sliced a fine line in Tom's calf. A trickle of blood traced his skin down into his muddy silk socks. "Might not be tonight. Definitely by tomorrow night."

Randy walked behind the tree and tested the slack at Tom's wrist then added a few more layers of tape.

"Should hold you until then. Must hurt being eaten alive. Shame I can't stay, but they won't come in with me walking around."

"You're just getting yourself in deeper."

"So he speaks. Well, I don't know that I could get much deeper. You haven't done me any favors on the Marston case and then you went and killed Sebastian Leonard and set me up."

"If I disappear, that gun's going to find its way to the cops."

"I'm betting I've got a few days before anyone misses you. They won't do anything for a week. No one will be out here until October and by then your bones will be picked clean. I'll have found the gun and moved on."

"You'll never get the gun, not out of there."

"Where's that?"

Tom snarled back as if he could be menacing while strapped to a tree in the middle of a massive swamp. The chicken stopped and looked at him sideways as if to ask what he was thinking.

"One twenty-five Coggeshall? Can't be that secure."

Tom flinched. Didn't he know getting the address was just a matter of calling Verizon? Maybe his men didn't believe Randy could memorize the circuit number. Maybe they didn't tell him about the night in the bar because they were afraid to be punished.

Tom didn't look scary now.

Randy had two days to get inside and get the gun. Two days might be enough, but there was something else he needed to know.

"What about the mosque?"

Tom turned his eyes to the darkening swamp.

Randy asked once more then folded a length of rope over itself. He wound up and whipped it across Tom's exposed midsection. The heavy braids hit like a fist and Tom blew out a mist of spittle. The tape kept him rigid, stretched upright for another blow.

The rope slapped this time, tearing a hole in the white button-down.

"Why'd you need me?"

Randy threatened again with the rope.

"Anyone could have planted those cameras."

Tom delighted in his secret, a wry smile at the corners of his lips.

Randy lashed the rope across his face, bloodying them.

He wound up and swung the rope like a baseball bat, lashing into Tom five more times, tearing the white shirt open. When Tom didn't respond, Randy hunted around for something more devastating. They spotted the fallen oak at the same time.

"Someone had to take the fall for the hit," Tom blurted.

Tom didn't need Randy to wire the mosque. He only wanted pictures of him going in so he'd have a ready scapegoat. It was more than just another murder they had planned. Killing an imam in America would make front page news. The cops would face enormous pressure to make an arrest and they wouldn't question the evidence Tom handed them.

Randy tromped through the scrub and kicked a branch off the weathered oak. He marched back and crashed it into Tom's ribs. The crack reminded him of the moment in the kitchen with Charles Marston. He'd lost control and battered him unconscious. He wouldn't make the same mistake.

Tom slumped to his injured side, straining against the tape at his neck.

Randy threatened with the branch, "When?"

"Tomorrow night," Tom blurted.

It was already five o'clock. Court would be in recess. He couldn't go straight to the cops. They'd never believe him. He could make an anonymous call, but he had a better idea.

The cold wire bit into his fingers as he twisted it off the chicken's leg. The bird scampered a dozen yards away through the underbrush and regarded them from there. The hen was grateful for her freedom, but she wasn't keen on venturing further into the swamp alone. She'd probably be there with Tom when Randy returned.

Randy hesitated, wondering if Tom was in any real danger. The coyotes wouldn't really eat a man alive. Not this time of year.

Chapter Forty-six

"You were really reaching yesterday. Don't you think?"

Cassie stopped short of the glass doors and wheeled around to meet Walter's smug face.

"I know you'll do anything to protect him, but vigilantes? Come on?"

Her foot stuttered toward the door then stopped. His barbs were getting worse. If she didn't teach him his place before Bart retired one of them would have to go.

"Lots of people have been dying in the city this year don't you think?"

"Your boyfriend has a lot to do with that," Walter snapped.

"Look at who's dying. The Berkeley Bangers were nearly wiped out. The same thing happened to the Cottage Street Killers."

"They're always killing each other. No news there."

"What about Scott Tomlin. An ex-cop turns up dead at a gang hit a month after he's arrested for killing a drug dealer. How do you explain that? He's no gang banger."

"He went nuts. But he's one guy, just like your boy."

"Wake up, Walter. It's all connected."

Walter stepped closer. "Open your eyes, Cassie. He's a punk and if you keep protecting him it's going to bite you, hard." Walter turned his back and headed into the maze of cubicles.

Cassie pushed through the doors and out into the parking lot.

Walter was the one blinded by prejudice. Whatever happened, he'd blame Randy because he was a convenient target. And now that he knew about Cassie's relationship with Randy, he'd never stop.

A large man with a goatee slammed the door of his van and crossed the wide lane toward Cassie's car just as she hugged the back of the Corolla and clicked the remote. She was so angry with Walter that she didn't pay any attention until he was bearing down on her. She flashed her head around behind her. It was well after deadline and most of the reporters had gone home. Walter hadn't come out, but even if he had, the scrawny jerk wouldn't be any help.

The man continued briskly forward. He came between the cars rather than turn down the lane toward the building. She'd never seen him here. Big as he was, he'd be more at home in production than on the news floor.

Normally she would have stepped back and let him pass, but she felt uneasy with him steaming toward her. She pulled her door open in front of him and jumped behind the wheel. She tossed her bag on the passenger's seat and quickly grabbed the door handle.

The door wouldn't budge.

Thick fingers gripped the frame. The man stepped around the door and positioned himself in the arc of the door opening. He ducked down to face her, one hand on the door, the other against the frame. No way she could close it now.

She eyed the horn.

Her cell phone was in her bag.

Fingers tapped the glass on the other side.

She turned and met a dark face. Thick glasses and the large nose made this man less menacing than the behemoth standing beside her.

He motioned for her to unlock the door.

Cassie shook her head.

"We just want to ask you a few questions, Miss Corcoran."

Charming as he pretended to be, no way she'd open another door. She'd interviewed enough rape victims to know better. He knew her name and he knew how to find her. She couldn't stop combing the city for stories. That meant trolling through seedy neighborhoods and talking to hoodlums who didn't like what she printed. She knew she should blow the horn, but she didn't. She motioned for him to wait, inserted the key and turned the car on. The guy in the door was ready to grab her until she reached for the window button and opened the passenger's window a crack.

"I don't give interviews. Definitely not in my car."

Cassie reached in to start the engine.

"We want to talk about Juan Martinez," the man said through the window before she could turn the ignition.

She knew she should start the car and drive away, but she was intrigued. "What about him?"

"Were you there? Did you see the men who burned him?"

The van in the next row could have been one of the vans Randy saw, the men on either side of her, the ones who poured gasoline on Juan. Cassie reached in her bag and pulled out her phone. The man behind her rustled, a movement she couldn't see. Cassie flipped open her phone and snapped a picture of the man with glasses.

She dropped the phone on the seat and reached for the key.

Just as she grabbed it, she felt the steel barrel press in against the base of her neck. She froze. She'd seen exit wounds from shots fired at this range. He couldn't miss with the gun pressed against her. She had nowhere to run and no one she could call to for help. She heard footsteps as the man by the window cleared the line of fire.

She could hear the medical examiner chronicling the damage: esophagus ruptured, larynx dragged out through the exit wound, cervical vertebrae splintered, spinal cord severed, death instantaneous.

"I wouldn't do that," the hulking man spoke from beside her.

"The phone."

Cassie gingerly picked it up and handed it over without turning her head. The two men were standing together now. The phone dropped to the asphalt and a heel crushed it to silicone splinters and useless components.

The man with glasses spoke again, his voice sharper, more demanding than his partner. Cassie tried to recall his features without looking.

"… someone was there. Make this easy. Tell us who your source is and we'll let you go."

"Not a chance. What's to stop you from killing me?"

"Cassie," he said smoothly, "If we wanted you dead, we'd have done it already. How many times do you rush in here with a story at one or one thirty? How many days do you sit in the courtroom on County Street?"

Sebastian must have felt safe surrounded by Sheriff's men. Four officers surrounded him when he was shot. Cassie provided no such challenge.

"I can't tell you."

The gun barrel pressed harder.

The smaller man tapped his partner's shoulder. Suddenly they were in a hurry. "Listen," he said, "print another word and we'll roast you like Juan Martinez."

The gun pulled away.

"Tell your friend to forget what he saw."

They slammed the door and rushed to the van as fast as they could without breaking into a run. Cassie locked her doors and leaned on the horn, not letting up even as she saw the van turn and speed away. There was no plate on the front. The rear plate was obscured by the car in front of hers. When one of the guys from classifieds stepped up to her window her knees were shaking so badly her feet were literally bouncing off the floor mats and she couldn't stop them.

Chapter Forty-seven

The muddy Chevy four-wheel drive could only belong to a gardener in the judge's neighborhood of somber brick homes with neatly-trimmed shrubs and air sweetened with freshly mowed grass. Randy left the pickup on a woodsy street that dead ended behind the judge's property then trudged downhill into the brush. He emerged into the judge's backyard under the lingering July sun and slipped across into the head-high bushes that trimmed the house. A narrow trail along the bricks led to a thorny barberry at the corner of the garage. The mulch was soft underfoot, the bushes and lawn lush from frequent watering. He settled on the mulch, hoping the sprinklers wouldn't kick on and soak him while he waited.

When the judge's new Lexus arrived just before nine o'clock, Randy was still dry. The judge hoisted himself out and huffed as he labored across the garage and up the stairs into the house. He slapped the garage door button and yanked the door closed behind him.

Randy sprung around the corner, ducked under the lowering door, high-stepped over the infrared safety beam and settled against the bumper of the Lexus. He noticed the shiny black tires first then the pristine paintjob and realized the LS he was leaning against was a newer version of the car the kids trashed the day Randy visited the judge's office. Hopefully, there wouldn't be a similar distraction tonight.

The judge had an after work routine as most people do. He'd likely stop at the fridge and bathroom then change clothes before he settled to watch television or read. Randy gave him plenty of time to settle in then crept through the kitchen to the study where the judge labored over a thick legal brief. The judge focused so intently he didn't hear Randy cross the floor and stand beside him. He never raised his eyes until Randy tapped his meaty shoulder.

Startled, the judge snapped his head around. The shock rippled through his bulk.

"Relax, Judge. I came to talk."

The judge's eyes flitted around the room and settled back on Randy.

"How'd you get in here? My office and now this. I've got expensive security systems," he groaned more loudly than necessary.

"I'm not here to cause trouble. Actually, I'm here to prevent it."

The judge pushed back in his chair and gave Randy the sideways glance he couldn't give an incompetent defendant in his courtroom. Utter condescension passed between them as the judge's eyes told Randy he was missing the obvious. It wasn't the muddy shoes or the ripped cargos. The judge barely looked at them. Instead, he eyed Randy incredulously as if he'd just lost his case by barging into the judge's home.

Couldn't he believe a defense attorney could break the law? The big fees made him comfortable, but who knew the law and how to avoid getting snared by it better than a defense attorney? The money for Tom's big waterfront home wasn't coming from the homicide cases that trickled into his office. His legal work brought him opportunities to create chaos. Tom created plenty of chaos and he profited handsomely from it.

"This about your defense attorney again?"

"He's not who you think he is."

The judge smirked as if Randy couldn't possibly know Tom Gold better than he did.

"I'm telling you he's dirty. He's bugged my house and my car. His thugs killed that kid by the airport. I saw them. He's planning to kill someone else tomorrow."

"How am I supposed to believe that? Do you have any evidence? A tape recording? Videotape? Any tangible link to the killing?"

202

Randy had rushed here without thinking. A tortured out confession wouldn't be admissible, but it would have earned him some allies. Tom spoke clearly about his plan once Randy threatened him with the branch. A little forethought, a basic digital recorder and the judge would have been convinced to help already.

Randy considered what he did have.

"So, do you have one of these bugs?"

He didn't.

"I can prove they're watching everything inside the new mosque next to one ninety-five."

"How so?"

"I have a receiver. They gave it to me to test the cameras I put inside."

"You put cameras inside the mosque?"

"He forced me to."

"You shouldn't be telling me this without a lawyer."

"Judge, I need your help. People are going to die—tomorrow."

The judge relented like a parent letting a kid get into trouble to teach him a lesson. Randy cautiously watched him dial the phone.

"Officer Tomlin please. This is Judge McKinnon."

There was a long pause before the judge spoke again. Then he related the situation over the line. He explained that Randy didn't want to come into the precinct. Randy hadn't made the request, but felt better for it. Four undercover officers would be waiting to meet the blue Chevy pickup at 5:00 A.M. on Beetle Street, two blocks from the mosque. Together they'd meet the imams before morning prayers and explain the situation. Randy would produce the monitor Tom Gold had given him and the police would help him remove the bugs from his house and his cars.

Randy left for Cassie's, hoping she'd let him in after he'd disappeared without a word that morning. One more day and it would all be over.

Chapter Forty-eight

The Beetle Street block between Ashley Boulevard and Acushnet Avenue was tightly packed at 10:00 P.M. Cars filled every available space along the curb. The few driveways on the street were packed three and four cars deep. The cops had chosen the rendezvous well, just two blocks from the mosque. They'd be completely out of sight from anyone watching it. A few extra cars here in the morning wouldn't draw any attention.

Randy drove back across town knowing he'd return early. According to Tom, the bombing wouldn't happen until 5:00 P.M., but the police needed time to sketch out the suspects and stake out the grounds. Randy would be waiting when the cops arrived at 5:00 A.M.

Upstairs, Cassie's door whipped open and she gave him a look that said she was glad he was ok and at the same time demanded to know where he'd been. She eyed the tiny holes in his new shirt and glared at his mud-slicked pants. His feet were still squishing inside wet sneakers and socks. Her eyes flicked down the length of the hall, back to his muddy feet, then inside to the cream carpeting. She didn't want his dirty feet inside, but she was uneasy leaving the door open and hesitant to abandon it.

Frail, indecisive, this wasn't the Cassie he knew.

"You ok?" he asked.

"Fine." She looked disheveled, anxious. "Where have you been?"

"You wouldn't believe me if I told you."

Tom Gold was faring much poorer tied to a tree deep in the swamp. Maybe he'd pissed himself waiting for the coyotes. Randy chuckled. With his hands tied, that was the way Tom would eventually relieve himself.

Unaware what he was thinking, she didn't appreciate his good humor.

She left him there reluctantly, the door open a crack as she rushed to the bathroom. She stormed back, traded his clothes for a bath towel and made him strip off his pants, shoes and socks right there in the hall. She wasn't the least bit squeamish seeing him in his underwear, nor was she amorous. She wanted him inside and she was all efficiency. When he'd wiped the muck off his feet, she sent him to the shower. He returned fresh with new sweatpants and a matching black T-shirt. He dropped onto the couch that doubled as his bed and watched her fold her legs underneath herself on the chair. She fixated on his face and he followed her eyes to a crusty trail of dried blood where a briar had sliced into his cheek. She hugged a throw pillow to herself. Seeing the blood made her even more skittish.

Randy asked what was wrong. When she didn't answer, he walked around behind the chair, put a hand on each shoulder and began deeply kneading her trapezius muscle. She rocked gently in rhythm.

"My friends read your article?"

She tensed. "They weren't happy."

He wished she hadn't written it at all.

She told him about the men she saw, her cell phone and the threat.

"It'll be over tomorrow. I'm meeting the cops in the morning and we're going to stake out the mosque." He told her what Tom said and how the judge had helped. Tom couldn't warn his friends that they were headed for a sting. If she stayed out of sight tomorrow, her next meeting with Tom's men would be through prison bars.

She took it all in, silent, rocking in sync with his massage.

Her hair hung down over his hands, mingling with his fingers whenever he repositioned them. The long fine strands smelled of strawberries. Looking forward, he admired the curves of her shoulders. Cassie was the kind of woman he should have pursued from the beginning, before he wasted so many years chasing Charles Marston. It was a wonder she let him touch her at all. She was terrified and needed his protection. Otherwise, her good sense would evict him. When she had her story and Tom's men were corralled, she'd be done with the man who'd killed three people and said he talked to God. It sounded psychotic even knowing how it happened.

"Unbelievable what they did to that kid," she muttered.

He knew Cassie was picturing a similar fate for herself. Reading her article had been difficult even after being there. Juan Martinez was burned so badly they could only run a file photo of a previous arrest. They also ran a wide shot of the crime scene that showed the yellow tape and a wide scorched area that testified to Juan's suffering. Martinez was a small time drug dealer, most recently acquitted of rape and murder. Cassie left little doubt he was guilty, citing a lack of evidence for his acquittal. She hinted about a life of crime leading to a violent end. She didn't say it directly, but Cassie believed the kid got what he deserved. She wasn't alone.

Juan Martinez and the imams seemed to be polar opposites.

Plenty of people wanted Martinez dead. Competing gangs, anyone from the neighborhoods where he was dealing, mostly the father of the girl he raped. The guy that punched the kid was out of control. He could have been the father. But how was he connected to Tom?

Randy's fingers slowed while he thought and Cassie stirred.

"What happened to your new clothes?"

"I wanted Tom out of the way."

"You didn't hurt him?"

"No. But no one's finding him before tomorrow night."

Cassie reached a hand to her shoulder and placed it on top of his.

"Thanks for staying with me."

Randy wouldn't have been anywhere else.

Her muscles were loose from fifteen minutes of rubbing. The skin under her shirt had to be irritated by now. She didn't complain and he didn't slip his fingers beneath the fabric. He eased his strokes, lightly gliding over her, not losing contact for fear of breaking the connection and being relegated to the couch. He'd never worked this hard for a woman and failed to get her undressed, but Cassie was busy reckoning with her encounter that day. His fingers meandered up and massaged the cords of muscle at the base of her neck, then wandered back to her shoulders, venturing forward, but never dipping low enough to risk a rebuke.

"Does it make you feel special?" she asked dreamily.

"What?"

"Talking to God."

"Terrified."

She didn't respond.

After seeing Hell, Randy's whole world shrunk from a grand place where injustice couldn't be tolerated, to a stage where the lights never went down and one's worthiness was calculated over decades. The rewards of Paradise and the torment of Hell contrasted so starkly that even the most insufferable earthly tragedy became insignificant. Life was chaos beyond control, the outcome uncertain, earthly achievements inconsequential, only one's actions mattered. Cassie could never comprehend the magnificent glory above or the savage demons below without seeing them for herself.

"Once you've seen Heaven, you'll do anything to get there." He hesitated. "The alternative is unimaginably brutal." His words sounded hollow, but he couldn't explain further, not after what she'd been through.

Randy's hands glided over her in silence. The old Randy would have plied her with a few glasses of wine. He'd be kissing her neck and caressing her breasts. Tonight, he kept strictly to her shoulders and neck. She didn't resist. He didn't advance. She reclined into his hands until he bent over, kissed her cheek and excused himself to the bathroom.

He ran water into his sneakers until it stopped running black then scraped the remaining peat from inside with his fingers. The blow-dryer warmed them enough so they'd be dry in the morning. The whine deafened him to anything outside the tiny room, but he knew it would prompt Cassie to get up. When he stepped out into the living room he heard his pants spinning in the dryer.

Cassie had settled into her bedroom and closed the door.

Randy slipped beneath the blankets on the couch.

Chapter Forty-nine

Randy waited for the hands of his new watch to read 4:30 A.M. before he strapped it on. He padded across the apartment and found his pants dry, but the bottoms of his sneakers were still damp. He skipped breakfast and waited until he was in the hall to put the sneakers on. Cassie didn't stir.

The downtown area was dark and deserted, but when he arrived at the mosque a few minutes later, he was stunned to see a row of cars parked outside. The sun wouldn't rise for another forty minutes, but the imams and the dedicated Muslims they brought to America were already about. An attack now would target the fanatics and zealots without affecting the community members who'd been drawn in by their rhetoric.

Randy scanned the area as he rounded the corner. The vans were nowhere in sight. Nothing moved among the low weeds under the highway. He parked on Coggeshall and flipped open the monitor to check the views around the mosque. Most areas were empty. He found the group of men together. They kneeled facing the camera, arms stretched out before them, faces an inch from the ground. Morning prayers were said before sunrise while the rest of the neighborhood slept.

Convinced the attack wouldn't begin until 5:00 P.M., he followed Acushnet Avenue and circled the Beetle Street block. The two dark gray Crown Victorias parked halfway between Ashley Boulevard and Acushnet Avenue weren't fooling anyone. They were the newest vehicles on the street. They might as well have had the city seal on the side and lights on top.

Randy left the truck running, double-parked and climbed down. He stuck his head in the window of the first unmarked. The uniformed officers up front were both mid-forties. Neither of them looked like they could run him down on foot.

"Randy?" the driver asked.

When Randy nodded, the driver signaled toward the back seat and rolled up his window. As soon as the door closed the driver shifted into gear and pulled away. Randy sensed he'd made a mistake.

"We're going to huddle up down here a ways," the driver said.

Behind them, an officer from the other unmarked jumped out and took the wheel of the truck. The two vehicles fell in behind and the convoy zigzagged out to Coggeshall. They drove a few blocks toward Fairhaven then turned down an alley. Randy had been to this building twice. He reached for the door handle, but there wasn't one. The door locks didn't work from back there. He stiffened his elbow to smash the glass, but they had already reached their destination.

Randy's hope to retrieve the Winchester and free himself from Tom Gold disappeared when the car stopped at the garage door. Tom played it smart and sent Randy headlong into his trap. But how did he control the action from the swamp? Could he know Randy would go to the judge? Could he know who the judge would call? Randy still had leverage. If they wanted their boss back, they'd have to let Randy go. In the meantime, Randy would get a look inside.

The garage doors raised to reveal an open area with two vans parked inside and a white Mercedes tucked in the far corner. The whole building had been hollowed out. The loading area was three floors high, framed by steel beams with a concrete wall tying them together. There were no windows in the huge space and only a few doors. Tom had built his fortress inside the brick shell of the building. Randy remembered the guard out front. He was fit and ready, but it was possible that the door and the elevators he guarded didn't connect back here. The concrete wall looked like it sealed off this part of the building from the rest. No wonder Tom was confident. He spent serious money making this place impenetrable.

The Crown Vic stopped twenty feet short of the two vans that had been pursuing Randy for the last week. The three men aligned beside them looked like they'd been embarrassed by his disappearance. They looked as hungry for payback as Randy was for being dunked in the river.

The other Crown Vic and the pickup stopped just inside. The procession waited for the door to lower behind them. This was Randy's best chance to escape. Whatever happened from here on, it would happen somewhere deeper inside the building, in a cell, if Tom had thought to have one built. The thugs sensed Randy's restlessness. The seven men arrayed themselves in a semi-circle from bumper to bumper before they opened the car door. None of them had drawn a gun. Randy had the SIG on his hip, but he couldn't outgun seven men. He couldn't kill one of them if he wanted any hope of redemption. The only way out was up and over the cruiser, but even then he'd be trapped inside the cavernous room with seven armed men chasing him. The pickup might crash the door, but he'd never get it started.

Randy stepped out. The nearest officer spun him around and cuffed him.

In that instant, he wondered if the judge had really called the cops.

The uniforms looked legit. The radio in the cruiser was switched off. How did Tom control legitimate police officers from the swamp? The judge could be Tom's boss in all this or Tom's men could have intercepted his call. Randy struggled to understand what the cops and the judge had in common and how Tom controlled them.

Randy let himself be led to the back corner of the cavernous room as the group shifted around him. The power lifter and the cops hung back, while the guy with the demon tattoos and the bigger guy with the goatee each grabbed an elbow. With the rented truck hidden, no one would know what became of Randy until they sent him or his body out into the world.

The group reflected in the elevator doors broke apart when they rolled open. Goatee took the SIG then Tattoos unlocked the cuffs and tossed them to the cops. They thought they had him, but Randy's ticket out was standing in a briar patch strapped to a tree. Sooner or later, they'd make a deal to free their boss.

With all these guys in such close quarters, Randy had no choice but to ride up to the fourth floor and follow them down a stark white hall. Ethan, the man from the shooting range, joined them there. This had to be Tom's second in command. They walked to the last of three doors, each with a fingerprint scanner attached. No one stepped up to the scanner. Instead, Ethan faced the top of the doorframe and said, "Open up."

The door clicked and Tattoos shoved Randy into a windowless cinderblock room. The floor and ceiling were poured concrete. The only features in the room were two vents at the base of the rear wall. He'd never find the tiny camera, but he knew it was there. They watched everything.

"I want to see your boss," Randy said before they shut the door.

"No, you don't."

"Humor me."

"No one disturbs the boss before ten."

The door slammed closed.

Sooner or later, they'd start looking for Tom and then they'd be more agreeable. Until then, he could only wait and wonder about their boss. The renovations to the building had to run a million dollars at least. Doubtful the city knew what had been done in here. Keeping it secret and working from the inside out would have tripled the cost. Engineering this project was an impressive effort itself. Pouring the thick concrete walls inside an existing building without knocking it down showed genius and a generous budget. Randy met with Heather Lovely in this building. He never guessed that the offices facing Coggeshall Street were a façade that masked what really went on inside.

Tom was a defense attorney. A well paid man, but how did he fund something this grand? His security company couldn't be that profitable.

The bigger question was why.

When Randy gave up wondering he turned his attention to the vents. Both were wide enough to reach his arm through and the screws faced outward. A dime from his pocket was all he needed to remove the first cover. The man behind the camera was surely watching, but Randy couldn't help himself. He tried to look casual, facing away from the vent as he worked the dime behind his back.

In a dozen minutes and almost as many scrapes on his knuckle, the cover pulled off and he reached inside. There he discovered the concrete wall was two and a half feet thick. Further progress was blocked by a heavy grate welded in place. Even if he was thin enough to squeeze into the vent, he'd get no further. He poked his fingers through the grate and bent back the sheet metal duct to reveal a murky pocket in the wall that housed the electrical and climate systems that serviced the building. There would be a service door somewhere below. The grid of one inch steel rod wouldn't let him out, but that door down below might be a good way in. He spun himself around and tried kicking the metal bars free of the concrete. They didn't budge. Whoever took the time to weld these bars had anchored them well. No one was getting out of this room except through the door.

Why Tom needed a prison cell wasn't apparent, but the room was pristine. Randy might have been its first occupant. He took the time to replace the grate even though he was sure he'd been seen taking it off.

At 6:30 A.M., the door clicked open. In walked Tom Gold.

No one followed him in and no one backed him up.

He'd showered, changed and looked well rested save the red streak below his right eye. Getting through the briars in the dark had cost him something. But how'd he get free of the rope and the tape?

Tom waggled his cell phone in answer. "GPS," he said.

"Did you bring the chicken? I missed breakfast."

The situation suddenly turned dire. Randy's leverage was gone and he was locked inside a fortress, sent here by the one man he thought might be able to help him. Tom stood with the door swung wide. He wasn't worried about letting Randy into the hall. None of the doors opened without assistance. There was a control room here somewhere. As long as Tom had a man in there, Randy wasn't leaving the building.

Chapter Fifty

Cassie heard the door close as Randy slipped out of the apartment for the third morning in a row. The night before he'd come in covered in mud with a story about Tom Gold blowing up the mosque. He'd told her to stay inside all day. The guys in the parking lot the day before were for real, but for all his talk about Tom Gold's persecution, Randy Black had a lot of time he couldn't account for. Why was he sneaking out before sunrise? Her parents would say he was playing her, trying to keep her out of the way. As nice as he pretended to be, she needed to know more. The story about seeing God jived more with the manipulative liar she'd heard about than the saint Randy portrayed. Randy Black would make her career. She just wasn't sure where his story would lead or how it would end.

If Randy was meeting the cops like he said, she'd be safe tagging along.

Cassie stepped out onto the balcony. Tom Gold had an office on County Street and a house somewhere in Marion. The pickup headed for Route 18. The office was out. She strained to watch the blue truck in the distance. When it failed to turn onto I-195, she knew where he was going. Tom Gold wasn't going to attack the mosque, Randy was. She couldn't understand why. He already faced multiple murder charges. Adding more mayhem to his record guaranteed a prison term. Charlie Marston said he was extremely volatile but remained serene on the outside most of the time. Cassie was finally seeing the Randy Black she'd been warned about.

Distressed she'd been so wrong, Cassie dressed quickly, took the elevator down and jumped in her Corolla heading for the mosque. If she snapped a shot of him going in, she could call the cops and still get her exclusive. She accelerated north. She'd take the picture, but she was already wavering about the call when she reached Route 18.

There was an open spot on Coggeshall directly in front of the mosque. The truck was nowhere in sight, but he wouldn't be foolish enough to park so close. She was surprised to find so many cars in the parking lot so early. She snapped a few photos and watched for a figure climbing the fence.

Two minutes passed.

He couldn't be inside already. She was just a few minutes behind. Surely it took longer than that to break into such a new building. She waited. A single man shuffled down the sidewalk in a daze as if he were dragging himself home to shower before work. She wondered if she'd misjudged Randy or if he'd gone to meet the cops somewhere else. A little convoy pulled out of North Front Street in answer to her question. Two unmarked cars and the same blue pickup Randy rented a few days earlier.

Randy told the truth about meeting the cops, but they were going the wrong way. They were driving away from the mosque east on Coggeshall. They should be driving toward a precinct to plan their sting, not heading for Fairhaven. Cassie started the Corolla and followed.

When they slowed and turned down a narrow alley, Cassie took the preceding turn up Mitchell, got out and hurried between the buildings with her Nikon. If Randy was helping the cops, this would be a career photo. She captured the second unmarked driving into the back of a brick building. This wasn't an official building. Maybe it was rented by the city for clandestine meetings like this one. She'd been following cops for months and never knew this building existed.

The truck drove in. Randy wasn't behind the wheel. She'd blow up the photo later, but it looked like a uniformed officer. The door closed and the vehicles were gone. She hadn't seen him, but she knew Randy was inside.

The building looked like any other office building, but the back wall had almost no windows. The center section was interrupted only by the double-width overhead door that closed behind the truck. The far side of the building looked like any other with a few scattered lights on in the offices.

When she circled around front, she stopped facing the revolving door. She'd been escorted out of this building after following Randy here. Most of the companies advertised on the front of the building were a sham. The security company on the fourth floor could be a front for the cops. Heather Lovely, the psychologist she'd followed to the cemetery, worked on the sixth floor. Losing her whole family so young must have driven her to work in law enforcement. Cassie wondered if she was a profiler or even a psychic, but her gut told her it was something darker.

She suddenly wished she'd listened to Randy and stayed home.

She turned the corner and followed the alley to the rear of the building trying to convince herself not to worry. If the police used the building for undercover operations, that explained the lack of tenants. Cassie reminded herself that Heather Lovely was a regular in criminal courts and she could be trusted. And with the city footing the bill, it made sense for the building to remain empty to keep these meetings from being discovered.

She hesitated at the back corner where she'd started.

A better picture was in order, but could she really publish it?

The question was answered for her when a strong hand clamped down on her bicep while its counterpart ripped the camera from her hands. For the second time in as many days, the man with the goatee took a camera from Cassie. This time there was no horn to blow for help. The big guy's fingers crushed into her arm and he wasn't letting go.

Cassie screamed. Pounding his chest with her free hand had no effect. He clamped a meaty hand over her nose and mouth. She screamed louder, pounded harder and then he spoke, "You want air, shut the Hell up."

Cassie obliged. The big overhead door opened and spit out the unmarked cars as she caught her breath. He hauled Cassie inside past the blue truck and into an elevator in the corner. The last thing she saw before the doors closed was her Corolla rolling in next to the pickup.

Chapter Fifty-one

Randy seethed at Tom Gold's figure in the doorway. He didn't block the passage. Rather he stood aside, daring Randy to rush out into the hall. Randy stood firm against the cinderblocks, but his eyes remained focused on his goal. Tom's nonchalance confirmed Randy's fear that the entire floor was secure. The elevator was the only way out and access was controlled by someone safely sealed away out of sight. Randy was no freer in the hall than he was in the cell.

The elevator doors slid open somewhere behind Tom and a woman's voice complained, "Watch your hands or I'll have your badge."

For an instant Randy sensed an opportunity to escape, but then he saw two men prod Cassie down the hall toward him.

Tom enjoyed her spunk. He stepped back while his men wrestled Cassie through the doorway. When they finally pried her fingers off the door casing, he stepped up and said, "Seems your friend is a bit confused about what's going on here. Maybe you should fill her in."

Cassie flashed a panicked look at Randy then Tom.

Tom shook his head and slammed the door. "Badges? We don't need no stinkin' badges."

The men laughed in the hall.

Cassie was embarrassed and angry but unhurt.

"Did they come to your apartment?"

Cassie inspected the cinderblock walls, avoiding his eyes.

"You followed me! Don't you ever stop being a reporter?"

She stooped in front of the vent, her back to him.

"After what they did to you yesterday? What were you thinking? You know I would've given you the story."

Cassie worked at the screw with a fingernail.

"Been there. Done that."

Cassie turned and he motioned for her to stand up.

She watched his hands suspiciously as he reached for her waist and pulled her to him. She didn't expect romance especially since he hadn't tried anything the night before. She seemed to understand that wasn't his idea. She was scared and confused but draped her arms around his neck and let him whisper in her ear.

He told her they were being watched and her head drifted away toward the ceiling. He squeezed a handful of her behind and her head snapped back.

She cleared her throat angrily, but he didn't loosen his grip.

He whispered softly, his lips an inch from her ear.

He told her what he found behind the vent and that the police were involved, but not officially. They were inside a fortress hidden behind the brick façade of an eighty year old office building. The cars were hidden inside, so no one would find them. Their only hope of getting out was Tom Gold opening the door and letting them go.

She told him how she'd been caught and that no one had seen her being dragged inside. She understood not to say anything aloud and they settled together at the base of the wall, legs extended. She kept hold of his hand and he wondered whether she was continuing the charade to convince the men watching them or if he was beginning to wear down her defenses.

Chapter Fifty-two

Randy wished they hadn't been so cozy in the cell. If he left Cassie alone and went with Tom, they could take her away and use her to make him cooperate. Once he left he could only hope to find her safe when he came back, but he had no other way out, so he followed Tom out the door.

Tom marched him down the hallway and through a set of glass double doors that clicked open for them as they approached. Randy veered right toward the small bathroom. Tom allowed him inside unsupervised and he quickly understood why. All he found inside were four solid walls, a toilet and a sink. No vent. No shower. No towel rack to use as a club. Short of cracking a pipe and flooding the building, nothing here would aid their escape. In a fit of desperation he imagined that the unseen man who controlled the doors could also shut off the water.

Outside the bathroom, Randy paused in front of a massive stainless steel door. A handprint scanner aligned beside a twelve-inch, polished wheel. Concrete walls extended eight feet on either side of the door then turned to meet the outer wall. Randy guessed the door was installed and a bank-sized vault was poured around it. The concrete was vulnerable to someone with time and tools, but the noise would alert them to an intruder long before he broke through. Randy doubted anyone had ever broken into the vault, but standing there he knew he was only feet from the Winchester.

Tom led him into an elegantly furnished room with a long mahogany table. They sat across from each other at the near end leaving the head and eleven other seats vacant. Tom waited in silence, reverence almost, for something to happen. When Randy asked what he wanted to talk about, Tom just raised his hands. Randy worried that he'd been brought there so they could take Cassie away. But when the door clicked open and Heather Lovely strutted in decked in a white suit and matching pumps, he knew he'd misjudged Tom. She traced her fingernails from the base of Randy's neck down his spine then back up to his shoulder. She trailed away toward her seat with her fingernails outstretched as if they hated to leave his skin.

Heather boldly took her place at the head of the table. Tom greeted her with a deep nod and waited. Randy looked back and forth in awe as he saw Tom's submissiveness. Heather was in charge!

"You've been quite troublesome," she said. "Unresponsive. Hard to keep track of. You even made off with Tom here and introduced him to the outdoors. Inventive, genius maybe, but a distraction from our work, nonetheless."

"What sort of *work*?" Randy asked.

"Freedom is a wonderful thing, but unbridled freedom for the masses slowly degenerates into chaos."

Heather was primed for a long-winded speech.

Tom looked queasy. He didn't like what was coming, but wasn't allowed to argue. Randy didn't need to listen to know she was nuts. He'd known from the moment he saw the white-on-white office.

"Liberals are a plague on our society. They support anyone with a cause no matter how depraved. Activist judges allow homosexuals to marry. They turn habitual criminals free. They're destroying families. Destroying our country. Now, our fine mayor *gives* land to a bunch of Islamic fascists."

"The Muslims agree with you on homos and crime," Randy said.

"Don't kid yourself. They'll put the fags in their place, but don't forget where this cult came from."

Randy sat stunned. "Cult?"

"Muhammad didn't fit in with the Jews and the Christians, so he went and created his own violent, bloody religion. Most of it he stole from the Bible. The rest he made up to keep his people in line."

"These people continually study and pray."

"And what about you? You're an Infidel. Do you know what they have planned for you?" She glared at Randy from her chair, her flirtatious lust now turned angry. "Don't be fooled. It's conversion or death for Infidels. Maybe subjugation if you provide an important service, but don't be blinded by all this crap about prayer and piety. They're taught to convince you with words. If that fails they turn to economic influence. If that fails they resort to the sword. In the end, you'll serve Allah or perish."

Randy stared back, disbelieving, wondering what she wanted from him.

"There are a billion Muslims that want every Jew wiped off this Earth. Who's next when they're gone? Bet your sweet ass it's you and me."

"So you're going to start a war?"

"Start? These bastards are gouging us for oil then taking *our* money, *our damn money*, and brainwashing children to blow themselves up. How do you fight someone willing to turn himself into a bomb? Someone willing to do anything no matter how profane? Only death will stop these people from killing us. Only death."

Randy wanted to shout how insane she was, but if he did, he'd never leave the building. Was he here to stop a holy war? In that moment he was positive that this was his chance to save people. Whether they were God's people he wasn't sure. Maybe the reverend was right, *people were judged by the light they were given*. That one imam might be as psycho as Heather Lovely. He might take advantage of the poor sheep, who dragged themselves into the mosque looking for a way out of poverty. That one imam deserved what Heather was planning, but not the rest.

Why did our government give the imam a platform to preach hatred? Shouldn't the CIA be shooting hatemongers like him?

What a horrible thought from a man trying to save himself. He knew God could hear his struggle, but he also knew this man was no better than Heather Lovely. He deserved punishment. No doubt they'd meet it in the next life, but they both needed to be stopped now. Randy couldn't choose one over the other.

Heather ranted on. However big the problem might be, Heather and her men were no solution.

"The only way to stop them is to kill them all. There are a billion of them and five billion of the rest of us. You might not know it yet, but it's us against them. They breed like disgusting vermin and if the rest of the world doesn't get serious about this, we're going to be overrun."

She was suggesting global genocide.

Heather Lovely's fortress was impressive, but she couldn't be serious. Her population numbers might be right. Islam might be growing at a furious rate, but no matter the fire behind her words, her ideas were absurd.

Randy sat upright when he recalled Middle Eastern dictators saying the same thing about exterminating Israelis. They denied the Holocaust. They were possessed by their conflict with the Jewish people as much as Heather was possessed with attacking them.

A filament of truth burned in Heather's speech.

Religion shouldn't inspire violence.

World leaders shouldn't incite people to hate.

Randy considered the genocide in Darfur.

Should he be helping Heather? Ludicrous!

Heather could see she had him thinking. She stood up and leaned toward Randy, bracing herself with her arms on the table, allowing the neckline of her button-down to hang open.

"Imagine a woman getting raped by ten men."

As his eyes traced the lacy white bra, he realized the visual was a prop.

"Now imagine this is *punishment* for walking in public unescorted. Imagine the government investigating and then punishing the woman! The men are allowed to rut around like pigs, pressing their will upon anyone they can take advantage of. Only the force of another man can stop them."

Appalling, but such things happened in the Middle East. He'd read half a dozen similar stories himself.

"Imagine this happening to your daughter or your granddaughter in forty years. This is what's coming. It's our damn fault if we don't stop them."

"You don't believe that."

"You know I'm right. The war has begun. It's them against us, but we're not fighting. Not yet. The one remaining superpower is handcuffed by political correctness. They terrorize, extort and murder and then if anyone resists, they cry religious persecution. They're sensitive to it because that's their mindset—Muslims versus the Infidels. The liberals can't imagine such a thing. And no matter how blatant it gets, they can never call it by name. By the time we wake up, we'll all be speaking Arabic."

Many in the world hated Americans, but he guessed it was more an Arab than a Muslim phenomenon. He reminded himself that she was a crazed psychopath and wondered what the kid in the tires had to do with her battle against Islam.

She sunk back into her chair, theatrically crossed her long legs and smiled seductively at him. Talk of genocide turned her on.

"I want you on the team, Randy. Our surveillance has never failed before, but you walk in and out of places like a ghost. My men can't keep track of you. I know they got lucky this morning, tricking you into the back of a police cruiser."

"Charmed. But genocide isn't my thing."

An orangey-tanned young man appeared behind the glass and made his way into the room. Slight, young, neatly dressed, a bureaucrat, not hired muscle. He placed a folder in front of Heather and left. He turned right at the glass doors. Randy listened. He used the fortified door at the end of the hall, not the elevator. There was the entrance to Heather's control room. The young man was working on the other side of the wall. Randy didn't have to pull back the drywall to know there was a thick layer of concrete behind.

Heather delighted in the contents of the folder before dealing the first photo to Randy. He didn't recognize the couple in the picture or the two closeups that followed. Heather was almost to the door when she turned.

"Show those to your cellmate. If she knows what's good for her—and them—she'll keep today's events out of print."

"Give him a day to think it over," she said to Tom.

The door slammed and she was gone.

Randy kept his eyes on Tom and listened. The elevator hummed upward. Tom was listening, too. They waited. When he couldn't hear the elevator, he brought Randy to join Cassie in the cell.

Chapter Fifty-three

The imam got out of his car forty minutes before sunrise and walked across the parking area. He strayed from the viewfinder a couple of times, but mostly he stayed in the frame. The chain-link didn't seem to be a problem and there was enough light overhead to make out his walk and his crimson turban. His friends would know who it was. They'd be certain it was him when they tried to find him later and could not.

The frame panned ahead to the nose of the McLaren and a darkly dressed man calling to the imam and hustling to catch up. The imam sealed his fate by turning toward the familiar voice.

A van screened the camera for an instant as it raced toward the men.

Appearing onscreen again, it screeched to a stop between the imam and the mosque entrance, the tire noise too distant to be recorded. The belly of the van slid open. A hooded man hopped out and blocked any escape toward the camera. The driver blocked the path to the mosque and a third hooded man from the McLaren converged and tackled the imam hard on the asphalt.

For all his hate-filled rhetoric about Jihad, the imam was subdued like a kitten. He offered no resistance to the three as they wrestled him into the van and sped away.

The camera followed the van toward Coggeshall Street without hesitation as it passed the McLaren and the lanky man running toward it.

Chapter Fifty-four

Randy expected one of Tom's goons to slip in overnight and plant another tracking device. He didn't want the hassle of another extended shopping trip, so he kept a sliver awake, attuned to any movement in the small cell. He watched Cassie stare numbly at the photos with a bittersweet mixture of hope and sadness in his heart. Her life changed radically when she saw the photos. She'd started the day overwhelmed with curiosity. Even when she was caught, she felt no more fear than a protester arrested for disturbing the peace. The photos signaled an entirely different threat.

Randy had been in a similar situation years earlier. He was younger then, struck by curiosity that drew him into the processing room at night. Unfortunately, Randy only saw the threat to the winery when he caught Charles Marston tampering with the filtration system. He never imagined he could lose his parents in the process. The threat to Cassie's parents was clear. Maybe Randy could make up for his failure by helping her save them.

Not only were the pictures a clear warning, they were a boon to their relationship. She'd been caught, but she believed him now. Only her visibility as a journalist kept her alive. Otherwise, she would have been shot and dumped or roasted like Juan Martinez, the kid who died at the airport.

The lights dimmed, encouraging them to sleep.

Cassie lay against his chest and they faced each other from just inches apart. Sheltered by their own bodies, they whispered late into the night knowing their lips couldn't be read. Cassie fell asleep leaning against him and he enjoyed the intimacy, though he'd had different ideas for their first night sleeping together.

When Randy's eyes cracked open hours later he was alarmed at how deeply he'd slept. His tailbone and shoulder ached from pressing against the cold concrete where he'd wedged himself into the corner. The left side of his neck had been stretched taught so long he couldn't right his head without wincing. Fortunately, the room appeared unchanged since he'd dozed off.

The concrete walls blocked any indication of the hour, but Cassie's growing restlessness hinted that dawn was near. Tom would return soon looking for an answer. If they wanted to get out, there was only one answer to give. He'd agree to cooperate no matter what assignment Tom proposed.

Breaking out, even trying to break out would seal their fate and probably doom the couple in the photographs. Still, he thought about the peculiarities of the building. Their cell was on the fourth floor, directly above his truck in the loading area. The thick walls and heavy door ensured there'd be no escape. The hall that snaked around the outside of the floor seemed strange as well. The doors all opened toward the center of the building except for the glass doors by the boardroom. Tom's bravado up here signaled that the thick outer walls secured the entire floor. He'd seen the fingerprint scanners and even then, no door opened without authorization from the man in the control room. At least now Randy had an idea where that room was. If he could con his way inside and decipher the controls, he could seize the whole building.

Randy relished the thought of wrapping duct tape around Tom's hands again, holding a gun to his head and forcing the operator to let him in.

Footsteps shuffled outside the door.

Cassie sat upright shaking herself awake, expecting someone to burst in, but the footsteps continued down the hall. A door opened nearby. Shouts erupted outside and the door slammed closed.

There was more than one cell on this floor. Heather Lovely owned cops and judges. Why not have her own private prison?

Cassie glanced back and forth from the folder to the door. She pressed herself against Randy in a futile attempt to hide.

"It's going to be ok," he whispered and kneaded her shoulder.

She straightened whenever he pressed into the knotted muscle, but she didn't complain and she didn't push away. Heather Lovely's insanity was binding them together more strongly than anything Randy could have done. They huddled on the cold concrete floor another hour without breakfast. Tom Gold never returned. It was Heather who finally pushed the door open.

"You've had plenty of time to think it over. Ready to talk details?"

Randy gave a solemn nod and she bid him into the hall with a white-tipped fingernail. She closed the door and led him a few paces from the cell where Cassie couldn't overhear.

"Ethan will give you the equipment you need when you get downstairs. You have ten hours to get everything set. I don't care how you do it, but when Ethan ignites the charges tonight, I don't want anyone to recognize that building as a mosque. No minarets. No dome. No turbans. I don't want anyone to remember the audacity of this mayor and these zealots. Understand?"

"Ten hours? How can I—"

"Figure it out. The whole place blows during evening prayers or you're on tomorrow's five o'clock news."

"It's not enough time."

"Don't screw with me. Get your friend, get on the elevator and get out before I change my mind."

Heather turned and walked away. She shared Tom's self-assuredness in these halls. She never looked back, not even a glance as she turned the corner out of sight.

The cell door clicked open when he reached for it. Cassie was surprised to find him alone in the hall. She came out reluctantly and waited as he stepped over to the door next to theirs. There was no window and no sound coming from inside, but Randy was pretty sure another captive was being held there. He knew he was being watched and didn't want to jeopardize Heather's offer, so he didn't try communicating with the person locked inside.

The rest of the floor seemed empty. They followed the hall past the boardroom and the vault area behind the glass.

The elevator doors slid open as they approached and closed once they stepped in, reminding them that every step of their exit was monitored. The car descended to the loading area and the doors opened when it stopped.

Ethan, Goatee and Demon Tattoos were waiting just outside the door with friendlier attitudes than they'd had earlier. Ethan handed Randy the SIG. The magazine was empty. Trust, it seemed, only went so far. Randy inserted the magazine and holstered the gun. Next, Ethan unzipped a black canvas bag and showed Randy how to attach the detonators to the explosives and switch on the tiny receivers. He didn't say anything about hiding the blocks of explosives or how he was supposed to move around a crowd of Arabs without being noticed.

Whatever angst Ethan had earlier, there was no trace of it now. No one changed their feelings so quickly. Heather couldn't order him to like Randy, but he hoped Ethan would accept him as part of the team. Once Randy clicked on the first receiver, his life was in Ethan's hands. Ethan would be watching on the monitor and he could detonate any charge the instant it was activated, blowing Randy and all the other explosives in the process.

Randy tried to put it out of his mind. He noted the placement of the elevators and the contours of the rear wall. They had been somewhere directly overhead. The hallway wrapped itself around the space, leaving the cells and the control room clustered together in the middle. The odd design emphasized security over all else.

They led him to the Chevy, which had been turned to face the large doors. Randy started it and waited for Cassie to drive her Corolla out ahead of him. He imagined the truck exploding as they rushed back to Cassie's apartment.

Chapter Fifty-five

Khan parked the van a block and a half from Cassie's building and waited. Ethan brought the monitors to life and the tracking screens showed what Khan could see out the window: the Chevy and the Corolla were parked in front of the apartment. There wasn't time to wire Cassie's apartment after her article about Juan Martinez and the vans, so they couldn't tell what was going on inside, but there wasn't much mystery about what these two were about to do.

The girl would run to save her parents. She'd cowered in that room all night. She was no hero, just a nerdy writer trying to make a name for herself by cozying up to criminals. She liked Randy, but she loved her parents. She'd run to them and when she dared come back, if she dared come back, she wouldn't print a word about Heather Lovely or Tom Gold.

Randy was a tougher call. He had a choice to make. He could do what he was told or he could abandon his old identity and run. Khan figured he'd run. He'd been a prick since the day he left the hospital and there was no reason for him to stop now. Ethan had faith. He saw the same idealism in Randy and Tomlin. Randy wasn't smart enough to see he was being set up. He wanted the girl. He wanted his life back. Somehow he'd convince himself that Heather would clear the way. Dumb schmuck.

It took them twenty minutes to get ready; time enough to grab something to eat, change clothes and run back downstairs. He'd probably been calming her down for most of the time. The girl appeared first, blonde hair flowing with an overnight bag over her shoulder. She hopped in the

Corolla and drove off. They tracked her on the monitors rather than waste someone following her. Randy was the key. He was still inside, probably working on a scheme to shake them. Ethan tracked the Corolla west on I-195, then north on Route 140. She was bound for Boston, scared out of her mind by the photos. She wouldn't relax until she was standing with her parents. She wouldn't be submitting a story from Boston. The pictures guaranteed that. After being in that cell, she'd probably never talk to Randy Black again.

Randy came out a few minutes later wearing a trench coat and reflective sunglasses. Neither was required that hazy morning. He carried the black bag, so there was a chance he was following orders.

"He'll have to do better than that if he wants to lose us," Khan scoffed.

The Chevy lumbered away to the highway and turned west. Ethan called Sid and a minute later the McLaren rolled down the block and parked where the Chevy had been. Khan drove over and picked him up.

"What a ride," Sid said when he was back in the van.

The McLaren was impressive, but Ethan was focused on the blip headed west. At first he thought Khan had called it, forty miles west through Providence and on to I-95 south to New York. They'd be rid of him then, but Heather would be livid. He resisted calling her as they scrambled to catch up with the signal, finally spotting the truck in a Home Depot parking lot half an hour later. They parked the van in the far corner so he wouldn't pass them when he left. Khan called the action from the driver's window while Ethan and Sid waited in back.

Randy took his time inside. A half hour passed and Ethan was thinking he could have slipped out back when they finally saw the black trench coat amble across the lot with a few sections of copper pipe and a cart full of boxes.

"What's he doing with all those boxes?" Khan asked.

"Small green boxes?"

Khan grunted.

"Nails and screws," Ethan said.

"Sweet," Khan called. "Too bad we're going to blow his ass up."

Randy was taking this job seriously. Packed around explosives, the nails and screws would fly through the mosque and rip apart anyone inside. Too bad the useless clay they gave him wouldn't propel anything.

Sid snapped his fingers twice by Ethan's ear. He cranked the volume on the television that had been silently monitoring the local news. The van they were sitting in flashed across the screen. The imam appeared next, standing stunned in the middle of the parking lot as hooded men surrounded him. After he was hauled into the van the camera lingered on the McLaren as a thin man that looked very much like Randy Black raced toward it and sped away.

If Randy had seen his car on the news, he wouldn't have headed to the second Home Depot to go shopping, but he couldn't get the broadcast in a rented truck and he couldn't have known about the kidnapping or the video. He was smart to break up his purchases so he wouldn't raise suspicion, but precious time was running out. In two hours, the cops would identify the McLaren and it wouldn't take long to trace it back to Randy.

The announcer broke in as the video ended.

"A note was delivered to us here at the station along with this video. The kidnappers demand the immediate withdrawal of all Muslims from the United States. They warn that Islam is a threat to all Westerners, especially Americans, and they will systematically hunt down Muslims one by one and treat them the way American hostages have been treated in the Middle East.

"One doesn't have to think back far to recall images of American servicemen killed and burned in the streets of Iraq. We can only hope that such a thing couldn't happen here in America.

"This station is cooperating fully with law enforcement in this matter. We'll update this story for you as soon as new information is available."

Ethan sat back and watched the red dot on another screen.

They had the cops' attention now. The explosion would draw half the police and firemen in the city. Randy Black was headed for disaster. By the time he figured it out, he'd be in cuffs.

Even the most liberal judges didn't offer bail for terrorists.

Chapter Fifty-six

Huddled in a corner of the loading area, the makeshift room reeked of latex paint. The plush red couch and the photo of the new mosque in the background looked enough like the imam's apartment to convince the audience Heather needed to reach. She strolled around behind the camera and took a long look at the bearded man centered on the couch. His head wobbled with the first vodka he'd ever tasted. The Taser burns wouldn't show, but they'd readied him to say what was necessary.

"Give him another shot," Heather ordered.

Tripp veered in front of the camera with a shot glass in one hand and a Taser playing menacingly in the other. He enjoyed his work a bit too much, as much as he'd enjoyed torturing frogs with a magnifying glass as a boy. After fifteen minutes with Tripp, the imam was as compliant as a schoolgirl. Tripp would have been perfect for the job if he didn't remind her so much of her brother. He had delighted in torture, too, but he chose his victims poorly. Not knowing when to stop had been his undoing. If Tripp showed he couldn't be trusted, he'd meet a similar, fiery fate.

The imam gulped down the shot without hesitation. He couldn't resist repeated shocks. He, too, saw the evil in Tripp's eyes. The shocks were just the beginning. He knew Tripp longed to get more personal.

Whitey zoomed in and cued him.

The imam faced the camera and apologized to the mayor and the people of New Bedford for what he had done. Converts had been persuaded to learn bomb making. Donations had been siphoned off and shipped to overseas terrorist groups. He spoke as if his entire goal in coming to America was to inspire new recruits to rise up against their government and cause mass hysteria. He hated America, but anyone in contact with his fledging organization knew the claims were ridiculous. Newcomers had ventured inside the mosque, but few converts had been made in the short time they'd been here. Not a single fanatic could be attributed to his work here, not that he hadn't tried. Still, the words would persuade viewers who digested their news with the same discrimination they used to select a microwavable dinner.

He spoke to the camera without a hint of remorse.

When he finished, Heather signaled Whitey to change the tape.

Tripp knew what was coming next. He rushed to the couch and kept the imam still by holding the Taser to his neck. Heather fondled the Glock she'd stuck in his mouth earlier. The doors were sealed. He wasn't going anywhere and he knew it.

Tripp punched two holes in the couch and pulled the imam's hands through behind him. His feet were already chained together, the shackles hidden by his long robe. When the wobbly imam's hands were secured behind him, Heather strutted in with her spike-heeled boots and kneeled between his legs.

"We're going to make sure you go to Hell. When we're done there will be no doubt. Relax and enjoy yourself." Heather signaled behind him. "These girls aren't virgins, but they're as close as you're going to get."

She rubbed herself against him, licking the fringes of his face all the way up and around his right eye then leaned back and circled her own lips with her tongue. His eyes widened as the most brazen woman he'd ever seen strutted back to join Tripp by the camera. She waited for two girls in black veils and sheer pants and tops to snuggle in next to him on the couch. She signaled Tripp to start the camera as soon as the girls hid the position of his bound hands. Whitey's hands reached out from behind the girls and massaged expertly augmented breasts. The tattoos disqualified Tripp from the role and he began fuming the moment Whitey's hands appeared.

Inebriated and confused, the imam watched as the girls explored his body with their hands. He'd been with women before and his reaction to their probing hands was undeniable. Tripp focused the camera in tight on the results of their exploration and captured the proof on film. Drunkenness consumed his shock and dulled his reaction so much that an observer would believe the renegade hands rubbing the girls were under his control. His reaction was natural. Short of running away, which was impossible, what man could resist the unabashed advances of two virtually naked women? Heather didn't know one.

He couldn't be very bright. All he had to do was protest. They could edit the tape of course, but it wouldn't have taken much to ruin the footage. Even a minimal protest would have delayed the release while Whitey edited. Maybe he didn't want to risk another round with the Taser. Tripp looked pissed standing behind the camera. He'd be glad to release his frustration on the cleric.

Now Heather had options.

She could release this tape to Al Jazeera and shatter the imam's hopes of ministering to the Believers or she could release the earlier tape and strike fear into every mosque across the country. Ideally, she'd bury his desecrated body face down in a garbage dump, beheaded and destined to burn in the afterlife. When they found his body, he'd be a prime example to any of his countrymen that dared pervert this great nation. That's the tape she should deliver to Al Jazeera. Too bad she couldn't be there when the body was found. Whichever way it played out, Heather would collect her fee as soon as the first tape was delivered and the bombs detonated.

Randy Black taking the fall would be an added bonus.

Chapter Fifty-seven

The Corolla pulled off I-93 and rolled to a stop underneath one of the last remnants of the raised expressway. Chris pulled the Crown Vic alongside and jogged around front toward the Corolla's driver's seat. Cassie's friend ripped off the blonde wig and gave a wide berth as he headed for the Vic. Surprise registered on his face as he backed away. Someone watching might think it was a carjacking until they saw the trade. As large as he was, educated as he was, Chris had plenty of career options, but he chose to give back to the projects where he'd been raised. He'd seen the violence, the drugs, the hopelessness and he wanted to be an example—a difference maker. Cassie's friend wasn't a redneck, but he wasn't expecting to meet a detective who was so young and so dark.

He didn't hesitate long. He jumped in the Vic and tore off south.

The driver's seat in the Corolla was already all the way back. Chris reclined the seat to squeeze in and still his head touched the roof. His shoulders pressed between the door and the passenger's seat. A few miles into Dorchester, he hauled himself out and admired the single family house just a few blocks from the beach.

He peeked under the bumper, curious about the tracking device Cassie said would be hidden somewhere on the car. Once the folks were safely stashed, he'd be back to check it out.

The Corcorans were glad to see a familiar face on the landing after their panicked call from Cassie. They trusted their daughter. Their bags were packed and they were ready for a few days on Cape Cod.

Chapter Fifty-eight

Randy ditched the Crown Vic just before noon and dodged through the doors of a pizza shop with a halal sign glowing in the front window. Ten minutes later he recognized two men with thick black beards and long black robes. He picked at a slice of pizza while they ordered and watched as they waited four long minutes at the counter for their lunch.

When they sat at a table by the door, Randy feigned an exit then dropped into the nearest chair blocking one of the men into a corner.

"Don't be alarmed. I'm here to help you."

The man opposite pushed back his chair ready to rush for the door and leave his lunch companion trapped against the plate glass window. Randy raised the SIG and motioned him to sit. Faced with the muzzle, he couldn't know the gun was empty. The other diners were attracted by the sudden movement, but returned to their lunches when he sat back down.

Twenty minutes later, three bearded men walked through the front doors of the mosque. Two headed to an alcove near the janitor's closet that hadn't been wired by Heather's crew. There Randy received a trickle of visitors who then left and mulled around the various areas of the mosque in search of the devices that were already planted. To the cameras these men appeared to be wandering and meditating a truer path to Allah. Each was assigned an area of the mosque. All paced back and forth over their assigned area with surprising calm and diligence.

The men found nine blocks of explosives. Most ringed the courtyard. A few others had been laid to destroy the minarets and the dome. Heather had told him too much. She hadn't meant for him to blow anything, but her ranting told him exactly where to find the live charges.

Randy risked his face before the cameras again and ducked into the communications closet at the back of the building. They'd used the same forwarder as in his house, a small black box with a black antenna and a connection to a telephone circuit. He yanked the phone cord and sprinted. When the receiving end went dead, anyone watching would know something was wrong. He'd have five minutes before they figured out what was happening. He prayed they were still following Cassie. If the men were at the building on Coggeshall, they could be here in two minutes.

Randy raced out into the courtyard. His haste alarmed the Faithful gathered there and they instinctively turned for the exits. If they made it outside and Heather's men were watching, they'd have detonated the bombs. It took a great deal of skill from the remaining imams, but they kept every last man inside the building.

The men calmed and began pointing to the devices Randy sought.

The first was camouflaged with a phony black speaker hung high on an inside wall beneath the dome. The case was packed with short screws and nails that would become shrapnel at detonation.

The communications closet housed the only ladder in the building. Running hard forty feet out of the courtyard and then down the long hall, precious seconds were ticking away. The alarm was raised by now. The man in Heather's nerve center was clicking on his systems trying to revive his video feed. Doubtful he was close enough to detonate the charges, but he and his comrades could get within range in minutes.

Randy prayed the only transmitter was with the men following Cassie.

Fairhaven Home Depot was ten minutes away.

The curious men clogged the opening from the hall into the courtyard and Randy came to a stop with the ladder, cursing them to move. Finally he opened a sturdy A under the speaker and climbed up. The whole unit lifted off and the detonator slid out of the explosive. He clicked the detonator off, carried the whole contraption down and separated explosive and detonator into separate bags. The men standing back in the center of the courtyard watched nervously, calmed somewhat by his comfort with the process, but they were agitated enough to bolt at the first sign of trouble. Randy wondered as he watched if he'd just taken the first step to end gambling, alcohol and unveiled female flesh in America.

He hoped not.

Another man stood nearby pointing at a spot along the wall. Randy rushed over with his ladder and climbed up. This cover was screwed down. He turned in a flash of panic toward one of his escorts and gestured for a screwdriver. The man understood, shouted something in Arabic and two men raced off down the hall Randy had traveled to find the ladder.

This bomb was just two feet from Randy's head.

Racing footsteps echoed down the hall and back.

Anyone watching would understand what was happening. They'd probably never seen anyone running here before. They didn't expect Randy to be inside yet, but all doubt would be removed once they saw the figure on the ladder defusing their explosives. Randy prayed that the building on Coggeshall Street was out of range of the tiny wireless transmitters.

A dark hand raised the screwdriver and Randy went back to work. The screws were driven in hard. The first and second came out reluctantly. His forearm cramped as he cranked against the hard plastic handle. Three. Four. The cover pulled away. This speaker was packed with four clay blocks. High in the corner, this one was designed to drop the dome. Easing down on the ground, he didn't dare breathe. He tentatively slid the detonator out. With only Ethan's quick demonstration to work from, he counted himself lucky to have separated the components without killing everyone in the building. He separated the two bags further, hesitant now to even lift the accumulating mass of grayish clay.

Two men hauled the ladder away and by the time Randy had hold of the bags, the ladder was in place under the next bomb. This one was lower, concealed behind a picture of an ornate mosque with foreboding sheer walls that could only have been financed in an oil-rich kingdom. A brick had been removed, its place filled with explosives, another attempt to drop the dome down onto those gathered in and around the courtyard.

Chapter Fifty-nine

The padded envelope wound its way from security in the lobby to the reception area then quickly made its way up to the news desk, thanks to the bold red lettering. Julie Kingston ripped open the biggest story of her short career interning at the news desk.

The letter called on law enforcement to converge on the mosque and arrest everyone associated with the religious teachings there. The author didn't admit to being involved in the kidnapping, but Julie had seen the earlier letter and CD. The packaging was identical.

Julie fumbled the CD into her computer and played it as fast as she could. When the movie finished, she jumped up to find the news director with the disc stuck on her index finger.

He nearly jumped out of his chair when he heard what the bearded man said. He dialed Homeland Security, said there wasn't a specific threat, and then the conversation calmed until he hung up the phone.

The director screamed and a reporter stuck his head into the office.

He didn't bother to play the video again.

"Get down to Coggeshall Street and get me a live feed from the mosque."

The reporter balked. "What's the angle?"

"Get down there and get me footage of anyone with a turban."

The reporter still didn't move. "I'm not here to showcase real estate. What am I supposed to say?"

The director pointed to his screen. "I've got footage of one of the imams admitting he was recruiting terrorists. We'll run it and cut to you to tell us nothing's happening out there. I'll feed the video to you in the truck if you need to see it. Just get down there."

Suddenly glad to be on the story, the reporter hustled out.

All over the city, media outlets were receiving the same package from the nondescript courier. By noon, Coggeshall Street would be awash in cameras and journalists.

Chapter Sixty

Whitey placed his thumb on the scanner, keyed in the code and slipped into the control room. Why he needed to key in the security code after scanning in, he couldn't understand. At least he had a private bathroom inside and almost never needed to leave during his shift. Working the camera for Heather had been strange. He still couldn't believe she paid him to feel up two hot chicks at the same time. Tomlin was right, Heather and Tripp were nuts.

Whitey was glad to be back directing the cameras planted all over the city. The guys practically fought over the night shifts when the customers thought they were alone in the privacy of their homes. Whitey missed some of the good stuff coordinating things from the day shift, but the other guys left him dozens of interesting recordings. He liked sleeping at night anyway.

After being gone over an hour, he did a perimeter scan and found two cameras in the building with movement. Tripp was lifting the girls into the van. They acted like pros for the camera, definitely high-end, probably fifteen hundred each. Fifteen hundred to handle a guy with no interest in sex. Whitey had never made that much in two hours, but lots of people were going to see that video. They didn't care. They were so high they wouldn't remember where the building was or what they did here. They were too hot for crackheads. Whitey assumed Tripp had slipped them something. Otherwise, they wouldn't have been so wasted in the afternoon. Tripp climbed into the back of the van, blindfolded them and started making up for the job he lost to Whitey by groping them in the cargo bed. The girls were oblivious to Tripp's hands and he took his time before climbing up front. Whitey opened the overhead door and closed it when the van was clear. He wondered what Tripp was planning to do with the girls.

Heather's voice came over the speakers. "Open up, damn it. Do I pay you to sleep up there?"

He couldn't respond and she knew it. He released the door. That was the only response she wanted anyway. Inside, the poor imam wobbled. He'd never had booze before and today he'd had enough to make Whitey puke. As much as he hated Americans, especially aggressive women like Heather, he was too drunk to be a threat. Whitey kept the monitor up even though he had over a hundred alerts to check. Tomlin had warned him to never lose sight of the boss when she was downstairs.

Heather swiped in front of the imam with a machete. Whitey thought he knew everything that came inside the building, but he hadn't seen the machete before. The blade sobered the poor guy up. His fellow Believers had been caught on tape many times hacking the heads off some poor slob from a tired European country. It was ironic for an American woman to turn the tables. Of course she wouldn't kill him. Heather wasn't one to forgo a payday. She couldn't finish him without a good camera running. The guy couldn't know. He huddled in the corner, paralyzed by fear.

Whitey wondered if this guy had ever watched his friends hack someone's head off. Maybe he'd held the camera. Maybe he'd used a machete himself. Positions were reversed now and the mighty leader shriveled into a whimpering sap. Whitey imagined being grabbed in some dusty wasteland and held with a blade to his throat. The imam believed he was about to die. He looked up and sputtered something about Allah.

Heather backed off when he did. She knew what she was doing. She'd pushed him until he was ready to die. As quickly as she stormed in, she signaled Whitey to open the door. She was into the elevator and back to the sixth floor in less than a minute, taking the machete with her and leaving the imam trembling alone, wondering what would happen when someone returned.

With Heather and Tripp gone, Whitey returned to his normal procedure, checking new alerts one by one. The screen was full of movements in dozens of buildings, typical daytime stuff that had been going on since he left. With luck he'd be caught up in fifteen minutes. He selected a screen full of minor alarms and was about to delete them when he noticed an alert in red text that stood out from the others. The link to the mosque was down.

Could it have blown while he was downstairs?

He called Ethan in the van.

"Where are you?"

"Coggeshall."

"You still got the Chevy?"

"Yeah, it just pulled up to a stop."

"Did you pass the mosque?"

"Ten seconds ago. We're swinging around."

"Everything ok?"

"Fine. A few reporters outside. Not enough so he'll have trouble getting in. What's the problem? We're just getting into position."

"Probably nothing. We lost the feed about fifteen minutes ago."

"It's not our boy. We've been following him for two hours. He thinks he's going to surprise our friends inside. Wait till he steps under the dome and sees what we have waiting for him."

Ethan guaranteed him everything was under control. They were in position. Randy would run in and they'd blow the place sky high. If the bomb didn't get him, one of the news cameras would catch him coming out. The footage would be everywhere. Someone would recognize him.

Whitey asked them to bring up the wireless monitor and check out what was going on inside. Ethan said he'd do it when they had eyes on Randy.

Whitey wondered if he should call Heather and Tom. They'd storm in and watch every keystroke, but that was better than disappointing them and winding up face down on the sidewalk like Scott Tomlin. The link dropping today was too much of a coincidence. Randy had found the mini-router at his house. He could find this one, too. Ethan was sure he wasn't inside yet, but that didn't settle Whitey. The moment he looked at the phone, it pulsed.

Chapter Sixty-one

The scrawny bearded creep downstairs couldn't have picked a better spot to begin his invasion of America. Heather's living room overlooked Coggeshall and two sides of the mosque five blocks away. They wouldn't notice her peering through the glass, but with her telescope she could see the color of their eyes. The video she sent had the media slobbering for the story. Two news vans had arrived and the cameramen raced to be the first with a live feed from the sidewalk. Their video would lend credibility to the story Heather created and this time she wouldn't have to courier it all over the city. The explosion would feed straight to the five o'clock news.

A blue pickup drove right in front of the building, down Coggeshall and made a right on Acushnet Avenue, just before the mosque. A beige van followed but stayed straight on Coggeshall, passed the mosque and spun around. It parked facing the mosque from half a block away. Ethan, Khan and Sid were in position. It was time. They'd let him get inside. They'd give him two minutes to start hiding his bombs. As soon as he stood under the dome, they'd blow the place and drop it on top of him.

What an idiot to try in broad daylight.

Heather zoomed her telescope in on the building and stood back. It'd take him some time to get inside. She watched with her naked eye for someone moving across the parking lot. The only way in with so many people watching was through the front doors. How he expected to get inside with the heavy bag she didn't know, but she was ready to shift to the telescope and see him up close when he appeared. She'd have to stand back to get the full effect of the explosion. She stepped to the corner of the window to try out the angle. Perfect. She could see the entire building.

A full minute passed.

She couldn't believe what happened next.

Dozens of men streamed out the double doors and raced away from the mosque. A thick line of bodies ran past the cars toward the street. Some filtered through the cars and scurried out to the sides, but most ran straight for Coggeshall Street as fast as they could.

She hit two buttons on her phone: the speaker and the speed dial for the control center. She shifted back to the telescope and angled it downward to take in the crowd. Her eyes followed the flow of bobbing white turbans as she stood helpless.

"What the Hell's going on?" she demanded.

Randy hadn't come across the parking lot. No one had crossed Coggeshall since the truck pulled up. If he wasn't inside, who started the panic?

Whitey hesitated too long.

"Aren't you watching?"

"No. The cameras have been out for —"

"Get Ethan! Blow it! Blow it now!"

Men scampered farther and farther from the building. The likelihood of hitting them now seemed slim, but maybe some doubters were left inside. They had to demolish the place before the bomb squad arrived. The explosives would give the lefties another chance to attack the military. Lefties hated weapons. Disarmament, disarmament. If they had their way we'd be facing these terrorist bastards with sticks and rocks. Stupid bastards. Their pressure would demand answers and high grade explosives had a way of leaving a trail. If they led here, Heather was out of business.

The crowd reached the sidewalk.

The men must have been screaming in terror.

A reporter backed away, terrified by forty screaming Muslims racing out of the mosque toward him and his colleagues on the sidewalk. Good for him. Let him know what real terror is. Maybe he'd stop cuddling up to these bearded assassins. He printed stories of diversity and integration, but in his heart he knew these men were dangerous.

The reporter skirted a tall communications van with satellite links on the roof, his eyes focused on the approaching mob as he retreated. When he stepped clear of the van, his body twisted grotesquely and bounced in the air. Heather saw the silver sedan coming for him as he backed into the street. The reporter wasn't so lucky.

The car bucked to a stop. The body sprawled out before it.

The mob stormed past the body wriggling on the asphalt.

Finally, the ground shook. Not as spectacularly as she'd expected. She swung the telescope up to the dome and witnessed the disappointing result. One of the minarets teetered and toppled onto the roof. The structure was so small that it wasn't even heavy enough to cave the roof in. The dome didn't fall. The rest of the building stood firm.

Zero body count.

A dismal failure.

Heather wondered if she'd have to return part of the fee.

"Shut it down," he'd said. "Terrify them."

She still had the imam.

The building would close for repairs. She could hack him to bits and scatter his fingers and toes inside. They were queasy about such things. Dead Muslims didn't want Infidels touching them. Grabbing him had been easier than planting the bombs. If they had to do it again four times over, it would be well worth the fee. The mosque wouldn't stand. Not here. Not in her city. She'd take them down with her own hands if she had to. She knew the one thing they feared was the afterlife. She'd pay whores to tear their bodies to pieces then she'd bury them in a toxic waste dump.

Suddenly a more terrifying thought dawned: where was Randy Black?

He knew where to find her. If he convinced the cops to search the building, they'd find the CDs, the money and the Winchester. The men she worked so hard to get control of would be run out of office and straight to prison. Her power would be neutralized and she'd have to start over again. She couldn't let Randy live long enough to talk.

If he never went inside the mosque, the cameras wouldn't catch him.

She could put the cops on him, but that would take time.

And what happened to the bombs?

Whitey was still on the line.

"Get me Ethan."

A second later he spoke on the same line. "I don't know what happened, boss. He never got inside."

"Get over there and find out."

"Now?"

"See all those people talking to the reporters? They know what happened. Go ask them!"

She saw him get out of the van and trot down the sidewalk toward the crowd. She steamed at his incompetence. For a second she wished she had a rifle mounted under the telescope, but the feeling passed.

Chapter Sixty-two

The fake beard and robe made great cover as Randy knifed through the crowd lugging the heavy bags. The gang of journalists exemplified a politically inconvenient truth. They reeled back in terror away from the screaming hoard crossing the parking lot. Americans publicly valued diversity, but privately they feared Muslims and the terror they represented. There would have been no such fear had a group of Catholics come running out of church. The journalists on the street would have dropped their microphones and rushed to help. Justified or not, the people on the street panicked. Only the cameramen stayed cool as they panned back and forth to take in the swarm that quickly enveloped them.

Randy wasn't sure where the screaming started. They'd all seen him diffuse the explosives. They were desperate to get clear of the building, but they didn't need to run at this point. They certainly weren't the most athletic bunch. Many of them ambled as if their legs were too long. Others bumped into each other and stumbled as they ran. The chaos gave Randy a way to get past the van that had been following Cassie without being seen. Heather's men didn't rush to surround the mob, so they hadn't figured it out yet. They were still expecting him to try and sneak in.

One of the reporters jumped back as the mob reached the sidewalk. The poor slob landed right in the path of a silver Taurus and it drilled him, flipped him up in the air and jerked to a stop eight feet too late.

He skidded on the asphalt and moaned. Randy darted around the man and the car. Someone behind him kneeled down to help. Randy couldn't. He kept running for the Avenue, up and over to the Crown Vic.

An explosion ripped across the block behind him.

Randy spun around in disbelief as the minaret rocked back and forth then toppled. He'd missed one. Hopefully it was the only one.

Randy turned the corner and broke into a run.

Cassie had ditched the coat and the dark wig. She lugged a black plastic case, the weight throwing her off stride as she ran to meet him. They hadn't left anyone to follow the truck or he'd be chasing her now. They assumed they knew where she was going and they had to know exactly where the truck was; they'd been following it electronically all day. Cassie had done a tremendous job. A night in Heather's cell and the threat to her parents gave Randy the ally he'd needed all along.

It was time for Heather to be surprised.

Randy loaded the bags and Cassie's black case into the trunk and weaved over to Belleville Avenue. They sped away from the commotion through the industrial wasteland toward Acushnet.

Chapter Sixty-three

Ethan lurked in Tom's shadow as the two men edged over the threshold. It wasn't good news. Once Ethan began the pitiful account of the day's exploits, Heather knew why he brought Tom along for cover. He overheard several men from inside the mosque tell basically the same story to the reporters. A newcomer with a fake beard and a black robe had saved them. He knew the bombs were inside and directed the men to search every room in the building. When they found the bombs the newcomer took them apart, nine in all. Unfortunately they'd missed one, but everyone got out safely. The reporters asked each man for a description of their rescuer and they all said a young man, tall, thin.

Randy Black.

Ethan the idiot had been following the truck all day. They had homing devices on the truck and the Corolla, but somehow with three men following the Chevy and surveillance tracking the Corolla fifty miles up to Boston, Randy Black appeared less than two miles from where the chase started. In all that time he could have walked!

The sponsor had to be contacted, but Heather had bigger problems than returning the money. The man who could put her out of business was within a few blocks of the building.

"Randy Black has to be silenced. Today!"

"He could be anywhere," Ethan blubbered.

"I can't expect you to do it. Now can I? You couldn't keep up with him when he had a homing device sewn into his shoe."

Ethan scowled, but quickly neutralized his expression. She couldn't afford his incompetence. She needed results. This wasn't a medical research facility where you could hide away for a decade. That's exactly what he'd done, but after ten years without results he lost his funding and they threw him out. She should have known better than to hire a failed scientist as an enforcer. Things happened fast here. If he wasn't smart enough or man enough to admit he'd screwed up, it was time for him to go. Tripp and Sid weren't far behind. The three of them weren't worth half what she paid them. She almost wished she had Tomlin back. He was hard to control, but he got things done.

"How about the N.B.P.D.?" she asked.

"If they catch him, his face will end up on the news." Tom said.

"And?"

"Every one of those guys from the news reports will ID him."

"That's ok. He planted the bombs and had a change of heart. He'll still go to prison. We've got enough on him to make sure of that. Don't we?"

"We do. But what's he going to say while he's locked up?"

He wouldn't live long enough to talk. The girl wouldn't either.

"Who's that reporter that's been all over the Marston case? Macedo isn't it?"

Tom knew the name immediately. "Walter Macedo."

"Let's give him everything we've got," she said.

Tom pulled a pen from his shirt pocket, but put it back when she glared. What criminal operation kept written records? Surrounded by idiots.

"Shoot," Tom said.

"Where are we with the football player from Minnesota?"

"Michigan. He's on board. He's got immunity, civil and criminal. He's good to go."

"Excellent. Make the call then hook him up with Walter Macedo." Heather waved a finger for emphasis. "I want this to hit the paper tomorrow. By the time the steel doors slam closed, I want Randy Black to be the most hated man in the city. If Walter Macedo can't deliver, find someone else."

Tom agreed.

"Whitey, you listening?"

An overhead speaker came to life. "I'm here."

"Cut me a CD of our friend sneaking into the mosque the night he planted those cameras. We still have that, don't we?"

"No problem. Give me ten minutes."

"Dup me a snatch-and-grab video, too."

"You got it, boss."

"Tom, I want you to package this stuff up and hand it to this guy Macedo. Tell him it gets in tomorrow's paper or he's never getting anything from me again."

Tom would get it right. He'd say what needed to be said and no more. There were more people she needed him to talk to—several more. Ethan stood by, his eyes roaming around the white on white furnishings as if he'd never been up here before.

"Ethan!"

He snapped upright.

"I need two things from you."

She explained that she wanted the Winchester stashed wherever Randy had been sleeping in the girl's apartment. He complained that he'd never been inside, that there were no cameras, as if Heather or Tom had been. Nimrod. She left Tom in her apartment to call some friends on the force and get the search ramped up, while she led Ethan down to the vault. He took the bagged Winchester and plodded for the elevator. She hollered after him that she didn't want to see him again until someone caught Randy Black.

Whitey had the CDs ready when she popped her head in. He was smart enough to wipe the prints off the discs and the plastic cases. Heather handled them through her silk scarf. Whitey was small, but he was going places.

Tom's envelope was ready to go when she walked in. The reporter would be bucking for a promotion as soon as he finished typing. Ron Morgan was on board. The detective on the Marston case was tickled.

Maybe things hadn't gone to shit.

251

Chapter Sixty-four

The Crown Vic hit fifty on Main Street. Randy took full advantage of the light blue official plates by zigzag passing over double lines with hard turns that made Cassie nauseous. He jerked the car into oncoming traffic. She looked away when he swerved back within inches of a Volkswagen. A collision would ignite the explosives in the trunk and vaporize them both, but Cassie wasn't leaving his side. The villain she'd been tracking had just turned her story upside down by risking his life to save forty people.

As much as she tried, she'd never seen the manipulative conman Charlie, Deirdre and Mrs. Marston described. From the day she snuck into the hospital, Randy had been a serene and thoughtful man. She saw no bizarre antics, certainly nothing she'd describe as evil. He'd been a mystery until Heather's threats seized her with fear for her parents. That night on the concrete floor she felt a glimmer of what Randy lost all those years ago. His loss had been devastating, life altering. When she woke up in his arms, she understood how he lost control and killed Charles Marston. If roles had been reversed, she might have killed Charles Marston, too.

Randy didn't deserve the crazy psychologist and her lawyer trying to kill him. He was turning himself around and he deserved a second chance. Cassie wished she could help, but didn't delude herself. She was here for the story developing in the seat beside her. All that remained was to see what became of Heather Lovely and Tom Gold. She might not be able to report what she saw, but she had to see it through. She tried not to watch as Randy gunned the engine and hung on around a tight curve.

Kelly Clarkson sang from Cassie's coat pocket. Randy turned a curious eye from the road as she answered her cell phone.

Bart sounded as uneasy as a semi-retired guy could. "Where are you Cassie? I've got Walter on the line. We need to talk."

Cassie steadied herself against the dashboard and tried not to look at the road. "Not a good time."

"Are you at home?"

When Cassie said she wasn't Walter snickered, "Good thing."

"Have you been talking to Tom Gold?" she asked.

Walter didn't answer.

"Are you aware there was an explosion downtown?" Bart asked.

Cassie had been only two blocks away. She knew what was coming.

"Anything to submit? People might want to read about that tomorrow."

"I'm working on a big story, Bart. I've almost got it."

"Working? Is that what you've been doing?" Walter asked. "Strange we haven't seen you in the building since Wednesday."

"Believe me Bart, it'll be worth it."

"Walter has some disturbing information. If I were you, I'd turn myself right around and get in here. Right this minute." Bart didn't trust Walter any more than Cassie did, but she wasn't giving him much choice. The paper had to print something about the bombing. They'd have pictures. Everyone would have pictures and they had to run them. If Cassie didn't have a story, Walter's was going to run beside the photos on page one.

"Walter doesn't know who he's getting his information from."

"Listen lady, I'm not screwing the biggest criminal to hit this city in a decade. Your boyfriend's killing witnesses, kidnapping clerics and bombing innocent people. Do you have any idea how much trouble you're in?"

"You don't know what you're talking about."

"Haven't you been watching the news?"

"I'm in a car, doing sixty."

"Where?" Walter asked. "I'll call it in and collect the reward."

Bart asked her to hang on. Angry voices barked in the background and then Bart's door slammed.

"Sorry about that," Bart said.

"What's he talking about?"

"He won't share his source, but he knows a lot about your friend." Bart went on to tell her that the police identified Randy's car in the kidnapping video. Walter had a story about a football player from Michigan and a video of Randy breaking into the Mosque on Coggeshall Street a few days earlier. "You need to get away from this guy. He's going to drag you down."

Randy kept on driving. The speaker wasn't loud enough for him to hear, but she rested her hand on his thigh in answer to Bart's comment.

He accelerated when they touched, never taking his eyes off the road.

"Walter's got it all wrong. I can prove it if you give me some time."

"Other outlets have the story. We can't be silent on this, but I'll keep your name out of it for now."

"My name?"

"Are you kidding? The police have called in Homeland Security. Every highway in the area is shut down. They want you both and they're not going to stop searching until they find you. Officially, you're a person of interest. Unofficially, it sounds like felony aiding and abetting. They say you've been hiding him. I wouldn't suggest going to your apartment if that's where you're headed."

"Walter's source is behind the bombing."

"Want to counter? Now's the time. Tomorrow might be the biggest news day of your career. Charles Marston was a blip compared to this."

"If you print Walter's story, you're going to regret it."

Her parents were hidden away, but Cassie couldn't incriminate Tom and Heather, not yet. Bart would run Walter's story. He had to, but it'd be ok. Everyone was going to follow that same angle.

She looked over as Randy eased to a stop on a wooded country road. Cassie followed him down a slope and into the forest. She was betting her career, her life, everything on what Randy had planned. She hoped she'd made the right decision.

Chapter Sixty-five

Officer Jim Grant waited for the forensics van and two black-and-whites to pass then blocked the street with his cruiser and turned on the lights. The sidewalks were packed this time of day. There was plenty of traffic heading down the hill toward Purchase, so he stood and waved the drivers east and west. Most gave him the obligatory wave, but several grimaced at the inconvenient detour. He caught a few smiles from women on the sidewalk, but nothing interesting enough to draw him out of the street.

Halfway down the block, the forensics guys taped off the McLaren and the search team went upstairs to the girl's apartment. Jim wished he'd pushed harder when he first came on the force. He had security for hours at the bombing that afternoon and now that the mess was under control, they dragged him over here to do the same thing. All the glamour of a traffic detail without the overtime. Walking the mall would be better than this.

In thirty minutes, Ralph came walking out with the detectives, proud as ever. He was just a lackey inside, but he'd come through the academy with Jim and he was already moving up. If Jim hadn't been caught sleeping in his cruiser half a dozen times he would be, too. Ralph gave a thumbs-up. They'd found the gun, bagged it and they were taking it in.

Jim had never served a warrant. He'd be pulling traffic duty until the car was printed. If he was lucky he'd be back on patrol in an hour or two.

He recognized Walter Macedo from the paper. All the cops read his stuff. Source names never got printed, but the officers knew the stories and they knew where they came from. Walter sidled up on the opposite side of the cruiser to fish for information. This had to be the biggest story in New England. Guy goes nuts, kills his buddy then tries to blow up forty Muslims. There were plenty of drugs and gangs in the city, but not many rampaging killers. The story was worth a few bucks and Jim had been standing in front of it all day. He wished he knew more about it.

Walter came right out and asked if they'd found the gun. He had to be connected pretty high up to know why they were here. Jim hadn't known until he asked his partner on the way over. If he didn't start getting better information, Jim was going to be directing traffic for a long time. Sharing tips with Walter Macedo seemed like a good place to start.

Jim told him they'd served a warrant and come out with something. He wasn't authorized to say what. Walter probably knew they didn't share those details with the guy waving cars. Sadly, Walter would know what was going to happen with this case before Jim.

"Is that the car from the kidnapping video?"

"Too early to tell," Jim said. They hadn't finished lifting the prints, but everyone Jim asked knew they didn't sell many of these. It was a slam-dunk. Randy Black was going away. Walter knew or he wouldn't be here.

Walter told Jim the state police had shut down all the highways around Southeastern Massachusetts looking for a blue Chevy pickup. Troopers were standing on I-195, I-495, Route 24 and both bridges to Cape Cod. He knew that Homeland Security had taken over the investigation of the mosque bombing. The story was going national for the evening news. Walter had a page and a half, maybe two pages in the next day's paper.

Amazing what this guy knew.

They'd handed Jim a glossy old mug shot of Randy Black before coming out. He'd popped some information up on screen on the way over, but that's all he knew about the case. That's why he was standing out in the sun directing traffic while the detectives worked to find the killer. Things were going to change for Jim. They had to.

Chapter Sixty-six

Randy hesitated twenty feet down the slope in dense undergrowth. Cassie was already tired of dragging her feet through the brush. She faced him hopefully, like he might forget the whole thing and turn back. Randy wished he could tell her why he'd come here instead of storming Heather's stronghold with the explosives. The chaos surrounding the mosque was just blocks away. Another explosion would bring a heavy response. Randy needed a quieter way in, but there was more to this visit than stealth. Judge McKinnon sent him headlong into Heather's cell. A year ago the judge's betrayal would have been met with a broken leg or a trip to the swamp. Things were different now. Randy was clinging to a thread of hope for salvation. Disarming the bombs was a good first step, but retaliating against the judge might bring lightning from above. He still wasn't sure what he'd do when he got inside.

The task ahead was bigger than stopping Heather, Tom and the judge. They reached deep inside the police department and the courts. Their police made arrests. Their court system protected their interests. Randy needed help from the feds, help he couldn't get with his credibility blown by the Marston murder. To stop Heather by himself, he needed to understand the organization and expose it. He knew where to dig for the answers he needed, but he was afraid of what he'd find.

Randy dropped the magazine from the P229. Still empty. He shook his head at his insecurity. No one had filled the magazine while he sped across the city.

Cassie leaned away at the sight of the gun. She kept her feet in place as a sign of trust, but she wanted no part in a shooting. He flashed the empty magazine to reassure her and shoved it back in. He eyed a dense patch of laurel and considered leaving her there until he was finished with the judge, but she'd get nervous out here alone, better to keep her close, somewhere he could get to her quick if there was trouble.

The cops and Heather's men would be looking everywhere for them. They might expect him to come back since he'd already visited the judge twice. If they did, the Crown Vic would be too easy to find. He left her there and climbed up to the car, promising to be right back.

There were four houses scattered within a quarter mile. Two shingled capes had faced each other across the road for sixty years. An elderly couple was not what he was looking for. The next house, a colonial with a two car garage, looked perfect. Big enough for a family, expensive enough so both parents would be working, not so expensive that the owners had money and freedom to do what they pleased. He backed the Crown Vic into the turnout and left it in plain sight. He listened for stirring behind him as he ducked into the tree line, but heard none.

Circling low on a path kids had used to sneak around this neighborhood for generations, he came up on Cassie from several yards downhill. She was still looking up toward the road. Only a city girl could let him get that close without hearing. He'd practiced stealth for years and he moved quietly, but not that quietly. He whistled, imitating a Bobwhite.

Cassie startled, turned and trudged downhill to the path, creating a ruckus with every step.

Farther along, they angled down and cut through the heavy brush to the edge of the judge's yard. The place was heavily alarmed to keep out defendants who disagreed with his rulings and to get help quickly in case they turned violent. The Omni-sense sticker on the window meant that it was Heather's men monitoring the cameras. They'd be watching the cameras closely today and if they saw him, it'd be the vans that came, not police cruisers. Going through the garage again would be risky. They'd know by now that's how he'd gotten in. They'd have new cameras or a few new sensors out there. He'd find a new way in when the judge got home.

He dodged to the edge of the yard and peered around the hedges at the nearest neighbor's house. The back windows were open to the breeze. He listened until something clattered in the kitchen then trotted back to Cassie.

Together they collected armfuls of fallen branches, crisp from the August heat, and they scurried low across the lawn, dropping them a few yards from the foundation of the judge's house. When the pile was large enough, Randy lit an oak branch. The leaves flared and the pile sparked to life. The breeze blew the smoke up against the rear wall and on into the sky as if the flames originated inside.

Randy hurled a stone against the bulkhead and raced for the woods.

The woman next door heard the clank and stepped onto her deck.

"Oh my God!" she cried loud enough for them to hear then she ran back inside leaving her sliding door wide open.

"Perfect." Randy led Cassie back up the slope.

"We can't just let it burn."

"It's not going to." The house looked like it was on fire to the woman, but in a few minutes the flimsy branches dwindled to little more than a smoking red spot in the manicured grass. By that time, the fire department was rushing toward them.

Randy backed Cassie up the hill. They slithered deep into a stand of young pines fighting each other for survival. They were hidden by overlapping green branches and successive ranks of trees that climbed the hill. Randy scraped the top layer of pine needles and twigs away, leaving a soft carpet that wouldn't betray their position if one of them shifted. It was an old deer hunter's trick. Deer possess exceptional hearing and smell, but poor eyesight. As long as a hunter didn't move and didn't make noise, they were nearly undetectable. The cops couldn't see them here and now they wouldn't hear them either.

In eight minutes a blue and white police car skidded to a stop out front and a young officer sprinted around back toward the smoke.

"Rotten kids," he cursed. He found a garden hose around the corner and soaked the remains of the fire. When the fire engine arrived, there was nothing but steam rising from the wet pile of ash. Ends of wet sticks jutted outside the fire's core.

Three firemen laden with heavy gear mulled around the back of the house with the officer. They seemed to be enjoying their fieldtrip. One lit a cigarette. Two others circled the house checking doors and windows, admiring the construction and landscape as they went. They found the woman next door on her deck. Randy couldn't hear what was said, but she had an embarrassed tone for reporting a false alarm. They soothed her nerves and she went back inside. Then the firemen came roaming back.

Someone finally had the idea to look for the punks who started the fire. The officer was the only one equipped for the job. The firemen wouldn't get far in the woods with their heavy protective coats. Cassie flinched as soon as the blue uniform reached the woods, but this was no search party. This guy wasn't going to find anything. Randy grabbed her forearms and held her low in the pines. The branches around them were so dense the patrolman would have to trip on their legs to find them.

He ventured twenty yards up the slope in an arc that paralleled the judge's property. Was he afraid to come further by himself? Randy wasn't sure what he'd do if the officer stumbled upon them. He couldn't let the judge get away with what he'd done, but the officer didn't deserve to be hurt either. He waited and wondered how far the young guy would come up.

The officer resorted to psychology. "We know you're up there. Don't make this worse on yourself. If we have to search the entire neighborhood we will. Don't make us do that."

He stood and listened, reluctant to move deeper into the woods.

"Don't make us take you down to the station."

His only hope was for someone to spook and break up the hill.

Cassie wasn't going anywhere.

Randy patted her hands and let go as the officer turned downhill.

The firemen wandered around for ten minutes then the fire engine was replaced by a second cruiser. The gray van arrived next followed closely by the judge. Cassie thought things had gone horribly wrong, but they'd worked out exactly as Randy had hoped. The judge had pushed off his commitments for the rest of the day, so there was no returning to the courthouse. As he settled into his study, Randy prepared Cassie for a long wait in the woods. They were both getting hungry, but patience was critical for what Randy had in mind. He handed her the keys to the Crown Vic and showed her the path that led up the hill to it. She'd go get it as soon as Randy got inside. If she found anyone standing around the car, she'd come back and hide in the woods until Randy found her.

The police sat in their cruiser in the driveway for over an hour, playing cards or surfing the Internet until finally the order came to leave.

Randy left Cassie on the hidden carpet and stalked down skirting the judge's backyard. The van was parked fifty yards down the street next to a patch of woods between houses so it wasn't apparent who they might be visiting. There were no cameras on the outside of the van. The men inside didn't think they needed protection. They were aggressors, riveted to the images coming from the judge's perimeter, searching for Randy Black, hunting the price Heather placed on his head.

Randy crept close to the van and settled in the bushes a dozen yards from the back door. Two cars and forty minutes passed before Mother Nature separated the two men inside. Tripp struggled up onto a path and followed it far enough so passing cars wouldn't catch his silhouette in the bushes. He stood where the path dipped past the trunk of a wide oak, exactly where Randy expected him. Good fortune brought Randy the smallest of Tom's four men, five inches shorter and forty pounds lighter than Randy. Once the stream started, he was helpless. Unaccustomed to forest sounds, he didn't hear Randy creep down the path.

When Randy planted his feet behind him, Tripp knew something was wrong. He looked back over his shoulder just as Randy grabbed a handful of his shirt and began a powerful swing for the demon's head that poked out from Tripp's collar. Randy missed the demon as Tripp turned, but his fist crashed into the side of his neck, folding his knees, and sending his body lurching forward.

Randy pulled him back to keep him from falling face first onto the wet leaves. He dumped his body trailside and found a Smith & Wesson 410 on his hip, a Sigma SW380 holstered at his back and a buck knife at his ankle. Like the demons on his arms, Tripp took pride in hurting people. Randy Zip Tied his hands tight and weighed the guns. He kept the bigger gun, the .40, in his right and the .380 in his left. He tossed the knife into the brush far enough that Tripp wouldn't find it before he finished. Tripp showed no signs of stirring when Randy left him and headed for the van.

Randy tucked the .380 into his belt, anchored his right foot against the bumper and confidently whipped the door open. The .40 poked in and he reached back for the .380 and swung it, too, into the open space. The hulking guy from the bar and the river sat at the monitors, his hands in plain sight on a keyboard. It made sense for Tom to set up his biggest guy with the smallest. Randy was glad Tripp had come out and not the power lifter.

By the time the muscle-bound thug turned his head, Randy had both guns trained on his chest. He lifted his fingers from the keys and held them there. His eyes held none of the rage he'd seen in Tripp's. He'd been caught and was ready to submit. Where Tripp would have reached for a gun and dove for cover, Sid held still while Randy climbed in the van and took a position behind him. He wasn't ready to die for Heather and Tom.

His arms bulged so huge he couldn't clasp his hands behind him. Randy Zip Tied them in front then added a second tie around his belt. He could unbuckle it, but for now it'd keep his hands where Randy wanted them. He left the hulk lying on his back.

Hauling Tripp's unconscious body through the bushes was a chore. Randy heaved him into the passenger's seat and duct taped his neck to the headrest to prop him up and keep the men from freeing each other.

The tracking device popped off the undercarriage easily. Randy tossed it into the bushes to give himself some extra time.

Chapter Sixty-seven

Randy rang the bell in three urgent bursts then angled the shoulder of his newly-borrowed leather jacket over the sidelight. Footsteps approached. The judge recognized the jacket and stepped up to the door.

"Hurry up, Judge. I've gotta go," Randy hollered.

The door swung open and Randy barged in with the P229 leading the way. He'd taken three loaded handguns from his prisoners in the van. The P229 was the biggest of the four and the black finish gave it a menacing look, but he didn't want to shoot the judge, not even accidentally. So he stood in another man's coat, three pockets stuffed with loaded handguns, and faced the judge without bullets.

The judge jumped back, stunned by the face in front of him.

After two hours alone in his study, he never expected to see Randy.

His eyes flicked upward toward the stairway, an unconscious habit borne of being careful on film. There was a camera up there watching the entry. Randy didn't give him the chance to signal for help.

"Your friends in the van won't be coming to the rescue."

The judge stood expectantly in the middle of the floor as if the phone were about to ring. The skinny kid in the control room knew the guys in the van were watching. Randy hoped he'd miss the next few seconds of footage.

Randy grabbed the judge by the collar and marched him down into the cellar. What he had in mind was too loud for outside. He hoped they hadn't bothered to wire the cellar.

The bare cement room was jammed with shelves. The judge labored past a baseball bat, an old lamp, and a shovel. He didn't reach for anything, just lumbered along until Randy pushed him up against the concrete wall beside the washing machine. The old man's sweatpants bulged to restrain an enormous gut. Sweat beaded on his bald head and he struggled for breath in the musty air. There was no fight left in the old man. He resigned himself to his fate. He leaned against the smooth concrete and waited to die.

"You set me up. Why?"

"You don't understand," the judge wheezed. "It's bigger than you and me. A lot bigger."

"You're fixing trials for them, aren't you? That's why they wanted a bench trial. You'd decide whichever way he told you. Tom, the cops, you're all just putting on a show for the court officers and the victims' families. Why? Why me?"

It wasn't money. Tom Gold hadn't asked for money yet. Heather put the players together, but Randy still couldn't understand why he'd been chosen as their fall guy.

The judge stared blankly.

"I know what your doing old man. Just standing there stalling, hoping your friends in the van will come rushing in. They're not coming. And their buddies back at home base probably aren't even watching those cameras upstairs. It's just you and me. And if I don't start getting some answers, it's going to be a long and painful night."

The judge swallowed hard.

Randy waived the gun, pulled back the hammer and took aim at the judge's right knee. The judge's hands shot up. He had enough trouble lumbering around on healthy legs.

"Let's try again. What does Heather Lovely want with me?"

"You fit the profile."

Randy lined up again and the judge hastily continued.

"You killed that guy Marston and they knew they could get you off."

"What does that buy her?"

"It's what she does. She gets paid to take care of problems the courts fall down on. Justice is blind, but victims' families don't care about due process. They know when someone's guilty and they want justice."

"And they're willing to pay for revenge."

The deal with the kid by the airport made sense to him now. Cassie said he'd raped some girl and gotten off. It was the girl's father he saw that night. He'd paid Heather big bucks to see the punk that raped his little girl get tortured and burned. Any father would want the same. Heather's service wasn't that different from Randy's vendetta against the Marstons. But she'd taken it to a professional level.

"Where do I come in?"

"Big projects get noticed."

He knew Heather had tried to kill him with the explosives, but he wasn't sure if the Marstons had paid her or if she was just deflecting blame for the mosque job. If she was really clever, she could have worked both sides. Charlie wouldn't have paid to have him killed, but after finding her husband in the foyer, his mother might.

The cameras were an excuse to get him inside the mosque so Heather could get pictures of him breaking in. She got her proof, but he stole the force from her plan. Randy realized then that Sebastian's death had been a meaningless ploy to keep him in line. Sebastian was angry at Marston and he made a mistake, but he didn't deserve to die for it. He felt so guilty he turned himself in. Where was the justice in killing him? Following Heather's logic, she deserved to be next.

"What about you? How'd you get mixed up in this?" Randy asked.

"I hired the wrong surveillance company."

"Heather's company. They're for real?"

"If you're a cop, judge, lawyer, or local politician. They record everything that happens in your house or office. Sooner or later they get some leverage. Once they've got you, they start asking for favors. Little ones at first. They pay for them and that only makes things worse."

"So they've got dirt on you, and those cops who picked me up. Can't you do something? Isn't there something you can do to fight back?"

"What am I going to do? Call a cop? That fortress of hers is impenetrable. They keep the videos locked up inside. A few cops got fed up and shot their way in once. They got upstairs, but we found them a few days later, dead of carbon monoxide poisoning. Anyone who crosses Heather Lovely winds up dead."

Separated from her goons, Heather Lovely wouldn't be hard to grab. She was tough, but she couldn't weigh more than one hundred thirty pounds.

"I know what you're thinking. Just forget it."

"What?"

"There's no getting to Heather. Sure you got Tom Gold, but that was easy." The judge smiled broadly. He'd heard about the chicken. "Listen, when she pushed me to throw my first trial I did some research. I found a family court judge who'd had her in court when she was thirteen. The judge never should have talked to me about it, but she was scared.

"You want to know why Heather's so twisted? Her brother was molesting her. He was a real piece of work. The parents found out, so he killed them. He put on a good show in court and the judge made a huge mistake. She gave custody to the brother and he molested Heather for another three years. Finally, Heather burned the house down with him in it. It doesn't excuse what she's doing now, but you can't help feeling for her."

The weird sexual advances were starting to make sense.

"The judge knew Heather was behind the fire, but she was too scared to tell anyone. Do you want to guess what happened to the judge when Heather turned twenty-one?" McKinnon asked.

"Heather killed her."

"Eventually. First, she hired a few guys to show the judge what Heather lived through for almost four years. It wasn't pretty when they found her."

"How do you know all this?" Randy asked.

"She is human. She's locked up in there and almost never comes out. When she does, she's glad for someone to talk to."

Heather was losing control.

If she wasn't coming out, Randy would find a way in.

Chapter Sixty-eight

Whitey watched from the corner of his eye as Tom studied an alert on the board then finally closed it after thirty seconds. Whitey closed seventeen alerts in the next thirty seconds, a brief interlude between streaming newscasts and video of movement in and around the buildings they were monitoring. He was glad to have Tom's company. A little insulation from Heather never hurt, but Tom was so slow with the alerts he'd be better off just watching the news broadcasts and playing back the good bits. In his defense, Tom was nervous as Hell. Before this morning they'd always been invisible to the media. They'd wiped out entire gangs and the newspapers blamed rivals. They'd killed dozens of murderers and rapists and it was always reported as street violence. No one ever assembled the entire picture. No one suspected a professional organization. Not until the bomb. Blowing up that minaret turned the world on its ear. Terrorism buzzed from Boston to Washington. The whole world was watching. Whitey guessed some rival Islamic group would take credit. He welcomed the proclamation, but had yet to hear it.

They were all desperate for news of Randy Black. Whitey could hear the tension in Heather's demonic voice when she shouted over the speaker. Randy knew enough about what they'd done to put them away. Worse, he knew about things in this building that weren't supposed to exist. If the wrong cops busted in with a search warrant, Whitey would be in a cell right next to Tom and the others. The longer Randy walked around on the outside, the closer those bars came to surrounding Whitey.

The local channels interrupted their broadcasts with something about the bombing or the hostage taking every thirty minutes. Shortly after the bomb exploded, Tom came in to help make sense of what was going on. He could have been worried Whitey would take off to escape the pressure, but even so, Whitey was glad to have him in the room. Just tracking police activity was a fulltime job. Whitey's CDs of the imam's confession ran on every station. Each channel added their own footage of the bombing and the crime scene investigators working the McLaren in front of the girl's apartment. They stayed so long Whitey wondered if they were milking it for publicity or if they truly didn't want to move the car.

While the cameras shot the outside of the girl's apartment, reporters talked about the gun found inside and the murder of Sebastian Leonard. The newsmen speculated wildly and Tom squirmed whenever they did. Sebastian's murder was the biggest hole left open. Nothing tied Randy to the murder until the police identified his prints on the Winchester. If they didn't, it was a life sentence searching for an inmate to serve it. Tom was too close to the front of that line. The media disagreed about what happened and who was to blame. Some reporters framed Randy Black as a murderous psychopath. Others assumed he had to get rid of Sebastian to go on with his life. Still others showed his home in Dartmouth, interviewed his neighbors and suggested that the police had it wrong.

Area highways were gridlocked. Helicopters showed solid, red brake lights on every major artery. Homeland Security was blamed on every channel. It was called an overreaction. It was called bungling. It was called a disaster. The blue Chevy pickup was found two blocks from the blast site after more than one hundred thousand cars were halted all over Southeastern Massachusetts to find it. Talk radio buzzed of bureaucratic incompetence.

It was an all-out manhunt. Randy's picture was on every television broadcast and newsstand thanks to Heather and Tom. Everyone with a badge was looking for him. Heather's friends were working harder, eager for the fifty thousand she offered. Whitey didn't have much hope for their guys. Randy had been at the judge's house. Tripp and Sid were right there, but they were just sitting there waiting for him to come back. Whitey argued that they should be driving around. Randy tried to burn down the house and didn't use enough wood. That was that. Tom wouldn't listen. When Tom told the guys to stay put, Whitey lost all hope that those two would catch him. Some flatfoot would trip over him or a housewife would see him outside her window. That's how it would end.

There was another alternative Whitey was trying to ignore. Randy knew the judge turned him in and went there to burn his house down. It made sense he'd come here to get even with Heather and Tom. The building was locked down tight and Whitey controlled everything from this room, but he wished Ethan and the guys were downstairs playing paintball. Tom, Heather and a prisoner weren't much comfort. The guard down in the lobby had no idea how much trouble was headed his way. Whitey kept checking the camera expecting to find him slumped on the floor.

Views around the perimeter played on the nineteen-inch right in front of Whitey. To his right, Tom's house, the imam in his cell and the loading area downstairs. The screen to his left displayed two cameras from the judge's house, tracking for the vans and a single view of Randy's kitchen.

Three televisions had Tom's attention. CBS, FOX and CNN were all covering breaking events. Tom had a screen for each. With two alert screens to deal with incoming events, the room shone with so much light from the monitors they didn't need the fluorescents.

The phone rang as if Whitey didn't have enough to manage.

Tom didn't move.

Ethan sounded worried. "Hey. I can't get hold of the babysitters. Something up?"

Whitey flashed to the monitor. The judge sat reading in his study like he always did. The van had moved six or eight feet. Whitey tried, but couldn't reach them on the radio or by cell. The monitor showed Ethan parked in Westport a hundred yards from the parsonage. Not a bad idea. Not a bad place to hide if you had thousands of cops hunting you.

Whitey wanted Ethan to come back to the building, but Ethan didn't buy his hunch that Randy was headed there. That and he didn't want to come back after Heather chewed him out. Ordering him not to come back could have cost them all, but Randy couldn't really get inside. That only happened once and they'd reinforced the doors to make sure it didn't happen again.

The judge looked too relaxed for someone whose house was almost burned down. Whitey got curious and opened all the cameras at the judge's and started working backwards. The system uploaded six frames a minute to save bandwidth. Whitey jerked the frames backward fifteen minutes then twenty. Room after room was empty. The judge sitting. An empty hall. Empty foyer. Empty stairs. Then the judge appeared in the hall. Someone stepped in and Whitey couldn't believe it. Randy Black. Inside!

"Tom. Tom. You've got to see this."

"Holy shit! When?"

"Thirty minutes ago."

Randy Black held a gun on the judge just inside the front door. Could the image in the study be faked? Was the judge dead on the floor? Not possible. Their gear was too good. Randy wasn't that smart. Not a chance.

Whitey clicked the button beside the image and the phone rang through the speaker. In the live frame, the judge reached over and picked up the receiver.

"Everything ok, Judge?"

"Fine."

"Has he come back?"

"No. No trouble." The judge got up and looked out the window. "Your van is still out front."

"That's good news. I'll check back later. Call us if you need anything."

"Will do. Thanks," Judge McKinnon said, and hung up.

Tom dialed his cell. Heather wasn't going to like this. The judge was covering for Randy. He may not be able to find Randy, but he knew exactly where the judge was.

"Ethan," Tom said into his phone. "We've got a problem at the judge's. Get there now. Fast. Check the van. Call us before you go in."

"You think he's helping him?" Whitey asked.

Tom just shrugged and pointed to the monitor.

The two figures stood in the hall for a few frames then backed toward the kitchen and disappeared. One frame they were together. Then only Randy. Then they were both gone. There weren't any rooms they couldn't see, but Whitey came up empty on every camera.

Tom had seen enough. He asked Whitey to zoom in on the gun.

The uploaded images had lousy resolution, but he found the right frame back at the judge's box and downloaded it uncompressed. The image came tighter and tighter until they could make out SIG SAUER P229 STAINLESS.

Tom called Ethan immediately.

Thirty minutes later Ethan stepped in front of the camera wearing a jacket similar to the one Randy had taken from Tripp. He coaxed the judge into exactly the same position Randy had held him in. He fired and the judge fell. He stepped up and fired again.

Ethan dropped his head and bolted.

Whitey began working the images on the box hidden at the judge's.

Randy Black would appear with the judge, but his gun never would. It was a small detail, but one of the lab guys could see the P229 in the photo and realize it wasn't the gun that killed Judge McKinnon. Ethan could pass for Randy with the camera at his back. Once the gun turned up at Randy's, it would just be another leg in his killing spree. The cops put him at the judge's house once today. Whitey was going to make it easy for them to believe he'd come back.

The timing of Randy's visit needed to be fixed to coincide with the gunshot. Whitey inserted a few hundred blanks to remove any trace of Randy's earlier visit. Fortunately the judge didn't move much once he settled into reading, so it was easy to erase his trip to the foyer. Duplicating an empty foyer was even easier. The hardest part was fudging the timestamps at the right intervals.

The cops would be there in twenty minutes, but they'd be busy with the body and the physical evidence. They wouldn't ask for the video for at least two hours. They couldn't hack into the onsite storage and they wouldn't be pushy about a few hours delay. They had enough on their plate tonight. When Whitey was finished, he would deliver a masterpiece.

Chapter Sixty-nine

Randy watched the rear view mirror as the Crown Vic pulled to a stop on the opposite side of an eight foot chain-link fence. The factory off Sawyer Street was the last place Heather's thugs would look for Cassie. They were nervous about cops today. They wouldn't approach the Crown Vic without knowing who was inside. She'd be safe there, close enough to call for help, close enough so Randy could get to her fast.

Randy pulled the van right up to the wide overhead door hoping he'd be so close the camera would be looking down on the roof rather than through the windshield. He checked his notes on the paper beside him and arrayed the recorders on the console. The tiny devices cost eight hundred bucks apiece at Best Buy, but they sounded so lifelike even Tripp was impressed.

Randy picked up the first, dialed Tripp's phone and waited. The line connected, but the person inside didn't answer right away.

"Hey, Sparky, let me in," Tripp's voice played from the recorder.

"Where the Hell have you been?"

"We had a little problem. We've been *tied up*."

"Funny. Where are you?"

Randy switched recorders. "We're at the back door. Can't you see us?"

The voice paused while he checked the camera. "I still show you in Acushnet." The matter-of-fact tone assured Randy he hadn't seen Tripp strapped to the passenger's seat with duct tape over his mouth.

Randy switched recorders again. "He smashed everything inside the van. Took every piece we had. Let us in. I think I know where he's going."

Randy waited but the man on the phone didn't ask. He keyed the recorder anyway. "Here. He's coming here. Now let me in. I need a piece."

Randy hid his face with Tripp's visor and waited. Seconds later the door rose and he drove inside. He parked the van where he'd seen it before and rushed across the loading area with his head low until he reached the door Tripp told him about. The guy upstairs expected Tripp to be in a hurry. Hopefully the images were grainy enough so he wouldn't figure out that he'd just let the man everyone was looking for into a fortress where he'd be safe from the police. He hoped Whitey would be intently focused on the outdoor cameras for the next half hour, trying to keep Randy out.

The overhead door lowered, sealing Randy inside.

Randy waited at the door to the armory and the man upstairs buzzed him in. A dehumidifier hummed in the corner. Wire mesh shelves lined the concrete walls, each topped with cheap red carpet that made the room look like the inside of an oversized jewelry box. Dozens of handguns lay in neat ranks. There were a few worn Glocks and SIGs probably reported stolen in the line of duty. There were also a bunch of throwaway revolvers worth no more than fifty bucks on the street. Tripp and his friends probably took them off small time hoods before killing them. They'd leave them at another crime scene later to convince the cops their work was gang related. If they were really lucky and the guns had a history, the cops would get a ballistics match on a past shooting or two.

Randy moved on to a cache of high-end weapons. He passed over a line of MP-5s and chose a SWAT version of the Saiga 12K. The shotgun had fewer rounds than the MP-5, but loaded with ten rounds of .000 buckshot it would be devastating indoors. He grabbed two extra clips, just as Tripp would do, and made a show of stuffing the extra magazines in his belt when he stepped outside the door. Randy didn't need the gun. He didn't expect to fire the handguns already in his pockets, but the delay rounded out his imitation of Tripp. He hoped he'd given the guy upstairs time to get busy watching something else. Having the Saiga along for protection was an unexpected bonus.

Back at the van, he grabbed two heavy black bags loaded with the explosives he took from the mosque and the tools Cassie bought him earlier. He stuffed the Saiga in with the tools and lugged the load over to the concrete wall. The vents three stories overhead all traced back to the same point in the wall. A lone door aligned closely with the vents. Beside it, three pipes protruded from the wall. Randy shifted down to the door, hugging the wall. None of Tripp's keys fit the lock, but he picked it in about a minute.

Tripp faced the windshield, squirming in his seat as he fought the Zip Ties. It'd take him a while to get free since he and Sid couldn't reach each other. Randy needed to get his work done before they did. He disappeared behind the door, wriggled out of Tripp's jacket and filled his pants pockets with the guns he took earlier. His legs felt heavy, but he needed his arms free with all he was carrying. He discarded Tripp's jacket at the base of the ten-by-ten concrete tower and faced the steel ladders that climbed six stories and the catwalks that provided a narrow work area on each level.

Half the space was filled with ductwork. A series of parallel conduits and copper pipes followed both sides of the ladder skyward. Dual two hundred gallon cylinders rested at the foot of the room. Each was topped with a black box that sent wires running somewhere upstairs. From the box came ten copper pipes each with an automatic valve and a typewritten label: 'Hall 5', 'Hall 4', 'Cell 1', 'Cell 2', 'Cell 3', 'Armory', 'Head 4', 'Head 5', 'Meeting 4', 'Vault'. There was no pipe labeled control room. If there had been, Randy would have triggered the valve manually and taken control of the building in minutes.

Randy and Cassie had been locked up on the fourth floor. Whoever was in the control room could have filled the cell with carbon monoxide with the press of a button. Lying to Heather had saved both of their lives. If Heather had suspected he would disarm the bombs, she would have killed him and dumped his body in the rubble later. He shivered with vulnerability at having survived merely on instinct.

He tightened the manual valve on both tanks and climbed the ladder to the fourth floor.

The men who installed the nervous system of Heather's fortress were professionals. Every angle was crisp. Every conduit was labeled. The ventilation ducts and electrical systems sealed inside two sets of thick concrete walls appeared to be completely secure. There were only two ways into the building and both were carefully guarded. With all her cameras and guns and hired muscle she never expected an attack in here. She'd never expect a single man to make it this far. That was the only explanation for making things so easy for him once he made it inside.

Two heavy power cables, two fiber optic links and dozens of category 5e wires met at the same point on the fourth floor next to the elevator. When Randy was in the boardroom meeting with Tom and Heather, the young guy had disappeared near the elevator. There was only one door. These wires and that door led to the same place: Heather's control room.

Two ducts piped air in and out of the room.

Randy set the heavy bags on the metal grating and stepped out onto the catwalk. He zipped open the tool bag and went to work hacking through the copper pipe that carried carbon monoxide up to the room labeled 'Cell 1'. The hacksaw worked slowly back and forth emitting a wheezing sound too low to be heard through the concrete. When he finally cut through, he worked a screwdriver behind the braces and pried them free. Down to the third, then second floors, the braces popped out one after another and fell lazily down to the concrete floor, jingling as they struck bottom. Soon he had enough play to divert the pipe into the duct beside the elevator.

Chapter Seventy

Ethan turned the corner onto Agawam and came face to face with two cruisers parked at the end of Randy's driveway. The street was only two hundred yards long and the van looked too much like Randy's to go unnoticed. He'd been driving the speed limit all the way from Acushnet, terrified to get pulled over with a murder weapon stashed in back. Heather and Tom might be able to fix it, but with all the publicity they might not. Faced with the cruisers he had to do something fast. There were only ten houses on the whole street. The cops had probably been waiting there for hours and they'd jump at a chance to search the van for Randy.

"Hey. Get me a box back there. Quick."

Khan didn't understand.

"A cardboard box. I need a plain old cardboard box."

"What size?"

"Anything. Neat. Clean. New looking."

Ethan checked his watch. 4:15 P.M., a reasonable time for a delivery. He wished they had a commercial decal on the side of the van.

The houses were all stonefaced monsters with no one outside. The neighbors were probably terrified after what happened to the Caulfields, and not likely to run outside and meet him. Ethan didn't have time to be picky. He couldn't risk driving by the cops, so he pulled into the next driveway. He parked in front of a red brick McMansion with white pillars spaced across the front and prayed no one was home.

He hopped out and went around back of the van like it was routine.

He picked up the clipboard they used for installation checklists, studied it and walked up to the four garage doors. There were no labels on the empty box Khan gave him, so the cops couldn't trace it back to them. He set the box down against a narrow section of wall between the doors and walked casually back to the van, reading the clipboard as if checking the address of the next delivery.

The cops bought it.

He turned left and wheeled around to the next block. More stone monsters. Manicured lawns with ranks of arborvitaes broke the neighborhood up into small green chunks. Ethan stopped long enough for Khan to dart out and follow an eight foot rhododendron hedge. He disappeared into a thin line of wild plants that lent privacy and a feeling of nature to the neighborhood. The occupants on both sides could see each other through the tangled brush, but the barrier was enough to make Khan's trip difficult.

Ethan drove a leisurely loop around the neighborhood. When he returned, Khan sprinted from the foliage. The house keys had been sitting on the back deck with a box of clothes and other things that had been dropped there. Khan returned the clothes to the bedroom and left the keys in the kitchen to contradict Randy's story in case he ever had a chance to tell it. He wiped the gun clean and stuck it between Randy's mattress and box spring.

The cell rang. Ethan clicked the speaker and set it on the dash.

"Where are you guys?" Whitey sounded nervous.

"Just leaving the house."

There was a long pause. Whitey fumbled with something. Normally he could work the screens, gizmos and switches without missing a word. "Get back here," he said with rustling and clicking in the background.

"What's going on?"

He hesitated. "I can't find Tripp and Sid. They came back a while ago. The van's downstairs, but they're not showing up on the monitors. Something's not right."

Ethan clicked off and hit the accelerator. Fifteen minutes to downtown.

Chapter Seventy-one

Randy pressed his head against the ductwork to steady himself as he stretched for the thermostat. Sharp bursts of conversation sounded from within and several quieter voices babbled in muffled tones. Randy assumed the room was only large enough for two men, and that the other voices were coming from audio feeds. He worked quietly, careful not to scrape the single screw that held the thermostat cover in place on the blower. He turned the wheel all the way up and the fan kicked on. He followed the duct back to where it met the concrete, stripped back the insulation and unscrewed the duct from the anchor that held it in place. The flimsy metal bent easily, just enough to slip the pipe inside.

With the duct open Randy could hear the men as clearly as if he were in the room. He recognized the news anchor's metered baritone. The men inside were monitoring news reports, clicking frantically on computer keys and barking instructions to each other. They were desperate to find him. Randy wondered if they'd ever realize how close he'd been to them before they passed out.

He worked the hacksawed end of the pipe into the duct and packed insulation around it to keep the gas flowing into the control room. He gripped the rungs and lowered himself three stories to the concrete floor as quietly as he could. Ten pipes sprouted from the huge tank like a two dimensional flower. Each had a valve with two wires leading out. The wires twisted together then consolidated into two larger cables that ran up to the control room. Randy snipped each pair. If the men upstairs wanted to stop the gas, they'd have to come down. Hopefully, the systems weren't sophisticated enough to warn them of the malfunction.

Each pipe carried a computer generated label. He found the one he needed and pushed the tiny metal handle stiffly upward. Randy did his best to ease it open gradually. Too much pressure and the sudden release would sound like a rocket launch behind the vent. Randy couldn't afford that. He needed them to stay in the control room while it filled with odorless gas from the bottom up. They'd stay focused on their work as long as Randy didn't alert them to his tampering here in the shaft.

He climbed the ladder to the fourth floor and listened to the gas hiss its way into the vent, flooding the lowest reaches of the room beyond the concrete wall. The turning fan covered the hissing somewhat. He hoped it was enough so they wouldn't notice. He pressed the insulation in tighter, trying to direct all the gas inside and keep the shaft safe in case he needed to come back.

Randy waited a full five minutes while the gas flowed.

The voices were gone now, silenced by the gas, the fan and the extra padding around the duct. He guessed the room was about fifteen feet square. It could take half an hour to fill up and longer for the operators to pass out. Randy was only thirty feet from the vault, but breaking through the concrete now would undo his work. The bag filled with explosives gave him an idea. He could give the gas time to work and expose Heather Lovely for the world to see.

He tucked the Saiga into the bag with the explosives, shouldered it and left the tools on the catwalk. He climbed steadily downward, ever conscious of the clink of his sneakers on each rung. If he appeared on camera roaming around the building, it would be the perfect distraction. The control room operators would be so focused on following him they wouldn't realize what was happening. When he reached the bottom, he jerked the manual control on the valve all the way open then pushed through the door into the vast loading area.

The van was still there and Tripp was still visible through the windshield. Checking on the big guy meant stepping center frame for the cameras. He turned instead for the only door in this room he hadn't used.

The narrow hall bordered the armory he'd entered earlier, snaked around the elevators, and ended at a heavy wooden door. The bare concrete transitioned to polished marble at the threshold. The P226 he'd taken from the power lifter was almost identical to the gun he practiced with. He pulled it from his pocket and hung tight to the wall around toward the guard desk. The P226 was loaded. He knew when he wheeled around the corner and faced the guard that he might be forced to shoot. The guard might jump from the chair, compelled to sacrifice himself by an overwhelming sense of duty. There'd be no time for warning shots. No time to shoot out his knee. Kill or die. Randy had saved dozens of people that morning. Dying might not mean damnation. After what he'd seen waiting for him, risking another murder wasn't worth it. He stepped forward, unsure he could pull the trigger. He reminded himself this wasn't about revenge.

Some nut jobs might say he'd done more damage than good saving those people that morning, but he felt lighter. The reverend would be proud. He'd tell him about it if he lived to see him again.

He passed between the matching tenant directories on the marble wall. This time he knew that most of the companies listed there didn't exist.

A few more feet.

He reached the gun around the corner, the front sight searching the padded red chair behind the desk, the pristine countertop, closed wooden cabinets. The cubbyhole behind the pillars was empty. He spun left. The grandfather clock, the glass doors, the sitting area, all vacant.

The center of the lobby afforded the men upstairs the best possible view of Randy, the bag and the gun, but it also afforded the most options for retreat if the guard popped up unexpectedly. He could be in the bathroom or making rounds somewhere. Heather wouldn't leave the lobby unguarded, not with her goons driving the countryside. He'd be in the building and he'd be back soon. Randy crossed straight for the entrance in spite of the cameras.

The revolving doors were locked in place. So were the glass doors on either side. The guard was somewhere inside. The lobby wasn't the place to wait for him. There was an office area on each side of the lobby, each with a different phony company name above the door.

Randy moved to his right. The lock jimmied simply and he was inside. He roamed past a long chain of tan fabric cubicles that ran down the center of the space like seats aligned for musical chairs. The calendar in the first cubicle charted 2004. The computer, a Compaq from that same year, had a screen saver swiping colored lines across the dingy monitor. The narrow office space trimmed the building front to back, camouflaging Heather's cement-walled fortress in the middle. Moving away from the door, the other cubicles were empty. No papers, not a stapler or a tape dispenser, not even a paperclip. The furniture was pristine beneath a heavy coating of dust.

Randy ducked down in the back corner and checked the contents of his bag. The remote trigger he'd taken from the van was the size of the remote control for a kid's car. Three switches were painted red, white and blue. The patriotic symbolism clashed horribly with the device's original intent. The bricks of explosive were wrapped in something resembling cellophane. They looked like the blocks he'd been given, but they were denser. The detonators looked much like what he'd been given too, but these had a dab of red, white or blue paint on them. They must have planned to blow the mosque in sections; the minarets one at a time and the dome as their finale. It hadn't worked out for them, but it suited Randy's purpose nicely.

His hand shook as he inserted the metal prongs of the first red detonator into the heavy block. He'd been closer to obliteration at the mosque. A flick of a switch by Ethan and he would have been blown to red-jellied goo. His purpose was clearer then. He'd been saving people. This was different. People could die. He was choosing to stay here and expose Heather Lovely. He could jump out a window and call a cop. They'd arrest him. He'd lose his chance to show the world what Heather Lovely was hiding, but he'd live and so would everyone else in the building.

He packed the first charge in place against a column then moved down between the next set of windows and planted another red charge. On he went, slipping into empty cubicles and working on the floor to keep himself from view. The painstaking work kept him from ruminating about the result.

As he planted the final red charge in the corner that bordered the lobby, something shifted behind him on the industrial carpet.

"Not on my watch, Tough Guy." The voice boomed from the door.

Randy let go of the charge. The remote and the rest of the explosives were behind him in the bag. Two detonators lay by his feet, prongs exposed but switched off, blind to the remote. He needed those if he was going to finish. He also needed to do something with the guy in the red blazer.

Randy dove for cover behind the cubicle wall.

Shots blared. Glass shattered. Two slugs zipped through the fuzzy walls and through the window panes out into the street.

Randy grabbed the remote from the bag and ran low for the corner, sliding to a stop with a view to two of the aisles. The .380 had spilled from his pocket back by the bag. It lay in plain sight. He drew the 410 from his left pocket and switched hands, the gun now in his right, the remote in his left.

Outside the window, an old man ambled away from the building, shoving off with his cane, hobbling, stumbling to safety at the corner of the next building. Two young men in jeans sprinted across Coggeshall, darting around traffic. Drivers honked. The men kept on and dove behind a parked car on the opposite curb. They wouldn't stay there long. They'd call the cops when they felt safe. They might be dialing already.

The guard stalked around the cubicles on the opposite side.

He stopped before he reached the windows Randy was working. He'd seen the charge and he wasn't getting any closer. At that moment Randy found his leverage.

"I got him. Down in the TechNow space in the lobby." The guard said.

Randy crept closer to learn the fate of the men upstairs. The guard didn't get an answer. They were passed out or they'd fled the control room

"What are you guys doing..." the guard began.

Randy sprinted down the aisle, along the windows, toward the far wall.

"I need help down here," he finished.

The radio dropped to the carpet and the guard hustled down the aisle to beat Randy to the corner. He crashed to a stop against a set of empty file cabinets. He ended up low at the end of the aisle, his gun aimed toward the windows waiting for Randy to make the corner headed for the door.

Randy had stopped twenty feet short. As the guard crashed to the floor, Randy vaulted the cubicle wall. The remote spilled from his hands, cracked on the desktop and bounced to the floor, tumbling into the aisle. Randy left it there and moved toward the door. The guard looked back, his body lying exposed in the aisle. He realized he was cut off. Randy blocked the door to the lobby. The only other exit, the windows, harbored a string of bombs. If the guard hadn't already seen Randy carrying the remote detonator, he'd know where to expect it. Panic flushed his face as he scrambled hands and feet for cover. He moved out of sight, but dangerously close to the explosives.

Randy emptied the 410, punching holes through the file cabinets and the fabric walls three feet high. The shots kept him down and moving toward the windows. When the 410 was empty, Randy pulled the P226 and emptied it as well. Randy stood up when he had the guard trapped.

"Ok, Asshole. It's over. Drop the gun and come on out."

"Dream on." He was moving down slowly, coming even with Randy across the cubes. He had a gun of his own and proven he'd use it.

"I'll give you three seconds." Randy picked up the remote and made a show of backing away toward the lobby.

Footsteps mirrored on the other side.

"Look behind you," Randy called from across the room. "Between the windows. That whole wall is coming down. Three, Two…"

The guard's head popped up.

Thank God. Randy was out of bullets and he was too close to blow the charges. The shell would come crashing down and who knew how many people were on the floors above. Randy kept his thumb on the remote and lined up the P229 on the guard's nose.

"On the desk," Randy said.

The gun clunked heavily on the laminate desktop.

Randy waved him to the corner and the guard marched stiffly around to the end of the aisle. Randy met him there and marched him to the door. Sweat poured down his neck, disappearing inside his blazer. He looked relieved to put his hands behind his back while Randy Zip Tied them together.

He was a problem now. He knew what was coming and he could tell the others. Randy thought about tying him up in the armory, but dismissed it as stupid. He couldn't put him in the van with the others. That was asking for trouble. He decided on the guard desk by the heavy pillars. The front doors were locked. Unlikely anyone was going to find him soon. A headshot would have solved the problem, but Randy sat him down behind the desk, opened a cabinet door and strapped him to one of the hinges.

Back in the office, he smashed the radio, picked up the guard's Glock from the desktop and dumped the empty P226 and the 410 under one of the desks. The Saiga was still in the bag along with plenty of blue and white detonators for what he had in mind.

Randy planted charges on the large beams at the front of the lobby. The guard shifted on the marble floor trying to get a view over the desk, but couldn't with his hands and feet Zip Tied. He wasn't going far. Randy detoured over to check him. He was permanently hunched with his back to the cabinet door, limited to a tiny arc beneath the pillars.

Randy hustled back to work.

A line of faces poked up behind the cars across Coggeshall. They watched him lug the bag across the lobby. Hustling down the hall he wondered if the walls would collapse on themselves as he'd planned or break away and tip outward on the crowd. If the people in the street had any idea what was coming, they would move back. Way back.

Chapter Seventy-two

The gunshots blew the timetable. The cops were on their way. The place was wired, but he needed to be up on four inside the vault. Instead he was standing in the lobby. He'd be the first schmuck the cops came across when they busted in. He pressed the call button between the elevators hoping the carbon monoxide had done its job.

Forty seconds passed. No whirring. No humming. No movement behind the shiny doors. Climbing up by the ducts would take time and he'd still need to blast his way in. There were three brick-sized charges left in the bag, plenty of power to get through the concrete.

There was a keyhole beneath the call button.

Randy ran to the guard and gave him a kick to get his attention. The guard gave up the keys immediately when asked. Randy thought the guy understood the hopelessness of the situation, but when he inserted the key and the elevator still didn't come, he knew it was something else. Randy rushed back to the guard desk.

"What's the deal?" he asked, training the Glock on his forehead.

"It's all controlled upstairs."

"Bullshit." Randy centered the sights on his kneecap.

"It won't move unless they tell it to."

A horn blared three strong bursts at the back of the building. The cops would have run their sirens, gotten out and pounded on the door or used a megaphone. Ethan wouldn't. He'd call upstairs to be let in. When no one answered, he'd get frustrated. Randy was almost out of time.

To the guard he said, "Why the keyhole then?"

"It was there before the systems upstairs."

"What's it good for?" He didn't understand, so Randy waved the key in his face. "Why do you carry it around?"

"At night they turn the override off. It's how we get in and out if there's no one upstairs."

They didn't build a fortress they could lock themselves out of. It didn't make sense. "There's got to be another way in. What is it?"

"Heather's got a key. She can go anywhere she wants."

Her key was up on the top floor. No help.

Randy gave up on the elevators. He kept the keys and hustled past the elevators and into the narrow hall that passed through the thick concrete wall. He'd climb up, blast open the duct and crawl into the control room. From there he might even be able to open the vault.

Metal crashed against metal as Randy stepped into the loading area.

The wide overhead door bulged in the center and tore away from the tracks. The rollers pinged off like buttons, spraying outward like machine gun fire. The door buckled and a wide bumper appeared beneath it. The van shrugged off the twisted metal, raced in and screeched to a stop. The shaft was thirty feet away and then he'd have to climb four stories with no cover and only one way out.

Randy stuttered in that direction then froze.

Ethan jumped down, covered himself behind the van's engine and drew his gun. Khan darted right and dove behind a lumber pile. They were working both sides, surrounding him without taking a moment to plan. The shaft was too far. One hit to the explosives and he'd be obliterated.

Randy turned back through the door and gunfire erupted behind him.

Out at the elevators again.

The cops would be out front.

The stairwell plaque was right in front of him. He'd missed this door last time. The stairwell didn't pass inside the concrete barrier, but it would get him away from Ethan and the others long enough to collect himself. Sirens screeched outside. Randy was the intruder here. They'd arrest him even if they weren't on Heather's payroll, but if he could get to the fourth floor and get into the vault he had a chance.

Randy raced up three sets of stairs.

Panting on the third floor landing he realized the door below still hadn't swung open. They should have been right behind. The only other place to run was out to the cops or inside the offices he'd rigged earlier. He hoped they weren't smart enough to be disarming his charges already.

The door finally burst open as he climbed to the fourth floor landing.

"There he is."

The booming voice belonged to the power lifter.

A gunshot echoed inside the brick stairwell.

They'd stopped to free Sid and Tripp from the van. That was the delay. Randy had a head start, but now there were four of them.

Randy reached the fourth floor landing, out of breath, his shoulder aching from the bag, his heart pounding oxygen to weary muscles. One floor up the stairwell was capped. Heather occupied the entire sixth floor. He could climb outside and crawl through a window then break his way into the elevator shaft, or maybe blow his way through the ceiling, but that wouldn't stop the cops from arresting him.

He kicked open the door and tumbled through. The bag hit the carpet just inside. Bullets ricocheted off the concrete behind him. Footsteps and voices chased upward as the four men behind him gained ground.

The phony office space was more of what he'd seen below, but smaller, much smaller. One narrow row of cubicles provided the only cover. He'd just burst through the only door. A cinderblock wall joined the poured concrete that sealed the interior. Randy was hemmed into a room with no cover that would stop a bullet. The only exits were fourth floor windows and a stairwell full of armed men.

Randy grabbed the Saiga, darted back into the stairwell and leaned over the railing. The twelve gauge boomed, the concussion reverberating up and down the concrete tunnel. The footsteps scampered back and stopped. Randy fired two more times and checked his ammo. He had two full ten-round clips and seven still in the gun. He could hold them off.

If he could bring himself to shoot them, he'd get two or three with the buckshot when they cleared the door. With a full magazine he might get them all. But he couldn't undo the day's work.

Randy pulled two empty file cabinets over to the door and lined them up against the center cubicle wall. A chair wedged in and took all the play out of the door.

Randy went to work measuring the room, trying to determine where the vault was on the other side of the wall. He had enough charges for one try. If he found himself in the conference room, it'd be over. He'd never beat the handprint scanner on that door and he'd never get downstairs to the other charges and back for another try.

Voices sounded at the door.

Randy turned and peppered it with buckshot.

The pellets didn't penetrate, but he earned enough time to plant the charges, insert a blue detonator and stack two bookshelves against them to direct the explosive force inward.

Randy moved all the way to the corner by the windows, behind the entire string of cubicles where he'd be protected from the blast.

Shoulders pounded against the door.

The chair bucked, but stayed in place.

Randy switched the black box on and flicked the blue switch.

Chapter Seventy-three

Officer Grant sprinted five blocks down Coggeshall when the dispatcher reported someone seeing Randy Black with a gun inside an office building at one twenty-five. When he got there the building was easy to identify. Faces peeked out from behind cars and the corners of buildings across the street. A few men crouched at bumpers on the near side, hoping to get a glimpse of the notorious killer through one of the windows.

Foolish idiots.

Grant shouted them back as he jogged to a stop.

He tried the doors and found them locked. He wouldn't have gone inside alone if they weren't, but he was tired of walking foot patrols and directing traffic. He'd have a ready situation report when one of the higher-ups arrived.

Glass lay on the sidewalk beneath four cracked windowpanes. The shots had come from inside the lower floor. The angle was impossible to measure precisely, but it looked as if at least one of the bullets had flown through the alley across the street and off toward the highway. No one on the street had been hit.

He ordered the onlookers back two blocks.

More officers arrived, lights blazing, sirens wailing. They angled their cars to a stop right in the middle of the street. They saw Grant waving the people back and joined him. Soon tape was stretched across the wide street and the onlookers were pushed farther and farther away from the building.

Traffic on the city side was turned back to Route 18. On the Fairhaven side, they'd have to loop around to Route 6 or work their way down to Belleville Avenue. Drivers honked and squawked at the cops behind the tape. If they knew bullets were flying across the street, they'd make the long detour and they'd be happy. Typical ungrateful citizens, annoyed at any inconvenience. They didn't care who was being shot at or why. They just wanted to go about their day without interruption.

Gunshots rang out again.

Grant dropped to the sidewalk and rolled against the bricks.

The shots sounded muffled, like they were on the higher floors.

Grant had seen the news from a pizza shop.

The senior imam from the mosque had been kidnapped and then shown with two hookers. If there were more Muslims here in the city already, they'd be rioting. They suspected Randy Black and they'd found him. It had to be the Muslims shooting inside. They'd have AK-47s. Grant wasn't going to challenge them with his Glock. They'd catch up with this guy, cut his head off and parade it down the street. Grant and the four men doing crowd control couldn't stop them. He could only hope to be part of the arrest when they were finished.

Grant kept an eye on the front door and waited for tactical.

A minute later he heard the sergeant on the radio. There was a hole ripped in the back door that looked like a car had driven through. They were going in. Grant hustled around back to join him, ducking the windows as he ran.

Chapter Seventy-four

The remote control clicked.

Nothing.

Randy worked the switch up and down, up and down. Nothing.

The black plastic case was cracked from the fall over the cubicles downstairs. He worked his index finger inside and snapped off the back panel.

Ethan and his men slammed the door. The file cabinets jostled inward and fell back into place with a pounding rhythm. They'd be inside soon.

Three wires floated free inside the box. Randy studied, stuck his finger in and held one of them down to a miniature terminal. He flicked the switch once, then repositioned his finger and flicked again.

BOOM.

Randy had never heard anything so loud.

Debris flew everywhere.

Splinters of wood shattered the entire wall of windows. Chairs flew. Seven cubicles flipped up against the windows. Still connected to their mates, the cubicles rolled up on their side. The twisted mess of gray walls looked like the spine of a poor soul twisted into a spiral. Concrete chunks bounded outward from the blast.

The file cabinets were buried, the exit blocked. Ethan and his men were safe in the stairwell, but they'd need to find another way in.

Randy had a new way out.

The blast tore a gaping hole in the wall and littered the inside of the vault with green bills. Randy collected his bag and crawled through the ragged hole and over a waist deep avalanche of hundred dollar bills. Green and white stacks, bound with elastics had packed a fifteen foot wide series of shelves before the explosion scattered them all over the room. The judge said Heather had made huge profits knocking off drug dealers, but Randy couldn't imagine she'd have thirty or forty million in cash. That's how she constructed this building and kept it quiet.

Randy wasn't here for money. He moved deeper inside.

The interior shelves were broken into velvet-lined cubbyholes. Each shelf had a name labeled across. Prominent names: city leaders, police, judges, congressmen. They had been packed with CDs in clear plastic cases. He'd expected to walk out with them all, a dozen, fifty maybe, but the scale of Heather's operation was unfathomable. Thousands of CDs littered the vault. Fallen cases crunched under his feet and he was destroying evidence with every step.

He grabbed a handful of discs.

Each had a number stamped on the case. No names just numbers. Heather's men were pros. They provided surveillance for customers and when the customers did something or said something they shouldn't, it was recorded here. That's how she got her leverage. These CDs were immensely valuable to someone comfortable with extortion. Heather took full advantage and ran her operation with the efficiency of a major corporation.

Randy avoided McKinnon's cubbyhole and rifled the others. He flipped through hundreds of cases until he stumbled upon exactly what he needed. Some of the CDs had a red sticker in the corner. One in twenty or maybe one in fifty. These were the ones with real value.

He emptied the shelves in turn, grabbing for the red stickers and discarding the rest on the floor. Hundreds of plastic cases rained down as he feverishly worked his way around the room.

Randy didn't hear the wheel spinning or the titanium bolts retracting. Florescent light cracked through the vault door brightening the room.

Heather Lovely stood in the doorway.

Randy dropped the bag of CDs. He'd left the Saiga just outside the vault, so he fumbled for the Glock in his pocket.

Heather fired first.

The impact slammed him back against a shelf. His feet slipped out from under him awash in a tide of plastic. His knuckles cracked against a shelf. The Glock dropped to the floor. Randy swam in a cascade of plastic cases. The vault door stood ajar and Heather was lining up a more careful shot— one sure to finish him.

Randy scooped up the gun and swung it around until the front sight settled on Heather's chest. He squeezed the trigger, but jerked the barrel to the right an instant before the gun fired. The slug ricocheted off the stainless steel door and out past Heather into the hall.

Heather dodged to safety behind the door and left Randy staring at the useless gun in his hands. It wasn't completely useless. It scared Heather out of the vault and bought him a few seconds to think.

Heather called out loudly from the hall.

"I'm on four. He's in the vault.

"Get your asses up here. Now!

"Take the elevator stupid."

The men from the stairs. They'd know how to work the elevator. He had what he'd come for. He needed to get outside before Heather's friends on the force dragged him off to jail. If they did, no one would ever see what was on the CDs. Heather would go on extorting and killing. What happened here today would just be added to Randy's rap sheet.

Blood leaked from his shoulder.

The bullet had passed through his pectoral below the clavicle. The shoulder burned, but he could breathe clearly. She'd missed his lung.

He pulled the remote from the bag and clicked the red and white switches. Nothing. He flipped it over, jammed the fingers of his left hand inside and pressed the wires to the terminals and held them. If Heather opened the door he was defenseless. He closed his eyes and hoped for the two guys in jeans he'd seen outside and the faces poking up over the cars.

He clicked the red and white switches again.

The world rumbled.

Explosions ripped through the first floor of the building.

Glass, desks, bricks, the entire shell of the first floor became one churning projectile. The charred, jumbled mass slammed inward and fired outward all at once. The structure above lost its support and crashed down to Earth. Beams ripped away from the inner concrete wall. Floors compacted down on top of each other like escalator steps disappearing into the rubble. The upper shell of the building fell away like a husk.

Without support from below, the outer walls of the sixth floor sagged like a floppy hat, held together by the thick concrete floor that isolated Heather's living space from the rest of the building. The concrete wavered then snapped in a jagged fringe around the stronghold Heather had built inside. Huge sections of her apartment rained down.

Down at street level, Officer Grant had saved dozens of lives by pushing them back. Waves of concrete and brick crashed down onto Coggeshall Street in a tide that rode up and stacked debris fifteen feet high against the buildings on the opposite side. Cars parked in the street were crushed flat. The crowd gasped as the building fell. The cloud of dust rose up and washed over everything for blocks.

Down in the lobby Gordon huddled behind the desk. The massive concrete pillars toppled together. The floor above broke away and slammed down at a steep angle, crushing the marble-topped counter, but forming a lean-to over him. The Zip Tie strapping him to the cabinet hinge saved him from being crushed. Anywhere else in the lobby and his body would have been compressed flat beneath the rubble and punctured by steel rods and jagged pipes.

A gaping hole ripped into the stronghold on the fourth floor. Computers fell away, dragged by their power cables. One monitor hung suspended against the concrete, hanging forty five feet in the air. Dusty air rushed in. Carbon monoxide swirled away. Tom Gold and Whitey would survive. The two legitimate employees of Omni-sense also survived. Debbie called in sick for the first time in a year. Rob was on a client call miles away, unaware that the state of the art monitoring center he bragged about was now rubble.

The first door the policemen broke through in the loading area was Heather's armory. When they found automatic weapons and dozens of handguns, they decided to stay put. The sergeant rationalized they were protecting the guns, but Grant knew they were also saving themselves. They'd be outgunned inside an unfamiliar building. When the explosion hit, the thick walls around the loading area held fast.

Upstairs, Heather Lovely knew it was the end.

She left Ethan, Tripp and Khan outside the vault door and headed off down the hall with Sid. With the control room destroyed, Sid was the only one strong enough to break through the door. One kick was all he needed to expose the imam where he lay recovering from the alcohol Heather had forced on him earlier. Heather stepped directly in front of the wobbly imam, pressed the gun to his chest and fired.

He sprawled on the floor.

Sid stood in awe as she pumped three more shots into him.

The imam was done spreading hate.

Chapter Seventy-five

Dread filled Randy's chest.

The guard lay trapped in the lobby.

So many people were watching out on the street.

More than he'd saved at the mosque. Dozens more.

Fresh air blew in through the hole he'd blasted in the vault wall. Bleeding to death wouldn't help. Randy dropped the Glock and grabbed a handful more red dotted CDs and stuffed them into his bag.

The vault door swung open and Tripp's angry eyes appeared over the muzzle of a satin black pistol.

Randy dropped to his knees, grabbed the Glock in his left hand and fired wildly. Tripp fired three times, shattering CDs, cracking shelves, but missing Randy completely.

The door swung closed.

He couldn't stay. The next time they opened the door, he'd be facing five guns, not one. They'd get smart and leave it open, dodging in to fire and back for cover.

CDs scattered underfoot. Randy slipped and stumbled his way to the hole. He tossed the bag through and fired two more times before shimmying his way out. The vault swung open as if they'd heard him escape. Gunfire erupted. Bullets whizzed past as he dropped to the floor, but nothing struck home.

The office space he'd been in earlier was now a jagged, six foot ledge. The barricade and the door to the stairs were gone. The cubicles and everything else inside had been ripped apart, twisted and dropped into a chaotic mess twenty feet below. Randy found the Saiga against the wall where he'd left it, grabbed the pistol grip in his left hand and fired toward the vault. The recoil nearly jerked the gun from his hand.

Feet shuffled out of the vault behind him.

Randy clutched the bag in his good hand and teetered out toward the stairs. The outer wall had been completely ripped away, leaving the stairs themselves and half of the top landing in tact. The crowd below cheered when they saw Randy moving atop the devastated building.

Randy made the stairs, turned and fired one last shot with the Saiga before tossing it to the rubble.

Tripp thrust through the opening and fired a shot as Randy took his first steps down to safety. The crowd screamed with the report. Tripp understood immediately that he'd been seen and ducked back inside.

Randy ambled down. His racing heart sent more blood pumping out the wound in his shoulder, soaking his shirt. He looped the bag strap around his neck and clutched himself with his good hand to slow the flow of blood as he climbed down.

The stairs descended into a thick cloud and ended at the third floor where they were filled in by the pile of rubble. Fire trucks arrived down the block, red lights cutting through the murk.

As Randy picked his way down, he saw an officer rush out the back of the building and start climbing toward him. Randy assumed he was one of Heather's men and angled toward the emergency vehicles parked on Coggeshall. He jumped over big blocks of concrete and brick still strung together in massive unruly clumps. His right arm hung useless, his left pressed hard to his chest to staunch the flow of blood. The debris shifted underfoot like unruly logs bobbing underwater threatening to throw him tumbling down the mountain of rubble.

The officer climbed faster, closing the gap, annoyed that Randy was moving away from him. He didn't pull his weapon, he couldn't with so many people watching.

The final descent to Coggeshall was a steep slope that shifted underfoot with every step. The officer rushed over the pile on all fours, eager to grab Randy and destroy the evidence he'd risked his life to capture. Randy's vision blurred. He choked in the thick dust and his shoulder throbbed, but he was too close to give in. He'd make it to an ambulance and hand off the bag. Then his Earthly work would be done.

A shot rang out from above.

A man in the crowd screamed and fell, clutching his calf.

Randy turned around to see Heather standing outside the vault, lining him up with a handgun. He was well beyond the gun's range, but a lucky shot would still be deadly.

The gawkers behind the barricades scattered for cover.

Randy ducked and hopped faster over the chunks of rubble. Twenty more feet and he'd be on undisturbed pavement. Emergency personnel waded into the rubble to receive him.

Heather's gun barked again.

The skin around Randy's left shoulder ripped open. The force threw him forward onto a slab of concrete. The whole six foot slab broke loose and surfed down over the pile. It reached bottom with a crash and stopped hard. Randy tumbled forward over a jumble of pipes, slicing his leg on a tie rod, rolling and crunching his way to the asphalt. He lay there blinking at the unfamiliar faces of the firemen that surrounded him.

Somewhere above, Officer Grant kneeled and fired three rapid shots.

Cassie shoved her way to Randy's side.

Someone screamed for the paramedics.

Randy tugged at the bag, his eyes on Cassie, but a corner of the canvas was caught underneath him and he didn't have the strength to pull it free. A fireman eased it from under him and turned to set it aside. Randy held fast. He didn't release the strap until Cassie took it from him.

He begged her to go. She hesitated then sprinted into the crowd.

Through the haze he saw Heather buckle. Officer Grant's bullet found her inside the fortress she'd built to protect herself.

Chapter Seventy-six

A week later two state troopers flanked Cassie down the hall to the I.C.U. Similar guards framed the door outside the room where Randy met Cassie almost two months earlier. A stack of newspapers lay on the guest chair. Each day she brought a new one and each day she read her coverage of the corruption scandal. The Times, the Globe, USA Today, they all ran her stories. The only source material was the CDs. She was the only citizen to see them before the attorney general seized them as evidence. Amazingly, the material hadn't been leaked and Cassie retained her exclusive.

Today she read the full page she'd written about a special man who'd been thrown off track by tragedy. How he'd gone mad with hate. How he'd wasted years of his life seeking revenge. And how he'd struggled so hard to turn it all around. He'd done it. He'd saved forty-four people from a savage bombing that would have set off a series of reprisals all over the country. He'd put an end to a group of criminals that killed with impunity. He'd shined the light on dozens of compromised officials. Big changes shook Massachusetts. One determined man touched so many.

The ventilator hissed.

The EKG beeped.

Cassie understood too late. Tears streamed down her face. She hid them as the nurse stepped in and checked the equipment.

"Keep talking to him, dear."

"Is it any use? Is he going to wake up?"

"Only God knows."

Printed in the United States
205270BV00003B/211-285/P